ADVANCE PRAISE FOR
WHEN THE FAR HILLS BLOOM

"*Far Hills* is a beautiful story of true love, loyalty, and betrayal. It gripped my emotions from the very beginning, and didn't let them go. Diane Noble is a master storyteller!"

—TERRI BLACKSTOCK

"*When the Far Hills Bloom* has everything I look for in a great novel— high drama, unexpected twists and turns, heart-tugging romance, and genuine, true-to-life conflicts. I not only fell in love with the characters, I fell in love with California in all her untamed glory. This is Diane Noble's best work yet!"

—LIZ CURTIS HIGGS

"Inside Tip of the Day: If you're looking for a great excuse to not do any housework, grocery shopping, or anything else for several days (if you can sleep), read *Far Hills*. This irresistible novel has an epic feel that made me think of romantic movies like *Far and Away*. I anxiously await the following two books in the series, as well as anything else that Diane Noble chooses to write."

—LISA TAWN BERGREN

When the Far Hills Bloom

When the Far Hills Bloom

Diane Noble

WATERBROOK
PRESS

WHEN THE FAR HILLS BLOOM
PUBLISHED BY WATERBROOK PRESS
5446 North Academy Boulevard, Suite 200
Colorado Springs, Colorado 80918
A division of Random House, Inc.

The characters and events in this book are fictional, and any
resemblance to actual persons or events is coincidental.

Unless otherwise noted, Scripture quotations are from the *King
James Version* of the Bible. Scripture also quoted from the *New King
James Version.* Copyright © 1982 by Thomas Nelson, Inc. Used by
permission. All rights reserved.

ISBN 1-57856-140-X

Library of Congress Cataloging-in-Publication Data
Noble, Diane. 1945-
    When the far hills bloom / Diane Noble. — 1st ed.
        p.   cm.
    ISBN 1-57856-140-X (pbk.)
    I. Title.
PS3563.A3179765W5   1999
813'.54—dc21   99-22462
                                                           CIP

Printed in the United States of America
1999—First Edition

10 9 8 7 6 5 4 3 2 1

Dreams, books, are each a world; and books,
we know,
Are a substantial world, both pure and good.

—WORDSWORTH, 1807

⸺◆⸺

For Lisa Bergren
Who passed to me her dream of this substantial world.
Thank you, my friend!

ACKNOWLEDGMENTS

God has blessed me with a circle of family and friends who surround me with love, encouragement, and prayer. My husband, Tom, and my daughters, Melinda and Amy, are at the top of the list. Tom's expertise on the history of the American West and, more specifically, the history of California, was invaluable. His love and encouragement never faltered. Melinda and Amy cheered me on from the sidelines, and our girls-only celebration in Santa Barbara at the book's completion was a joy.

Kudos and heartfelt thanks to my editor and friend Lisa Bergren, whose astute editorial direction and "California Dreamin'" did much to shape this book. Thanks, too, to Traci DePree and Paul Hawley for their wonderful hands-on editorial skills. And to Mary Lou Herrera, Arabian horse breeder and real-life "horse whisperer," thanks for reading the manuscript and advising on all the horse-related action.

Continuing thanks to Karen Solem, my agent, for her always well-placed words of advice and enthusiasm for my work.

To my LoveKnot writing sisters, warm blessings and thanks for always being there.

And to Liz Curtis Higgs, my beloved friend, deep gratitude for listening, advising, praying, and sharing as I worked—during the months I lived in Spain and during the long summer of writing after I returned. Her loving support—another midwife effort!—did much to bring this work to life.

Bless you all. And to God be the glory! For without him this book would never have been written. It is for him I write.

Though the fig tree may not blossom,
Nor fruit be on the vines;
Though the labor of the olive may fail,
And the fields yield no food;
Though the flock may be cut off from the fold,
And there be no herd in the stalls—

Yet I will rejoice in the LORD,
I will joy in the God of my salvation.

The LORD God is my strength;
He will make my feet like deer's feet,
And He will make me walk on my high hills.

HABAKKUK 3:17-19
(New King James Version)

ONE

Rancho de la Paloma
May 1861

Winds from the east were already kicking up a wild warmth, clearing the air of mist and dust, etching the skyline against the rays of the rising sun. Another day of scorching heat was in store, fed by the desert winds, and if many such days followed, the already pale green grass would soon turn golden, then brown. Days like today matched Aislin D'Ary Byrne's spirits.

In the distance, a rider approached from the direction of a neighboring rancho, and Aislin stood as she recognized Jamie Dearbourne. Tall in the saddle, shoulders broad and proud. He kicked his dark stallion to a gallop, yanked off his hat, and waved to her as he rode.

The sun slipped over the San Jacintos, bathing the windswept lands of the Big Valley in light. Aislin caught glimpses of Jamie through the cottonwood branches as he rode, and the sounds of falling dirt clods and rocks told her the sorrel was climbing the final and steepest part of the trail.

Minutes later, Jamie swung one leg over his saddle and dismounted with a soft thud of boots on the ground. Aislin watched him from where she'd perched atop the stone wall around the fort they had built as children.

He swept off his hat and gave her a mock bow. "M'lady," he said. His eyes crinkled at the corners when he again lifted his gaze to hers and a slow and crooked grin took hold of his face. A grin she couldn't resist. Had never been able to resist.

"Jamie, this is serious." But she found it difficult to remain solemn; it was always that way in the presence of Jamie Dearbourne. She smiled in spite of herself. "Oh, Jamie…" she murmured, shaking her head slowly. "Can't you understand how difficult this is for those who love you? You act as if you're leaving on a holiday—not a journey of twenty-five hundred miles."

He sat down easily beside her on the rock wall, stretching out his lanky legs, crossing his feet at the ankles. "Can it be that I'm finally hearing that you might miss me?"

Her heart was about to break, but she bit her lip to keep the tears from spilling. "It's not our war. Not your war. I don't understand your reasons for going."

"But you didn't answer my question." He was grinning at her, and the way the morning sunlight hit his face caused her heart to catch. "About missing me, I mean."

He glanced at her hand, which rested in her lap. She imagined what it would feel like to have the comfort of his rough, warm hand wrapped around hers. But he hadn't held her hand since they were children when the gesture held no more meaning than sweet friendship.

"Your family and mine will be praying for your swift journey back to us," she said, still not willing to answer his question. "You know that."

His eyes seemed almost merry as he beheld her. "The war is my duty, sweet Aislin. The duty of every red-blooded Southerner. My mother's family lives in Tennessee. If you're about to argue with me about my being a Reb…" He laughed heartily.

She saw the spirited gleam in his eye. He'd been caught up in the jubilant rush to arms and glory, and especially the honor of the battle, just as so many young men in the East had been. How it had reached all the way to California, she couldn't guess. But it was so like him. He'd fight the Federals single-handed if he had the chance. It always had been that way with Jamie, and probably always would be. But that was part of his charm, part of what she loved about him. Some people, including her sisters, thought him cocky. She saw him as strong.

"I'll be coming back for you, my sweet, if that's your worry." His eyes twinkled.

"Jamie, you're heading into grave danger," she reminded him, "and you seem to be paying it no mind."

He laughed. "And you're no different than when we were children. Always reminding me of my place. Reminding me God hasn't placed me in charge of his creation and all the people in it." He laughed again.

"I wish you would see that this is no laughing matter." But even as she spoke, Aislin knew Jamie's feelings about duty. He would not turn his back on a fight. He would see it to an honorable end—though she suspected that duty came second to proving himself through his triumph.

She stood abruptly and walked to an outcropping of boulders nestled among some scrub pines, buckthorn, and manzanita. Before her spread a view of her father's rancho, stretching to the jagged peaks of the San Jacintos like a pale green-gold sea. When she spoke, she didn't turn back to him. "I thought life would always go on the way it is now."

"Nothing can stay the same forever, Aislin."

She turned toward him again. Though he was a man of twenty-two, his expression was as playfully roguish as it had been at twelve. His shock of unruly wheat-colored hair, ears that stuck out slightly, and the glint in his dark eyes only added to the illusion.

Aislin's heart caught; she turned away from him. "I will miss you, Jamie."

Behind her, a low chuckle rumbled from Jamie's throat. "Aha. There it is at last. I never thought I'd live to hear those words." There was a soft crunch of boots on stones as he moved toward her, and a moment later, he reached for her shoulder and turned her toward him. She raised her eyes to meet his.

"Is there something more you've been wanting to say, Ceallach?"

His use of her nickname caused the back of her throat to sting. When she was eight and he was ten they had set about building this fort, pretending it was an ancient Celtic ruin in the heart of Ireland. Jamie found the name in a Gaelic book belonging to Aislin's father, read its meaning—warrior maid—and said if she had to have a Gaelic name, she needed one that fit her better than Aislin, which meant flower. She always wondered if he'd chosen it because he didn't think her pretty or if he simply valued strength more than beauty.

"How long will you be away?"

"From all reports, the war will not last long. The Yanks may think they can crush the Rebs." He laughed. "But everyone knows the South will enjoy a swift and decisive victory."

"That's what folks here say, but…"

He placed a fingertip on her lips to shush her. "I'll be coming back, Ceallach, I promise." It was the first time Jamie had touched her with such intimacy, and she blinked in surprise. He stepped closer again. His dark eyes had lost their boyish look.

This was a Jamie she had never seen.

He touched her cheek. So light. So loving. He was closer now. He nodded again, slowly. "There's so much I want to tell you, Ceallach."

She cleared her throat and swallowed hard. "You do?" she managed, hoarsely.

"I want to speak to your father before I leave…about asking for your hand in marriage."

She stared at him. She had loved Jamie for as long as she could remember and had dreamed of the day he might tell her he loved her too.

"Ceallach, I want to marry you. I mean, if you'll have me." His words rushed out as if he had been planning them for an eternity, holding them inside for nearly as long. He raised a brow as if asking a silent question.

"Oh, Jamie!" She caught both hands to her face and, speechless for once in her life, felt her eyes fill with tears. "Oh, Jamie!" she repeated. When she recovered her breath, she said, "You know my father will say yes. He's always said that we should marry. Our families have counted on it."

He touched his fingers to her lips again and looked almost shy as he beheld her. "I love you, Ceallach," he said quietly, still gazing into her eyes. "It doesn't matter what our fathers planned…or what our coming together will cause for both ranchos. All that matters is our love."

Aislin bit her lip, not trusting her voice. She looked up into his face, that face filled with quiet confidence. Sighing deeply, she smiled into his eyes.

"But you haven't said whether you love me, Ceallach." He let the question hang. And then he raised her hands and brushed them lightly with his lips. "Do you love me enough to spend a lifetime with me?"

She touched his face. "I love you enough to spend all the days of my life with you! But…"

"Do you have doubts, Aislin?" He didn't look worried.

"I don't want to wait," she said. He smiled, almost as if he expected her words. She went on. "Let's marry now, Jamie. Before you leave."

He dropped her hands and turned to look toward the distant hills. He didn't speak, as if considering her request. She moved to stand beside him, circling his waist with her arm. "I'm afraid for you, Jamie. If I let you go…" Her voice caught and she didn't finish what was in her heart. That if she let him go, he might not return.

"It isn't the right time," he finally said. "For marriage, I mean."

"Jamie, look at me." He turned toward her again. "It's the war, isn't it, that's so dangerous after all? I mean, you sense it too?"

His eyes couldn't lie. He nodded finally. "Yes, Ceallach. I don't want to make you a widow."

She caught Jamie's hands in hers. "My heart will belong to you whether we're married or not before you leave. And I promise I'll wait for you, no matter how long." As she spoke, Jamie's crooked smile returned.

Jamie reached into his vest pocket and pulled out a small cloth drawstring pouch. He pulled it open and, lifting Aislin's left hand, slipped a thin gold ring onto her third finger.

"God be with us," he whispered as he drew her into his arms, "while we are parted and bless us when we meet again."

She stood on her tiptoes and wrapped her arms around his neck as he kissed her.

"I love you, Jamie Dearbourne," she whispered when she could breathe again.

August 1861

Jamie arrived in St. Louis, trail-dirty and bone-tired, planning to be in the lively riverside town just long enough for a bath and a haircut and a decent night's sleep in a real bed. He took a room above a saloon just off the boardwalk for one night only.

After a soak in a bathtub he'd ordered brought to his room, he headed down the stairs and into the saloon for the biggest slab of buffalo steak the cook could fit in his frying pan.

Even before he entered the dining room, Jamie could hear laughter and the sounds of raucous voices. Three rough but friendly looking men sat in one corner near the door. He heard snatches of bragging about life on the Santa Fe Trail as he stepped past their table and gave them a friendly nod, knowing what trail life was like.

"Sit yerself down, boy," said the oldest of the three, a man with coarse gray hair and bad teeth. He gave a nearby chair a short kick in Jamie's direction.

"Don't mind if I do," Jamie said as he sat.

"Name's Madden," said the man, reaching across the table to shake Jamie's hand.

"Jamie Dearbourne. Glad to make your acquaintance."

"This here's Dwyer," he nodded to a somber-looking man with leathery skin and thin lips. "And the kid there goes by Neal." He grunted a laugh. "Long as I've known him, he's never said whether it's his first or last name."

"Doesn't matter, does it?" said the young man, sounding surly. He was sandy-haired and as leathery-skinned as the other two.

"Where you headed?" Madden asked.

"Plan to join the Confederacy. Soon as I cross the Mississippi."

"Do you now?" Madden said, though not in an unfriendly way. "Me and my partners here talked about it once..." He laughed. "For about a half-minute. Then decided just about anything is better'n being shot at."

Jamie grinned. "Can't say as I blame you. Some are called...some aren't."

"Some might take offense at your attitude," said Neal, with something that looked like a sneer. "There're some who think everyone's called, whether they agree or not."

"I guess they've got a right to their opinion," Jamie countered. The other three men didn't smile.

"You better mind yourself, son," said Madden, looking around the room.

"What do you mean?"

Dwyer leaned back in his chair, studying Jamie. "I hear tell there're those buying and selling folks to the military."

Jamie laughed, though now slightly nervous. Suddenly none of the three looked as friendly as before. "What do you mean?"

"They come across young men, traveling alone usually. No kin in sight. Nobody who'll miss 'em. Might hit 'em over the head. Hogtie 'em. Ship 'em down the ol' Mississip' and sell 'em to the highest bidder."

Jamie narrowed his eyes. He didn't want to jump to conclusions, but it was clear he needed to get away from these men. He rose to his feet, only to find there was someone else standing behind him. A hand as big as a hamhock pushed him back into his chair.

"Now, you do as we tell you, and you won't get hurt," said Madden.

Jamie felt the barrel of a gun in his ribs, obviously coming from Dwyer, sitting to his right. He sat up straighter and glanced around the room. No one was paying the least attention to him, to the men at the table, or to the gun in his ribs, for that matter. The whiskey flowed and the men around the bar were laughing and talking. Someone was playing a tinny piano in the corner, and several of the men nearby were singing, their voices loud and slurred.

Even so, Jamie figured, these thugs wouldn't try anything here in front of everyone.

"What's the matter?" Madden said with a grin that showed his brown teeth. "Cat got yer tongue?"

The others laughed.

"I need to be going," Jamie stood again, only to be slammed into his chair once more by the hulking presence standing behind him.

"You'll leave with us, son," said Madden. "When we're ready to go. And we ain't ready. Not yet."

Jamie watched for a chance to make his move. He planned to drop and roll to the floor, hoping to draw attention to his plight before the gun in his ribs was fired. He waited for the piano player to stop, even for a moment. That would be his signal.

The men appeared to have let down their guard and were laughing with each other, seeming to pay no mind to Jamie. The piano stopped. Jamie dropped to the floor, just as he had planned.

He held his breath, waiting for the explosion of gunfire. There was none.

He scrambled to standing, ready to lunge. But Madden, blocking his path, gave him a slow smile, then nodded at the other two men. Dwyer grabbed one of Jamie's arms, Neal, the other. The big presence who'd been standing behind him was a giant of a man, towering over the others, greasy hair falling in strands to his shoulders.

"Don't let them take me," he implored the suddenly silent room. All eyes were watching the group. But the expressions were disinterested. "Don't let them take me!"

"My son can't seem to keep hisself outa trouble," Madden said with a shrug. "His brothers here are always havin' to haul him outa places he shouldn't be. Usually from too much wine, women, and song..."

Some of the men at the bar snickered.

"It's not like that!" Jamie shouted. "These aren't my kin."

"He's also a little tetched," said Madden. "Don't even know his own family."

Jamie struggled again, kicking and howling, but to no avail. Suddenly he was dragged through the saloon doors, backwards, out into the hot, humid night. The men chuckled as they hauled him, still kicking, down the boardwalk. His boot heels clunked against the wooden planks in rhythm with the men's tapping boots as they walked.

"Looks like we bagged ourselves another'n," said Neal proudly. "Makes ten this month."

An argument ensued over the exact numbers. They showed no more concern for Jamie than if he were a sack of grain they were dragging to the river.

A breeze off the Mississippi carried its odor into Jamie's nostrils long before they reached the wharf. By the time the barge loomed in the dark night, he had been thrown to the ground, hogtied, and readied to toss into the hold.

Minutes later the heavy door of the hold slammed closed. Utter silence met him.

Jamie was aware only of the darkness and the greatest fear he had ever known.

September 1862

Aislin knelt in the courtyard, clipping spent roses from the bushes near the fountain. By winter it would be time to prune the branches, making them look barren and sad for a while, but come spring, they would burst forth with a froth of blossoms, unless the dire predictions of drought came true. She wondered if Jamie might be home in time to see them in full bloom.

She hummed to herself as she worked and pictured meeting him in this very courtyard. He would stride toward her in his Rebel uniform, the gray matching his eyes. The scent of roses would fill the air… She sighed and moved to another rosebush.

"Aislin, lass?" MacQuaid Byrne's voice was solemn when he called out to her. He hesitated on the stone terrace that led into the courtyard, his gaze never leaving her face. "It hurts me to bear such tidings as this."

Frowning, she stood, then brushed off her hands. The look on her father's face nearly caused her heart to stop. "Jamie…" she whispered. "It's Jamie, isn't it?"

He nodded, looking as still and quiet as she ever remembered seeing him, his face lined with sorrow. "Spence has just now come to see you. He'll tell you everything."

"Oh, Papa…" She stood abruptly, letting her hands drop. It had been seven months since Spence rode East to search for his brother. She had never stopped believing that Jamie was safe, even though both families worried when no word reached them of Jamie's arrival. Even when Spence left, she had refused to consider that Jamie was anywhere except with his regiment. He was simply too busy to write. Jamie was courageous…fearless…strong. He was invincible.

MacQuaid drew her into his arms. "Oh, my poor, sweet lass," he said.

He was still murmuring words of comfort when Spence's voice broke into her thoughts.

"Aislin?" he said softly. Through a blur of tears, she saw Jamie's brother striding across the terrace. "I'm so sorry…" he said, once he stood in front of her.

She nodded, but couldn't speak. Not yet.

Her father gently squeezed her shoulders before letting go. "I'll leave you two alone. Spence has already given your mother and me the details. But I am certain you will want to hear it firsthand, lass."

When he left them, Spence took her elbow and they moved to the stone bench beneath the century oak at the far end of the courtyard. "Tell me everything," she said, once she was seated.

Spence sat across from her on another stone bench. He bent forward earnestly. "I followed Jamie's trail to St. Louis. I heard from others he'd first gone there."

Aislin nodded, recalling the trail Jamie had told her he'd take.

"I found those who remembered him, remembered what happened to him."

A lump formed in Aislin's throat. "Go on," she whispered.

"I found the saloon where he stayed for just a short time." Spence shook his head. "Some dirty business went on there."

Aislin was almost afraid to ask what business, but she had to know. "And Jamie got caught up in it?"

Spence nodded slowly. "Not of his own accord." He hesitated as if trying to decide how much to tell her. When he spoke again, his voice was low. "Jamie was accosted."

"Accosted?" she frowned. "I don't understand."

"A group of thugs, an outlaw Rebel band, was being paid so much a head to get folks signed up to fight. Didn't matter where a victim's loyalties lay, he was forced into a Reb uniform."

"Go on," she whispered.

"They got Jamie. Took him by force. I followed their trail. They were headed to Fort Donelson. That's where the fighting was—also where the Reb colonel was camped." He paused. "It's also where Jamie escaped. Near the fighting."

"Escaped?" She leaned forward, her heart pounding. "So there's a chance he's alive then?"

Spence shook his head. "No, Aislin. There's not." His voice was hard when he went on. "He was shot in the back as a deserter."

Aislin dropped her face to her hands, letting Spence's words sink into her heart. But she did not yet weep. Her grief seemed too great, too deep. "No," she said softly, as if to herself. "It can't be…"

"I saw his grave." Then his tone softened. "He wasn't running away from the fight. He was a Reb at heart, at least he was when he left here. But true to Jamie's spirit, he was going after the thugs who'd captured him. He wanted to see that justice was done, even if he had to take on the entire Confederate Army to do so. It was a matter of honor."

She finally looked up at Spence, his face blurred by her tears. "So like him," she whispered.

Just then, Camila and MacQuaid stepped onto the terrace. Josefa, the maid, stood behind them, holding a silver tray with tea and small cakes. But the thought of taking tea, even though it was her mother's cure for everything from dyspepsia to melancholy, was more than Aislin could bear.

She took a deep breath and stood. Without a word, she blindly pushed past her mother, her father, and Spence, who'd stood when she did. Her father reached out to grasp her hand, but she brushed it aside. "I need to be alone," she cried as she hurried up the terrace stairs. "Please…I'll be all right."

When she reached the entry hall, her sisters, who'd obviously heard the sad news, stood white-faced. Even Sybil, whose heart often seemed made of stone, was sniffling. Sybil started toward her, but Aislin waved her away. Brighid's pretty eyes were red-rimmed, and she reached out to give Aislin a hug. But Aislin shook her head. "Please, I must go," she whispered, and hurried out the front door and down the wide stone stairs.

She ran straight to the eastern corral, saddled Silverheel, and moved the horse into an easy canter as they headed across the fields. The sun now beat hard on her shoulders, and its heat scorched her face. She nudged the mare lightly in the flanks with her heels, turning her toward the trail leading to the place where Jamie had asked for her hand. Small stones rolled down behind Silverheel's hooves, and clouds of dust rose as the horse worked his way upward.

Minutes later, she dismounted, turning Silverheel loose to graze on the dry grass beneath the scrub oaks. She faced west, looking out over the dry rancho lands.

The drought, just as predicted by the Sobobas, had indeed settled across the region, and now there was little water to quench the land's thirst or bring seeds to life.

A hot wind lifted her hair from her sunburned face. Dry and harsh, it beat through the pines behind her and bent the dusty limbs and leaves of the scrub growth before her.

She thought she heard Jamie's voice in the sound of it. "Ceallach," it murmured. "Ceallach."

But it was only the wind. It would be a long season of suffering.

Spence Dearbourne urged Ruffian, his bronze sorrel, up the small hillside. Moments later he reached the top and saw Aislin standing near the rock wall. She was looking across the valley below, now shimmering with heat in the autumn sun.

If she had seen him ride up the trail behind her, she gave no indication. He dismounted and strode toward her. "Aislin?"

She drew a deep breath and turned. Her eyes were watery and filled with pain. "I came here to be alone," she whispered.

"I started to let you go, then I remembered how it was when I found out Jamie had died. I wanted to talk to someone who knew him…who loved him as much as I did. But I was alone." He walked to the wall, near where she was standing, and leaned against it.

Aislin turned away from him.

"I wanted to talk about Jamie. About his goodness and honesty. His decency."

Her gaze was fixed on some distant spot.

"It might help to tell me your feelings, Aislin. Tell me about times you spent together."

Now he had her attention.

"It was here Jamie asked me to marry him," she said. "We played here as children. Pretended this was a castle in Ireland." She laughed softly, sniffling at the same time. "Though neither of us knew what an Irish castle might look like."

He gave her his handkerchief. "I remember that you and Jamie wanted the place all to yourselves. Your sisters and I couldn't decide exactly why. We'd come up here when you two were off riding elsewhere." He grinned. "We'd nose around, trying to figure out the strange Gaelic words we saw carved here and there."

"Ceallach…" she whispered.

"Yes," he said. "That was one."

"It means warrior maid."

"I know," he said. "I looked it up after I found it. I figured it was your name."

"Jamie gave it to me."

He nodded.

"We had plans to build our home here, on this hill, when Jamie returned," she said, now walking toward another of the rock walls. She trailed her fingers along the tops of the granite stones. "We had such dreams…"

"I know," he said.

She turned to look at him, her gray eyes still shimmering with moisture. "You do?"

"Jamie told me." He paused. "He loved you, Aislin."

"It seemed we always loved each other. Even as children."

He wanted to ease her sorrow, but he didn't have the words. He could only try. "We all loved Jamie; not the way you did, but we did love him."

She looked stricken. "Oh, Spence. I'm sorry. You lost your brother," she said. "I wasn't thinking. Your parents lost a son…"

He reached for her hand and held it tight. "Don't apologize. Don't ever apologize for your grief."

She was crying openly now, her face wet with tears. "If only I could have stopped him from going."

"He wouldn't have listened. You know Jamie. He was as stubborn as they come."

"Always the hero."

"Yes, always." He smiled softly at her. "Do you remember what I used to call him?"

She shook her head, wiping at her nose.

"Saint Jamie."

She grinned, quiet suddenly. "Saint Jamie? It's been a long time since I've heard you call him that."

He nodded. "But it fit him. He could do no wrong."

She drew in a deep breath, wiping her cheeks with her fingers. "Oh yes. He was always first with the answers—even when no one asked the question."

"Can you imagine what it was like living with a brother who was not only a hero, but a saint?"

"You never seemed bitter," she said.

"I loved my brother. And he loved me"—he chuckled, and she raised a quizzical brow—"as long as I knew my place."

"Jamie did have a way about him," she said, "a way of taking charge."

He laughed again. "I also called him Little Emperor. That he hated more than he did being called Saint Jamie."

Her gaze searched his face as if reaching into his thoughts. "It couldn't have been easy living with a brother who's both saint and ruler."

Her words surprised him.

"You didn't hate Jamie for it?" she continued.

"How could anyone hate Jamie? He might have been more than a wee bit arrogant, as your father would say. Perhaps more willing than the average man to have his own way, but his heart was made of pure gold. He loved fiercely and honestly."

She was quiet for a moment, and there was the faintest dusting of salt on her cheeks where her tears had dried. "But what about you, Spence? Growing up with Jamie as your older brother?"

"Do you mean, was it hard to live up to Jamie's example?"

She nodded.

"You grew up around the two of us. What do you think?"

She smiled, and to Spence, it was as if the sun had risen for the second time that day. "You had your own way of going about life, Spence. You were never like Jamie at all." She frowned, as if calling some distant memory to life. "It seems you've always had a different kind of strength…" Her voice fell off as she searched his face, seeming to grasp for something out of reach. "A strength of spirit somehow that far surpassed your brother's. I think he knew it too."

No one had ever said such a thing about his brother…about himself. Spence swallowed hard. The moment seemed sacred, and he knew Aislin's words would long be etched in his soul. He reached for her hand, pressed her fingertips tenderly, then let it go. "Thank you," he said simply.

She looked down at her ring, and turned it with the fingertips of her opposite hand. His heart went out to her. "Is there any way you could have been mistaken?"

"I talked to a man who saw the shooting. He said there was no mistake. Jamie died in the woods near Fort Donelson. This man wasn't the only witness to the killing."

"But are they sure it was Jamie?"

"I gave him Jamie's description. He knew my brother had come from California, knew too many details about him to have been mistaken. I'm sorry, Aislin. I'd hoped otherwise too. But it was Jamie."

"Spence?" She was crying again. "I don't want to be alone."

"I'm here." And he was, now standing very near her.

Her eyes caught and held his. He thought his heart would break with the look of her misery. "Would you hold me, please?" Her voice was husky, broken.

Without a word he gathered her into his arms and felt her tremble against his chest. He rested his cheek on the top of her head, and held her while she cried for his brother.

Two

Pueblo de los Angeles

Barely one month later Hugh Dearbourne, patriarch of Rancho Dearbourne, flicked his whip over the backs of his two high-stepping grays. The carriage rattled along the rutted road leading from the Big Valley to the dusty Pueblo de los Angeles.

He popped the whip once more, and the carriage tongue jangled as the team moved forward. Overnight, eastern desert winds had swept the air clean, now giving him a rare view of the distant pueblo. It looked like scattered toy blocks, just like a set he'd once made for his son Jamie. Only these squat blocks took on the hue of burnished sienna in the slant of the morning sun.

The carriage swayed, and he headed the horses onto a smoother side of the dirt road. He had made a decision that would forever change the Big Valley, and as he considered it, it struck him that instead of relief, he felt burdened. He hoped that by the time he reached Pueblo de los Angeles, he would feel greater peace. Or at least indifference.

He was lost in thought as he rode closer to the pueblo. The wheels squeaked with each turn, and as the minutes passed he considered the past…and the future he was carving out for himself.

He'd lived through the devastation of Jamie's death. It had changed him. He acknowledged that. But he'd also lived through years of hiding a deep and growing bitterness. Hiding painful memories involving one he had once loved more than life itself, hiding a heart that had turned to stone.

He thought of MacQuaid with his generous ways, his know-it-all bearing, his way of assuming he could make decisions for them both

16

because of their friendship. MacQuaid, who had never known the personal tragedy that Hugh had experienced.

Within minutes Hugh would sign papers to ensure the realization of a dream. That of political gain. Power. He smiled to himself. He'd been criticized for giving up his British citizenship and adopting this land as his own. But he had no regrets. He'd met people in high places, played their political games, and now they promised to see his star rise. He wondered if Governor was too great a dream.

He reined the grays to the left, heading them toward the main street through town. A few nondescript trees with brown leaves rattled in the dry wind among the clusters of squat adobes. Perhaps they were sycamore or elms; Hugh couldn't tell, nor did he care about their identity. All he knew was that they were planted by newcomers from the East who hated the barren desert landscape of southern California.

Give him the wild open spaces any day. Trees made him feel he might suffocate. Especially planted too close together.

For months the Land Commission had been hounding MacQuaid Byrne to provide proof of La Paloma's boundaries, refusing to accept his records. MacQuaid had fallen into deep debt, spending thousands on legal fees. And still the Byrnes were in grave danger of losing at least half their land, the very land that contained the rancho's precious water supply, the San Jacinto River and all water rights.

The Dearbournes had little grazing land but much in the way of cash resources. La Paloma had no cash resources, and land enough for tens of thousands of head of cattle. Because MacQuaid had long dreamed of joining the families and the lands, he still thought there was opportunity to save both ranchos, make them prosper.

But there wasn't such an opportunity. There would never be.

MacQuaid would never know how and why he lost his beloved rancho. By the time he figured it out, it would be too late. But it wouldn't be too late for Hugh. He was a powerful man on his way to political gain. It was all that remained to live for.

He didn't grieve for MacQuaid Byrne. Everyone knew the heyday of the California rancho was over. One by one, the ranchos were falling into disrepair because of the high cost of proving land ownership. It was a matter of time before Rancho de la Paloma fell with the others. Hugh simply planned to profit from the inevitable.

Nor did he grieve for his family, or concern himself with how Spence and Sara might feel about losing their home. Nothing really mattered now, not even Sara or Spence. Especially not Sara or Spence.

He set his mouth in a straight line and again turned his attention to driving the team, flicking the whip over the grays' backs.

The carriage rattled along, and he turned his musings to Spence and Aislin. MacQuaid had pushed him into trying to get Spence to propose to Aislin. He'd said it was the only way to save the ranchos. Hugh dreaded putting on a show for Spence, trying to convince his son to do the very thing that would complicate—even destroy—his scheme. But he had no choice; MacQuaid would undoubtedly come asking questions later. He was afraid to tip his hand. He wanted no suspicion cast his way.

If Spence and Aislin did marry, Hugh's plans would be destroyed. But he was betting the young people would not wed. Everyone knew Aislin still pined for Jamie. And Spence wasn't the type to force a woman into a union without love, for any reason. He knew the young man well.

Of course, if they did agree to a cordial union, a few well-placed words about Jamie would cause both Aislin and Spence to have second thoughts. Even if he had to wait until their wedding day to manipulate the outcome, he would do it. No, he had no doubt. They would not marry.

He headed the team down the dusty street past two mercantiles, four saloons, two churches, and the Butterfield building and halted the team in front of the town's single bank with its fancy oval sign stating the partners' names, Fitzwalter and Boothe. After he stepped from the carriage, he took a moment to smooth the dark cloth of his jacket sleeves and adjust his hat before bounding up the stairs, onto the wooden walk, and into the bank building. The bell above the door announced his arrival.

Bertrum Fitzwalter looked up from his desk behind the customer window and gave him a quick nod. "Come in, come in," he said, motioning Hugh to follow him through a door at the back of the small room.

Hugh removed his hat, straightened the shoulders of his jacket, and followed the smaller, rotund man. This was his third meeting with the two men in the room behind the counter where they met most of their customers. He understood that only the most privileged customers were given this preferential treatment. He straightened his shoulders again and, with a sense of dignity, took his seat across the long mahogany table from Farley Boothe, bank president.

"I understand you've come to a conclusion," Boothe said without preamble. He fixed his small, dark eyes on Hugh. His coloring, his narrow face, and his shrewd wit reminded Hugh of a red fox. He liked the man. Had from the first time they met.

"I have," Hugh said. "I am ready to sign."

Boothe and Fitzwalter exchanged pleased glances. "You're making our position in this transaction much easier," said Fitzwalter, thumbing through a stack of papers on the table. "And as we've said in the past, you will be amply rewarded for your contribution."

Hugh gave them a slight, dignified smile. "Yes."

"You understand, now, Hugh, what your position must be?"

"Of course." He drew in a deep breath. He tried to dismiss the thought that he might be betraying MacQuaid Byrne. The demise of Rancho de la Paloma was inescapable, he told himself for the hundredth time. There was nothing he or any of the other rancheros could do to stop it. There was also no reason not to profit from the inevitable. "Of course," he repeated. "I understand."

"Let me review our agreement," Farley Boothe said, "because, as you are aware, we can't possibly let all the ins and outs be put to paper. Some must simply be understood." He gave Hugh a piercing and knowing look.

Hugh nodded. "I understand."

"Let me continue, then. You are promising to work toward the financial demise of Rancho de la Paloma, through whatever means you choose."

Hugh swallowed hard and nodded again. "Yes."

"You are promising the delivery of the same rancho into our hands. When you have accomplished this, thus saving the State government time, trouble, and money, you will then be paid fair market value for Rancho Dearbourne."

"And don't forget," Hugh said quietly, "the political office. Whatever appointment might be available at that time."

Both men met his gaze. "Yes," said Farley. Hugh hoped it wasn't a smirk he saw cross the man's face.

Then Fitzwalter laughed. "You're getting the high end of the bargain. You probably don't need to do much to bring down MacQuaid Byrne's rancho. He seems to be heading along that road quite nicely all by himself. Just see to it that he doesn't reverse the process."

Hugh nodded quickly. "Of course."

"Political cronies of the governor are being noted," Farley Boothe mused as he leafed through his papers. "You will be amply rewarded. Believe me."

"Good," he said, though he felt strangely bereft.

The papers were thrust in front of him. And a pen.

He dipped the slender implement into the inkwell, then scrawled his signature across the bottom of the page. He signed another copy of the note, then upon their direction folded it and placed it in the hidden pocket inside his coat. Over his heart, he thought grimly.

Bertrum Fitzwalter stood abruptly and reached out to shake his hand, as if they expected him to leave as quickly as possible. Farley Boothe took his elbow to escort him to the door.

He deserved more respect, but they were treating him like a Judas. Or maybe it was how he saw himself. No matter. He hurried to the carriage, anxious to be away from the men, the bank, the accusing eyes he imagined from passersby. Within a few minutes he was on the road back to the Big Valley.

No one knew what he had signed away today. No one would for a long time.

⎯⎯◄►⎯⎯

Spence headed into the corral at Rancho Dearbourne. He had just swung a saddle onto Ruffian's back when he was summoned to his father's library by the foreman, a big man named Conrado. He unbuckled the tack and lifted the saddle over a nearby rail. He hurried around the side of the two-story hacienda, let himself in a back entrance, and, minutes later, rapped on his father's door.

"Come in," came the gruff call from inside. Spence pushed the door open. His father sat behind his desk, looking dignified as usual. "We need to talk about how you see your future with Aislin," Hugh said without preamble.

"It's been only a month since we found out about Jamie."

His father interrupted. "We're not here to discuss how long it's been since Jamie's death. We're here to discuss the future. MacQuaid and I both feel it would be for the best if you and Aislin marry."

Spence's hands fisted. "You and MacQuaid are giving her no say in this. You expect her to marry the brother of the man she loved to save the ranchos. Do you think she can ever forget that?"

He was surprised to see his father lean back wearily. "MacQuaid had another post from the Land Commission. They're threatening to call in his loans. If that happens, he loses everything…we lose our grazing land, that which he allows us to use."

"And the obvious solution—loaning him enough to pay off his debts—will not work?"

"You mean, could we pay off his debts?"

"Yes, exactly that."

His father shook his head and smiled, as if at Spence's simplistic thinking. "The debts are far beyond what we could manage."

Spence wondered if that was true, but he didn't question his father aloud.

"You're counting on Aislin and me to help in what way then? We marry. The lands become united. We still have MacQuaid's debt and not enough cash to pay off the loans. I don't see how our marriage would solve the legal mess that both ranchos are in."

His father hands, fingertips steepled, remained motionless. "There is a loophole," he explained patiently, as if Spence somehow should have known. "When you marry, MacQuaid and I will draw up the legal documents to present you the lands as a wedding gift. They legally will become one."

Spence narrowed his eyes in thought, and nodded. "I understand. But won't the debt remain? The legal problems with defining the property boundaries?"

"The loophole," Hugh repeated, "makes the difference."

"What exactly is this means of escape?"

"Lands given as a gift no longer bear the burden of personal debt. An obscure clause was written into the 1849 constitution."

Spence leaned back in his chair, stunned. "If that's the case, why are other rancheros not pursuing this?"

His father laughed, looking uncomfortable. "Part of our jointly incurred debt was from the hiring of lawyers to research the law. The debt must be unsecured. Most people did use the land as collateral in the early years, at least until bankers tried to collect on the disputed lands. The odd thing is, because MacQuaid's rancho was in such dispute, the bank refused to use the land. He's being charged twice the interest rate for his loans, but the loans are personal."

"There's still the problem of boundaries…proving MacQuaid's legal property lines." Something didn't make sense with his father's argument, but he didn't know exactly what it was.

"We'll go on fighting to prove his northern boundaries, just as before, but Rancho Dearbourne has no such problem. And more important, we have no disputed water rights. Both ranchos could survive without the acreage in dispute, as long as we have water."

"The ranchos are to be our wedding gift," Spence said, watching his father carefully.

"You will run them," his father said, surprising Spence.

"I will be in full control?"

His father answered by shifting his gaze elsewhere.

"Legally then," Spence continued, "we'll have one large rancho belonging to the new Mr. and Mrs. Spencer Dearbourne. But in reality, father, if I know you, La Paloma will continue to be run under Mac-Quaid's control. Rancho Dearbourne, under yours. No matter what you'd like for me to believe right now."

His father didn't answer. Spence noticed a faint sheen of perspiration on his forehead. He had the strange sensation that Hugh was leading him to the only conclusion he wanted Spence to consider.

"And what do Aislin and I get out of this…ah, union?"

His father laughed, though the sound was hollow. "You will have the satisfaction of helping your families."

"And if I refuse?"

Hugh's eyes bored in on his. "I can't imagine that you would consider such a thing. You want to save the ranchos as much as I do—as much as Jamie would have…" His words didn't match the look of triumph in his eyes, again as if he wanted Spence to conclude exactly that. Refusal.

Spence stood so abruptly that his chair tipped backwards and banged to the floor. "You underestimate me, Father. I'm not Jamie, but that doesn't mean I don't want to save the ranchos." His hands were clenching into fists again.

"Is that right, Spencer?"

Spence flexed his fingers, and he forced himself not to speak until his breathing was normal. Why did his conversations with his father always take this turn? "I've heard enough," he finally said.

His father arched a brow. Again, there was a look of triumph in Hugh's expression. "We'll see," he said.

THREE

The next morning, Aislin looked up as MacQuaid Byrne strode toward her in the oak-shaded courtyard. She was sitting alone on the stone bench beneath the gray-green leaves. Her father handed her the envelope, a thick cream-colored parchment with the Rancho Dearbourne insignia stamped into a crimson wax seal.

Her sisters peered through the window above the terrace, their expressions curious. Their mother appeared and quickly turned them away. It seemed the entire family knew, and was asking for, the sacrifice only Aislin could make to save the rancho.

"So our letter has arrived, Father?"

"Aye, lass," MacQuaid said. His worried expression didn't escape her. The ranchero's legal troubles were taking their toll, and her father's last hope for saving La Paloma lay in the letter's contents.

She stared at the letter in her hands, knowing full well what it contained. "You are asking the impossible of me."

MacQuaid acknowledged her words with a slight nod. "The question is," he said sadly, "how much do you love this land?"

Before she could answer, her father turned and left her alone to read the letter in privacy. She flipped it in her hands, unwilling to open it quite yet. It struck her as odd that one piece of paper could hold so much weight against her future, against the future of La Paloma. Then she laid the missive on her lap and stared at it, unwilling to slide her finger beneath the wax seal to pop it open.

So instead, she raised her eyes to the canopy of oak leaves above her, focusing on the lacy, dappled pattern of sunlight and shade. The gnarled trunk rose majestically toward the heavens, a silent, living sentinel, as much a part of Rancho de la Paloma as any of the Byrne family.

Only a few weeks ago she had received the news of Jamie's death beneath its branches. Strange that another life-changing event should occur beneath them today. Finally, she turned her attention back to the letter, unfolded it, and began to read.

> *My dear Aislin,*
> *You are as aware as I am that the Dearbourne*
> *and Byrne families most anxiously await the*
> *opportunity to bless our betrothal and marriage.*
> *This is a matter you and I need to discuss.*
> *I will call on you this evening. At that time I*
> *will speak to your father if we reach a satisfac-*
> *tory conclusion.*
>
> *Yours faithfully,*
> *Spencer Dearbourne*

Aislin swallowed hard, staring at the letter, letting the words sink into a bleak reality. The threat of tears stung her eyes. The tone of the letter was so cold, as if the writer had no comprehension of how she might accept such a proposal.

"Lassie?" Her father's voice broke into her thoughts. She looked up as MacQuaid walked across the courtyard. "Aye, but you're lookin' glum, lass," her father said as he sat beside her. He glanced down at the crumpled letter on her lap. "I'm sorry for my earlier gruffness."

She nodded. "You understand better than most how dismal the thought of marriage is to me."

"Spence Dearbourne is a good man," her father countered. "He'll be good to you, daughter."

"I have no doubt that he will, Papa."

MacQuaid reached for the letter, scanned it quickly, then handed it back to her. "Is it the lack of affection in his words, or is it the man himself, lass, that you object to?"

Aislin looked up at her father in surprise. "Perhaps both."

Her father met her gaze evenly. "You're thinkin' he may have written this from obligation, not from any caring for you?"

"It's as if he's discussing a change in the weather, not a lifetime commitment."

MacQuaid stroked his beard in thought.

She hurried on. "Next you'll tell me that it's for the good of La Paloma that I marry Spence. That bringing together Rancho de la Paloma and Rancho Dearbourne will cause the entire Big Valley to be ours. That it will make the joined rancho invincible, and that we'll come to love each other in the years ahead, and have children and grandchildren who will make you proud."

MacQuaid laughed lightly. "It is you who have a manner of runnin' away with thoughts and puttin' words in others' mouths, lass." His tone turned sober. "But as for what you just said, oh, that it could be that easy, lass."

She wondered at the sadness in her father's face, in his voice, and squeezed his hand.

"You're the most like me. It's my spirit I see in your gray eyes, and your grandmother's, my own sweet mother's face lookin' back at me when you smile. You were named for them both, you know, your grandma'am and her own sweet mama as well."

Aislin nodded. She loved the reminder. Though she'd heard the tale told again and again through the years, she never tired of it.

"Aislin D'Ary Byrne, prettiest name this side of heaven." With his thick Irish brogue, he pronounced it with pure Gaelic perfection. *Ashlin.* He made it sound like a breeze whispering in the mountain pines. Then he laughed. "Though it was your sweet mama's idea."

"What does all this have to do with my marrying Spence?"

"You are strong. Like me. You have the strength of this oak tree we're sittin' under."

Aislin looked up at the massive trunk that spread its leafy branches over them. Already a hundred years old, the tree would probably outlive them all. She smiled, glad to know her father had seen that kind of tough endurance in her.

"In marryin' Spence Dearbourne, you'll be partners in the running of the ranchos." MacQuaid was no longer looking at her. Instead, he seemed to be focusing on something far away, something Aislin couldn't see. And when he spoke, it was as to the wind. "'Tis no secret. I've been pushing Hugh and Spence to approach you about the union."

She touched his arm. "Is there something more that you haven't told me?"

He again turned toward her. "The drought is worsening," he said. "The river flows now, but there's no snowpack in the mountains to make the water last. For the cattle. For irrigation."

"I've heard Indian legends of their signs," she said quickly. "It's been a dry year, but that happens from time to time in California. Maybe there's no substance to our fears." But even as she said the words, she knew they were empty.

She stood and moved to stand by the fountain, her back to her father. His footsteps crunched on the gravel path of the courtyard as he approached. She didn't turn toward him, just watched the water trickle over the fountain's top tier and into the pool beneath, indistinguishable from the other droplets that had already fallen. If rain didn't come soon, they would need to stop the water's flow. She would miss its music, just as the plants that circled its base would miss the moisture they needed to survive.

Her father, standing close to her now, glanced at the letter clutched in her hand and nodded slowly. "The choice is yours, child." He sounded tired. "But you know the consequences."

Consequences? Her family's survival…or their ruin. What kind of a choice had she been given?

She reached for her father's hand and held it in both of hers. "Papa, I care about you. I care about this land. But is there no other way?"

Her father's eyes darkened from someplace deep inside. "I would not ask this of you, child, if there were." He circled one arm around her shoulders, and for a moment they stood watching the splash of water in the fountain. "Aye, of this one thing I'm sure."

She looked up into his beloved face. "What is that?"

"'Tis not an easy road, what I'm askin' you to do. That is, if you say yes. But God will be with you, child, no matter which way you choose."

"You don't have to remind me of its difficulty, Papa. Or of God's care." Though she wondered how God could be in this. She considered next what it would be like to enter into a marriage without love. How could God be in such a union? "According to the letter, Spence will call on me tonight," she said after a moment.

"Will you see him?"

Again, her choices played in her mind. *Her family's survival…or their ruin.* And when it came right down to it, no matter what her father said, there was really no choice at all.

She fixed her gaze on her father's eyes. "I will," she said.

Then without another word, she hurried from the courtyard before he could see her tears.

Later the same afternoon, Spence headed to the barn to saddle Ruffian. After mounting, he headed east toward the mountains, hoping to clear his thoughts as he rode. Tonight he would call on Aislin. Tonight they would make decisions that would affect the rest of their lives, decisions muddled by his own pent-up feelings of rejection and anger.

How could he marry Aislin, when she still mourned his brother? How could such a marriage of convenience benefit anyone, except, of course, his father and MacQuaid Byrne?

He pictured his mother's soft, pretty face. What would she do without a home? Or the Byrnes—Camila, Sybil, Brighid, and Aislin herself? What if they lost their rancho? Where would they go?

He had entered a wide canyon leading into the high country, and, surefooted as ever, Ruffian picked his way upward, his hooves drumming on the hard and dusty trail.

Where did sacrifice end and following one's own heart and dreams begin? Thin strips of white streaked across the eastern sky. They weren't rain clouds, he knew, but they dimmed the skies enough to match his somber mood.

He drew in a deep breath. *Father, we've got some things to talk over,* he said aloud to the Friend riding next to him. *You know I want to flee from this place…flee from my father's home…*

He rode on, and in the distance, the rush of Strawberry Creek blended with the sounds of pines whispering in a soft wind.

If I should stay…to do my father's bidding…I will do so only if it's right in your eyes.

Ruffian, choosing his path, moved smoothly up the trail as if by rote.

No matter the circumstances, no matter the earthly gain, Father, all of it is meaningless compared to doing your will. But your way is unclear.

If I relied on feelings, I'd leave this land, the only home I've ever known, right now. Never to look back.

He shook his head. *But, Lord, how can I know what you would have me do? Show me, I pray. Just show me the way.*

Beloved, you are mine…

My presence will go with you, and I will give you peace.

But it's answers I need, Lord. Not peace. Then he chuckled. *Well, Lord, I take that back. I do need peace.*

I will instruct you and teach you in the way you should go.

I will counsel you and watch over you.

But it's specifics I need right now, Lord!

Trust me, my beloved son. Trust me…

He continued his conversation with God as he rode to the crest of the mountain, through the forested flatlands, and onto a knot of boulders on a bald dome overlooking both ranchos. Odd how this place, which belonged to neither rancho, gave his soul the greatest sense of rest. *Yes, Lord, you do give me peace!*

He slid off Ruffian's back and stepped to the edge of the rocky precipice. On both sides of the trail, lupines and poppies shot up among the Indian paintbrush and buckthorn.

In the valley below, a honeyed light from the California sun spilled across the golden, drought-singed lands of the two ranchos, his father's smaller spread and the massive acreage belonging to the Byrnes, Rancho de la Paloma.

Lands that might someday belong to him. Together with Aislin. Their children, grandchildren.

But she doesn't love me, Father! How can such an alliance be?

He heard Ruffian nickering softly behind him and thought about remounting and riding as fast as he could away from the place, away from the Byrnes and the Dearbournes. He'd been east once, looking for Jamie. He liked life on the trail, the freedom it gave him.

What would it be like to simply follow a trail, any trail, according to whim?

Ruffian nickered again, and Spence turned to watch the big sorrel. Horses were usually silent unless another horse was nearby. He hadn't heard anyone else on the trail, so his curiosity caused him to step closer.

Ruffian was nosing into the brush, pushing gently at something obscured from Spence's view. He headed immediately to the place, just a few yards back down the trail. The nickering continued, followed by yet a softer sound.

He pulled back some buckthorn branches and bent closer into the brush.

There in a small patch of dried grasses lay a small, frightened mustang foal. The horse, a fawn-colored dun, appraised him with silent, frightened eyes and struggled to get onto its spindly legs. One leg was swollen twice the size of the others.

Spence broke off some branches and moved closer into the brush. It was a wonder that the helpless foal hadn't been dragged off by a mountain lion. He touched the foal, limb by limb, inch by inch, and some of the fear left the animal's eyes. His eyes took in Spence's every move.

Spence quickly found the injury: distinct double fang marks on the swollen leg. Rattlesnake bite. He pulled out his knife and sliced the flesh over the fang marks. The foal kicked and struggled. But Spence calmed it with his touch, then bent and sucked the poison from its leg and spit it into the dirt.

The foal quivered soundlessly, and Spence touched the velvet between his eyes, stroking, speaking softly, almost as if to a child. He wondered about the foal's herd. Recently, hundreds of wild mustangs had moved from the eastern California deserts into the upper valleys of the San Jacinto near Sapphire Lake, and no doubt this foal was part of that herd.

The Soboba Indians said the horses knew of bad times ahead, times of death and drought that no one else knew. That's why they'd come.

A beat of hooves sounded in the distance, just as Spence finished tying a handkerchief around the foal's leg.

He was surprised to see the rider. The last person he expected to see in this place. The last person he wanted to see anywhere.

Aislin Byrne.

She slowed her mount and slid from the saddle a short distance from where he knelt, then headed toward him, moving with a natural beauty and grace that had always reminded him of a wild deer. Her dark hair hung in a single heavy braid; it caught the sun as it swung to the beat of her stride.

Today, he considered her in a new light. The pale spray of freckles across her nose. Her spirited face. Her expressive gray eyes. Odd that he would think of it now, but Aislin, and every bit of her gray-eyed grace and freckled spunk, had captivated him since they were children. But she had always belonged to Jamie.

If she felt the same dismay he did about their encounter, she didn't show it. She quickly knelt beside him and turned her attention to the foal.

"He's beautiful." Her voice was filled with awe as she rubbed the little animal's neck and laced her fingers through his mane. "What happened?"

"Snakebite."

"Do you think you got to him in time?" Her voice was barely more than a whisper.

"It must have happened only minutes before I found him. He fell from the pain of it, which kept the poison from moving to his heart. There's some swelling, but I think he'll recover. Right now he's more frightened than anything else."

"He's not very old."

Spence nodded. "Only days, it appears. But healthy."

"You think his dam is nearby?"

He shrugged. "A wild horse is frightened to be away from the safety of the herd. I don't know which instinct would be stronger for a mare. Staying near her foal or staying with the herd."

The exhausted foal now closed his eyes and lay, spindly legs outstretched, his sides heaving. Aislin stroked him again, gently, with her fingertips. Then she stood, brushing off her hands.

He stood when she did, and they stared at each other for a long moment. She was close enough to touch, and he took a few steps back and turned toward the vista of the valley below. He wondered how many times through the years, when he stood too near her, he had found it necessary to look away to breathe normally again.

"This is awkward," she finally said, causing him to turn back toward her. "Seeing you here, I mean."

He couldn't agree more. "You received the letter then?"

"This afternoon." Her words came out in a sigh. A sigh of resignation. "When I rode up here, I certainly didn't expect to see you. I just needed time to think."

"Please," he assured her quickly, "we don't have to speak of it now."

She laughed lightly, and the sound of it was a welcome break from the tension between them. "Oh, Spence. I can see by the look on your face that you're in no hurry to draw this thing to a conclusion. Am I right?"

"Are you?" He skirted around an answer.

She was looking up at him now, considering him through those gray eyes. There was something tender in her expression, and he figured it was because she somehow reminded her of Jamie. She touched his arm. "It's unfair, what they've asked of us," she said finally.

"I said exactly that to my father," he said.

"So you feel it too? The lack of honor in it, I mean?"

"I know you still love Jamie."

Now her gray eyes lost some of their brightness, and her smile faded. "It's unfair to ask you to marry someone who's still in love with your brother."

"That, too. Yes."

She pulled her gaze away from his scrutiny and turned toward the view of the valley below them. Her words were almost lost in the wind. "I had to wonder at the tone of your letter."

He stepped closer. "And why did you wonder?"

"There's no caring in it." She turned back to him now, her eyes filled with pain. "Marriage should hold, at the very least, some caring between the two…well, those who plan to marry." Her words were halting, and he knew it was hard for her to speak of such emotion to him.

"Yes, it should," he finally said. She gazed up at him with an expression of complete trust, and the slant of the late afternoon sun touched her face, causing his heart to catch unexpectedly. "I didn't think you would want flowery, meaningless words at such a time."

"Because of Jamie."

"Of course, Aislin. Always because of Jamie."

She laughed softly, though the sound was filled with more sadness than joy. "You know me well, Spence."

He didn't laugh with her. "What our families are asking us to do is for them, not us."

"I know. But it's also for the land."

"Can you take me as your husband, for all our time on earth, for the sake of saving the ranchos?"

She looked surprised. "I'd do almost anything to save La Paloma."

This time he did laugh, a short, bitter sound. "That's where you and I differ, my dear. I'm not so in love with Rancho Dearbourne that I would sell my soul to save it."

She stepped backward, but her gaze remained locked on his. For several heartbeats, she said nothing. Just stood there with eyes that told him she was attempting to search his soul. "Because of Jamie," she finally murmured, almost as if to herself. "Also because of Jamie."

"What do you mean?"

"The land was always meant for him."

"Yes, of course."

"It makes me wonder if, out of your own resentment, you might want to turn your back on it now?"

Her clear assessment of his inner struggles almost took his breath away. *How does she know this about me, Lord?*

"It's crossed my mind," he said.

She smiled. "It's different for me."

"I know."

"But even so, Spence, I looked for some sign of affection in your missive. I couldn't find it." She gazed up at him again. "We've known each other all our lives. I thought we were friends."

"I hold you in the highest esteem."

"You see? There you go again."

"There's something wrong with esteem?" He was teasing her now, and he could see by the light in her eyes that she understood.

"Maybe we will marry without love. But we can at least be honest about those other qualities we see in each other."

"From the first time I saw you toddle across the yard of La Paloma, Aislin," he began, "your good qualities became too many to number." She glanced up at him in wonder, as if she thought he was teasing again. What he didn't say was that from the time any of the two families' five children could talk, Aislin and Jamie had been paired off, either by choice or by their parents' design. "It's true," he added, letting his gaze linger just a moment on her face. "Your beauty and grace were evident to me even as a child."

She colored slightly. "I'm asking only for friendship—whether or not we go through with this."

He stepped back slightly and turned away from her. "And it's your opinion that we have a choice?"

For a moment she didn't answer, and he thought perhaps she hadn't heard him. "No," she said finally. "In *my* opinion we don't. But it's your opinion that matters, Spence." She let her voice drop.

She moved closer to him and followed his gaze to the ranchos, just below a rugged descent of nearly five thousand feet, rife with boulders the size of small barns, and a thick copse of buckthorn, manzanita, and scrub oak. The view stretched eighty miles to the south toward the barely visible edge of the Pacific Ocean, just a thin strip of silver shimmering in the late afternoon light. And nearly all of it would belong to the two of them…if they married.

"Spence, look!" Aislin interrupted his thoughts. She shaded her eyes and gazed southward. "Look, over there!"

He squinted in the direction she was pointing. First he saw nothing. Then through the thick foliage, there was movement. Very slight, but movement nonetheless.

He grinned. Nearly hidden in a small canyon below them, some two dozen wild horses were grazing, ears flicking nervously.

She nodded excitedly. "It's got to be the foal's herd."

He turned to her and grinned, raising a brow. "Shall we?"

She knew immediately what he was proposing. "Can you carry him?"

He nodded. "With your help."

Aislin smiled at him as if their charge were the most important task in the world. All other concerns seemed to have faded from her mind as they walked back to the foal.

Spence lifted the small leggy bundle and carried it like a sleeping child, Aislin at his side. They climbed carefully downward to the nervous herd. A few nickers carried toward them on the breeze. A big stallion circled the group, ears back, eyes wide. A tall dun mare stood off to one side. The foal's dam.

"Silently…" Spence reminded Aislin. "Move as quietly as possible. If they bolt, we have to start all over again."

She nodded, and they continued their descent.

Finally they were within a hundred yards of the mare. Spence laid the foal in the shade of a live oak. The foal seemed weaker now, probably from lack of nourishment. Spence unwrapped the wound. The bleeding had stopped, but the leg was still swollen.

Silently, he crept back to where Aislin waited. Together, they hid in the thick brush. The mustangs obviously smelled their presence, but eye contact would frighten the horses away, so they remained where they were.

A few of the mustangs near the outside of the herd nickered. Ears flickered forward, then back again. The stallion paced nervously, his body always staying between Spence and Aislin's hiding place and the wild horses.

"They're beautiful…" breathed Aislin. She was lying on her stomach, elbows propped, chin resting on her hands. "I've never seen anything so magnificent."

"Have you ever seen a mustang so close?"

She transferred her gaze to him, and he thought there might be moisture in her eyes. "Only the foal," she whispered.

They turned their attention to the dun mare, who was now nickering to the foal. She stepped closer, one ear forward, one bent back nervously. The rest of the herd stood perfectly still, ears flicking, tails swishing. Only the stallion continued his lookout.

Finally, the mare reached the foal. She bent her long neck and nosed against him; he nickered softly. She pushed against him, hard. Spence whispered that the mare was silently telling the foal to lean into its mother just as hard, lean and attempt to stand. The foal instinctively obeyed, but his legs wouldn't hold him.

Aislin groaned softly. "Come on, fellow."

The mare licked her foal's face, then nudged him again. This time he took longer to make the attempt, but finally, slender legs wobbling, he stood.

Aislin's eyes were filled with the witness of a miracle. She reached for Spence's hand, and her touch, so trusting and natural, fanned to a flame a spark that had flickered unnoticed in him for a long, long time.

The foal seemed stronger now and took several wobbly steps toward the herd. "Watch this," he whispered. It occurred to him that his lips were close enough to kiss the pink shell of her ear. "Watch what they do," he said, swallowing hard.

As if at a silent signal from the dam, or perhaps the stallion, the herd moved as one around the foal and mare.

"Oh, Spence…" she murmured. Still clutching his hand, she gazed at him in wonder. Words weren't needed.

After a moment, they crept back through the brush to the top of the mountain. Below them, the mustangs continued their silent vigil over the injured foal.

"You go on ahead, Spence," she said with a nod to Ruffian. "I want to stay a few minutes. I still have some thinking to do…about our future."

"I understand," he said. He swung a leg over Ruffian and looked back down at her. "Tonight then?"

She nodded. "Yes, I'll be waiting for you."

Long after Spence was out of sight, Aislin stared after him, aware of the soft thud of Ruffian's hooves on the trail, their slow plodding unlike the gelding's usual spirited canter. And she wondered about the plodding in Spence's own spirit, so matching hers.

Even when he'd ridden from sight, his image filled her mind. Spence carrying the little foal. The light in his eyes as he watched the wild herd. The look of him riding off on the bronze sorrel, so like another time he'd done the same. And strangely, the place in her soul, so long frozen, seemed not so cold as before.

But almost as soon as she recognized the transformation, she caught her breath in surprise.

It was Jamie she loved, Jamie she would always love.

In this very place they had met to say their final good-byes on the same day Jamie rode east. She remembered how Jamie rode to meet her on a tall, dark stallion, its hide gleaming in the sun. How he'd swung out of the saddle and moved toward her with a bold, broad-shouldered grace, his gaze locked on hers. He had gathered her into his arms, and she had felt the beat of his heart as their lips met.

Then Spence had arrived, seemingly from out of nowhere.

She and Jamie had turned toward him, their arms still wrapped around each other, their faces still warm with passion.

She remembered a kind of sacred beauty in Spence as he halted Ruffian and sat there, still in the saddle, staring at the two of them. He had seemed bathed in golden light—his hair, his bronze sorrel. Behind him, a stand of pines had whispered in the breeze, and farther on still, the mountains had jutted upward to form stern, snow-covered peaks.

And she remembered the hue of the sky. Bitter blue.

How could she forget? It was the last time she saw Jamie.

She had never thought to ask Spence why he had stared so solemnly, then turned in utter silence to leave them alone.

Strange that she thought of it now.

FOUR

A harvest moon was rising by the time Spence headed to La Paloma. He considered heading Ruffian down the trail, skirting the Byrnes' spread, and instead turning north to the main road out to the barren lands of the desert, far removed from the Big Valley. The thought of drifting on without facing discussion of the arranged marriage was inviting.

Then he considered Aislin.

Even on the day Jamie left, he'd wanted to take her in his arms, comfort her, make her path easier. Perhaps, if he was brutally honest with himself, he fancied that she might turn to him. It hadn't been an honorable thought then, and it wasn't now. It had been a mistake then, and it would be an even greater mistake now. Aislin's heart would always belong to his brother. It didn't matter that Jamie was dead.

What a bitter lesson he'd learned that day.

From a distance, he'd watched Aislin ride up the high country trail to the bald mountain. And he'd followed, thinking Aislin might need him because Jamie had just left her.

He'd had the witless notion that she might need comforting. Or perhaps he merely hoped she might need him.

He had met the two of them on the trail wrapped in a tender embrace. In that one instant, their expressions told him more than an entire lifetime of words might have. In that one instant, any hope of need, of love—oh yes, especially love—had died a swift death.

And he'd been ashamed of imagining she might need his comfort. Ashamed that he'd wanted to be the one to gather her into his arms.

So he'd continued watching her from a distance, before and after the news of Jamie's death. He had weakened only once—the day he told her of Jamie's death—in his determination to keep his distance. Holding her in his arms, even for those few minutes, had nearly broken his heart.

But before they knew that Jamie would never come home again, he had watched as she awaited his brother's return. Watched as she raced Silverheel across the fields…as she danced to the music of guitars at a fandango…as she expressed her opinions at a book reading in his mother's parlor.

He'd watched the way she lifted a brow and said precisely what she thought, not what she was expected to say. The way she made no bones about preferring to ride western style, legs akimbo, and could rope a steer as well as any of her father's vaqueros. He'd watched her eyes brighten with the desire to win whether in a game of chess or in a horse race, no matter her opponent, male or female, young or old. Yet never once did she lose her feminine appeal.

He'd watched would-be suitors who were clearly willing to give the saddles off their horses just to see her smile. She rode with them. Sometimes danced with one or two. But never had she raised her eyes in a way that might be construed as anything other than friendship.

Just as she'd never raised her eyes to his in such a way.

And if these same young men had looked past her beauty, past her lighthearted, even coquettish behavior, and stared into her eyes with the same understanding Spence had after Jamie's death, these young men would have seen a dark sorrow in her gaze.

And they would have kept themselves at a distance.

Just as Spence had.

He urged the gelding up a small incline, and the horse, sensing Spence's intention even before a signal, halted at the crest. There before him lay La Paloma, the hacienda, outbuildings, and corral fences bathed in a moonlit sheen. Without hesitation, and allowing himself no further sentimentality regarding Aislin Byrne, Spence nudged Ruffian in the flanks. Within minutes he rode under the high Spanish-iron horseshoe gate leading into the rancho.

As he headed from the stables past the kitchen garden and henhouse to the front of the imposing adobe, he passed an olive grove through which he and Jamie had raced with the three Byrne sisters; it was here that Jamie had let Aislin win a footrace only to have her rub his face in the dirt when he boasted about it; it was here a few years later that Jamie had boldly smacked his lips against Aislin's round, pink cheek.

Spence had watched the stunned, bright look cross her face, followed by that quirky half-smile of hers. It was the first time he had considered that she might love his brother. And almost simultaneously, Spence had chased Aislin away from Jamie, pretending he was about to yank her long braids when he had no intention of doing so at all.

He pushed the memories from his mind as he bounded up the stairs and onto the wide verandah of the two-story adobe, then rapped the heavy brass knocker at the thick Spanish door. He received a hearty greeting from MacQuaid and was ushered immediately into the front salon. As they seated themselves, there was a rustle of fine cloth and soft footsteps, and both men stood as Camila entered the room.

"It is good to see you, Spence," she said in Spanish.

Spence bent to kiss both her cheeks, European style, and she patted his when he'd straightened. "You're looking well tonight," he answered in Spanish. He and Jamie and the girls had labored over Camila's Spanish language lessons during their childhood, and even now he tried to match her pure Castilian pronunciation.

She smiled and nodded approval as they continued their brief conversation. Finally she said, "Aislin asks that you await her in the courtyard. She will join you presently."

MacQuaid stood and took Spence's hand once again, shaking it with his right, then covering it affectionately with his left as he spoke. "May our Lord's blessings be yours, son," he said, then added almost under his breath, "God knows ye'll be needin' it."

Spence gave him a slight smile. "Yes, sir. I do believe that's true. We both will." A moment later he exited the room and made his way toward the terrace.

Darkness had fallen now, and luminarias cast an orange glow around the base of the fountain. Spence continued along the path until he came to the small stone bench beneath the oak tree. He turned as

Aislin moved through the archway. She halted at the terrace, her gaze meeting his from across the courtyard.

She made her way down the steps and skirted the empty fountain. She was dressed in a pale lilac that seemed to him the color of the exact moment between sunset and dusk. As usual, her hair was unadorned. It hung in one thick plait down her back. Her eyes were luminous, and, as she drew closer, they expressed both wariness and sorrow.

He nodded to the stone bench, and she walked over to settle onto it. He followed and sat beside her.

Spence cleared his throat nervously. "When I left you on the mountain, you said you wanted to think about the future."

"I did." She studied him a moment before going on, her gray eyes narrowed in thought. "Today as you rode away from me—" she paused, still searching his face. "A memory returned. A memory of the last day we both saw Jamie."

He knew exactly the memory she was talking about.

"You came upon us…standing together."

"Yes."

"Why didn't you say anything?"

He laughed lightly. "I had intruded. I merely wanted to leave you alone to say your good-byes."

"Did you follow us there, Spence?" she persisted.

"It doesn't matter now," he said.

She reached for his hand. "We must have a foundation of honesty. Perhaps there's no love. But at the very least, we can strive for honesty."

He raised a brow. "Why is this so important to you?"

"I need to know there's caring between us." Her tone was solemn. "When you followed us that day, there was such anger in your expression, as if you couldn't bear finding us together. I remember other times in our childhood when you seemed perturbed at me."

"Perturbed? That's a mild way of putting it." He smiled. "We fought like bobtailed cats most of the time. All of us did. Even Saint Jamie."

She smiled into his eyes, even at his reference to Jamie. "I want there to be affection between us in this marriage."

"You just said marriage, as if you're giving me an answer about the betrothal."

She studied him for a moment. "I'm not, at least not yet."

He saw the concern in her gray eyes. "You're worried I'm carrying some sort of animosity in my heart…toward you."

"Yes, Spence." She was still staring up at him. "You've kept a distance through the years, as if you don't…well, care for me…even in friendship." She stood, and moved to the fountain, her back to him. He sensed she didn't want him to join her, so he stayed seated, but leaned forward, elbows on his knees, hands hanging down loosely. After a few minutes, she turned back to him, seating herself on the fountain's outer ledge, and folded her hands in her lap.

"What do you think of me, really, I mean?" she finally said.

He took a deep breath, caught unprepared by the question. He laughed out loud. "Oh, Aislin," he said, still chuckling, "that's the last question I would have expected. I thought we'd speak of our families' expectations, even of the fact that, though we save the ranchos, it will be years before we're even consulted about the running of them…"

An indignant look crossed her face, and he wondered if she thought of him as some sort of rogue. "I thought we'd both have questions, Spence," she said quietly.

He looked at her curiously and nodded slowly. "Maybe so. But the one question you don't need to ask is what I think of you."

"And why is that? I think it's a completely natural and very fair question, considering where this courtship will lead."

"We've been friends since we were children riding around the countryside." He hesitated slightly. "I care about you." No, that wasn't entirely accurate either. He tried again. "I have great affection for you. Our families have been friends for years—our fathers go back to seafaring days. My father worked for yours. You and Jamie—"

She cut him off. "That's just the point. Jamie and me, Spence. Your brother's memory can't be overlooked in our relationship." Her expression was filled with misery. He couldn't stand to see it, so he looked away.

"I'm more aware of that than you think, Aislin."

She looked directly into his eyes, her gaze seeming to bore through to his soul. "Ours is to be a union born of necessity."

"Yes, it is."

She looked at him a moment longer as if puzzling through more questions in her mind. Around them, the music of the night rose, the songs of crickets and frogs blending with the rustle of oak leaves in the breeze. Finally, the young woman seemed to settle something in her mind and she nodded slowly. "To save both ranchos."

"With no sons to inherit the land, your father has chosen you, his firstborn daughter, and me, the son of his best friend, to someday take over the running of the La Paloma and Dearbourne lands."

"Our properties will come together as one."

"Yes. Both stronger for the union. To save both ranchos for the families." He wondered where she was going with her thinking. "Someday it will be ours, together."

"It all sounds perfectly reasonable," she said. "I love this land, and I will do anything to save it."

"Including marrying a man you don't love?"

Aislin didn't answer his question. She merely said, "We've gone over this before."

He rose and stepped toward her. After a moment he touched her under the chin with his fingertips, tilting her face toward his. Now she was looking directly into his eyes, and hers seemed filled with a hidden pain. "What else are you considering?" he asked softly.

She surprised him by moving backward out of his reach and smiling up at him. "We both know where this is leading. And because of that, I have one more question."

He frowned at her teasing tone. "What is it?"

As he stood there, wondering about her thoughts, she reached up and gently touched his jaw with her fingertips, turning his face toward hers.

"What I ask you now, my dear friend," she began, her voice low, "is more important than any other question I will ever bring you."

He stared at her, and quoted her own words back to her. "Though we don't love each other, at the very least, we can be honest."

"Yes," she agreed, then paused with a frown furrowing her brow. "Can you marry a woman who still carries the memory of your dead brother in her heart," she finally asked, "and may until the day she dies?"

"Oh, Aislin…" he muttered, then drew in a deep breath. "You don't have any idea how often I've asked myself the same question."

"And have you an answer?"

"No, I'm sorry. I don't." He reached for her hand, lifted it, and touched his lips to her knuckles. She watched him intently, and he knew that this very moment she was wishing he was Jamie.

For several minutes they listened to the mournful sounds of an owl that called from the rear of the rancho and some coyotes yipping in the distant hills.

"Aislin…" he began, wanting to explain how he'd always felt about her, about Jamie, about the two of them.

Before he could get out the words, Aislin released her fingers from his clasp, put her hands on either side of his face, and pulled him toward her. Then she kissed him softly on the lips. Her skin smelled of soap and orange blossoms and her hair held the scent of wild sage. Breathing in her fragrance and relishing her soft lips on his, he forgot all his grand intentions of keeping her an arm's length away. He pulled her closer, his heart ready to burst from his chest.

She melted against him, and he felt the soft thud of her heart against his chest. "Oh, Aislin…" he murmured against her lips.

She pulled back to look up at him, her eyes shimmering with tears. And her expression was one of sorrow, yet, strangely, also something akin to hope. She swallowed hard and touched his lips with her fingertips, staring at him, unblinking. Then, abruptly, she left him, her long skirt swishing at her ankles as she walked across the courtyard, the swing of her long braid accenting each step.

"Aislin," he called after her. But she did not turn, now stepping, head high and back picket-straight, across the upper terrace and into the house.

Aislin hurried up the stairs, and a still small voice spoke to her from a place of great and cold darkness inside her.

YOUR SEASON OF MOURNING IS OVER, CHILD. I WILL GIVE YOU THE TREASURES BORN IN DARKNESS, IF YOU WILL ONLY LET ME, PRECIOUS DAUGHTER. I WILL SHOW YOU HIDDEN RICHES IN SECRET PLACES...

She fell on her window seat and buried her face in her arms. "I cannot give up Jamie," she sobbed. "I cannot!"

I WILL GIVE YOU BEAUTY FOR ASHES... THE OIL OF GLADNESS FOR MOURNING, MY BELOVED!

"No! I cannot give up Jamie," she cried. "I will not!"

She cried, pushing all thoughts of Spence from her mind until it was only Jamie she could see, only the memory of his voice that she could hear.

But instead of relief, she felt only deeper loneliness.

The following morning, Aislin pushed open the door of her father's library. MacQuaid was sitting behind his massive oak desk, a warm fire crackling in the fireplace. When he heard her footsteps, he removed his spectacles, looked up, and smiled.

"Come in, come in." He walked a few feet to the fireplace and pulled a leather wing chair toward his and motioned to her. "Please, sit down, child."

Her father turned in his chair toward a nearby window. The library faced the center courtyard, its fountain with its ring of rose- and herb-filled pottery, the massive live oak in the corner, spreading its thick moss-green canopy over it all.

"Spence told me you have not reached an agreement."

Aislin remained silent.

MacQuaid settled back and closed his eyes in thought. He released a heavy sigh. "Lass," he said after a moment, his eyes now fixed on hers, "how long will you go on with your mourning?"

"You know it's not just that—"

MacQuaid cut in. "You need to start living again. You can't go on this way for the rest of your life. Jamie would not have wanted it.

"For a year and a half, I've seen you throw yourself into the work of the rancho. You ride our lands with the expertise of a vaquero, checking on cattle and strays, overseeing the planting…" He smiled at her sadly. "I've tried to appeal to you on behalf of the rancho and your family. But perhaps you should think about the life God's given you. Do you think he wants you to bury that life right along with Jamie?"

She started to speak, but he held up a hand.

"Perhaps I'm goin' too far, trying to convince you. Forgive me." He paused. "But there is something else you need to consider, lass." The worry that had etched his face during the past few years seemed more pronounced. His shoulders sagged, and he rested his forehead in one hand without speaking.

"What is it, Papa?"

He settled back into his chair and went on as if she hadn't spoken. "When your mama and I first came to this new land, we planned on a quiver full of sons…to inherit and work the land for generations to come. We brought together your mother's Spanish blood and mine of the Irish. And in this wild new land, we thought we were beginning a kingdom all our own, such as could never be ours in either of our native lands."

"And all Mama delivered you were daughters." She laughed again at the irony. "Three daughters."

But MacQuaid did not laugh with her. "All that lived were daughters," he reminded her quietly. Then he leaned forward in his chair. "You are our firstborn, Aislin, and I've never regretted that you weren't a son."

He turned toward her again. "Sybil is a fair beauty, but she is flighty and selfish. And sweet as she is, Brighid is more interested in how to teach an Indian child how to read than in how to run a rancho. It is only you I can turn to now." He looked into the fire as if searching the flames for the right words.

"Something else has happened since yesterday?"

"Aye, child."

"What is it?"

"The Land Commission has issued an ultimatum. They're usin' my debt as a weapon. They're demandin' that it be paid immediately."

"Or what?" Her voice was a whisper.

"The first penalty will be to take over the disputed part of La Paloma."

"The San Jacinto River?"

"Aye, lassie."

"They can't do that!"

"I'm afraid they can, child. I have been informed that, as is the usual government arrangement, squatters will be allowed to move into that part of the rancho until the settlement is made. While we try to settle our legal battle with the State in court, these..." MacQuaid's face turned red, and he fell silent for a minute, trying to control himself. "...these vagrants will be using up our precious water supply."

He stood and walked to the oak desk, looking under a stack of papers until he found what he was looking for. "Have a look at this." He handed a letter to Aislin.

She quickly scanned it before handing it back. "The squatters will have more rights than we do to the river."

"According to the letter, yes."

"They can dam it up if they see fit."

Her father's voice was low. "Aye."

"Papa, what will we do? By summer..." Her voice fell off as she pictured the lands, the cattle, the crops, if there was no rain by next summer. "We can't survive without water. Not for any length of time."

MacQuaid let out a deep sigh as he settled back into his chair. "I need your help now more than ever." He was watching her intently.

She pictured Spence, his face, his kiss.

"You must make your decision."

Aislin drew in a deep breath. "I know it's expected."

"More than that, it is necessary. Absolutely necessary."

She walked to the window and stood with her back to him. "Are you certain that if I say yes, Spence will go through with the wedding?"

She turned to him as he spoke. "Has he said he will not?"

"No, not exactly."

"But you're thinking he's lookin' for a way out?"

She nodded slowly. "I think he'd rather attempt taming a clutch of rattlesnakes than marry me."

MacQuaid didn't laugh. He removed his spectacles and polished them slowly with his handkerchief. There was a knock at the door, but before he crossed the room to greet the newcomer, he said softly, "I've asked Spence to join us."

She took a step backward. "Don't try to force this on us so quickly, Papa. Please."

"It is not my intent to force you." His weathered, lined face softened. "I simply have a story to tell you. One you should hear before you make your decision. I thought it only right you hear it together."

The rapping sounded again. Aislin seated herself in front of her father's desk while he stepped to the door.

"Spence," he said a moment later, extending his hand to shake the younger man's.

Spence hesitated only a heartbeat when he saw her, then strode across the room. "Aislin," he said with a curt nod, before seating himself near her.

MacQuaid pulled his chair from behind his desk, centered it in front of them, then settled heavily into it. "Now," he began with a deep sigh. "What I have to tell you, neither your mother nor I have ever discussed with anyone. Not in our family. Not among our friends."

She leaned forward slightly. "What is it, Papa?"

"I was not the first man your mother chose to marry."

Aislin frowned. "What do you mean?"

"Just what I said, lassie. Your mother was once in love with someone else."

Aislin's first reaction was that of disbelief. She glanced at Spence and could see his reaction was the same.

"Your mother once loved someone very much." Her father's voice was gruff with hidden emotion. "Someone who left her for another."

"Father, this is too personal—" But MacQuaid help up a hand.

"Hear me out, lass. It may make a difference in how you see your present circumstances." He rested his gaze for a long moment on

Spence's face, then continued. "My sweet Camila, young and beautiful, was once betrothed to a man she loved with all her heart. According to her, the very sun rose and set in his eyes.

"They had known each other since childhood, loved each other for as long.

"The wedding plans were made. And, children, they were grand. Camila's father was once a wealthy man, and his place in Barcelona society was nearly that of royalty.

"The guest list was set, invitations delivered, food prepared, the celebration ready to begin, when—" His voice broke off, and Aislin saw the despair, the sadness on behalf of her mother, written on his face. He reached for his handkerchief, blew his nose, then continued, "Her betrothed disappeared.

"No one knew where he had gone. A search went out. Everyone was sure he had met with foul play. After all, everyone was certain of their love for each other."

"Sir," said Spence. "I'm not certain I should be hearing this…"

MacQuaid held up both hands. "Hear me out. You'll understand in a moment." He paused, studying their faces. "Turned out that Camila's betrothed had left her for another. He never returned to apologize or explain."

"Oh, poor Mama," Aislin murmured.

"And, even worse, his new bride had a child a mere six months later. That new bride was Camila's cousin, a girl she had loved and admired since girlhood."

Aislin fell back in her chair. She pictured her mother's pretty, loving face, and wondered about the heartache she'd never known existed. "Oh, Papa…" was all she could manage.

"Not too long after, I sailed into the harbor in Barcelona. I had been invited to her father's home to negotiate a fee for shipping olives to Charleston. When I saw your mother, I was awestruck by her serene beauty…especially that within her heart. I asked her father if I might call on her, never dreaming that he would say yes."

MacQuaid looked wistful. "I didn't realize that she had been cut off in shame by Barcelona society. Her father seemed to sense that I would not judge his daughter for something not of her doing.

"That evening was the first time I saw her alone. Well, not exactly alone. There were her ever-present aunts who stood guard over her honor. But we could speak freely. She told me what had happened, adding that she would never love anyone again. I understood, but I also hoped and prayed that my love for her might be a balm to her soul.

"That night I asked her to marry me."

Aislin sat forward. "And she said yes?"

Her father smiled. "Aye, she did—after makin' it clear she would never, could never love me. She asked me if I still wanted her under those conditions."

"I'm glad you said yes, Papa."

"Aye, lass. It was the best decision I ever made."

"But you loved her." She gave a sidelong glance toward Spence, whose expression remained as unmoved as carved stone.

"You aren't understanding me, child. It's your mother I'm comparing you to, not me. She started this marriage with a heart so full of pain that there was no room for love."

Aislin didn't answer right away. She thought of the tenderness she witnessed between her parents, the little gestures that said "I love you" a dozen times a day.

Spence's voice broke into her thoughts. "She loves you now," he said.

"She does." MacQuaid's expression softened.

"You are thinking that Spence and I might grow to love each other in the same way."

MacQuaid drew in a long breath, not looking at either of them. He stared into the fire. "I thought you might at least try. For yourselves. For the families...the ranchos." He paused. "Your father and I, Spence, don't want our lands splintered a dozen ways if you should die without an heir..." He let the thought hang.

Aislin gasped. "You are talking about a union that has the coldest reason ever for being. Far worse than simply keeping the land intact."

He suddenly laughed. "Coldest ever, lass? How about your mother marrying me to get away from Barcelona society? I have no doubt that was one of the appeals of my proposal and that escape weighed heavily in your mother's decision. What else would she have seen in this old Irish sea captain more than twice her age?"

"Papa!" Aislin couldn't help smiling. "You're the most handsome ranchero in all of California."

"I couldn't agree more." Camila's soft voice, with its musical inflection, broke into the conversation as she entered the room.

"Ah, sweet Camila," said MacQuaid. "And how long have you been standin' at the door, listenin' to our chatter?"

"Long enough," she said simply. She moved across the room and sat very near her husband. "Long enough to know when someone's fishing for compliments from his daughter. Old Irish sea captain?" She laughed, meeting his gaze, then turned to Aislin and Spence. "You should have seen him back in those days. He was so filled with charm and strength it made my eyes hurt to gaze at him."

She looked back into her husband's face. "And that charm and strength still move me today. And love, Aislin. Yes, there is a deep and abiding love we share."

"How did it happen? When did you know you loved him after all?"

For a moment Camila didn't answer. Then she looked into Mac-Quaid's eyes as if searching for her answer. Finally she smiled, not moving her gaze from his face. "I remember the moment well. It was right after I told him that you, daughter, were expected. It was aboard the ship, *Spiritus Sanctus.* We had just anchored off the California coast.

"His face seemed to glow from within. I saw in his eyes his love for me, for the child growing within me, for this land and new life he'd brought us to. And I knew that God was directing him—directing us—and something leapt up inside me. And I knew. I just knew. Oh, how I loved him!" She touched his face. "Oh yes. There was no longer any doubt."

Aislin stood, brushing the folds of her dress. She walked slowly to the window, her back to her parents. Presently she heard Spence move to stand beside her.

Her voice was low as she whispered, "We will talk about courtship. We will come to a conclusion that will benefit us all."

She looked up to meet Spence's gaze. He understood; she could see it in his eyes. "Maybe it's time to live again," he said. He took her hand. "Will you let me help you?"

She nodded, unable to answer. Quick tears filled her eyes.

FIVE

Three weeks later, the afternoon sun was on its downward slant when Aislin strolled out to the corral to watch the arrival of the vaqueros and a herd of wild horses as part of the rancho's annual harvest celebration, or fandango, set to begin that evening.

She leaned against the corral fence to watch. It was a sight she and her sisters had relished since girlhood. The prancing horses, decked with silver-trimmed bridles of rawhide and horsehair. Saddles of gleaming tooled leather. The proud men dressed in full costume: black broadcloth, ruffled white shirts, and high-heeled boots. They wore high-crowned white sombreros trimmed with silver-braided bands, and crimson sashes were wrapped around their midsections.

The men were in high spirits, as they always were when the fall branding and counting were done. Some reared their horses, letting the beasts dance sideways on their back legs, and the air filled with whoops and shouts and horses' whinnies. Later their *señoras* and *señoritas* would arrive wearing colorful gored skirts and bright flowers in their hair, and by evening, the small pueblo by the river would be alive with the sounds of their music and dancing.

Aislin climbed up the two rails of the fence to sit at the top. She chewed on a piece of straw while she watched a few of the vaqueros practicing with their lariats. The ropes snapped and whirled through the air. One of the ranch hands had let some mustangs into the corral for roping.

Puffs of dust rose and drifted off to the east. Aislin breathed in the smell of the earth and livestock, enjoying the feel of the breeze lifting some strands of hair that had fallen loose from her braid. Bracing her weight with her arms, she leaned back, closed her eyes, and let the autumn sun beat on her face.

"One of my favorite sights."

The low voice caused her to start. She straightened and glanced up to see Spence leaning against the nearest fence post. His back was to the sun, so she couldn't see his face clearly. His legs were crossed at the ankles. His hat was pulled low, and he looked at her from under the brim.

She shaded her forehead with her hand and squinted in his direction. He was looking out at the vaqueros who now had herded several dozen more mustang mares, colts, and fillies into the corral. The stallions had been separated into another corral. The air was filled with laughter and calls as the men tried halfheartedly to calm the frightened, bucking and snorting, wild-eyed horses.

"There's Fraco Ciro," he said, though his eyes were on the nervous mustangs, not the men. "Insolent as ever."

Aislin turned to watch the silver-haired vaquero with the haughty bearing and granite face. He was leaning against the fence on the opposite side of the corral, his black gelding with its silver-tooled saddle standing outside the fence.

"I would have thought after what we did to him," she said, "he'd never return to La Paloma. But he's been back every year since."

"We probably should have done more than put a straw dummy in his bed."

"After the way he treated that colt." All signs of amusement faded from Spence's face.

The silver-haired vaquero had tied a sack of tin cans to the colt—the man's method was to break all horses with fright.

"The dummy looked just like him," Spence said with a self-satisfied grin.

She laughed. "He should've; he was dressed in Fraco Ciro's own clothes."

"I've never seen anyone so angry." He stared at Fraco from across the ring. "He deserved worse."

Aislin couldn't suppress her laugh. "Do you remember how Fraco poked at the dummy with his rifle, yelling in Spanish for the man to get up and get in his own bed? He ranted on and on, until he threw himself on the straw body, ready to teach the trespasser a lesson. Then he flipped it over…"

Now Spence was laughing with her. "Only to see the grinning face we'd painted with lamp oil and soot."

"While we hid in the loft, peering down, as quiet as mice." She squinted at him.

"*I* was quiet," he reminded her. "You and Jamie were snickering." He met her eyes for a moment.

"Giggles always seemed to get me into trouble sooner or later," she said with a laugh, trying not to let her heart consider the words he'd said, *You and Jamie…you and Jamie…* But before she could say any more, she noticed that Spence's attention was riveted to Fraco and his treatment of a bay filly, one of the wild mustangs brought to the rancho earlier in the day, part of a herd rounded up for the wild-horse race that would take place on the final day of the fandango.

She climbed off the fence and moved closer to Spence, leaning her elbows against the top rail. His eyes narrowed as he watched the unruly filly and Fraco, whose attention was focused on the small animal.

Fraco Ciro quickly mounted his gelding, entered the ring, and wound his way through the herd, toward the bucking filly. Spence bolted from the fence and headed toward the herd, winding quietly, slowly, among them. From time to time, he touched a mare or filly gently on the neck, and they calmed noticeably.

The vaqueros had fallen quiet as they watched. Even Fraco turned and stared at him in silence. He held a whip in his hand, his hard eyes challenging Spence's authority.

Without a word, Spence moved closer to the filly. Her nostrils were flaring and her eyes were filled with wild fear. Both ears were skinned back to her head, and she snorted once more and arched her neck, giving Spence a challenging look.

He continued moving slowly among the other horses, at the same time circling the little filly at a distance. She stopped her bucking and watched him, one ear cocked forward, the other still flattened. Spence moved to a small chestnut mare near the filly and stopped, rubbing the mare's neck, patting down to the forelegs, slowly, lightly touching and crooning words neither Aislin nor, she was sure, any of the others could hear.

Curious now, the bay filly sidled closer to Spence, still nervous, but quiet. Slowly, he turned his attention to the little bay. He met her gaze, and walked even closer. The filly didn't move. Then Spence reached out his hand for her to nuzzle. Both ears flattened again, and she stepped backward.

Spence didn't follow, but he began speaking to her again and rubbing the neck of the chestnut mare who was now following him.

Fraco said something that Aislin couldn't hear to some nearby vaqueros. There were immediate answering snickers, raucous remarks, and catcalls. The sharp sound of the laughter frightened the filly again, and she bolted, heading straight for the vaquero who still held the whip in his hand.

The filly kicked against the fence, then reared with a frightened whinny. Fraco nudged his big gelding forward, his hand poised for action.

Spence stepped between the massive black horse and the bay filly. The black reared, almost throwing Fraco from his back. But Spence didn't move; he merely held up a hand to the vaquero and gave him a steely-eyed nod. Fraco turned the gelding back to the gate, leaving Spence alone in the corral with the wild mustangs.

The filly bucked wildly, but Spence moved quietly toward her once again. This time she recognized him and quieted, though one ear was still flattened.

He held out a hand again. This time she nuzzled it, nickering. The sound she made was almost babylike as Spence now touched her neck, rubbing it and speaking as if to a child. For several minutes, he stood with the filly, touching and whispering. When he stopped, both her ears were forward, and she nickered once more as she trotted behind Spence back to Aislin's side of the corral.

Their eyes locked when Spence at last stood before Aislin, the fence all that separated them. The horse's velvet nose nuzzled his hand.

"She's scared," Aislin managed.

Spence swung a leg over the fence and stepped down. He removed his hat to rake his fingers through his hair. His hair was more the color of honey than wheat in the sun like Jamie's, and it was plastered in a wide ring where his hat had been.

"I didn't ride over to tame horses today," he said.

"I figured you'd come for the fandango," she said, with a light teasing laugh. She enjoyed him more each time they talked. A blackbird sang someplace, and a puff of dust lifted from the corral. Among the mustangs, a colt nickered only to be answered by another on the far side of the herd. Spence leaned back against the fence, crossing his ankles as if he had all the time in the world. And wanted to spend that time with her.

He put on his hat and pulled it low again, over his forehead. "The fandango?" He grinned slowly. "Maybe."

She followed his gaze to the herd of mustangs, and could see him searching for the bay filly. She was aware of his nearness as she had never been before, aware of how he seemed to watch her with new interest.

"If not the fandango, then…?"

He laughed, still watching her. "I figured maybe we ought to make some plans for the wedding." He gave her a half-smile and slightly cocked his head.

"Well, yes…" she stammered, feeling her cheeks flush with warmth, surprising her as they did. "You are right. Folks might be asking about our plans, the date and such, when the announcement is made."

He shifted his weight and she thought he might be stepping closer to her. He didn't, and for some reason, she felt herself blush again. "I thought maybe Christmas," he said. "If you're so inclined."

She was still staring into his face, now struck by its power and gentleness, his rugged jawline, his kind eyes. "Christmas?" she whispered. She pictured pine boughs and candles, and sighed. It was a pretty thought.

He lifted his hat and raked his hair again. It struck her that for as long as she'd known him she'd never seen such a light in his eyes.

She shrugged one shoulder. "Christmas, I suppose then," she said. "If that's agreeable with you."

"I like a woman who knows her mind." He replaced his hat and studied her a moment.

"Don't fuss at me just because you were the one to set our wedding date, Spencer Dearbourne," she said with a grin.

"I've always liked that about you, Aislin."

"Liked what?"

He studied her a minute without answering. "Everything," he finally said. "Everything."

The sun now cast long shadows, and Spence's stretched into the corral, disappearing in the dust. There was something about the shape of it that reminded her of Jamie. Maybe the elongated look of it, the narrowness of the shoulders. She moved her gaze from Spence's shadow to the solid reality of him, standing in front of her. And she pushed Jamie's image from her mind.

Spence caught her hand. His touch reminded her of how he'd gentled the horse. His fingers rested on her third finger. On Jamie's ring.

"I won't ever ask you to remove this," he said. "But I would like to add one of my own tonight when your father makes our announcement."

Aislin stared at the ring. The blackbird sang again, and the late afternoon breeze caught a few loose tendrils of her hair and lifted them from her face.

She nodded, glad he understood. "Thank you."

But when she saw his disappointment in her answer, she bit her lip, and her eyes strayed from his face.

In a heartbeat, he touched her cheek with his fingertips and turned her face back toward his. He didn't speak, but just looked into her eyes with more tenderness than she thought possible.

Spence watched Aislin move down the dusty road leading to the hacienda. The setting sun caught her dark hair and turned it the color of burnished copper, her plain brown dress to gold.

But still, she wore his brother's ring, and Spence felt like a thirsty man who saw water on a desert landscape and on closer examination, found it to be liquid heat on dry sand. He needed to be cautious of his feelings for her, he reminded himself. Her smiling face. Her soulful eyes.

Just as significant as the ring that clung to her finger, that glimmer from deep behind her eyes, perhaps from her soul, told him the core of her remained true to Jamie, even now.

Spence wondered how long the desert landscape would be his. How long would he thirst for a love, shimmering, beckoning, a love that turned out to be merely a reflection of a love for someone else?

Aislin headed from the corral to the house. Every year for as long as she could remember, the Byrne rancho had hosted an autumn celebration in the middle of California's windy, clear, and warm Indian summer. Other ranchos held fandangos throughout the year, but none could compare to theirs. It was always held after the choicest of the La Paloma herd had been driven to the farthest corner of the rancho, some thirty miles from the hacienda itself, for slaughter by the Soboba Indians.

Her mother often recounted to her daughters how, even during the first year they spent in the one-room adobe while the ranch houses were being built, MacQuaid had insisted that they share the bounty of God's goodness. They had invited everyone within a day's ride of the rancho, Soboba families, vaqueros, seasonal workers, neighbors, and friends from as far away as the central California coast.

It had turned into a housewarming. She'd heard the tale many times. Their new friends brought food and furniture to help the young family through their difficult first months in their small dusty home. New friends in a new land. Hope for the future. God's abundant blessings. All came together for a harvest celebration that first year. And her father had declared that, no matter what the circumstances, no matter whether the cattle on the thousand hills were fat or lean, this was a time to celebrate God's care.

This year was expected to be the finest celebration ever. With the announcement of the betrothal and coming wedding, Aislin knew that the feasting and dancing would carry on for days. She also knew that, though it wouldn't be openly talked about, there was in everyone's mind cause for even greater celebration. That of two ranchos saved. That of two ranchos becoming one.

She reached the hacienda and let herself in a back door. Preparations were in full swing. She passed Josefa carrying a load of bedding.

Aislin took half her stack of blankets and followed her up the stairs. Buena met them on the landing and smiled gratefully. One wing of the upstairs bedrooms had been set aside for the women, and for days Aislin had helped with washing, starching, and ironing the embroidered bed linens.

She chuckled as she headed down the hall. Sybil was nowhere in sight. No surprise. Her sister had tried her best to get out of all preparations. At one point she complained that she would much rather help with the ironing than churn the great amounts of butter needed for the meals as she had been directed. But after lifting the heavy, hot iron she quickly and quietly went back to the churning under Josefa's eagle eye. It was Aislin's guess that making sweet butter was the last of Sybil's contributions to the celebration.

The men would sleep downstairs on mats, with saddles for pillows, saddle blankets for bedding. They would be scattered throughout the main salon, the dining room, MacQuaid's study, and every hall and room between. Her father insisted he knew best where to place the excess furniture to accommodate the two dozen men and older boys who would sleep there. He directed his strongest servants to move the heavy furniture into corners and hallways.

She smiled as she headed to her room. The weeks of planning menus of beef stews, fire-grilled beefsteaks, and beef ribs were finally over. Pots of frijoles and onions already simmered in the outdoor kitchen, and cornmeal dough was ready to be patted into plate-sized tortillas by Consuelo and baked by Josefa. Sides of beef hung in rows in the cool keeping house, and barrels of green coffee beans had been roasting all afternoon, filling the adobe with their pungent fragrance.

She sighed when she reached her bedroom. For weeks, the entire household, from the youngest to the eldest, had been given chores to complete before the first carriage rolled under the horseshoe gate. The fifty guests would be staying three days and nights.

She should be deep-bone weary from the household chores. Yet she wasn't. Rather, she was as giddy as a schoolgirl, feeling as feather-light as a butterfly in spring.

Stunned, she paused, her hand resting on the door handle. For the first time, as she thought about how different it would be if she and Jamie were announcing their betrothal, the familiar ache was not there.

When did it happen? When did Spence begin filling her waking thoughts, her dreams at night?

She pictured him now, as he had looked at the corral, and she swallowed hard. *Spence?*

By twilight, Spence stood, hands in pockets, feet spread, on the wide verandah, just outside the open double entry doors. He kept an eye on the wide staircase beyond the foyer, waiting for Aislin to descend. From time to time, his attention turned to the arrival of the guests as carriages rolled to a stop under the covered portico. Because of the mild autumn evening, the tall ballroom windows were open on both sides, one set to the courtyard, the other to the front verandah. The soft strains of a guitar carried through the ballroom window to where he stood.

Harnesses and reins jangled as the rigs moved on to the stables, and wheels crunched along the gravel as each new carriage rolled into place. Children laughed and called out as they raced though the front door ahead of their families.

MacQuaid and Camila flanked the entry, greeting the newcomers as they arrived. There was a flurry of activity as the household servants hurried about, carrying their burdens of carpetbags, hats, and wraps to the guest-room wings. The night air was already filled with murmuring voices and soft laughter as families from the outlying ranchos and pueblos caught up on news.

A banjo and fiddle joined the guitar, and the beat of the music picked up. Spence left his post on the verandah and moved inside, past the foyer and staircase, into the ballroom itself.

Two men Spence didn't recognize were standing in the doorway of the ballroom. Snatches of their conversation drifted toward him as he passed. Talk of war. The older man glanced over as if inviting his views.

"The Johnny Rebs are heading to victory, don't you think?" he stated, rather than asked. "Thoroughly routing the Federals. The war will soon be over and the boys on both sides heading home."

The younger of the two, whom Spence heard the older man call Hyrum, looked bored. He raised an eyebrow. "That's the prediction," he said. "But history tells us if there's one thing man cannot predict, it's war." Then he chuckled. "Maybe two things. A woman's the other." They both laughed.

"War can't be taken lightly, by either side," said Spence without joining their laughter. "There are men dying on fields filled with blood. So filled, the fields have turned into lakes. The blood of men, young and old, cries out, and it's a pity no one hears it. That's the only part of war that is predictable. Killing and lakes of blood."

The men were looking at him intently. "Sounds like you've seen it firsthand, boy," said the older man.

"Close enough," Spence said, then started to move on.

The greasy-looking Hyrum squinted at Spence. "You one of the Dearbourne boys?" He looked slightly uncomfortable with the question. He slicked his hair back nervously.

"There's only one son." Again Spence tried to move on.

Hyrum stepped closer and stared in Spence's face. "You had a brother, right?" Again, Spence noticed the flick of uncertainty in his eyes.

"Yes."

"I heard what happened," Hyrum said. "You went back after your missing brother and found out he was dead."

"I have no desire to discuss my brother," Spence said, looking around. His mother still wept at the mention of Jamie's name. He didn't want this conversation overheard. "Who are you?" he finally managed.

"We're visiting out at the Douglass Rancho. On our way north to the gold fields." The gray-haired man was still looking hard at Spence as he spoke.

"You're about ten years too late." Spence tossed the words over his shoulder as he turned to walk away. "The Gold Rush is over."

"We heard you were in a rush yourself," said Hyrum, causing Spence to halt abruptly. "When you left Fort Donelson."

Spence turned toward them again, his curiosity heightened. How could they know where he had been?

"We were heading through the hills of Tennessee several months ago just after you," the younger man went on. "We heard about the California boy out a-lookin' for his brother, only to find that he had been killed." The mention of Jamie was like a blow to the stomach.

"So you heard," Spence said, staring hard at the speaker.

"The folks were still talking about how broken up you were when you heard the news. Heard you busted up some folks you thought mighta been involved."

No one in California knew what he'd done. He'd made sure of that. The men obviously got their information from the source. "What are you getting at?"

"That you coulda saved your grief." The older man stepped closer. "You rushed off with the wrong conclusion, boy. You shoulda asked around a bit more before hightailin' it back to California."

Spence met the man's hard gaze with his own. "You telling me you know something about my brother? About his death?"

"We might," said the young man.

"What is it?"

"Only that he might not be dead. That's all."

Spence's hands fisted. "You'd better not be lying to me."

"Why would we wanna do something like that?"

"Perhaps to get paid for information." His words were brittle. "You heard about my brother, about my coming for him, figured you'd make a quick buck by selling information. And it took you a year to track me down. End of story." He was breathing hard. *That had to be it. Jamie couldn't be alive. Couldn't be!*

"You're supposin' quite a lot," the older man said. "We were headin' west anyways. And as I said, we're friends of the Douglasses. You can ask them, if you don't believe us. As to information…" He shrugged. "Don't have anything special. Only that you left a few stones unturned."

Around them rose the noise of the fiddles and guitars, the clamor of voices, sometimes a ragged spurt of laughter. Spence grabbed the man's lapels. "If you know anything," he growled, just inches from the man's face, "you'd better tell me now. That is, if you want to live through the night."

Now both men laughed and backed away from Spence. "Hey, son. Calm down, now," said the older man. "You just calm yourself down." They exchanged a glance.

"Well, now. Maybe we don't know so much after all," the younger man added. "We're not as smart as we look." He exploded in laughter.

"Get out of here," Spence growled. "If you know what's good for you, you'll get out now."

The men looked at each other once more, shrugged, then headed to the foyer and outside, falling in with some vaqueros sauntering toward the corral.

His hands still fisted, Spence walked to the verandah. He needed fresh air. Lots of it. He moved to the farthest end of the long porch and leaned up against a pillar. Jamie alive? Could it be? What if…?

Light footsteps sounded on the wooden floor behind him. He turned. It was Aislin.

Her hair had been swept into a crownlike affair, and the effect of it, together with the upturned tilt of her face and pale lace gown sweeping from her small frame, was regal.

"I saw you having words with those two men," she said. "What did they want?"

Six

Spence was surprised Aislin had noticed the men who'd told him Jamie was alive. He wondered how much she'd overheard. He stared at her but couldn't speak.

She tilted her head and grinned. "Why, Spencer Dearbourne, I had no idea the sight of your intended might give you the vapors." She fluttered a lace fan in her left hand, her eyes meeting his over the top.

She had never looked so beautiful.

How could he tell her about Jamie?

He reached for her right hand. "Aislin…" Her name came out in a croak.

He couldn't tell her! Not now! After all, there was no proof. None whatsoever.

Now she was frowning. "Spence, what's wrong? You look as though you've seen a ghost."

His knees went weak, and it wasn't from the ruffians' news of Jamie. It was from gazing into her upturned face. It was from considering that she'd never look at him this way again if he told her. He lifted her chin to keep her face tilted toward his. Then he bent his head and touched his lips lightly, tenderly, to hers.

When he pulled back, she was staring up at him. Then she laughed, a soft, musical sound, and reached up to touch his cheek.

"Aislin…" he began again, meaning to tell her before any more time passed. But still the words wouldn't form. So instead of speaking, he drew in a deep breath and offered his arm. She took it.

They strolled back into the hacienda, and though he didn't look down at her, he sensed her gaze.

For a moment they stood watching the dancers, laughing and

whirling to a Virginia reel. Brighid looked over and waved, showing a dimpled smile. Sybil opened her fan and flicked it back and forth, her eyes flirting over its black lace with the tall, handsome son of a ranchero.

Beyond the girls, MacQuaid and Camila moved from couple to couple, sometimes stooping to greet children, sometimes shaking hands, always smiling and laughing with their friends.

The strum of guitars now turned soft and romantic, the Spanish melody lifting into the balmy air. Spence looked down at Aislin, and within a heartbeat he had pulled her into his arms. She laid her hand lightly on his shoulder, and they began to move in rhythm, slowly, around the dance floor.

He drew in her fragrance, and thought of the incongruity of the person who made up Aislin Byrne. The same young woman dressed in simple homespun garb who had talked with him at the corral today, now was so exquisitely made up in dress and demeanor that everyone else in the room paled.

She seemed to sense his reverie and pulled back to meet his eyes. There was such trust in her face.

Trust.

And he knew he had to tell her.

The guitars played on, and they floated around the ballroom. Her small feet moved gracefully to the music, and her delight showed on her face. She gazed up at him as they turned. It struck him that a new expression graced her face, and now—because of his news about Jamie—just gazing into her eyes was like trying to look at the sun. Or trying to get a drink from a waterfall. His eyes, his heart, his mind, ached with a kind of longing. Longing for something unattainable…because of Jamie. Again.

The music stopped. He tore his gaze from hers, then escorted her to the side of the room. He didn't trust his voice to speak. Not yet. So without a word, he strode to the terrace and leaned against the iron banister. Luminarias placed on the stone surface of the verandah flickered orange and gold, casting strange, moving shadows across the pots of palms.

Within minutes Aislin followed and stood silently near him. Beneath them in the courtyard, children played tag under the live oak, and a group of women sat on stone benches, talking, near the fountain.

"You can't go through with this, can you?" she said quietly.

He leaned forward, hands on the railing. He didn't face her.

"It's not too late to change Father's plans to announce the betrothal tonight."

"We need to speak privately," he finally said.

"So, I'm right. You are reluctant…" Her voice dropped.

He turned to her, desperate to keep this awful secret his own. "There's something you need to know. Something that may change everything." The courtyard had just emptied, and he glanced toward the small bench under the century oak.

She reached for his arm, and he escorted her down the steps. When they were seated, she turned toward him. "Tell me, Spence."

He looked into the night and didn't speak for several minutes. "This is difficult for me, and I'm not certain I should even tell you…" *Oh, Lord,* he cried silently. *Help me do the right thing, the righteous thing for Aislin, for Jamie, if he's indeed alive!*

"Tell me," she repeated.

"It's about Jamie," he said.

"Jamie…?" she breathed. Her face suddenly turned as pale as ivory in the moonlight. "You mean it has to do with his memory."

"No. It has to do with the flesh-and-blood Jamie." Her expression held so much sorrow that he thought her heart was surely ready to break. "The men you saw me with earlier… They told me they know something about Jamie, about him being alive. Something I didn't uncover when I was in Tennessee."

She stood abruptly, her hand covering her mouth, and he thought she might faint.

"Maybe you should sit down," he suggested and reached for her hand.

"How? What?" she uttered as she sat. "Oh, Spence…" she cried, her eyes filling. "Oh, Spence!"

He lifted her fingers to his lips, then held them against his cheek. It was a gesture of comfort, nothing more. But she pulled her hand away, staring blindly at him.

"Jamie? Alive?" She leaned forward. "Tell me everything! Everything the men said."

He drew in a deep breath and related the conversation. Then he added, "I'm not certain they're telling the truth, Aislin. There's no way to know."

"Unless we go to Tennessee ourselves," she said.

He had known that would be her conclusion. He nodded solemnly. "Yes," he agreed quietly.

"But the ranchos...our marriage..." Her voice fell off helplessly.

"Of course I can't ask you to marry me now," he said quietly, not looking at her.

She didn't speak for a moment. Soft guitar music drifted through the open doors and windows of the hacienda, mournful and slow moving. "I've never tried to hide my feelings for Jamie," she finally said.

"You've been honest with me."

"Just as you've never hidden from me your feelings about your willingness to marry without love," she said.

"Without romantic love," he corrected. But even as he spoke, his words seemed hollow and false.

"We need to leave immediately," she said. "For Tennessee, I mean, to look for Jamie."

"We can't, Aislin. Not yet."

She stared into his face, as if disbelieving what she had heard him say. "We must."

She stood, and he reached for her arm, imploring her not to leave. *Not yet. Please, Aislin. Not yet.* But she shook him off. There would be no stopping her, just as he had known from the beginning of their conversation. But he tried once more to reason with her. "Let's send an agent on behalf of the family. I failed once to get to the truth. I don't want to fail a second time." He paused, looking into her eyes. "Besides, the men may be trying to sell us information, though they know nothing. They didn't seem exactly trustworthy."

She gazed at him in the moonlight, shaking her head slowly, slightly, as if uncertain. For a moment he hoped Jamie's pull was no longer like that of magnet to iron. "I must go myself, with or without you," she said.

"What about the ranchos? It's October. Even if we found Jamie alive it might be too late to make a difference for the ranchos."

She lifted a brow and gave him a heartbreaking smile. "As soon as we find him, Jamie and I will marry, no matter where or when."

"I'll go with you," he said. "But promise me you'll delay leaving until I can make further inquiries about the men who brought the news. Let's make sure they're reputable before we act." She looked at him evenly, obviously not ready to promise anything. He sighed. "I'll find out as soon as possible, Aislin. I promise."

She reached for his hand and folded it into her own. It was such a trusting gesture, and again he felt his heart ready to break.

"There's something else," he said. "What if we don't find Jamie in time? What if…the news is wrong…and he's not alive?"

"You mean, what will we do about the rancho?" When he didn't answer, she stood. "I can't ask you to step in again on behalf of your brother," she said, her voice little more than a whisper. "I can't. I won't."

He pushed himself from the bench and moved toward her. When he stood directly in front of her, he put his hands on her shoulders. "I agree," he said. "Your heart belongs to Jamie."

She nodded solemnly. "Yes," she said.

"You said this was important," MacQuaid said, peering into his daughter's face.

She nodded. "Of the utmost importance, Papa." She glanced across to Spence, who sat beside her in the library, his parents and hers both present. "But why don't you tell what's happened, since you heard the news firsthand?"

The room grew silent except for the sound of Spence's voice as he related the conversation with the men from Tennessee. When he had finished, Sara Dearbourne's quiet weeping was the only sound. "Oh, that it could be true," she cried. Her eyes had so long been filled with sadness, but now, when she met Aislin's gaze, they were filled with fresh pain.

And Aislin noticed the bright look on Hugh's face. Along with the joy that his son might be alive, was an expression of profound relief. She watched him carefully. His firstborn might soon be home to take his rightful place at his father's right hand. Jamie, the son to lean on, to cherish, to hold before Spence as the ideal son to emulate.

She winced at the thought, and glanced up to see if Spence saw in his father's expression what she saw. He faced his father, appropriately attentive, but he worked his jaw. And she knew that he saw it too. She reached for his hand.

Hugh cleared his throat. "I say we get the men in here. Ask some hard questions. Find out exactly what they know."

The others agreed, and Spence left to corral the men and invite them into the library. While he was gone, the conversation centered around the joyful news that Jamie might be alive.

"No less a miracle than Lazarus being raised from the dead," Hugh said more than once, with Sara, sitting beside him, agreeing and dabbing her eyes with a handkerchief. She was a pretty woman, big boned and sandy haired, with soulful eyes that stood out in her pale face.

"*If* it's true," cautioned MacQuaid. He was frowning, and looked uncertain whether to consider the news at all.

Aislin brushed away the thought that he might be the one with the clearest head among them. Camila didn't speak, but met her daughter's eyes across the room with a questioning look.

Presently, Spence returned with the two men, who slouched into the room, hats in hand. They were not invited to be seated.

Hugh stood and strode toward them. "I understand you may have news of my son, James."

The men exchanged looks. The older man spoke first. "I don't know where you got that idea."

Spence stepped forward. "Tell my father what you told me."

The younger man shrugged and laughed. Then he stared at Sara Dearbourne, an uncomfortable expression crossing his face. "I don't remember sayin' any such thing. Do you, Jake?"

The older man gave the younger a long, studied look, then his face split into a smile. "Well, now, Hyrum. It wasn't *quite* like that. As I recollect, this fellow over here," he jerked his thumb toward Spence, "approached us when we was discussin' the war. He asked if we'd ever been to Tennessee, Fort Donelson. We said no, we hadn't, then he went on to tell us about his dead brother."

Spence stepped forward as if to grab the man by his collar, but his father put a hand on his arm to restrain him. "Now, I suppose you two wouldn't be out to make some money, would you?"

The men glanced at each other. Jake seemed to take the natural lead. "Whataya have in mind?" he asked.

"You tell us," said Hugh, "what it would take to jog your memory."

"Well, now. I'd say…" Hyrum's voice fell off as he glanced at Spence's face. It was filled with raw anger.

Aislin hands grew clammy, and she wiped them on her skirt. It was obvious the men were playing with their emotions, but perhaps they did know something about Jamie. "Please," she said. "Tell us what you know."

The older man, the one called Jake, cleared his throat. After a long pause he named a dollar amount.

Sara gasped, and Aislin and Spence looked at each other. "I'll pay it," said Spence. "From my own pocket, not from the rancho's coffers." He didn't even glance at his father.

"Well, now," said Hyrum. "That's a horse of a different color, ain't it?" Uninvited, he strolled to the chair nearest Aislin and sat with a heavy grunt. Then he turned to MacQuaid, still seated behind the desk. "Write out a note," he said, "made out in the brother's name." He jerked his head toward Spence.

MacQuaid did as directed, and a moment later, the document was signed by Spence. He met Aislin's gaze as he completed the last flourish of "Spencer Dearbourne."

Hyrum took the paper, folded it, and placed it in his pocket. Then he looked over at Aislin. "Somethin' tells me, missy, that you've got more than a passin' interest in James Dearbourne," he said.

"Where is he?" she asked, narrowing her eyes. The man made her stomach queasy, but her burning desire to hear anything about Jamie made her ignore her own discomfort.

Then Hyrum began to spin a tale about bodies rising from the dead, a tale that Aislin, with a sinking heart, knew could not be true. After he had droned on for a quarter of an hour, Hugh held up a hand. "It seems Spencer has made an error in judgment. I don't believe you have anything new to add to what we already know about my son James's death."

Aislin saw Spence's jaw working again; his fisted hands, his expression, the slope of his shoulders, all reflected his anger. He didn't move his eyes from the greasy-haired man.

For a moment, the room was silent. Then Sara began to weep again; this time the sound was deep and filled with the anguish of a mother's heart. Both men watched her nervously, then looked back at each other.

Then Jake laughed, a low, coarse sound. "Well now, folks. You can't fault us for trying. We're just a couple of fellers tryin' to make a buck." He looked across the room at Hugh. "We'll give your boy here back his IOU, and call us even."

He jerked his head toward Hyrum, who stood to join him.

"Get out of here!" shouted MacQuaid. He stood, and pounded his desk. "Get out of my sight. Get out of my house!"

The two men sidled toward the door and backed out.

Aislin met Sara's gaze and knew Jamie's mother suffered even more than she did. Aislin went to her, knelt in front of her, and gathered her into her arms. Camila joined them, and the three women cried together. In the background, the men discussed what was to be done with the two ruffians.

"I'll make sure they're gone," Spence said, and without so much as a glance in Aislin's direction, he stepped out of the room.

When the door opened, the sounds of talking and laughter and music floated into the room. It seemed too mournful to bear.

Spence followed the men as they galloped from the hacienda, waiting on a bluff until he saw them disappear into the night on a trail leading alongside the San Jacinto River.

By the time he returned to La Paloma, the house had quieted. The younger children had been taken upstairs to bed, and many of the women had followed and were preparing for bed in the guest bedroom wing. Spence joined the men as they carried their saddles and blankets into the house, choosing bunking spots in the great room, MacQuaid's library, or the hallways.

He had just dropped his saddle onto the great room floor when he noticed Aislin slipping through the ballroom, across the entry and verandah, and down the steps. He was far enough behind her, once he decided to follow, that he didn't call out.

She headed to the stables, and he worried that she might have taken a notion to search for Jamie, head east alone, even though there truly was no evidence that he was alive.

Minutes later, Spence let himself into the same dark barn. The smell of fresh hay and horses seemed one with the place. He had been there often and knew his way around even in the dark. Feeling his way, he moved toward the tack room. Lantern light seeped under the wide door leading into the carriage room.

He hesitated, knowing that he would find Aislin inside. But as he was deciding whether to follow, the wide door squeaked open and she stepped through, backlit by the glow of a lantern.

He was caught in the same light. She looked momentarily surprised, then started toward him across the hay-strewn wood plank floor.

"What are you doing here?" She walked closer, and he stood perfectly still, too stunned by his rapidly beating heart to move.

"Aislin, you aren't planning to go east to see for yourself, are you?" He noticed that she had not changed into traveling clothes.

She bit her lip, and he could see that she was trembling.

"If I could take it all back—I mean, I should never have mentioned what the men said in the first place. All it did was cause more heartache." He longed to pull her into his arms but kept his distance.

"You are an honorable man, Spence," she said simply. "That's why you told me. You could not have done otherwise."

How close I came to not telling her. "You're not thinking of going to Tennessee?" he asked again.

"One of the fillies threw a shoe this morning. I wanted to make sure she was all right."

He didn't believe that was the only reason she'd come. "And is she? All right, I mean?"

She nodded slightly, her eyes on his, and didn't move. She just stood there, looking younger and more vulnerable than he thought possible. Aislin, who had always been so strong. How she must love his brother!

"Promise me," he said, "that you won't take it upon yourself to search for any further news about Jamie." He knew her well. The same fearless woman who rode the rancho lands, bareback and hatless, would think nothing of heading east with the first guide she could find.

She met his gaze without blinking, brought her fingertips to her lips, then gently touched his. He wasn't a crying man, but the gesture made his eyes sting.

Before he could speak, Aislin turned and slipped away as silently as she had come.

SEVEN

Aislin stepped outside the stables, closed the door behind her, and fell against it. *Jamie!* It had always been Jamie who was tucked away in her heart, even after death.

How could it be that Spence was now stirring her so? How was it she now found herself watching his face, his every expression? Wanting to guess his thoughts, to know his feelings? To touch his jaw and look into his eyes?

She drew in a shaky breath. This new ache in her heart was different than anything she had felt for Jamie, and it frightened her. She closed her eyes and drew in a few more steadying breaths of the evening-scented air.

Then almost without thinking where she was headed, she hurried down the path toward the corral where Silverheel waited. She was conscious of nothing except the sting of the cold night air on her cheeks and wanting to get as far away from Spence as possible.

An owl moaned from the top of a live oak, and some little night creatures skittered in the fields. Bats fluttered around her, their high-pitched whistling calls piercing the night.

The moon was high, lighting her path, and she ignored the brambles and low crooked branches grabbing at her skirts and petticoats. Impatiently, she yanked the cloth each time it was caught, heard the tears, but moved on without hesitation. She headed down a small bluff, around a stand of cottonwoods, then on to the corral itself.

Silverheel nickered a greeting and moved toward Aislin, raising her head and shaking her mane in the moonlight. She rubbed the velvet nose, then buried her face in the mare's long mane. Aislin hadn't ridden bareback since girlhood, but as she stood there murmuring to Silverheel,

she was overcome with the desire to ride the mare with complete aban-
don, through the moonlit fields, along the banks of the San Jacinto.
Maybe then she could quiet her mind's clamoring emotions.

Silverheel stood steady and tall, and Aislin, in one swift motion,
stepped onto the lower rung of the fence and swung onto her back.
Moments later they were cantering across the fields, past a spit of land
leading to the river, then onto the riverbank itself.

The horse understood the slightest pressure from Aislin's knees and
slowed to a walk as they neared the river.

Before them was a sheltered cove where the river lay still as it pushed
into an eddy. Around the crescent-shaped beach were low-slung native
willows and some tall eucalyptus planted decades earlier. Aislin dismounted and, letting the mare graze, pulled back some slender willow
branches and entered the peaceful place.

With a deep sigh, she settled onto a large flat boulder in its center.
Her feet ached, and she quickly removed her shoes. She stretched out
her legs and leaned back slightly, propping herself with her arms. For a
moment she listened to the gentle music of the river, the rustle of the
willow leaves in the breeze, and the far-off croaking of frogs downriver.
Small ripples lapped against the sandy shore.

Spence's image pushed into her thoughts unbidden as she gazed at
the moonlit water. She thought of the wistful quality she'd noticed in his
face, the strength in his jawbone and chin, the way he absently pushed
his hair from his forehead, the gesture giving him an endearing, boyish
look, though nothing else was boyish about him at all. Far from it.

But Jamie! Again she tried to conjure up his image. She couldn't call
his face to mind, and again she was frightened and hung her head.

A sudden crack of twigs in the brush broke her reverie. She sat
upright, pulling her legs beneath her tattered gown.

She heard it again, and her heart skittered into her throat. She
thought of the wild game her father had hunted on the rancho. Bears,
grizzly and black. Cougars. Wolves. No, she thought, whatever was out
there moved carelessly, loudly breaking branches as it moved; this
sound—a crunch of footsteps on sand—was more human than animal.

There was another rustle in the brush, followed by silence.

"Hello there!" she called out, even as the hair on the back of her neck stood on end.

There was a muffled greeting from the other side of the willows, and when the branches parted, she could plainly identify the form of a man in the moonlit clearing. He was holding a rifle by his side. A moment later, a second man stepped forward.

Jake and Hyrum, the men from Tennessee.

She regarded them solemnly, and her fear made her stand abruptly. "Gentlemen," she said with a brief nod as she backed away from them.

"Well, well, well," Hyrum said, appraising her. She didn't like his look.

The older man, Jake, bowed with a flourish. "Pleased to see you, ma'am. I heard rustlings over here and thought we might have a visitor of the most unwelcome sort. Our camp is just over yonder."

"I must confess," she said with a nervous laugh, "I was thinking the same about the rustling on your side of the willow trees."

They moved closer, and Jake nodded to the granite boulder. "Mind if we join you?"

"You're welcome to it," she said. "As for me, I was just leaving." She moved toward the opening in the willows.

"I noticed you didn't seem convinced that we were lying about James Dearbourne," Jake called after her.

She spun around. "You didn't seem to mind taking advantage of a grieving family."

"But you still believe the man's alive," challenged Hyrum. His eyes glittered in the moonlight.

"What I believe is not your concern," she said, and turned away from them again.

"There were some unanswered questions," Jake said. And she noticed his voice sounded kinder, almost sorry.

She halted, her feet frozen to the spot, her heart threatening to freeze just as solid. "What questions?" she whispered when she could speak. She turned. "What are you talking about?"

"It's true that James Dearbourne was reported dead," said Jake. "And that witnesses saw him shot in the back."

"But an old woman was spreading the rumor that the grave is empty," said Hyrum with a smile that wasn't altogether unkind. "She's known to be tetched in the head, so no one paid much mind to her rantings."

"And that's what gave you the idea that you could sell the information?" Her heart was pounding in both fury and hope. "The rumor of an empty grave?"

Hyrum shrugged. Then he brightened, as if suddenly remembering something he'd forgotten. "And we heard the same thing from a Union soldier on his way to Fort Tejon. Ran into him in Santa Fe on our way to California. We got to talkin' about what we heard. He said some old woman at Donelson was rantin' about a man bein' buried alive. She tells every soldier who passes through that she saw him risin' from his grave in the night, then bein' carried off in a Reb uniform. She described your James Dearbourne to a fare-thee-well. She even knew he was from around here because he was rantin' and ravin' about wanting to come home."

"That's the information you were going to sell?" Her heart was still pounding. It was a place to begin. Fort Tejon was less than a week's ride from the rancho.

"That's about the extent of it." Jake stepped closer, and this time she didn't back away. "I'm fairly well ashamed of what we tried to do," he said quietly. "Miz Dearbourne reminded me too much of my own ma." He paused, looking at the ground. "Don't get your hopes up, missy. That ol' woman near Fort Donelson was tetched. Even the soldier on his way to Tejon knew it."

"But he paid her enough mind to at least notice…to remember," she countered.

They both nodded, and Jake cast a glance at Hyrum.

"Why didn't you tell this to Jamie's father and brother?"

"The old woman wasn't to be believed," said Hyrum with a shrug.

"And neither was the Union soldier," agreed Jake. He looked again to Hyrum.

"I wouldn't trust a Union soldier even if he said black was black and white was white," Hyrum growled.

"What's the soldier's name?" she asked, knowing now what she must do.

Hyrum and Jake exchanged another uneasy glance. Finally, Jake said, "Billy, I believe it was. Billy Melcher."

"Billy Melcher," she repeated.

"That's him, ma'am. Tall fellow. Bald as an eagle."

"And an officer, too," added Hyrum, as if frosting a cake.

Billy Melcher. At Fort Tejon.

She headed to the opening in the willows, preparing to leave.

"Ma'am?"

She turned to face them once more.

"You know we didn't get a penny for what we told you tonight." Hyrum was looking properly humble, his head inclined slightly. "We'd be much obliged…I mean, if you think what we said might truly help…"

"You're asking for payment after all?"

"Well, now. Not exactly. We just thought, well, since we've been so forthcoming—"

"I don't carry any money with me, gentlemen," she said, interrupting. "And as you said, even the officer's words about Jamie are questionable. I don't believe I owe you a cent."

The men laughed, low and menacing. "Well, now, it certainly don't hurt to try, does it?" called out Jake as she left them. It was the second time they'd used those words tonight.

She could still hear their chuckling as she slipped back through the willows and hurried toward Silverheel. In one swift motion she mounted. Then, urging the horse to a trot, she considered the distance to Tejon. It would be dangerous, no doubt. But it was a journey she knew she had to make, no matter the danger. To find Jamie, of course. But also to rid her heart of that instant of dismay she'd felt when Spence first told her Jamie might be alive.

A mist had flowed inland off the distant Pacific and lay flat against the land. Silverheel wove in and out of the trees and scrub brush, and Aislin didn't hurry the animal. She had much to think about, and by the time she reached La Paloma, she had gone over every detail. Details she would tell no one. Not even Spence. Especially not Spence.

Lamplight no longer blazed from the rancho as she dismounted by the front verandah. She slipped into the dark house without lighting a lamp, the hazy moonlight enough for her to find her way upstairs.

Spence couldn't sleep. He was bedded down with the other men in the great room off the entry. Light snores rose, and he turned toward the courtyard window, yanking his blanket up over his shoulders and adjusting his head on the saddle. The full moon was waning now, and a light mist had rolled inland off the Pacific. He stared out at the courtyard in the ghostly light, observing its mocking shadows, the dark outline of the century oak.

He couldn't erase from his mind the image of Aislin's face when she first heard that Jamie might still be alive. That spark that was at once hope and astonishment and desperate longing.

After their meeting in the carriage house, Spence had remained there, trying to sort out his feelings. Now, he stared through the window into the bleak courtyard, his mind filled with a whirl of contradictions— the friendship with which he had always regarded Aislin…his physical attraction to her…his intense fascination with her—and now, his sinking realization, once more, that she belonged to Jamie. Still. Always.

He adjusted the saddle beneath his head, only to find it even more uncomfortable. At last, he turned over, away from the mist-shrouded courtyard, wishing his thoughts could be as blurred until finally, he fell into a restless sleep.

Aislin quietly moved through the entrance hall and into her father's study. She had changed into traveling clothes: homespun trousers, a simple white shirt, and an embroidered vest sent years before from relatives in Spain. A black woolen cape was her only covering and would have to serve as a blanket as well. One plain dark skirt and an extra blouse were neatly packed in the carpetbag by the door. She wore her black felt Spanish hat, small-crowned and flat-brimmed without ornamentation, except a tie that would allow it to hang on her shoulders when not needed.

As soon as she silently closed the study door behind her, she moved to the desk and lit a candle. Then holding her breath, she carried it across the room and set it on a table. She removed a painting from the wall, revealing a hidden safe. She knew the combination well, and turned the knob until she heard a resounding click.

The safe door sprung open. She planned to leave a letter in the safe, knowing that her father probably wouldn't open it until it was time to pay the vaqueros on the final day of the fandango. By then she would be nearly to Fort Tejon.

She set the candleholder back on the desk, sank into her father's chair, and reached for his pen and a heavy piece of parchment. She dipped the writing instrument into a well of black ink and scrawled,

> *Beloved Papa and Mama,*
> *I have discovered more information about the*
> *circumstances surrounding Jamie's disappearance,*
> *and find it necessary to leave La Paloma with*
> *immediate dispatch.*
> *After speaking again with the men from*
> *Tennessee, I believe there is a greater truth to be*
> *learned about the rumor that Jamie lives. There is*
> *an officer in Fort Tejon who may shed some light*
> *on the mystery. I go now to find this man.*
> *I will return in a fortnight. Pray me godspeed.*
> *Your loving daughter,*
> *Aislin*

She fanned the letter to dry the ink, then folded it into thirds, melted a dab of wax over the flap, and pressed the La Paloma insignia into the pliant surface.

Quickly now, she moved to the safe, pulled out the funds she would need for the journey, placed them in a leather waist pouch and fastened it into place beneath her vest. She replaced the small stack of bills with her letter, then closed the safe, twisted the knob, and lifted the painting back into its place.

After one more glance around the room, she snuffed the candle and tiptoed into the hallway. Once in the dark entrance hall, she stooped to pick up the valise and moved silently through the doorway to the outer verandah.

She smiled to herself, wondering why she felt no fear at all. Instead, she felt exhilarated, more alive than she had been for a long time. She hurried to the mare and led her to the barn for saddling. Then she gathered some cooking utensils and bedding her father kept for the cattle drives. One more stop at the small building that housed the kitchen for salt pork, jerky, flour and salt for biscuits, and fruit preserves, and her food supplies were complete.

It was nearing dawn when she at last roped the valise and the large bundle of supplies firmly in place behind the saddle and headed Silverheel down the road leading from Rancho de la Paloma.

The only sound in the predawn light was the quiet clop-clop of the horse's hooves beneath her, a drumlike cadence that matched the beating of her heart.

Spence woke suddenly to the sound of a horse's whinny outside the hacienda, then decided it was just his imagination. Who would be riding near La Paloma before dawn, he wondered, then turned onto his back, adjusted the saddle beneath his head, and stared into the ashen light.

Unbidden, his thoughts turned again to Aislin.

"Oh, Lord," he prayed, "I don't understand why, but I'm drawn to her…unexplainably drawn…even though I know her heart will never turn from Jamie, especially now that his image has been resurrected.

"Why now, Lord?" His mother's weary, sorrow-filled face came to his mind, followed by the image of Aislin gathering her into her arms.

For a long time, he considered that God's ways were often as mysterious as a mist-covered valley, and that at other times they were as clear as a mountaintop view newly washed by a passing storm. Most of the time they were somewhere in between.

The sound of distant horse hooves plodding on the road leading away from the rancho drifted through the window. Briefly, Spence wondered at the sound, then fell again into a restless sleep as the hoofbeats grew faint, then disappeared.

EIGHT

Aislin kept Silverheel in an easy trot for the first few miles away from the hacienda. She rode alongside the river, stopping from time to time for Silverheel to rest and drink. She reached the Sierra Madre foothills and turned due west toward the pass that would lead north to Fort Tejon on a little-known Indian road, Trail of Rocks, she had ridden many times with her father.

Day was now beginning to break, and before her, a dark layer of clouds hovered over the flat landscape that stretched to the ocean, fifty miles distant; behind her, a pearl gray mist was the only sign of dawn.

Aislin nudged Silverheel's flanks and headed for the crest of a small incline. Pebbles and clods of dirt rolled downhill as the mare's hooves tore at the loose, dry soil as they moved toward a clearing bordered by a few scrub oaks and buckeye. She rubbed the horse's long, graceful neck while she looked across the valley toward La Paloma. For the first time she allowed herself to consider that her family might lose the rancho.

She swallowed hard, considering her promise to her father—he would be greatly disappointed. But she and Spence had agreed that marriage between them was not right or proper under the circumstances. A twinge of regret crossed her mind, but as quickly as it landed there, she pushed it away.

She nudged Silverheel to head again down the hillside to the main trail, but as they turned, Aislin's gaze fell upon the distant mountains, now backlit by the rising sun. The mists below them had turned a luminous pink.

Halting the horse, she pulled the flat brim of her hat closer to her eyes and gave the hills one last long gaze. Though she planned to be gone but a fortnight, she wondered what it would be like never to look upon this beloved sight again.

Silverheel half skidded, half walked down the trail, and within minutes they were back on the main trail. Gradually the terrain evened out, and she urged the horse to a trot. They passed vast rolling herds of cattle, lean and rangy from grazing in drought-stunted fields. As the sun rose higher, red-tailed hawks soared as they hunted for prey, and scrub jays squawked from the live oaks that dotted the nearby hills.

By midday she had reached Mudd Springs a few miles east of the mission at San Gabriel. She rested Silverheel, letting the big gray graze in the dried grasses near the barely trickling spring, then mounted and rode hard across the farthest western boundary of La Paloma.

Soon the mission rose out of the haze, surrounded by cattle and small Indian pueblos, its distinctive arched bell tower pointing heavenward. She didn't slow, but instead crossed a wide, empty arroyo to the north of the mission and headed into the treacherous pass. She was no longer on her father's land.

The trail followed a dry riverbed and snaked through canyons and ravines, becoming more hostile, steep, and rough as they went. After an hour, the trail disappeared, yet she continued northward by dead reckoning.

She had climbed to an elevation that made her lightheaded when she looked back to the valley floor. A tea-colored cliff rose to the east, and a deep, forested canyon dropped to the west. Beyond were tree-covered mountains, no two alike, fading into the now slanting sun like ragged and torn petals of a dusty rose, one behind the other.

Steadily, they climbed. The air was fresher now and had lost its dry, dusty feel. The trail hugged the cliff, and Aislin pressed her knees against Silverheel's flanks to urge her forward. Ears slanted, the mare danced sideways from time to time, and Aislin closed her eyes, not daring to regard the plunging precipice to her left.

When they reached a wide overhang, she halted the gray and reached back for her canteen, took a long drink, wiped her mouth with the back of her hand and replaced the cap. Then she turned again in her saddle and with her heels gently kicked the horse to a trot.

Trail of Rocks. An Indian name. She had heard they used this trail north when they wanted to disappear into mother earth. And she could see why, she thought grimly, questioning the wisdom of using it herself.

The trail narrowed again, and she slowed Silverheel to a walk, not daring to look toward the canyon, stark except for some jutting boulders clinging to the steep sides and gnarled trees bent from the wind tucked in among them.

The cliff on her right was close enough to touch. She could feel it radiating heat. They rounded another curve, the trail hugging the mountain, and she saw a vertical shard of granite atop a massive stone dome, framed by a sweep of pine forest in the distance.

Castle Keep, she murmured to herself. She remembered the landmark from riding this trail with her father.

Castle Keep. Yes, that's where she would make camp her first night on the trail.

⋘══⟫

Spence awoke to the growls of a grizzly being headed to a pen in the yard behind the house. Spence's neck hurt from the saddle, and he stretched, rubbing the spot to relieve the kink, then rolled off his pallet. The sounds had awakened most of the others, and there was laughter and speculation about the bull-and-bear fight that would be held later in the day. Several of the men headed outdoors to see the beast.

It would be a full day. MacQuaid made sure there were few idle moments during his fandangos. Soon after the growls died down, Spence heard the commotion of bulls being forced into pens.

He grinned. The growls and snorts were an unspoken invitation for guests to gather for an outdoor breakfast of potatoes, grilled beef, eggs, and coffee while watching the animals rage at each other.

He sauntered out to have a look and carried his enameled coffee mug over to the pit behind the barn where the fight would be held later.

He had just turned back to the house when some costumed vaqueros rode past the bull-and-bear pit, flaunting their silver-encrusted saddles and exquisite horsemanship as they headed to the eastern corral with a small herd of the mustangs. They stopped in front of the guests and cast their loops across the necks of a nervous and spirited stallion, a dun mare, and a couple of young reds.

Fraco Ciro, dressed in a splendid crimson brocade jacket, was lead rider. His eyes briefly met Spence's as he roped the distressed stallion. Spence turned away. The horse wouldn't be harmed, but Fraco, with his cold look of defiance, had spoiled the beauty of the pageant for Spence.

The sun was high when the bear-and-bull fight began. Spence hadn't seen Aislin all morning, and now he threaded among the watchers, searching for her. He wasn't surprised by her absence. Since childhood, she had thought the practice barbaric. The bear had just taken a savage swat at the bull's throat when the vaqueros herded the mustangs to the racecourse. Spence followed with the other guests, still watching for Aislin. Sybil, with two of her friends, sat in the shade of a live oak, near the course.

He sauntered over to ask if Sybil had seen her sister. Sybil glanced at him and shrugged at his question. But one of her friends, a plain girl with a kind smile, was more helpful. "I thought I saw her with Buena in the kitchen this morning," she said, "though it was only from the back." But the more she talked, the less certain she was. "Of course," she finally admitted, shrugging one shoulder prettily, "it could have been someone else."

The third girl was of no help. "I didn't think Aislin was here at all," she said.

Sybil rolled her eyes, and finally stood in front of Spence. She tucked her hand in the crook of his arm and strolled with him a short distance away from the others. "I thought Papa was going to announce your betrothal last night."

"He was," Spence admitted. "But we heard a rumor about Jamie."

Sybil halted immediately, touching his arm with her other hand. "What rumor?"

"We don't believe there's anything to it, but two thugs who were here last night, guests of the Douglasses, tried to sell us some information about him." He briefly told Sybil what had transpired in her father's library.

As high-flown as Sybil usually was, the flash of anguish in her blue eyes surprised Spence. "How is Aislin taking it?" she asked.

Again he was surprised by the young woman. He'd watched her behavior for years, the way she teased and tormented both Aislin and Brighid. Could it be she had finally matured into a giving and caring young woman?

Then a half-grin lit her face, and she brushed a strand of hair back from her eyes. The illusion of a grown-up Sybil was gone, and in its place was the dreamy-eyed, flighty Sybil, just as always. She shrugged again as if she didn't care. "I would guess that if my sister's missing, she's headed east to look for Jamie," she said. "I know my sister."

"You're wrong, Syb. When I saw her last, she seemed as convinced as the rest of us that the thugs were no more than petty thieves trying to sell false information."

She shrugged prettily again and gave him an exaggerated sigh. Then she waved at a young vaquero and looked over at her giggling friends to see if they had noticed her brazen act.

"Syb?" Her actions didn't match the troubled expression in her eyes. "If you see Aislin, tell her I'm looking for her, will you?"

"It won't matter," she said sadly. "You've lost her again."

"What are you talking about?"

"It's always been Jamie. Aislin won't change."

"I just want to talk to her," he said. "Tell her, will you?"

"Of course," she finally said and strolled over to her friends without a backward glance.

Spence wandered through the small groups of still-gathering guests. But Aislin wasn't among them. He turned to make his way back to the house just as Camila Byrne headed his way. He waved to catch her attention and strolled closer.

"How are you doing, Spence?" She touched his cheek gently, her actions mirroring her concern. And it struck him that the entire Byrne family might assume that Aislin had jilted him because of the false rumor about Jamie.

But he knew Camila's words sprang from a heart of kindness toward him as Jamie's brother. "I'm concerned about Aislin," he said instead of answering her question. "Have you seen her?"

"No, she probably just wants to be alone. I am sure she needs to answer the many questions that remain in her heart."

"I'm certain of that," Spence agreed. "I suppose we should wait to find her until she wants to be found." He smiled at Camila and took his leave a few minutes later.

By the time the sun was hanging low on the horizon, the aromas of roasting venison and lamb carried from the brick oven at the rear of the rancho. The guests were drifting back to the house and onto the terrace. Spence milled among them, speaking with a group of men about the war. The conversation did little to take his mind away from Aislin. He found himself glancing toward the staircase as if she would descend at any moment. Finally, he could bear it no longer.

Excusing himself from the group, now discussing the land commission's unfair practices, he headed to MacQuaid's study and knocked.

"Come in."

He pushed the door back and stepped into the room. He was surprised to see MacQuaid in a disheveled state. The older man sat white-faced at his massive oak desk, his hair wild, deep circles beneath his eyes.

"What is it?" Spence hurried toward him, leaning over the desk. "What's happened? Is it Aislin…?"

MacQuaid lifted his head almost as if not remembering he had just called out for Spence to enter the room. He blinked rapidly, rubbed his eyes, then nodded. "Aye, son. Come in. Sit down."

For a moment neither of them spoke, then MacQuaid let out a deep and tired sigh. "What do you know about this, son?" He handed a folded sheet of paper across the desk.

Spence took the letter in his hands, unfolding it as he settled back into the chair.

As he read, his heart plummeted. So the lure of Jamie had been too strong after all. When he finished reading, he looked up. "I knew nothing about this. Aislin didn't say anything to me about leaving."

MacQuaid let out a deep sigh and leaned back in his chair. He closed his eyes wearily, then reached up with one hand to rub them. "I know my daughter. She will have taken Trail of Rocks, an old Indian trail."

"I know the way," said Spence.

"It's the most dangerous trail she could have taken." He shook his head again. "If she would simply have told me, I would have gone with her myself."

"And I," said Spence. "If only she'd asked."

MacQuaid blinked, then focused on Spence. "Will you help her now, son?" He paused, his brow still furrowed. "Even if she's on a quest to find Jamie?"

He was aware of where MacQuaid was headed with his reasoning, but felt powerless to stop it. "Of course I will, no matter the reasons." He shifted his gaze away from the older man's scrutiny. "I care for my brother too," he said quietly. "If there's any chance he might be alive, I'll lead her to him myself, if it's in my power."

"Even though you love her?"

Spence looked at him in surprise. For a moment he didn't answer. "How did you know?" he finally said.

"I've known for a long time, son." He gave Spence a weary smile. "Do you think I would have orchestrated your betrothal without such knowledge?"

Of course, he wouldn't have. The arrangement hadn't been merely a business deal, at least from MacQuaid's perspective. "Aislin doesn't know, and I don't want her to know. Her heart still belongs to my brother. Once, I thought it might be different, but by her actions since hearing that there's even the faintest hope that he's alive, I see he has the same hold on her as always."

"Go after her, son," MacQuaid said. "I'm sure she's taken the Trail of Rocks. It's the only way north she knows."

"I'll go," said Spence, standing.

MacQuaid walked to the door with Spence, his arm draped around his shoulders. Spence couldn't remember ever receiving such a kind gesture from his own father.

"Find her quickly," MacQuaid said. His expression was so full of weariness and sorrow that his face seemed more crags and shadows than flesh. They reached the door. "Is there anything you need? You may be on the trail quite some time."

"You mean, if we find out that Jamie is alive?"

"Aye, that is my meanin', son."

Spence drew in a deep breath, considering. He had convinced himself that Jamie was not alive, and the truth of MacQuaid's words slid through him like a knife. "If that's the case, we'll head east."

"Just get word to me. Let me know where you've gone and why."

"I will, sir."

MacQuaid strode across the room to his desk, rifled through one of the drawers, then came back with a small leather pouch. He handed it to Spence. "You may need this."

Spence pulled it open, and saw the bills inside. He knew how financially strapped the rancho was and handed the pouch back. "I can't take this."

"I insist. It's my daughter you'll be caring for. I will not have it any other way."

"But the payroll…" He knew MacQuaid had this much money in his hands for only one reason. The vaqueros would come for their pay on the final day of the fandango. But there was a look on the proud man's face that told Spence not to refuse.

"I'll take good care of her," he said, taking the leather pouch again.

"Tell her for me that I would have stopped the sun from settin' if I thought it would have helped her." The big man was staring straight at Spence with a look that made him stop in surprise. He'd never seen an expression of such profound compassion and gratitude from his own father. It took him a moment to comprehend that MacQuaid meant it for him.

"It will take me at least a full day to overtake her," he said. "I'll leave immediately." He turned to let himself through the door.

———◆———

For Aislin, the following day was much like the one before; the air grew thinner and colder as she climbed. The trail had nearly disappeared, and even Silverheel seemed to follow some inner direction. The big gray was becoming more accustomed to the routine and seemed to have lost some of her skittish behavior.

Aislin leaned back in the saddle and tried to enjoy the sheer beauty around her. Wildflowers flanked their path, miniature violets and lupines, and, tucked away in the shadows, crimson snow flowers poked their heads up through patches of wet pine needles. The trees were larger here, spaced farther apart than at the lower elevations. The heavens were so blue it almost hurt her eyes to gaze into their depths. She breathed in the pine-scented air, listening to the songs of birds she hadn't noticed before.

Silverheel shied away from a chipmunk that crossed the trail, and Aislin reached down to pat the horse's neck, absently, still deep in thought.

Then she heard the sound of hoofbeats behind her. Frowning, she halted the gray and listened carefully.

There it was again. One rider. Perhaps two.

She kicked Silverheel to a gallop and headed for the cover of a thick stand of pines. They reached the crest of a bluff, and she slid from the saddle. Holding the reins in her hand, she looked back down the trail.

There, winding along the most distant portion of the trail that she could see, a bronze sorrel laced in and out of the pines. Its rider was bent low over the saddle, as if in deep concentration, a tracking kind of concentration. Tracking Silverheel's trail.

The rider's face was hidden beneath his hat, but she knew from the proud set of his shoulders who it was. *Spence.*

She watched him examine her trail for a few more minutes, then reluctantly, she turned away, remounted, and let Silverheel choose her path. Finding Jamie was something she had to do alone.

She headed to the place her father had shown her years before, a shallow mountain valley filled with broken granite where a trail couldn't be followed. The Devil's Postpile. The place Indians lost trackers.

Spence was no longer in sight, and she slowed the big gray, relieved she had thought of the Gabrieleño Indian trick. It had taken her on a roundabout detour, but the result was worth it. Spence had obviously lost her trail.

The sun was slipping behind the mountains, and in the pale dusk she glanced around for a campsite. Silverheel sensed water and headed for some lush undergrowth even before she gave the signal.

The horse wound among the sharp cylindrical granite rocks and some boulders standing as large as houses as she gingerly made her way toward the water. They drew closer, and Aislin let out a sigh of relief. Between boulders, she could see a clearing with a soft and sandy spit of land jutting into a small beaver-dammed pond. And there was an abundance of tall, pale green grass for Silverheel. The perfect resting place, she thought wearily, and urged the horse onward.

They had just rounded the last of the giant boulders when Aislin spotted the smoke of a newly set campfire. The campsite itself was hidden from view. Not yet spiraling skyward, the smoke was rather a lacy fog, filling the air with the scent of burning pine.

In her alarm, she halted Silverheel too quickly with a yank on the reins, and the big horse reared and whinnied as the bit cut her mouth. She quickly slipped from the saddle and rubbed Silverheel's neck, crooning words of comfort until the horse stood still once more.

"I didn't think you'd ever get here."

She looked up in surprise. Spence stood, lolling against the trunk of a pine, ankles crossed as if he'd been waiting all day. His hat was pulled low against the slant of the setting sun.

He grinned at her.

For a moment, Aislin didn't move. She wanted to run to him, feel his arms around her. She wanted to circle her arms tightly around his neck and plant kisses all over his face. She wanted to tell him that no matter how he saw Jamie, how Hugh saw his elder son, it was Spence's heart and soul that shone more intensely than the first rays of the morning sun. And it was Spence who had come to fill her own life with that light. As Jamie never had.

But she didn't say, or do, any of those things.

If Jamie was truly alive, it was to him she was pledged.

Instead, she stared at him in utter silence, drinking in everything about him. "Hello, Spence."

NINE

Spence led her immediately to the cook fire and sat her down on a flat-topped rock. His voice was polite but laced with anger. "You had no call to run off by yourself."

"But, it's because of Ja—"

"Yes, I heard," he interrupted. "The reason doesn't matter. Do you have any idea the dangers a woman alone can face out here?"

"Of course I do." She stood and glared at him. "But in the event you've forgotten, I can take care of myself." She started to walk away from him, but he grabbed her wrist and sat her down again, and still holding her hand, he sat on a another slab of granite across from her.

"It doesn't matter why. It doesn't matter who." He turned her hand palm-side up and felt a pang of regret for treating her in such a brusque manner. "How did you do this?" Her palm was torn and bleeding.

"I slipped on some rocks. Took a bit of a tumble." She held her chin at a defiant tilt.

"I told you I'd help you look for Jamie," he said. "If that's what you wanted to do."

"I didn't think it would be seemly."

"Seemly?" He frowned, at the same time assessing her. She had been on the trail for two days. Long strands of hair had escaped from her braid, her cheeks were smudged, and her trousers were scraped and worn, probably from the same fall. "Why would my help be unseemly?"

"If Jamie is alive, it's Jamie I'll marry when I find him. It isn't right to ask you to accompany me."

"I am his brother."

"You were also going to marry me only a few days ago." She looked at him evenly.

"That was a few days ago," he said. "This is now. And I want to help." He didn't give her a chance to argue. "What did you find out? I mean after you and I last talked?"

"After we spoke in the carriage house," she began, and he noticed the high color in her cheeks beneath the trail dust, "I needed to get away, to think things through. So I took Silverheel for a ride. Headed down to the river." She paused. "I ran into Hyrum and Jake. They were camped nearby."

"What did they tell you?"

She frowned in concentration. "It may not be much, but it's something, Spence. Something more than what we've known before."

He nodded his encouragement. "Tell me."

"They said that they'd run into a soldier named Billy Melcher who was on his way from Fort Donelson to Fort Tejon. He told them he'd heard of a man near Donelson who was taken from a grave in a Reb uniform. He was alive. At least that's what the old woman said. And from the description he gave, it sounded like Jamie."

"That was all?" He was surprised she had been taken in by such sparse information.

She frowned, noting his disapproval, and her tone held a sad sharpness. "I didn't ask you to join me or to judge me, Spence."

Behind him Ruffian nickered at Silverheel, then all was quiet again. He stood and tossed another two dry branches on the fire. Sparks flew into the twilight sky. When he sat down again, he gave her an apologetic smile. "I'm not judging you, Aislin. It's unlike you not to reason things through completely before acting. You are anything but impetuous."

She laughed lightly, breaking their somber mood. "Yes," she agreed. "That's one thing I'm not." She laughed again. "Maybe that's why this feels so right. I felt free when I left La Paloma. Free of obligation,"

"To me?" he interrupted.

"I didn't mean that, Spence."

"It's weighed heavy on you, hasn't it?"

"Do you mean the betrothal to you?" She smiled softly.

"How many times have you told me you'd do anything to save our land? I know our plans weighed heavy—"

She shook her head, but she was grinning. "Would you let me finish?"

It was his turn to smile. "Yes, please. You were about to tell me about that sense of freedom you felt when you left."

She leaned closer. "My betrothal to Jamie had been planned by our parents almost from birth. I've asked myself if Jamie and I would have loved…and planned to marry…without those ideas instilled in us. Or were we somehow feeling the weight of responsibility and carrying out their wishes?"

"Leaving La Paloma," he said, "even as much passion as you feel for it, is part of your search to find those answers? To discover some sort of freedom along the way?"

"Yes," she said, looking surprised that he understood.

"But it's Jamie's ghost you're chasing, even as you search for those answers."

She nodded. "I may find him. Find him alive."

"And you still plan to marry him, even with what you've just said?"

"Yes. I plan to marry him if I find him alive. I always keep my promises."

"To save the rancho?"

"No. Even you said there has to be another way."

"For love then?"

She turned away from him, now staring into the fire. For a moment only the pop and snap of pitch from the pine branches could be heard.

"Is it love, Aislin?" It hurt to ask, but it hurt worse not to ask.

She was facing him again, and the glow of the firelight played on her cheeks. "If friendship, deep friendship, is love, and I think it is, then yes, I will marry Jamie for love. And don't you see? Because we'll be free of expectations, there will be great freedom in our marriage."

"What if there's more? More to love, I mean?"

She gave him a short laugh. "More?"

"Yes. What if there's a love so strong that without it, your heart feels squeezed dry?" Their eyes met, then she let her gaze drift to the cook fire without answering. "Would it be right for Jamie, for you both," he persisted, "to settle for anything less than that kind of love?"

"It's time to fix supper," she said. She stood and reached down to brush off her pants and winced as her palms touched the rough cloth.

"Let me see to those," he said, gently taking her hands in his for closer inspection. "Sit down again—"

She arched a brow.

"Please," he added, and she sat.

He swabbed her palm with cold water from the creek. Then as she sat waiting, he crushed a handful of nettles, another of wild spearmint, and added a cup of silt from the creek bank to make a poultice. He worked with gentleness, just as he had with the wild filly at the fandango. And it struck Aislin that she was acting like that mare—running from home, running to Jamie when in her heart all she could think of was Spence. But it was too new and frightening, these feelings that stirred within her.

He insisted she sit with her hands immobile while the poultice drew out the pain. She never moved her gaze from him as he greased a skillet and set it on some flat rocks to the side of the fire. Without a word he headed again to the creek where he'd left a string of fresh-caught rainbow trout, cleaned and scaled.

"When did you have time to fish?" she asked incredulously.

He grinned. "Your father knows you well, Aislin. He said you might try to lose me by heading through the Devil's Postpile—he drew a map of a shortcut. I arrived here at least an hour before you." He dredged the trout through a pile of cornmeal, then dropped them into the skillet beside some biscuits. The grease spattered and hissed.

She had been staring at his every move since he had applied the poultice to her hands. He cleared his throat. "Your father sent a message to you, Aislin."

"I hated to leave without so much as a good-bye."

"He understood."

"I left so much undone. Both ranchos are about to be lost." She drew in a deep breath. "I wish there were something we could do. Perhaps go to Yerba Buena ourselves, implore the Land Commission once more to extend the deadline."

"It's been tried, Aislin."

She was silent for a long moment, the sizzling grease in the frying pan the only sound.

"Besides," he said quietly, "is it the rancho you want, or Jamie?"

"Maybe both."

When he didn't comment, she looked down at her hands. "I have gauze in my satchel," she said. "The pain is gone now. I'll wash off the poultice, if you'll wrap my hands."

He removed the baked biscuits and flipped the trout, the splattering juices raising sparks in the darkening sky. Then he headed to Aislin's satchel and rummaged among her things, breathing in the feminine fragrance of lavender among them. By the time she had finished washing off the poultice in the creek, he had cut two strips of gauze.

Aislin sat again on the rock, and he knelt before her. He took first one hand, then the other, patting them dry, gently, carefully.

"You said my father sent a message," she said, looking down at her hands.

"He said that he would stop the very sun from setting if he thought it would help you." He was holding her left hand, winding the gauze around her palm. When she didn't respond, he glanced up and caught an unguarded look crossing her face. It reminded him of her father's expression as he'd left his study the day before. A mix of compassion and gratitude.

"So would I, Aislin," he said without looking at her. "If I had the power, I would stop the very sun from setting for you, if you asked."

With her unbandaged right hand she reached for Spence's face, but when their eyes met, she withdrew, letting her hand drop to her lap.

"I do believe the trout smells done," she said, breaking the mood.

He finished wrapping her right hand and stood. "I guess we know who's getting out of washing the skillet tonight," he said.

Late afternoon three days after their meeting at the Devil's Postpile, they reached the summit near Fort Tejon. The long mountain shadows were falling upon their trail. The fort itself lay in a mountain valley, barely visible through a small clearing in the pines, probably an hour's hard ride from the summit.

"We'll arrive by midmorning," Aislin announced, sliding from Silverheel's saddle. She stooped to make quick work of removing the saddle, and ducked her head while unfastening it so she wouldn't have to look in Spence's face. For three days the tension between them had mounted. She felt it, and she knew he did too, though nothing had been said.

Spence, still atop the sorrel, was watching her, a look of concern on his face. She stopped unfastening the tack and glanced up at him.

With a sigh, he swung his leg over the saddle and slid to the ground. A shaft of late afternoon sun crossed his face as he sauntered toward her, then just as quickly, it disappeared. "If you would rather go on tonight, we can get there before sundown."

She shook her head. "Let's rest here and head out first thing in the morning."

He gave her a quizzical look, then turned away to lift the saddle from Ruffian's back. A few minutes later, he led both horses to a small patch of grass near a stream and picketed them to graze.

When he returned, Aislin had already gathered twigs and leaves for kindling and now was heading into a stand of cedars and pines for some dried branches. He joined her. But as they worked, neither spoke. Finally, when they arrived back at the campsite and piled the wood near the fire ring, he took her hand to inspect her palm, which was healing nicely.

"We're nearly to Tejon," he said, not letting go of her hand. "If we find out Jamie's alive, I'll be with you. I'll help you look for him, even if we need to travel all the way to Tennessee." She started to protest, but he quickly went on. "Don't tell me anything more about it being unseemly."

She was grateful for his words, but he didn't understand that being near him awakened feelings she'd never before experienced. Feelings she didn't understand. Feelings she feared. She pulled her hands away from his. "When we find Billy Melcher, we'll decide," she said finally.

Spence stooped to pile the kindling in the center of the fire ring, then set short pieces of pine over the twigs in a tipi shape. Aislin watched his profile as he worked.

"Has it ever occurred to you that I don't want Jamie to be found alive?" she said suddenly.

Spence dropped the piece of wood he'd been holding and spun around. She stared at him, wishing she could retrieve the words.

He frowned at her for a long moment, and his voice was low when he finally spoke. "What did you say?"

"I said I don't want Jamie to be found alive." She settled onto the same log where she'd earlier put Silverheel's saddle. Then she covered her face and began to weep.

She didn't look up when Spence sat down on the log beside her. He made no move to touch her, to comfort her. When he spoke it was with the same low, flat tone. "So you've decided to search for him because you feel guilty?"

Still weeping, she nodded her head without looking up.

"And you'll marry him for the same reason, if you find him alive…marry him to try to make up for wanting him dead." His words were not a question. He knew her heart.

Again, she nodded. She couldn't tell from his low tone whether he was angry or appalled. She didn't want to look into his face and see. She wouldn't blame him for getting up and leaving her this minute. Riding off to leave her alone in her bitter, selfish misery.

She waited for him to leave. When he neither stood nor spoke, she ventured a look at him to find he was staring into the darkness. Aislin wondered if there was any limit to friendship. If there was, she was sure she had crossed the barrier to the other side. She had just told Spence that she hoped to find that his brother was dead. There could be no for-giveness for such thoughts.

She now stood, her face wet with tears, and she wiped her cheeks with her hands. As she did, she realized that she had succeeded in turn-ing the trail dust on her face to mud. Without another word to the stone-faced Spence, she headed through the brush to the spring. It wasn't far. Even in the darkness, she spotted it because of some telltale high-growing fern and berry brambles. She knelt before it, thinking of Jamie, her guilt washing over her again.

She reached into the clear pool of water, filled her hands, and brought them to her face. Unable to bear the pain of her guilt, she wept again, her hands cool against her hot cheeks.

Suddenly she felt Spence's arm around her shoulders. He was kneel-ing beside her.

"Aislin," he said, holding her tight. "I understand."

She looked up at him, her eyes still watery. "How can you?" she groaned. "How can you understand what it's like...the guilt...?"

He didn't move his gaze from her eyes, and she saw in their depths something she should have seen before, should have known all along. "You?" she whispered raggedly. "You?"

There was such sorrow in his face that she didn't think she could bear it. "Oh, Spence," she cried.

"I felt it too." His voice was hoarse. "When the men said he might be alive"—he closed his eyes a moment—"I didn't want it to be true. I saw the joy in my mother's and father's faces...and in yours, Aislin." He shook his head slowly. "Especially in yours." His voice broke, and he didn't go on.

They were still kneeling by the spring-fed stream, its gentle bur-bling the only sound in the darkening forest.

Aislin looked into his anguished face, and she understood every-thing he had just told her, and more. She knew the scars he carried, some so deep that even he might be unaware of the hurt that caused them. But she knew. She had watched and cared all along.

"I thought I loved Jamie," she whispered. "His was the only love I'd known." She looked down. "At least, I thought it was…" She didn't finish. "And I mourned for him."

"I know you did, Aislin. It was real."

"Then something happened." She moved her gaze again to meet Spence's. "I began to consider that my life wasn't over. I opened my heart to other possibilities. When you and I…" She hesitated. "When we talked of marriage the sun was about to rise again after a long, dark night." She bit her lip and halted. "Then just as I settled into the wonder of that light, that joy"—she paused again—"we found out Jamie might be alive." She sniffled. "I was glad, so very glad, when we first heard it. Then I thought about the rest…that new joy…" Her voice trailed off miserably.

Spence touched her cheek. "I know," he said simply.

For a moment, neither one spoke, then he grasped both her hands and helped her to stand. They stood looking at each other in the twilight.

"Aislin," Spence finally said, "I understand why you think you must marry Jamie if we find him alive. It's the same reason I must search for him."

She drew in a deep breath. "We'll get through this together," she said, attempting a shaky smile. "We'll find him, if he's alive."

Around them the sounds of crickets and tree frogs began their cacophony of night music. Once in a while, there was the splash of a fish jumping in the stream, followed by ripples lapping at the shore. Spence touched her hair above her ear where it smoothed back into a braid. For a moment he stroked it, the same way he gentled a wild mustang.

And at last her heart was still.

The night passed slowly. She'd placed her bedroll near the fire, but by midnight, the coals had turned to ashes. She slept in her clothes and used her cape for a blanket, but still she shivered, turning first one direction, then the other on the hard ground. Her dreams were filled with images of Jamie, alone, suffering, calling out to her. She tossed on her bedroll and finally woke in the deep predawn darkness.

The stars were just beginning to fade, and she stared heavenward.

Oh, Lord, she breathed. *Help me find my way. I'm so filled with guilt and sadness that I can't bear it. Oh, Father, help me! Help me find my way to Jamie. You know if he's alive or dead. If he lives, lead me to him.*

But her prayers seemed to go no further than the tops of the pines around the clearing. *Oh, God! Help me.*

SEEK ME FIRST, MY BELOVED. SEEK ME FIRST...

A slight breeze stirred the needles of the pines, and Aislin turned on her side, wondering why she felt so alone.

Spence rose before Aislin, set the wood for a fire, and lit the kindling. Aislin yawned and stretched, then turned to watch his profile as he worked. When the fire blazed orange and red, she hurried from her pallet, wrapped her cape around her shoulders, then stood, holding her hands over the flames. Spence dumped some coffee in a blue speckled pot that he'd already filled with creek water, and set it to boil on a rock near the center of the fire.

"Did you sleep well?" he asked, though it seemed from his look that he knew the difficult time she'd had. Maybe it had been the same for him.

She rubbed her hands over the fire and gave him a sleepy smile. "I'm just hoping for a bath and a decent bed tonight at the fort."

He grinned. "You'll be treated like royalty, probably given the best bed in the officers' quarters. I'm sure they don't get many women passing through the fort."

"Ah, it's a luxury just to think of it. A hot bath to soak my aching bones. A decent bed instead of the hard ground."

He snorted. "If I know Aislin D'Ary Byrne, and I think I do, you'll charm the entire population at Tejon. They'll be at your beck and call, giving you the finest accommodations the U.S. government can provide." He laughed again.

She chuckled. "You *do* know me, Spencer Dearbourne."

They stared at each other across the cook fire, the unspoken tension suddenly hanging between them. Then Spence pushed himself up and, without another glance, he headed toward the horses. The set of his shoulders was stiff, and his gait was purposeful as he moved away from her.

"Spence..." she called after him. When he didn't turn, she followed him into a small clearing where the horses were grazing in the morning sun. He had already started inspecting their hooves as he did every morning before beginning their ride.

"Spence," she said again, and this time he turned, letting go of Silverheel's foot.

She took a few steps closer. "What I said last night..." His gaze was now locked on hers. "About Jamie, and how I wished..." She couldn't finish.

Spence nodded, understanding. "Yes," he said simply.

"I just want to tell you that we can't add more guilt because of any feeling between us."

He didn't answer.

She took a deep breath. "We are practically family. We've been friends through the years. There is nothing in our relationship to worry over."

He gave her an assessing look but said nothing to agree or disagree.

"Absolutely nothing." Now there was a hint of amusement in his eyes, and somehow it gave her courage to go on. "We had a moment of thinking there might be more...I mean just the hint of something more than, ah, friendship," she added wisely, "when we planned to marry."

Still he said nothing.

"And the way I see it, no matter what we find out about Jamie, we will leave it at that."

A slow, crooked smile crossed his face. "All right, my friend. Shall we head to Fort Tejon?" He squinted at the rising sun, then looked back at her, its light falling strong on his face.

She remembered what he'd said the first night he found her—that for her, he would stop the sun from setting if he had the power.

The only reason she might want the sun stopped in its tracks, she thought whimsically, would be to see Spence's beloved face in the morning light. Always.

TEN

Spence eased Ruffian into a smooth three-beat canter, and Aislin followed mere yards behind on Silverheel. Fort Tejon lay ahead of them, basking in the late morning sun, surrounded by low-slung, rounded hills, brown-velvet smooth. Aislin, suddenly in a hurry to be done with whatever news Billy Melcher might have for them, kicked Silverheel's flanks. The horse responded and soon galloped ahead of Spence on Ruffian.

Spence grinned as she raced by, immediately urging the bronze sorrel to keep up with the mare. For one lighthearted moment, Aislin felt like they were children again, competitive, carefree, joyous. Her hat flew out behind her, held only by the neck tie, and over the beat of hooves she heard Spence laughing as he urged Ruffian to overtake them.

Minutes later, still laughing, they slowed the horses, finally halting by the road leading to the fort. She pushed some strands of hair back into her braid and replaced the black wide-brimmed Spanish hat.

Spence smiled his approval as his gaze flicked over her. "Are you ready?"

She gave him a quick nod and nudged Silverheel into an easy walk. This time, Spence pulled the sorrel up beside her. They had gone only a quarter mile or so when a uniformed rider headed toward them. They halted again as the man approached.

"Greetings!" he said, slowing to a stop in front of them.

Now that he was close, Aislin could see his carrot-hued hair beneath his hat and that his face was more freckles than not. She couldn't help smiling at him.

"What brings you folks out this way?" he asked pleasantly. His horse skittered sideways, and the young soldier seemed to have difficulty controlling the energetic beast.

"We've come looking for information," said Spence. "We'd like to see your commander."

The man shook his head. "I'm sorry; Captain Adams is away from the fort. Took some troops north for a few days. Won't be back until the end of the week."

Aislin let out a sigh of disappointment. "Is there a second in command?"

The young soldier's gaze moved to her. "Yes, ma'am. Lieutenant LaMott." The soldier's horse danced sideways again, and he drew up the reins to steady him. "Problem is, he's taken some troops into the Valley of the Horses, just up yonder. Won't be back until nightfall."

Spence shot a glance at Aislin, who nodded slightly, then looked back to the young man. "Do you have a soldier here by the name of Billy Melcher?"

The soldier squinted his eyes in thought, then shook his head slowly. "Not that I recollect."

"He might be new, part of a detachment recently arrived from the east," Spence said. "Fort Donelson in Tennessee."

"I heard him described as a tall fellow," Aislin added, "and bald. It's said he's an officer."

"Well, now, that may explain it. We've got troops headed this way. Don't recollect where they hail from." He laughed, gesturing eastward. "Just know they're from the other side of the Rockies. And they're expected any day now."

"Do you know if they traveled through Santa Fe?"

He gave Spence a strange look. "Well, I do know for a fact they took the Oregon-California Road, then headed south through Utah after they reached Bridger. Last we heard, they were camped at Mountain Meadows, letting their livestock feed and rest in preparation to cross the desert." He paused, frowning. "They'd have traveled a thousand miles or so out of their way to pass through Santa Fe," the young man stated. "I'm fairly certain they would not have done that."

Spence turned to Aislin. "Hyrum and Jake did say Santa Fe?"

"Yes," she said. "I'm certain it was Santa Fe."

Spence turned back to the soldier. "Could there have been a reason they might have begun on the Santa Fe Trail, then cut north, taking the Cherokee Trail into Utah?"

The red-haired man obviously relished dispensing information. He drew himself taller and jutted out his chin. "Well, now that you ask, yes, that could be a possibility all right. These particular troops are looking for wild horses to take back to the army. That's the whole reason they were sent west in the first place. They might've zigzagged all over the West scouting for mustangs."

"For the war?" Aislin asked. "That's why they went, after the horses?"

"Yes, ma'am. The Federals are hurting for horseflesh. Rebs, too, we hear." He paused. "From the way I heard it told, the troops will return to Santa Fe with as many horses as they can herd. So you'd be right as far as the return route."

"These wild horses," Spence said as if mulling something over, "say, if a private citizen could get a herd to New Mexico, he might find himself a wealthy man, is that right? I mean, the demand is that great?"

The soldier laughed. "You bet your boots, there's a demand. If I could get out of my duty here, I'd take a herd east myself." He looked wistful. "I'd be a rich man."

Aislin broke in. "Do you know how soon these troops are expected to arrive?"

"No, ma'am. I don't," he said, looking truly sorry. "Some of the others inside," he nodded to the buildings that made up the fort, "well, they might be of more assistance. They might have heard something more recent than I have."

"If you'd take us in and introduce us, we would certainly be appreciative," Spence said.

The soldier grinned. "Well now, sir. I'd be happy to help you and the missus out in such a way." He straightened in the saddle again.

Aislin smiled. "That would be very kind of you. But we're not a mister and missus, not even close."

She shot a sideways glance at Spence, whose face remained impassive.

Spence then introduced first Aislin, then himself, and the soldier did the same.

"Sergeant Scotty MacPherson at your service," he said amiably. "Why don't you follow me, and we'll see how we can help you out? Fact is, we'll put you up for a time, if you'd like. You two look like you've been on the trail a spell."

"Yes, thank you," added Spence. "We could use a place to rest and clean up."

A few minutes later they followed the soldier down the slightly winding road, across the parade grounds, past the three main buildings, long squat adobes, and on to the corral at the rear of the complex. The three dismounted in front of the stables and turned their horses over to a couple of even younger soldiers for feeding and watering.

Fort Tejon itself was surprisingly large. Aislin had expected just a few dusty buildings, but it resembled a small town, with its officers' quarters, headquarters building, smithy, mess hall, and rows of barracks to shelter what appeared to be hundreds of men. Soldiers milled about, glancing at them curiously as they passed.

Scotty led them into the general headquarters building, asked another soldier at a desk which guest rooms were available, then led them upstairs to the officers' quarters. Then they were given time to rest and bathe before the noontime dinner, the main meal of the day.

Aislin's room was bare except for an iron-framed bed, plain white broadcloth curtains at its single window, and an Indian rug on the floor next to the bed. She spent an hour soaking in a tub of tepid water that Scotty had ordered delivered to her room.

Promptly at noon, Spence appeared at her door to escort her to the officers' mess. He had washed and shaved, and she smiled her approval as he stood before her.

She hooked her hand under his elbow, and they strolled down the hall and descended the stairs to the officers' dining room, where Scotty MacPherson met them at the door.

Two officers were already seated, and Scotty escorted Spence and

Aislin to the same table. The men stood to greet the newcomers, shaking hands with Spence, then remaining on their feet as Spence pulled back a chair for Aislin and she took her seat. Scotty exited the room as soon as the introductions had been made. Spence seated himself directly across from Aislin.

The taller, more distinguished-looking officer, a man named Captain Everett, caught Aislin's attention first. His hair was silver, and he sported a waxed mustache.

The second gentleman, Lieutenant Shirley, was younger than Captain Everett, though his washed-out wiry hair was no indication. His small eyes shifted uneasily as he talked, which made Aislin nervous for the poor man, who seemed more shy than untrustworthy.

As the four made small talk about the history of the fort and the '57 earthquake that had demolished every building on the property, other officers drifted into the room. Soon it was filled with the low tones of civilized conversation and laughter.

A staff of three Gabrieleños soon began to serve dinner. In response to her curious look, Captain Everett told her the ingredients of each dish as it was served. A steaming platter of *puchero* stew made of green corn, potatoes, and beef was brought first, followed by a large bowl of frijoles, served with a spicy roasted pepper sauce that made Aislin's eyes water. Finally, the youngest Gabrieleño brought a *totopo* bread made of dried ground yucca and cornmeal. The small rounds of flatbread had been roasted instead of baked, and were served with sweet butter and honey.

"We hear there's a troop from the east heading here," Spence said as he spread butter on a small round of *totopo*.

"That's right," said Captain Everett.

"We're looking for a man named Billy Melcher," Aislin explained, then went on to tell him why.

Both men looked sympathetic. "I'm sorry," said Lieutenant Shirley, "but I have never heard of an officer by that name." He took a bite of stew, chewed for a moment, then wiped his mouth with the cloth napkin. "And I served with most of the officers in that division."

Aislin's heart dropped. She had hoped to find out something by now. She glanced across the table at Spence, but he seemed lost in thoughts of his own. She had just taken another bite of *totopo* when a boisterous voice sounded outside the room.

She and Spence looked up in surprise as another officer strode across the room to join them. The tall, distinguished, dark-haired man heartily greeted them both, introduced himself as Lieutenant LaMott, then sat beside Aislin.

"I hear from Scotty that you're looking for a man named Billy Melcher," he said. One of the Gabrieleños set down a new platter of stew. LaMott ladled a hearty portion onto his plate.

"Yes, have you heard of him?"

"May have," he said, stabbing a piece of stew beef with his fork. "May have."

Aislin looked to Spence, who was concentrating on the conversation of the other two officers and didn't turn.

"Can you tell me where?"

His eyes were sad when he looked back to her. "Billy Melcher is the name in a bawdy song," he said. "A song sung mostly in saloons. It's not likely you would have heard of it."

By now the table had fallen silent, and Aislin felt her cheeks redden. She dropped her fork.

"I've heard that name pulled out of the air more than once," Lieutenant LaMott said gently. "Usually when someone's trying to figure out a quick name to use, if you know what I mean."

Aislin remembered the glances Hyrum and Jake had exchanged the night they'd told her about Billy Melcher, their shifty-eyed looks, their final plea for money. *It doesn't hurt to try*, they'd said twice that night. It didn't hurt anyone but her.

She put her napkin on the table and stood. "Excuse me, gentlemen," she said and ran from the room.

She was heading up the stairs to her quarters, when she heard the fall of footsteps below her at the base of the stairs.

"Aislin!" Spence called, and she turned toward him. "Please, wait!"

He took the stairs two at a time until he reached her. "I'm sorry. I'm really sorry."

Hot tears filled her eyes. "I was such a fool. Only the young and innocent have never heard of…that name. Think of it. Not even young Scotty MacPherson had heard it."

Spence wiped her tears with his fingertips, then pulled out his handkerchief and dabbed at her cheeks.

"No matter what I said about Jamie last night, I want to find him alive. I didn't realize how much until we arrived here, and it seemed that we were so close to learning he might be alive." She paused. "Do you think there's still hope…hope that he might be alive?"

He didn't answer.

"Shall we continue our search for him?"

"I said I'd help you, Aislin…" He took her arm and turned her toward the hallway leading to a balcony overlooking the parade grounds.

"Why do I get the feeling you're about to add 'but'…?" She shot him a glance and studied his profile for a moment, the line of his forehead, his nose, his lips. His brow was furrowed deep in thought, and she turned away.

They headed to the French windows at the end of the hall. Spence held open one door, and Aislin stepped out onto a planked porch that ran the length of the building. Two large sycamores flanked the area, providing a canopy of dappled shade against the warm autumn sun.

They stood by the railing, Spence leaning slightly forward, his weight supported by his hands, Aislin standing beside him, and watched a group of soldiers exit the mess hall and head to their barracks. Scotty MacPherson glanced up and gave them a wide grin and a mock salute as he headed toward the stables.

Finally, Spence turned, considering her quietly for a moment before speaking. "There is something else we need to discuss," he said.

She lifted her eyes to his. "I know. Heading back to see our families through the drought, the legal problems. We need to do what we can to help." Chasing after a dead man's ghost wouldn't help either family, she thought grimly.

He lifted a brow and gave her a crooked smile. "Do everything we can, *except* marrying, to save the ranchos?"

She didn't answer. "We spoke earlier about finding another way. No one should marry for those reasons."

"And I think I have. Found another way, I mean." His words spilled out, almost as if he couldn't wait to tell her, as if he wanted her to share his excitement. "Horses, Aislin!" he declared, almost with a roar. "Wild horses!"

"Mustangs." She grinned, considering his words. "Herds of marvelous, wild, and wonderful mustangs!"

He was facing her now. "Aislin," he said, his voice dropping. "Think of it! We can herd horses even better than the Union army. We can take them to Santa Fe. Sell them to the highest bidder."

She remembered he'd once said that mustangs make the best military mounts because of their sturdiness, agility, strength.

"They'll want them broken," he said. "And broken wild horses fetch a far dearer price than any other." The light in his eyes said he couldn't wait to get started. "After we round up the horses, we'll head across the Tehachapis to the Mojave Road and the Old Spanish Trail. We'll drive them all the way to New Mexico. It will take us at least two months, depending on the weather."

"We can't do this alone, Spence. We're talking about hundreds of horses."

He nodded. "More likely thousands. We'll lose close to half along the way, so we'll have to start with at least four thousand."

Aislin settled into a nearby chair. "Four thousand?" she breathed in awe. "We can't possibly—"

"I've already figured that out." He pulled up a chair beside her and leaned forward. "We'll send someone back to the ranchos. Someone we can trust. Have our fathers choose their best wranglers to join us to round up the mustangs and get them east. We'll pick a meeting place. Probably in the Valley of the Horses. You and I, possibly a scout or two from here, can go on ahead and spot the healthiest herds."

"You've given this some thought."

"I have," he agreed. "What do you think?"

"What about our search for Jamie?"

He was silent for several moments while he studied the troops that were gathering for drill on the parade ground. Finally, he turned to her again. "Aislin, I went to the place where Jamie died. I spoke with witnesses…"

"You believed then that he was killed. And you believe it now."

"Yes," he said quietly. "It's only because of two thugs who deceived us that we held out any hope at all." He sighed deeply. "We'll hold all the feelings we've talked about, including our guilt, our sorrow, even hope, in our hearts forever. But those feelings won't bring him back. Even hope alone won't."

"He still seems alive to me." She finally admitted it to herself. "If there's anything I learned from this Billy Melcher business, it's that."

"I know," said Spence. "And I will honor your feelings for him."

She let out a pent-up sigh. "Let's get back to the horses. You asked me what I thought of the plan."

His eyes had lost some of their luster, she noticed, and when he spoke, his voice sounded tired. "And what do you think?"

"How long will it take? I mean, do we have a prayer of a chance of making it back in time to save the ranchos?"

He studied her thoughtfully a moment. "A chance? Maybe not. But a prayer of a chance?"

She smiled, getting his meaning. "We'll pray those few thousand mustangs are willing to move fast," she said. Then she added, "It may be the one thing that will save our lands."

"It will be a hard ride, even after we get the herd together."

"I figured it would be."

"This morning you mentioned you were tired of sleeping on the ground."

She smiled again. "I suppose you're about to tell me I can't expect a cot on this trip."

Now he grinned. "No, nor a bathtub."

She chuckled.

"But wait till it's your night watch—then your back won't hurt from the cold, hard ground."

She raised a brow. "Because I won't be sleeping?"

"You got it," he declared, enjoying the way her luminous eyes opened in surprise.

"Won't the wranglers keep watch?"

"One of us, meaning you or I, will keep watch over the wranglers."

"Every night?"

He nodded. "Every night. We'll be herding a small fortune in horse-flesh. The closer we get to Abiqui, where we'll auction them, the more valuable they'll become."

"Because they'll be broken?"

"And because they're closer to their destination—Santa Fe."

"So we'll face Indian raids?"

"Yes."

"Outlaws?"

"Yes."

Aislin sighed. "And I suppose Union troops."

"Yes. That's why we must stay clear of Santa Fe—where the troops station. They might commandeer the herd, promising to pay us later. Only later might not come, or at least not come in time to help our families." He paused, looking at her carefully. "It will be perilous, Aislin. Are you sure you want to go through with it? You could head back to La Paloma and tell the families what we've planned. I could go on alone."

She sought his eyes and gave him a wide smile. "I could indeed," she said.

He threw his head back and laughed out loud. "I thought not," he said, looking extremely pleased. "I thought not."

At supper that night, Spence, with Aislin at his side, spoke to Lieutenant LaMott about assigning Scotty MacPherson to a temporary duty—first, to deliver a message to Rancho de la Paloma; then, to lead into the Valley of Horses as many vaqueros and wranglers as the ranchos could spare. The Lieutenant agreed after Spence promised to send Scotty back with a small herd of broken mustangs. Scotty, after receiving directions to Rancho de la Paloma, left before dawn, heading south on the road to Trail of Rocks.

The sun was high by the time Spence's and Aislin's saddled horses were brought to the front of the officers' quarters. It was with a feeling of mutual satisfaction that they mounted up and rode from Fort Tejon. Within the hour, they were winding along the steep trail of the foothills, heading to their first view of the massive Valley of the Horses.

Aislin was in the lead when they rounded the last low hill before reaching the long straight stretch into the Valley. Frowning, she drew Silverheel to a halt. A few moments later, Spence halted the sorrel beside her.

"Might be difficult to find even one horse in this," she said.

Spence's shoulders sagged, and he nodded in agreement. There, spread before them like a lake of cream that had been whipped into frothy peaks, was the densest fog that Aislin had ever seen.

"Tule fog," said Spence. "Typical in the dead of winter. Not now."

"I've heard travelers tell of it," said Aislin. "They say it can lie on the ground for weeks at a time."

"So thick you can't see your hand in front of your face."

She let out a sigh. "Or a herd of mustangs, even if they're only feet away."

Without another word, they urged their horses back onto the trail and down the long straight stretch above the valley. Aislin's heart was pounding as Spence disappeared into the fog. She followed the slow clip-clop of Ruffian's hooves, because, though man and horse were only a few feet in front of her, she could see nothing but ashen white.

ELEVEN

Camila moved down the length of the verandah toward her husband, who was standing beneath the arbor. The grape leaves had long ago withered, died, and blown away with the dry winds. But still the tenacious vines remained on both ends of the verandah, a testament to determination.

MacQuaid turned as she moved toward him. "I saw you gazing off into the distance."

"Aye," he said sadly. "That I was indeed."

She stepped beside him, circling her arm around his waist, and looked out at the mountains to the east. "And what is it that is holding your attention?"

"I've been thinking about what we will do when we leave this land." His voice was flat, and she knew it hurt him to say the words.

She touched his jaw and gently turned his face until he was looking only at her. "That's what I wanted to talk to you about."

"About where we'll live?"

"*Sí.*"

He searched her eyes. "How did you know…I mean that it has come down to this?"

She gave him a gentle smile. "I saw Noe arrive with the banker this morning. I knew it must be nearing time."

His gaze swept the mountains again, then he shook his head slowly. "To lose it now, after all we've done, after working so hard…" His voice choked and he couldn't go on.

"Husband," she said, drawing herself up tall. "You listen to me now!" In all their years of marriage she had seldom spoken so sharply to him. He gave her his full attention. "Do you remember when we first sailed into the harbor, the day Rancho de la Paloma became ours?"

"Aye, how could I forget that moment?"

"We spoke of our dreams for this land, how we would build, raise our children here, begin a new life."

He nodded, but his gaze returned to the distant mountains. "Aye, that we did, lass."

"We looked to these same hills with hearts filled with joy that God had given us this land. We knew that the land was on loan from him, for us to tend and love and fill with playing children, for him. I remember us standing on board the *Spiritus Sanctus*, the wind in our faces, the sun on our shoulders. We knew that not every day, or every year, would be easy. Far from it, we knew the work ahead might bring sorrow or death." She thought back to the stillborn son she'd lost all those years ago.

MacQuaid must have known her thoughts, for he reached for her hand and squeezed it. "And we've known both," he said quietly.

"We have," she agreed.

He swallowed hard. "Where will we go? We will have lost everything!"

Camila touched the sides of his red-bearded face with her hands, looking deep into his eyes. "We have not lost each other," she said. "Nor our children. Nor the love of God!" She gestured out to the sweeping land. "I said a moment ago that he lent this land to us for a season. And now it appears that our season here has passed."

MacQuaid started to speak, but she touched his lips with her fingertips. "Let me finish," she said softly. He gave her a gentle smile, and she went on. "I have never told you this, but I was never happier than where we first lived on the rancho lands."

He looked at her incredulously.

"It is true. The one-room adobe where Aislin was born."

He chuckled. "You found joy there?"

The sting of tears filled her eyes. "Aye," she said, knowing how he loved to hear her say the Irish word. "Aye, that I did."

"It was a Basque shepherd's cottage."

"But it was filled with such love. Did I ever tell you how I sat by the window facing the mountains and rocked Aislin in her cradle, waiting for you to come home for your midday meal?"

"Na, lass."

She laughed. "I knew that the minute you headed through the door, you would kiss my cheek, then hurry to the small wooden cradle. You could not wait to lift the child into your arms."

"I remember," he said.

"And you would hold Aislin to the window, facing the mountains. I remember how you told her that God says, 'Lift up your eyes to the hills, from whence comes your strength.'"

He swallowed hard, and she nodded to him slowly, her gaze never leaving his.

"Think about what you told her. She did not understand a word of it, but I did. You said to lift up our eyes to the hills, his creation…to him, the Creator." She paused. "He didn't say to keep our eyes on the work of our hands, this rancho, even the cattle on the hills, or the land we've cultivated. He wants us to look far beyond those things."

MacQuaid was watching her carefully. "I canna believe that God gave us this land only to take it back again."

"You told me when our baby boy died, that in the Bible, Hannah said to God, 'You have lent me this child, and now I give him back to you.' Is a child any different than land?"

He shook his head. "I think a child is far more important."

"If a child is only on loan to us, how much more temporary is something like land? God gave it to us for a season. Perhaps that season is over."

"I canna give it up so easily as you seem to," MacQuaid uttered, turning away from her.

"Husband," she said, placing her hand on his, "is the small cottage still there?"

"I haven't ridden out that way for years," he said, his voice low. "It very likely has fallen to ruin."

"I want to see it."

"Why?" he said, his voice almost a growl. "I wouldna take my wife, my family, to live in such a place. Not now!" She knew he was too proud to cry, but there was an awful catch in his voice.

"It is a place I treasure in my heart," she countered.

"Because it was our first home? Because it held Aislin's cradle?"

"No," she said, thinking how she had come to America as his bride, though she had not loved him. Not then. "Those were not the reasons I was thinking about."

"Why then?"

"Because it is the place where our love grew from just the seed of something good into something as solid as an evergreen, as a century oak. Something that will last until our Lord calls us home."

"Ah, my lass," he said, and finally his voice broke. He gathered her into his arms, resting his cheek on the top of her head. "It was one small room," he reminded her, "with a dirt floor and no glass in the windows."

She laughed lightly, still resting her cheek against the soft cloth of his shirt. "I swept that floor, sprayed it with water, and swept it again until not a speck of dust could be found. When Aislin began to crawl, I didn't want her knees to be dirt stained."

He pulled back and looked into her upturned face. "That was then, this is now, lass. We had newly arrived. We lived there only while we constructed this house. The adobe was filled with dreams for our future. That was what made it bearable."

She sighed deeply. "Have we no dreams left? Is life so harsh as to have taken them all?" She paused, her eyes still on his.

MacQuaid glanced up at the solid structure of the house, and his gaze softened. "Aye, what dreams we had then," he murmured, more to himself than to her. "Do you remember how we figured where to put the windows so we could always see the view from our bedroom?"

Camila laughed lightly. "Oh yes. You said you wanted our children to look to the hills for their strength."

"And it was quite a feat, because we also wanted the house to catch the evening breezes." He rubbed the smooth, whitewashed adobe wall. "Never will there be another house such as this."

"I have loved it as much as you do."

He moved his gaze to the bare-branched sycamores. "Once the yard was green with grass, and the roses bloomed, and the wild lilacs made the place smell like heaven."

She smiled. "And it was filled with children, ours and the Dearbournes'. They played tag and blind man's bluff and sang and laughed and squealed as they ran."

"I wish I could hear the music of their laughter again," he said.

"I believe your Irish melancholy is filling you with an aching emptiness that cannot be filled. You are looking more to the past than to the future."

He turned to her, studied her face for several moments, then smiled finally. "You are a wise women, Camila. God smiled upon me when he brought you into my life."

She lifted one of his broad, rough hands to her lips. "It is I who am blessed," she said softly. The wind from the east blew the dry leaves beneath the sycamores, rattling them like old bones. Her husband's long sigh nearly broke her heart, and she knew he had more to tell her. She did not let go of his hand. "Have they given us a date we must leave this place?" she asked, knowing they surely must have.

"Aye, my lass, they have. The bank will take possession of the land in only a few weeks. The cattle, what's left of the herds, everything…"

She smiled up into his face. "Then we must go immediately to the small adobe. We will need to work to get it ready." She hesitated. "We will be allowed to live there, though even that land is no longer ours?"

He winced at the thought. "We have as much right as any other squatter on government land," he said, his voice low. "But there's only room enough for the family to live there."

"That is all we will need."

"We must let our help go. The house servants. The cowhands. I have already told Noe he is no longer needed."

She reached her arms around her husband's neck, forcing him to look into her eyes. "We have each other, MacQuaid. Our God is with us. We will look to him now, just as we always have."

He nodded, unable to speak.

"We will seek him first. Nothing else matters right now."

"Ah, my Camila…" He tenderly pulled her into his arms. "Hold me," he said.

She circled her arms around his waist and pulled tight against him. "I am here," she said. "I am here."

Two hours later, Camila mounted a rangy blood bay and settled onto the sidesaddle, her preferred way of riding, as MacQuaid swung a leg over the richly tooled saddle on his chestnut mare. They headed west along the foothills leading to Mystic Lake, now a dry lake bed in the middle of a long flat valley. She followed her husband on the narrow trail as it wound along the side of a dusty streambed.

Soon they climbed a small bluff, and she recognized the road leading to the adobe. The fragrance of warm earth and dried sage filled her heart with memories. It had been spring when they'd first come here, Mystic Lake a blue mirror nestled among the wildflower-covered hills, the distant mountains snowcapped, and the grass beside the trail as tall as a horse's flanks. She had never seen anything so lovely.

But now, even in drought, the otherwise brown hills were dotted with sturdy live oaks and beavertail cactus, giving the land a wild and harsh beauty. The wind had swept the air clean, turning the sky a deep purple-blue.

They rounded another curve, and MacQuaid slowed the chestnut mare. She brought the bay even with him, and they halted together. There, some one hundred yards ahead, stood the squat adobe.

MacQuaid had been right—it had fallen to ruins. The door swung in the wind at an angle, pulled loose from the uppermost hinges, screeching in an uneven rhythm. Most of the whitewash had long since disappeared, leaving the crumbling adobe bricks an odd speckled combination of red, brown, and white. The place was surrounded by dandelion weeds and the ever-present cacti, nearly as tall as the windows themselves. The single century oak that Camila remembered well stood tall and proud behind the compact building, as if consciously sheltering it until their return.

Without speaking, MacQuaid urged his horse onward, then halted and dismounted at the front door. Camila, still seated atop the bay, waited, watching her husband's reaction. If he wept in despair at their circumstances, she would give the proud man his privacy. He stepped into the adobe and disappeared inside.

When he didn't return after several minutes, she urged the bay closer, then dismounted near the chestnut. Cautiously, she moved across the threshold.

MacQuaid didn't turn when she entered the room. Instead, he continued leaning against the window on the east side of the small dusty room. She stepped toward him and wrapped her arm around his waist. The view was just as she remembered: the windswept fields, the rugged hills at the base of the majestic peaks that seemed to rise nearly to heaven. Even the house at La Paloma could not boast of such a vista.

She felt his rhythmic shaking, and at first she feared the worst, that her proud husband was beginning to weep, though attempting to keep the emotion from her. Then the distinct sound of a low and rumbling chuckle became clear, and she looked up into his face in wonder.

"What do you find humorous?" She glanced around at the decaying old adobe, its interior far worse that what she had observed outside.

"Ah, my sweet lass," said MacQuaid. "Our lives began here. And here, they may very well end. But is it so tragic that we must look out this window for the rest of our lives?"

"To God's hills?" she added.

"Aye, to those very hills."

He turned to her then, and she saw a new light in his eyes—a light of hope. It was then she knew they would be all right after all. "We will need one more room," she said, "for our daughters."

He nodded. "I will see if someone will help me build it. I have no money to pay hired help."

"But we have friends," she said.

"Aye, we do, and they know I would do the same for any of them."
He paused. "And I was just thinkin', lass, as I gaze at the hills, that I will
offer my services as overseer of La Paloma to the new owner. That will
bring in enough money to feed us, perhaps to buy back a small herd to
keep for milk and beef for the table."

"I will plant a garden."

He looked at her tenderly. "It is a long way to the river," he
reminded her, "to fetch water, I mean."

"We have three strong daughters. Carrying buckets of water is a
good way to build strength—especially strength of character."

"They will think it an adventure at first, perhaps. But later…?"

"I have no doubt that Brighid will adapt well. Sybil is another
matter."

"She will assume she can still order her fashions from New York."
His face had fallen, and she knew his pride was tugging at him again.

"She will dress as fashionably as ever, but she will learn to sew. We
will all learn to sew." Then she glanced around the room, hands on her
hips, assessing all that needed to be done. "You will need to see that all
of our beds are transported here by wagon."

"We haven't room for more than one," he said sadly.

"When the second bedroom is finished, the beds will fit nicely." She
smiled. "Until then, my love, we will sleep outdoors. It is warm enough,
and we certainly do not need to worry about rain. We will bring enough
bedding to see us through the winter."

She was still turning a slow circle, assessing their new home. "And
we can fit one small kitchen table there, by the window we love."

He nodded. "I will build shelves for dishes and pans. And a brick-
oven kitchen outdoors."

"And we will bring the parlor stove for one corner."

"I think nothing more will fit into this small space," MacQuaid
said.

"We will bring the cradle, the Byrne family cradle," she added
softly. "Here it first held Aislin, and perhaps someday it will hold a child
of hers." Their eyes met, and she knew they were both thinking of their

daughter and wondering if she would ever marry. "I wonder what our firstborn will think of this place."

"We must be careful that she does not blame herself, that had she married Spence our circumstances would be different." MacQuaid's expression softened as he thought of Aislin. "Aye, 'tis ironic that in the end it would have made no difference whatsoever. I was wrong to have pushed her as I did."

"She is like you, though, and I doubt that she will settle easily into this place."

He studied her face. "So you don't think I will? Ultimately, I mean."

Camila didn't answer. Her husband might accept it for now. But she knew he was trying to give her hope with all he had said. He wouldn't accept their meager circumstances for long. "I meant that Aislin might be unwilling to let go of the land. She might continue to fight, yet find it will accomplish nothing in the end. Just as you have found. And as for you, I fear you will join her."

He sighed with weariness. "Never fear, lass, there will be no fight ahead. I've used it up, the fight in me, the hope, too, every bit of it." He gave her a gentle smile and touched her face. "It is here that God has put us for a season, and it is here I will stay, with you, with my family. And I will look to his hills for strength."

"But that strength may give you hope to dream again."

The light that she had noticed in his eyes earlier had faded again. She saw that much of what he said had been for her sake, and she loved him even more for it.

Her eyes filled, and he pulled her into his arms. "My Camila," he murmured, then his voice choked and he could say no more as he buried his face in her hair. This time he wept.

TWELVE

Sybil Byrne paced the Persian carpet in her bedroom on the second floor of the hacienda. Her mother had left her just minutes ago after delivering the news that she could take only two practical frocks to their new home. Some of her favorite gowns and hats would be packed away in trunks and stored, for how long her mother hadn't said.

She drew in a deep breath of impatience. She had to admit to herself that her annoyance had more to do with what her friends would think of the Byrnes's reduced circumstances than with the circumstances themselves. After all, how bad could the new home be?

Her mother and father hadn't told her or Brighid any of the details about the new adobe, only that it had been their first home after arriving in California. Knowing how both her mother and father enjoyed the finer things in life, it should be more than adequate. She pictured the fine-cut Venetian crystal, the ornate gold-trimmed dishes from England, the sterling cutlery from Boston, the Valasquez oil painting hanging in the dining room. Of course, their new home would not be as large or as elegant as La Paloma, but it would certainly be equal in comfort.

Losing the rancho lands didn't bother Sybil nearly as much as losing the hacienda. What good were the lands anyway, especially now that the drought had robbed them of their beauty?

To Sybil, the drought's worst consequence was her worry that the dry winds and lack of moisture would make her skin wrinkle prematurely. She constantly scrutinized herself in the mirror, checking for the first signs of crow's-feet around her eyes. Now that she thought about it, she would of course insist that her extensive collection of fashionable hats from New York not be packed away. A young woman had to be careful of her skin, and there was nothing like a hat to keep the harsh California sun out of one's face.

She opened her tall, imported French wardrobe and scrutinized her gowns, riding clothes, and jackets, trying to decide which to pack away, which to take. She started to frown, then remembered frowning caused wrinkles, and sighed again instead.

Finally, she pulled out a long, elegant visiting dress of lapis poplin; at least that's how the frock was described in *Godey's Ladies Book* when she'd ordered it. She let her fingers trail over the scallops on the edging, and touched one of the dozens of soft black-velvet buttons that trimmed the sleeves and ran in double rows from neckline to hem. Yes, it was wise to take at least one visiting dress, she decided. Just because they were moving to the new adobe didn't mean that her social life would end.

Next she pulled out a blue-and-white striped silk walking dress. Her fingers lingered over the smoothness of the fabric, then she folded back the outer coat to admire the underskirt. It was edged with Irish lace, layer upon frothy layer of it. She held it slightly away from her to get a better look and let out another satisfied sigh. She'd cajoled her father for weeks before he finally consented and ordered it for her; it was probably the most expensive of all her clothes. She couldn't bear to put it into storage. It would accompany her to the new adobe.

Now that the two dresses were chosen, she set about looking for the perfect jewelry to take, her favorite gold pendant earrings, her pearl drop necklace, and her locket. Oh, and she mustn't forget her bustled crinoline. She only hoped her mother understood that the fine imported French undergarment certainly didn't count as a dress, though if she were to admit it, the cagelike garment took up more room than three frocks together.

She pulled open the miniature chest that held her jewelry, wondering if she dared try to take the entire chest with her. She looked through the top drawer until she found the earbobs, then the pearl drop necklace. She rummaged through the velvet ribbons, cameos, and pearls, until she finally found the locket. It had belonged to her grandmother in Barcelona and was fashioned of pure gold in a Spanish filigree.

She sat down on the corner of her bed and opened the locket. It had a miniature painting of her grandmother, but it seemed the likeness could have been her own. That's what had prompted her mother to give the heirloom to her.

Sybil studied the face of her grandmother, painted when she was just a young woman. The shape of her face was a perfect heart, and the tilt of her chin was aristocratic. Sybil liked that and tried to imitate the tilt herself.

The other side of the locket was empty, but Sybil had long fantasized that someday the tiny frame would hold a miniature painting of her beloved. She didn't know yet who her young man would be, but she enjoyed thinking of him simply as her beloved. At different times and stages of her life she had fancied herself in love with Jamie, then with Spence. She'd long known, even before Jamie's death, that both brothers were in love with her sister Aislin, though she couldn't imagine why.

And she had also fantasized that she could easily have taken their hearts from Aislin. Either one. Perhaps both.

Then as she grew older, she realized that she wouldn't have accepted either even if they had begged for her hand on bended knee. No, she had known years ago that neither of the young men was sophisticated or debonair enough for her.

Even now, each season when the latest *Godey's Ladies Book* arrived, and she pored through the pages looking at the fashionable drawings of ladies and gentlemen, she knew it was one of *those* gentlemen she fancied. She looked at the empty place in the locket. She had long ago decided that it would be filled by the likeness of a gentleman from New York, just like in the *Godey's* drawings.

She sighed, picturing such a man. Tall, slender. No ranch clothes for this man. *No, sir.* Dressed in the latest coat and top hat, he would escort her, his new bride, to New York, where they would ride in a carriage drawn by a team of prancing grays to a fashionable establishment of the finest reputation for *haute cuisine*. She didn't know what that meant, but it sounded elegant. She sighed romantically again and turned back to her wardrobe.

She was so busy pondering her imagined life in New York that it took her a few minutes to realize that there was quite a commotion outside her window. Finally, she heard the cacophony of voices and strolled to the window to peer into the yard below.

A rider dressed in Federal blues had just dismounted. Her mother and father had obviously hurried outside when they saw him, and her sister Brighid was now heading toward the group. Several of the household servants followed, all speaking at once.

She immediately forgot her dreams of her New York beloved and, gathering her skirts above her ankles, hurried into the hallway, down the stairs, and across the verandah and raced into the side yard.

The tall young man, who had removed his hat, was bowing slightly to her mother and sister. Then he shook hands with her father. The sunlight caught his hair, and Sybil suppressed a giggle as she neared the group. His hair was of the brightest orange she had ever witnessed, and when he turned to her and met her eyes and gave her a slow gentlemanly smile, she almost snickered in a most unladylike manner at his bumper crop of freckles.

She stopped beside her father and looked up into the young man's face, noticing that his ears stuck out, though in a way that somehow fit his contagious grin.

"Miss," he said to her with a most genteel tone and gave her a nod.

She bobbed her head just enough to be polite, and her father said, "Sybil, this is Sergeant Scotty MacPherson from Fort Tejon. He has brought news of Spence and Aislin."

"Sergeant, this is our daughter Sybil."

She smiled at the young man finally, and noticed that he seemed to be appraising her. So she brightened her smile, letting her dimples show. He was not her kind, but it wouldn't hurt to have another beau fall at her feet.

"Sybil," her father said, and she realized that while she was woolgathering, as her sisters called it, he had probably spoken her name more than once. "Sybil," he repeated.

"Yes, Papa?"

"Would you find Buena and ask her to serve tea in the courtyard?"

"Yes, Papa."

Then MacQuaid turned to Brighid. "Lass, would you show the sergeant to the guest room at the end of the hall? See that there is fresh water in the stand and clean towels."

Brighid nodded her assent, and the group began walking toward the front of the house. MacQuaid turned back to the young man as they walked. "Please, Sergeant, take some time to refresh yourself, then we will meet in the courtyard to hear your news."

The sergeant smiled again, and it seemed to Sybil that it lit his entire face. "I'm much obliged to do both," he said. "I have more to tell you than you can imagine."

"Before you retire upstairs," said Camila when they reached the verandah, "at least tell me that Aislin and Spence are in good health."

"That they are!" he declared. "I left them in finer spirits than when I found them."

She touched his arm. "You don't mean they have news of Jamie Dearbourne, the young man they set out to find."

The sergeant's smile faded. "No, ma'am. That was not their good fortune. It is something else entirely…"

"You can tell us after you have refreshed yourself," said Camila kindly. "I just needed to know that my daughter is safe."

"She is," he said, "and in good hands with a capable traveling companion." With that, he entered the house with the group, then followed Brighid up the stairs.

Sybil stood in the entry, watching her sister lead the young soldier across the landing and up the next flight of the stairs. At the top, the sergeant seemed to sense her stare and turned to meet her gaze. He looked slightly puzzled, then winked and turned again to follow Brighid, who, it seemed to Sybil, might have added a bit of a chassé to her walk.

An hour later Sybil joined her mother, her father, and Brighid in the courtyard. Her father had sent a rider immediately after the sergeant's arrival to let Hugh and Sara Dearbourne know that news had come of Aislin and Spence. It would be another hour or more before they might arrive.

Brighid had piled her braids onto her head in a most fetching look, and Sybil suddenly wished she had dressed in a fresh frock, perhaps added her pearl drop earrings. Her own hair was drawn up as usual in a sophisticated French twist, and the earbobs would have added a stylish touch.

Then she laughed to herself. Why would she want to go to such trouble on behalf of a mere sergeant? A grinning, carrot-topped, silly-eared sergeant? She gave her sister a haughty look and settled back into her chair, crossing her feet at the ankles so as to show off her silk-embroidered slippers.

Sergeant Scotty MacPherson loped into the courtyard minutes later and greeted everyone again with another amiable smile. Sybil noticed he had more freckles than she had thought before, now that the trail dirt had been washed from his face. She tried not to stare.

He sat nearest her mother and father, who shared the iron settee under the oak tree.

"I was sent here by your daughter and Spence Dearbourne," he began, "to tell you of a plan that they are readying to carry out."

MacQuaid held up a hand. "Before you tell us of their plan, can you tell us if they found out anything about Jamie Dearbourne? They did tell you why they traveled to Fort Tejon, didn't they?"

"Oh yes," he said. "They asked me about the man they were hoping to find. It seems they had met a couple of scoundrels here at your rancho who told them about an officer who knew of Jamie Dearbourne."

"Was the man there?"

Scotty shook his head. "No, he was not. There was no one by that name, nor had there ever been."

"So they found nothing more about Jamie than they'd known before," Camila added softly.

"Spence told me that he was sure his brother died at Fort Donelson." He hesitated.

"But Aislin is still not convinced?" MacQuaid asked.

"No, I'm afraid not. You can see it in her eyes." He sounded sorry.

For a few moments, no one spoke, then Sybil fixed her gaze on Scotty MacPherson. "You were about to tell us about their plan." She enjoyed the way his eyes fixed right back on hers.

He cleared his throat. "Well, yes, indeed I was." He leaned back and crossed his long legs, one ankle resting on the opposite knee. Somehow his legs reminded Sybil of a grasshopper's, and she tried to suppress her smile. Surely he must have read her mind, for he winked again. This time she felt her cheeks turn pink.

"While they were at Tejon," he began, "the talk was everywhere about the need for horses in the war. I was the first to mention that we have men scouting for mustangs in the desert, also in the Valley of the Horses just north of Tejon. The hope is to round up as many of these horses as possible and move them to Santa Fe.

"Then others talked about it as well. The need is great, the price per head is getting higher each day.

"Aislin and Spence plan to capture several thousand of these mustangs and move them east."

Her father let out a slow whistle, but Sybil noticed his eyes were bright with interest. "Go on," he said, leaning forward. "Please, tell us the details."

"They left the same morning I did, heading north into the Valley."

"To scout for the herds."

"Yes. The plan is for you and Spence's father to send as many of your wranglers, vaqueros, anyone, everyone you can spare, to the Valley. We'll meet them near the lake at the southeast end of the Valley."

"Why is the army not in on this?" MacQuaid asked. "You said they have troops out scouting the desert and the valley as well."

"The army needs horses any way they can get them. If the army troops are lucky enough to herd five thousand, only half that will survive the trip to New Mexico. We need many more than two or three thousand horses for our army, sir."

MacQuaid nodded. "So the more, the better."

"Yes, sir." He paused. "There's something else."

"What's that?"

"The army will pay an even higher price for broken horses."

"And we know just the man who can get horses ready to ride faster than a person can blink."

"That's what your daughter said about Spence Dearbourne. He wasn't in earshot, but she told me he has a way with horses, also with spotting herds that no one else can find."

"Spence Dearbourne has been known to talk to horses," Sybil said, rolling her eyes.

"Maybe there's nothing wrong with that," said Scotty quietly, and she flushed, knowing he'd spoken the truth.

"Especially if the result is worth thousands of dollars," said MacQuaid. "I think I'd learn horse language in a hurry." The group laughed, then MacQuaid sobered as he went on. "Our circumstances have changed here since Aislin and Spence left. The bank is calling in my loan. They've taken steps to force me off my land." He paused. "We're in the process of losing everything, including every man who has worked for me through all these years. But they're free to accompany you on their own."

MacQuaid nodded slowly and went on. "Very truthfully, 'tis a good plan, but I don't think it will do us much good. Any help young Spence can bring will be too late."

"I'm sorry to hear about your circumstances, sir," said Scotty.

Sybil looked to her father, hoping he would answer with a word of hope. But instead his voice became even more solemn, "As I said, Sergeant, 'tis too late for me. Perhaps it will not be for Spence's father. His circumstances are not quite as dire."

"I'm sorry, sir," said Scotty.

Sybil looked first to Brighid's face and saw that tears had filled her sister's eyes. Then she moved her gaze to her mother, who gave her a gentle, encouraging smile.

"I want to go," Sybil heard herself say. There was an audible gasp from her mother and a giggle from her sister. "I want to go," she repeated.

"You want to go…where?" her father said, frowning in disbelief.

"I want to go with the trail hands, the cowboys, whatever they are, to New Mexico."

"You can't fit all your dresses in a trail satchel," said Brighid. "And how will you take a warm bubble bath each night?" She collapsed with laughter.

"Shush, now, Brighid," said their mother. "Sybil, tell us why you want to go."

She tried to find the words, but they wouldn't come. In truth, she didn't know exactly why. She shrugged. "Can it be that bad? Aislin is going. I would accompany her. In fact, it doesn't look proper for a young woman to be on this kind of a…an adventure…with only men."

"Spence is almost family," her mother countered. "He will protect her with his life, if necessary."

"We know that, but does anyone else? If I go, then everything will be fine and proper. We would each be a chaperone to the other, to outsiders at least." She knew by her mother's expression that her reasoning made sense.

Her mother glanced at her father, and she saw a curious twitch of a smile touch both of them.

"Carrying buckets of water is a good way to build strength," were the curious words her mother uttered next.

Her father's face broke into a wide smile. "Aye, that it is, my lass! Just as you said."

Then he turned back to Sybil, who was now sitting forward, wondering why on earth she had blurted out her strange request. "Papa?" she said. "Why are you laughing?"

"Oh, my sweet darlin'," he said, "I think you have decided on a fine plan for your future."

"I have?" Now her voice sounded small, even to her. She truly had expected her mother and her father to say no, now that she thought about it.

"An excellent plan," he repeated. "And I'll send you with my blessing." Then he looked over at Scotty MacPherson, whose mouth seemed to be hanging open slightly. "And I do believe, young man, you are going to need my blessing as well."

"Well, yes sir. Thank you, sir." Scotty swallowed hard, his Adam's apple bobbing. "I think."

MacQuaid and Camila exchanged glances again, but Sybil barely noticed. Now she was busy planning her wardrobe for the journey. She wondered if she should take the silk walking dress or the velvet-buttoned visiting dress. She knew better than to think she could take two. Then it occurred to her that the crinoline would be difficult to pack, and either dress would look dreadful without the wide hoop.

She let out a long sigh, and glanced up to see Scotty MacPherson staring at her. "Wha—"

Her mother interrupted. "Are you listening, Sybil?"

"I—I'm sorry," she stammered. "I was just thinking about…about the trail."

"Scotty was just telling us about his hometown," her sister said gleefully.

"Your hometown?" Sybil repeated politely, wondering why her sister seemed so full of giggles. And why should it be so important to her? "Where are you from?" she asked again, meeting his eyes.

He grinned. "Well, now. I hail from New York."

Thirteen

Sybil watched with growing dismay the rapid collection of supplies for the mustang roundup and trek east. It took the few house servants left at La Paloma little more than twenty-four hours to gather from the rancho's larder all the remaining dried meats and hams, preserves, corn and wheat flours, coffee, tea, and salt; pack it into barrels; and load it into a cook wagon.

By the morning of departure, two days after Scotty's arrival, nineteen wranglers from La Paloma had volunteered for the trek along with thirteen vaqueros, led by the stone-faced Fraco Ciro. From the Dearbourne spread, another half dozen hands rode onto the rancho to join the group just before daybreak. All told, there were thirty-eight hands, forty-one counting Scotty MacPherson, Sybil, and the cook.

Her mother and Buena had helped her pack a meager selection of sensible clothes into a small trunk that would be placed in the rear of the cook wagon. To her horror, no frilly dresses were allowed. Grim-faced, she agreed to two split riding skirts, one heavy cloak, two plain shirts, and two unadorned hats, one straw, one felt. Buena had offered her an old poke bonnet, but quickly withdrew the offer when she saw the look on Sybil's face.

By dawn, the mounted riders had gathered with a small remuda of an equal number of horses, to exchange in the event of lameness or to provide rest for those being ridden at the start.

Sybil swallowed hard, fighting her welling tears, as she kissed her mother and father and Brighid. She glanced at Scotty, who was already atop his horse at the head of the group, and he gave her an encouraging nod as she gracefully mounted Rachelle, her buttermilk palomino.

As soon as she was atop the spirited mare, she lifted her chin in such a way that her family would remember her bravery and mettle, not her tears.

Scotty shouted the command, and the company began to move out. She rode beside him, and it suddenly struck her that they provided a rather romantic sight: he in uniform, she beside him on the prancing palomino. Of course, he was someone she would normally not give a second glance, and she would have to suffer his inelegant looks and mannerisms for a time. Although she had to admit, as she glanced at him from the corner of her eye, he did cut an imposing figure. With the abhorrent exception of the way he angled the bill of his army hat heavenward.

They rode at an easy trot while still on rancho lands. The better road to the Valley of the Horses, the only one that would accommodate the cook wagon, ran parallel to the Trail of Rocks toward Fort Tejon. So the group first headed westward, skirting the foothills of the Sierra Madres to meet up with the road that veered north into the mountains.

Sybil had heard her father and Scotty discussing the route during the last few days, the stopping places for watering the horses, the best campsites for the massive group. But she had paid little attention, leaving the details to Scotty and the ranch hands.

They had been on the trail a little more than two hours when she figured it was time to stop for water. She looked around for a spring, and when she didn't spot one, figured her canteen would have to do.

She and Scotty were still in the lead, so she veered Rachelle to the right, out of the way of the rest of the company, still thundering behind her. She easily dodged the remuda and riders and headed for the shade of a live oak nearby.

The group slowed, then halted a ways ahead. She was just taking another swig from her canteen, when the nearly forty riders all craned in their saddles, looking back at her. She gave them a dainty wave, but no one waved in return.

Now, Scotty's horse thundered toward her, its hooves pounding the packed dirt. He drew his horse to a halt in front of her, his face red and angry.

"What do you think you're doing?" he roared.

She held up the canteen. She figured he should have been able to tell that for himself, so she gave him a bit of a smirk as she delivered the words. "I was thirsty."

"You don't ever pull out by yourself," he barked.

She blinked in surprise. "I'll do whatever I please whenever I please," she said raising her chin. "And you have no call to speak to me in such a manner."

He stared at her in silence for a moment, and she wondered if he might grab Rachelle's reins and lead her back to the company like an errant child.

Instead, he barked again. "Let's go! You're wasting precious time."

"I'm not through resting," she countered evenly and raised her brow to show her superiority.

He glared at her another long minute, then abruptly turned his dull brown horse to head back to the company. She really didn't want to stay in the shade of the oak any longer, but she figured she would stay just long enough to make a point. She would be traveling with this incorrigible man for several weeks, and she needed to let him know that he could not pull rank over her in any way, shape, or form.

Scotty yelled the signal again, and the company moved out. Scotty was in the lead, the cook wagon to one side. And behind them thundered the hooves of the ranch hands' horses and those of the remuda.

A cloud of pale gold dust rose behind them. She marveled at the density of such a cloud, then did a quick calculation. Nearly forty wranglers on horseback. At least that many horses in the remuda. More than three hundred individual hooves, beating the dirt on the drought-ridden, thirsty, dusty plains!

And she must ride into that dust to keep up with the outfit. Or wait hours for the dust to settle.

With a heavy sigh, it came to her that she had not proved one iota of anything to Sergeant Scotty MacPherson by defying his order. All she had done was show him her own green stupidity. He was probably laughing right now at what she faced by heading into that dust. Well, she would show him. She would give him no call to laugh. *No siree!*

She replaced the cap on her canteen and stuffed the container into her saddlebag. Then, pressing her heels into Rachelle's flanks, she headed after Scotty and his band of horse herders.

She tried to catch up to the rear of the group, but by now they had quite a lead on her. And the closer she got, the more difficult it was to breathe. She figured if her eyes and mouth were filled with dust, so were Rachelle's. She regretted that the animal had to pay for her own stupidity, so she slowed, hanging back a good half mile.

She coughed and hacked, trying to spit the dust from her lungs and mouth. Her eyes stung and watered as she peered into the pale gold gloom of it, squinting to see the barely visible rear of the company. Her mother had insisted that she tie her father's red kerchief around her neck for the trail. Reluctantly, now, knowing how grotesque it would look, she slowed Rachelle to a walk, and took the piece of cloth from her neck; she shook off the thick layer of dust from its folds, then retied it in a triangle over her face so that only her eyes showed above it.

She reached for her felt hat, planning to pull it as low as it would slide over her forehead and tilt it over her eyes. Her fingers touched its brim, then recoiled in surprise. She lifted it from her head to have a look. The hat was no longer black, but brown with a quarter-inch layer of dust. She beat it against her thigh, only to have the dust rise in another small cloud.

She sneezed several times, then replaced the hat.

The company was at least a mile ahead of her now, and Sybil looked around, feeling alone and sorry for herself. For a moment, she considered turning Rachelle back to La Paloma.

Then she pictured how it would look to her family. She could almost hear the whispers: "Poor little spoilt Sybil wasn't tough enough for the trail. Turned back before she was a day's ride away from home."

She sniffled and swiped at her watery eyes, noticing her tears had turned the dust on her face to mud. Taking a deep, shuddering breath, she nudged Rachelle into a canter.

She had gone only a short distance when she saw a rider swing away from the company and head her direction. Even through the swirling dust, she could see the blue uniform.

In a heartbeat, she tilted her chin upward and assumed the easy posture of the expert horsewoman she was. But when Scotty slowed the brown gelding in front of her, forcing Rachelle to halt, she knew by the young man's expression she hadn't fooled him for a minute. But he at least had the grace not to laugh, or even smile.

"There's a cutoff up yonder," he said. "If you'll follow, I'll lead to it. We'll beat the troops to our nooning place."

She gave him a curt nod and, still sitting tall in the saddle, followed him into the Sierra Madres. An hour later, they waited on a bluff above the main trail, and just as Scotty said, they were well ahead of the troops, as he called the company.

After the too-brief nooning of salt pork and cold biscuits, the company was back on the trail. By nightfall, they were well into the mountains on the road leading north. Scotty called for them to halt near a small creek.

Sybil slid from the saddle, grateful they were stopping. By now the mountain shadows had fallen deep and dark upon their trail. Sybil made quick work of removing the saddle from Rachelle, trying to keep out of Scotty's way. She didn't want pity, and she was determined to make her own way through this ordeal.

Because the forested terrain provided no large single clearing, Scotty ordered the company to split into smaller groups. The cook wagon pulled to a small meadow, just beyond the main campground, and the remuda was let loose to graze in the same meadow as the wagon. Sybil walked Rachelle to the meadow, then headed back through the brush to the place where she planned to set up her bedroll.

She ached from the day's ride and limped slightly from a crick in her lower back, but she halted abruptly. Scotty was near the space she had claimed for herself, and he had cleared a circle nearby as if he was about to set out kindling for a fire.

He didn't look up as she walked closer. "You'll need to gather firewood," he said.

She put her hands on her hips. "I thought the hands would be doing that for cook," she said evenly. "Why do we…er, why do I need another fire here?"

He chuckled, still laying sticks of kindling in the shape of a tipi. "You'll figure it out by morning."

"Oh," she said quietly, thinking of the cold, hard ground and the night ahead. With a heavy sigh, she slouched into the woods and half-heartedly gathered an armload of firewood.

But when she returned a few minutes later, Scotty shook his head at the bundle of dried twigs she laid before him. "I can see you're lacking in the ways of the woods, Miss Byrne. Follow me."

He led her into a dark copse of pine, past some with slender trunks and into a forest of taller trees, larger in circumference, with fallen branches rotting beneath them. The woods smelled of loamy soil and pine, not altogether unpleasant.

"This will do," he said, kicking a long, round branch. "And this, they're neither too new nor too old."

She nodded.

"If it's falling apart, it's rotting. Probably filled with wet fungus. Won't burn. If it's newly fallen, it may still be green. Needs to weather some before it'll burn."

She reached for the pieces of pine, then stumbled after him as he toed one branch, then another. Too tired to argue, she stooped to pick up each one. His armload was as full as hers, and she bit her lip to keep from complaining about the heaviness of hers. Her back ached with the effort. When she could carry no more, they turned back to camp.

He quickly arranged the twigs and branches in a larger tipi than the kindling wood, lit the twigs, then stepped back as the flames licked upward. Sybil watched as he then lined the fire circle with stones. As soon as the branches had caught, he added larger ones, then squatted, his weight on his toes, and poked at the fire with a stick until he had it arranged to his liking.

There was a small boulder a few feet away, and she settled onto it wearily.

"There's no time to sit," he said, though not unkindly. He pulled out a Bowie knife and was proceeding to sharpen it.

"I'm tired."

He turned toward her, the rhythm of the small scraping sounds of the knife and flint blending with the crackling of the fire. "You may be my charge, Sybil, at least according to your father. But I'll not be your nursemaid."

She looked at him and blinked.

"It's been a long day." She knew she sounded petulant, but she was too tired to care.

Scotty didn't look sympathetic. "You may not have had to work for your supper on your father's rancho, but that part of your life is over." He was looking straight at her now, a twitch of amusement playing at the corners of his lips.

She stood abruptly, hands on her hips. "What is it you would like me to do?" she muttered between clenched teeth.

"You ever cooked your own supper before?"

"I thought that's why the cook wagon was along."

He chuckled. "I prefer fixing my own vittles when on the trail."

"Well, I don't."

He ignored her and pulled a greasy skillet from his mess kit. He chuckled again, tossed his knife so that it landed point down in the hard-packed soil, then poked at the fire with a stick. He was still laughing to himself when he stood, brushed off his pants, and faced her. "Have it your own way."

"But we've got a cook wagon," she protested again.

He shrugged, and called back to her with a laugh. "Do you want stew with heaven-knows-what in it? Or do you want to see firsthand what goes into the pan? Your choice, Miss Byrne."

"What do you mean, 'heaven-knows-what'?" she said as she trailed behind him to the edge of the clearing.

"You feed this many people on the trail…you throw in everything from soup to nuts, or in this case, from squirrels to possums," he said lightheartedly. He yanked on a makeshift pulley, and a sack of supplies fell to the ground with a thud.

She looked up in wonder. She hadn't noticed that he'd swung any supplies heavenward. "Squirrels?"

"Yep."

"Possums?"

"Even the tail," he said. "Sometimes the feet."

She shuddered. "And what do you plan for dinner?"

"You'll see." Whistling to himself, Scotty then rummaged for the exact ingredients he was searching for. Moments later, he proceeded to show her step by step the art of biscuit making in the wilderness.

Sybil stood back, hands still on her hips, for the first few minutes. Then he cocked his head her direction, indicating that she was to take over. Tentatively at first, she stirred the lumpy mixture, as he added water from the canteen. He set the skillet on some rocks he had earlier moved into the fire and dropped in a scoop of grease. Within seconds it sizzled and spit as it melted. Then he took the pan of dough from her hands and dropped a few lumps of dough into the skillet. Fascinated, Sybil stepped closer to the fire and took her turn, dropping several more spoonfuls beside his.

She caught him watching her face as she worked, and she couldn't help giving him a small grin. She considered that perhaps he just wanted to be alone with her; maybe that's why he'd suggested they not partake of the squirrel and possum stew. The thought caused heat to flood her face.

Still whistling, he went back to his knife sharpening. Within a few minutes the biscuits were done and he had whacked off a hunk of salt pork from the supply bundle that seemed to hold unending surprises.

By the time they sat by the fire for dinner, darkness had fallen completely, and Sybil was glad for its warmth.

"You ever fished before?" Scotty asked suddenly.

She shuddered, thinking of the innards she'd seen when her father cleaned a mess of trout. "No," she whispered, and her stomach lurched.

"Are you planning to fish tonight?" It was almost worse than the thought of rodent stew.

"I'm planning fresh trout for breakfast," he said. "Do you know how to shoot?"

"Do you mean shoot fish?"

"I do. And shoot well, I might add, otherwise you'll leave no flesh."

"So you have to shoot them in the head." She imagined the difficulty in such a thing. Her father had once tried to teach her to shoot tin cans on a fence post, and she never hit a single one.

He cocked an eyebrow and grinned. "No. Not the head."

She frowned, not seeing the humor in it.

"You have to aim for the eye." He tossed more limbs on the campfire, and a fine spray of orange sparks rose into the black sky. He was still chuckling as Sybil tried to take another bite of biscuits and salt pork. Then she pictured fish innards and rodent stew, and, covering her mouth quickly, she ran for the woods.

Sybil fell asleep almost before her head touched her bedroll. She'd placed it near the fire, but by midnight, the coals had turned to ashes. She was bundled in her clothes and two heavy woolen blankets, and because she'd never been so tired in her life, she barely noticed the cold hard ground until the ash-gray dawn. By then she was chilled to the bone.

To her surprise, Scotty had kindled a fire and caught enough trout for breakfast well before daybreak lightened the wan purple sky. Sybil squeezed open one sleepy eye, observing him as he stirred coffee into a pot of boiling water. Then trying to exit her pallet with grace and dignity, she gasped as she took a step, then bent double trying to take another. Every bone in her body ached. She hobbled to the fire, moaning and clutching her back.

"You take a chill last night?" asked Scotty nonchalantly.

She nodded, her teeth now chattering. Her back hurt from the hard ground, and she didn't know which made her more uncomfortable, feeling as cold and brittle as an icicle or feeling she would never again stand straight.

He gave her a quick grin, and made a tsk-tsk sound.

"What's that for?" she demanded.

"Well, seems to me if you were cold, you should have done something about it."

"I was too tired to notice the chill." She huddled closer to the fire. "It didn't hit me until this morning. By then it was too late."

"Too late?" Scotty didn't look up. "Why didn't you just add some wood to the fire?"

"Now you tell me," she said, her voice petulant. Then she turned and hobbled into the woods, her own foolishness making her angry.

"You'll find a suitable place for washing just beyond the bank of ferns to your right," he called out, then added, "though it's as icy as a melting glacier."

She couldn't be sure, but she thought he was chuckling to himself as he fried the trout. *Trout!* Their slimy, colorful innards came again unbidden to her mind. She covered her mouth with both hands and hobbled as fast as she could for the creek.

Three days later, the company moved down the mountain valley to Fort Tejon. It had been exactly one week to the day since Scotty MacPherson had left on his mission to Rancho de la Paloma. He drew himself up tall as he led the riders into the fort, proud that he had accomplished what he'd set out to do. The travelers would feed and water their horses, then spend the night in some empty barracks before heading down the trail into the Valley of the Horses.

Miss Byrne, of course, would be put up in the officers' quarters, just as her sister had been a week ago. He glanced at her profile, noticing how her pampered skin was now pink from the burning sun, and how the tail she'd pulled her hair into was swinging in rhythm with her horse's hooves. His eyes lingered for a moment on the narrow scarlet ribbon she'd tied around it.

An hour later, while the ranch hands cared for their horses and cleaned up in their rooms, Scotty headed into the officers' headquarters to report to Captain Adams, newly returned to the fort.

He stood at ramrod-straight attention and gave his tired-looking superior officer a snappy salute.

"At ease, Sergeant," the captain said, then asked for a report.

Scotty related the details, including the numbers of ranch hands and the whereabouts of the meeting place in the Valley of the Horses.

Captain Adams turned his chair to look out the window, and Scotty stood waiting to hear what he would say. It didn't appear to be good news, judging from the older man's expression.

"You've received orders to go east," he said finally and turned again to face Scotty. "They were carried here from the newly arrived troops out of Tennessee."

"Those scouting for horses?"

"The same." Captain Adams paused. "Many of the men we have here have been overlooked for the war effort. We're a long way from the fighting."

"Yes, sir." Scotty's heart was hammering. It had been a fluke that he'd been sent to California in the first place. He had always figured it was his mother's prayers that kept him in the army but out of the war. He held his breath, waiting to hear what else the captain had to say.

"Son, you are to report to your regiment in Santa Fe in sixty days. You'll receive your papers with all the details as you leave."

"Yes, sir." His voice was little more than a hoarse croak.

"You will be seeing combat, Sergeant."

"I thought so, sir."

"There's something else, son."

He nodded, waiting. Whatever it was couldn't be worse than what he'd already been told.

"On your way east, your orders are to accompany the Spence Dearbourne party and see to it that they deliver their mustangs to the U.S. Government and no other."

Scotty frowned. "What do you mean?"

The captain sighed wearily as if tired of giving orders. Scotty wondered if the captain had been ornery before he came or if the California wilderness had drawn out his cussedness.

"The prime motivation for the Spence Dearbourne party to herd the horses and head them to Santa Fe is for profit."

"Of course," Scotty agreed with a crisp nod.

"Have you observed any sentiments from the family, sentiments leading them to support one army or the other?"

"You mean, are they Southern sympathizers?"

"That's exactly what I mean."

Scotty considered the question. Of course there had been comments and questions about the war. It was no secret that the two rancho families' sympathies were with the South. "You would need to ask them where their true loyalties lie, sir."

The captain gave him a hard look as if he knew Scotty was avoiding giving a straight answer. "Your orders are to help the party with their roundup, gain their friendship and trust, and make sure the herd is sold to the Union representative in Santa Fe."

"Will this Union representative give the Dearbourne party a fair price for the horses?" Scotty knew that horses and cattle were often commandeered for the good of the government. Payment, if any, was too often promised but not delivered.

The captain met his gaze and nodded curtly. "You have your orders, Sergeant. I will see to it that the paperwork is completed by morning, including the name of the commanding officer you are to report to in Santa Fe. You will continue on eastward with his troops."

Scotty again stood at attention and snapped a crisp salute. "Yes, sir."

The older man seemed to be studying him. "God be with you, son," he said unexpectedly. And it occurred to Scotty that the captain didn't like giving this particular order any more than he had liked receiving it.

Scotty nodded. "Yes, sir," he said again. "And with you as well, sir."

FOURTEEN

Jamie Dearbourne slipped along the trace, through a muddy marsh and into a tangled wall of berry vines. He had lost count of the weeks since his escape, lost count of the number of days he'd been running. He only knew that it was autumn because of the blood-colored leaves on the maples and the spent and ragged cornstalks in the fields where he sometimes slept.

It might have been summer when he escaped from the Union prison in Elmira, New York; he had no exact recollection. Only that it was hot, and the bogs around the prison were maggoty and slimy the day he left. And he remembered the mosquitoes, great clouds of them, filling his nostrils and mouth as he ran, as if death itself was at his heels.

It was nearing dark now, and Jamie headed into the gloomy shadow of pines to hunt for a resting place. The air hung clammy and cold, and he shivered, clutching his rags to his chest. He wondered if there might be a farmhouse nearby, or troops, though he hadn't heard a volley of gunfire for days now. He wanted to light a fire with one of the few matches he had left, but he didn't know if he would rather be cold and safe or warm and fearful.

A sure way to be discovered was by the smoke of a lone campfire. He knew that firsthand. He shivered again, deciding to postpone the fire awhile. He sat heavily on a stump, letting his head fall into his hands.

After a time he looked up and realized there wasn't much light left to hunt game for supper. *Game.* Just a highfalutin name for rodents. A squirrel if he was lucky, a mouse if not. Perhaps a bird or a lizard. Though in reality there wasn't much difference in the flesh on any, especially if he didn't light a fire to roast the thing.

There was a skittering in the wall of berry vines. He pictured a fat pheasant roasting on a spit, and his stomach growled in response to the thought. Maybe the need for a fire would win over his fear after all.

He lowered himself to his belly to crawl along the ground, snakelike and silent, as he peered into the brambles. There was another faint rustle, and he held his breath, listening again, trying to tell if it was a rodent or ground bird. Now he pictured a plump quail and readied himself to make a lunge for it.

Then the thought of quail brought another image, unbidden, terrifying. The image of the wild open lands of California. Two boys, he and Spence, rode like small hurricanes across the fields. The sounds of their hoofbeats and laughter had caused a hurricane of beating wings as hundreds of quail took flight.

Their squat bodies couldn't fly far, and just as quickly as they had spooked, they landed in a flock. One plump male took sentinel duty on a high branch, watching out for the others, especially for their chicks, the mature males and females gathering them under their wings to ensure safety.

He had laughed at the birds and their odd behavior, the way their heads bobbed as they walked, the way they called out *Chi-ca-go!* as they scratched at the ground. Spence had defended them, he remembered now, and had an extraordinary fondness for them.

A fat brown bird peered out at Jamie from under the tangle of vines. It stared, unblinking. His stomach growled, and he moved his arm farther into the brambles. But the bird remained out of reach, skittering backward as Jamie's arm moved toward it.

His cheek was on the damp earth now, so close was he to the ground. And he was so tired, so very tired and hungry. He gathered all the strength he could muster and made one last lunge toward the bird. It beat its wings and flew upward through an opening in the vine patch. Upward and out of reach.

The sound of its beating wings brought back his memory of home, of laughter, of his family. Without moving his face from the damp earth, he began to cry, his tears mixing with the peat and decayed leaves beneath his face. But he was not conscious of where his cheek lay. He thought only of the terror that always accompanied his thoughts of home. Terror that he wouldn't find his way back.

He curled into a ball and sobbed into the cold, damp night, until he at last fell into a deep and dreamless sleep.

The next morning he woke surprised that he no longer felt hungry. He'd heard once that a person starving to death no longer felt hunger pangs, and he wondered if he had reached that state. His ribs showed pitifully through stretched skin, and his arms and legs hung stringy and sinewy from bony sockets. But surely, there was enough meat left on his bones to see him through another few days.

He tried to recollect when he'd last eaten. Was it yesterday he'd caught the lizard, or the day before? He unfolded his stiff, cold limbs and stood, rubbing the place in his back that still pulsed with pain every morning.

The woods were as gloomy as they'd been the previous night; a mist had condensed and dripped from the leaves, a steady sound almost like rain. He was reminded of his thirst and wiped some of the larger leaves against his palms, then licked the moisture off them.

Soon he slipped silently from the thicket and back onto the narrow trace he'd been following for days. He figured it was some ancient Indian trading route, and as near as he could tell from the sun, it seemed to be leading him directly west.

The sun slipped up behind him, warming his back and shoulders. A big doe with small hooves and elastic sinews soared from a thicket near where he walked and bounded across the trail in front of him. He was startled by the noise she made, and his heart pounded long after the creature had disappeared into a stand of plush pines to the south of the trail.

He was tuned to the sounds of the trail, just as he was alert to every sound that might mean danger. A rustle of leaves could mean the scurry of wildlife or the presence of a Union scout.

He walked all morning until he came to a creek sheltered by willows and roots and fern. The water spilled down a series of moss-covered rocks where he knelt. He bent deeper, the pain increasing, until he could turn up his face to where the water cascaded and catch it in his mouth. He drank deeply, swallowing until he was satisfied.

He avoided looking at his reflection. He'd seen it before in similar waters: his long stringy beard and greasy hair, his startled eyes in dark sockets. Such an image could belong to any of Elmira's prisoners, yet it was him, Jamie Dearbourne. He was always ashamed and shocked when he saw it—it was better not to look.

That night, he still had not caught game for supper, but he hadn't seen a farmhouse all day, so he chanced lighting a fire for warmth. Again, he noticed his lack of hunger and was mildly disquieted by his growing weariness. Perhaps tomorrow, he thought, he would rest longer into the morning before moving on. And tomorrow, maybe he would find game.

He lay down near the small campfire. Banks of fern sheltered his resting place, and shivering, he pulled his tattered coat over his chest. He looked up at the stars, trying to conjure Aislin's image, thinking if he could but dream of her, the nightmares of his capture and the accompanying cold sweats would be kept at bay. But she had long ago joined the remote company of people in his past whose faces and voices he couldn't reassemble, not even a fragment of a smile or tone, and it frightened him.

He tried to remember what it felt like to ride across the rancho, Spence at his side, or Aislin. But when he imagined he was looking into their faces, all he saw was a ghostlike darkness.

He pushed the recollections from his mind when a cold moisture covered his neck and his pounding heart pressed hard against the inside of his ribs. And when the terror came again, the terror of never finding his way home.

He finally fell into a restless sleep. Toward midnight he dreamt Spence was gentling a wild stallion.

The horse bucked and snorted and screamed until Spence circled the beast three times, looking away as if he didn't care whether the horse bucked or not. When the horse noticed he wasn't being watched, he calmed, then stood perfectly still while Spence walked toward him. His brother whispered something to the animal that Jamie couldn't hear. The beast settled, its restlessness and fear gone.

Sometime after midnight that night Jamie awoke, feeling strangely calmed. For the next week as he struggled onward hour by hour, he tried to find within his heart the words his brother had whispered to the stallion.

Finally he lost hope of recollecting, realizing the words were as distant and faint as the people in his past.

The weather changed and grew colder by the day. One morning there was frost on the trees, and Jamie's feet and hands were numb when he awoke. He knew if he was going to survive he would need to head for civilization to find warmer clothes, perhaps a blanket for the nights, boots for the storms to follow.

He came to a river, wide enough to be the Ohio, he thought, but too wide to cross. He left the trace he'd been following and headed along the riverbank as it meandered south for a day, then west again. He figured he must be in Kentucky, or close to it.

For the first time, he ate plentifully, finding the fish easy to catch with a net he fashioned of slender branches woven and tied with strips from his tattered pants. But his belly was now swollen from food, causing him more discomfort than the slow starvation from before.

One morning he woke covered with a light snow that had fallen during the night, and he tried to pray that he'd come upon a farmhouse soon. But praying didn't come easy. He hadn't turned to God since his first days at Elmira when he had cried out for a deliverance that didn't come.

He set his face like flint and moved ever westward along the river, his feet now bleeding through their rags. Dogs would have an easy time trailing him, he thought grimly as he pressed on.

At dusk he spotted a house in the distance. He climbed to a bluff above the river, thinking he would observe the place for a few days. Watch to see who lived there. If it was a family, he likely didn't have as much to fear, particularly if there was not a man present.

The first morning, just past dawn, a woman did indeed come

from the house. Behind her trailed a child of perhaps two years. The woman worked at a washtub for several minutes, then hung several shirts and what appeared from a distance to be baby dresses on a line stretched between two barren trees. She then returned to the house, not to appear again until the wash was flapping dry in the afternoon breeze.

Jamie was pleased to see the clothes on the line, yet it briefly occurred to him how low he'd stooped to consider stealing from a woman. He brushed the thought away. This was war, and Northerners were the enemy. Woman or not, he'd take whatever he needed, gladly. Perhaps she had a firearm he could steal from her as well. And food.

He watched the house for two more days. Carefully hiding his cookfire, making sure it was under the cover of the nearby dense forest, he continued his meals of roasted fish and wild onions.

On the evening of the third day, he was fairly certain that no one else was in the house with her. Just a thin woman and a baby. He had studied the house well enough to figure out the lay of the rooms inside. He would wait until dark, until he was fairly sure the woman and child were sleeping, then slip into the house, steal what he needed, and be on his way before she woke at dawn.

He waited until the moon was high enough to give him light to follow the trail and also to navigate the interior of the farmhouse. His feet had healed some during his days watching the house, but now that his weight again pressed fully on them, he could feel the warmth of fresh blood oozing into the rags that served as shoes. By the time he'd reached the door to the house, he knew that he'd left a trail of blood behind him. Anyone who happened by in the daylight would see that someone had entered the woman's house.

She hadn't had a visitor for three days; he only hoped she'd not have one tonight.

He was in front of the house now, and stopped to catch his breath. The steep hike down the bluff, fighting the pain in his feet with every step, had sapped his energy, and he leaned against a rickety fence post to steady himself. The pickets wobbled slightly, and he noticed for the first time, now that he was closer, the rundown look of the farmhouse. He figured it was because the woman's husband was away at war.

He drew in a deep and ragged breath, then limped to the door. He tried the latch. It was fastened securely from the inside. Probably bolted. He put his weight against it, but didn't have the strength to make it budge.

He hobbled to one of the two windows that flanked the door. The shutters were drawn, but not clasped. He carefully folded them back and checked the window. Surprisingly, with winter coming on, there was no glass. Another sign of a house suffering from neglect.

Jamie leaned against the house for a moment, to gather his strength. Then he hefted himself upward and over the sill. With the shutters open, the moonlight streamed into the room.

It was the first such room that he'd seen since leaving home, and for a moment it stunned him and he couldn't move. There was a rocking chair by the fireplace. A quilt was folded across it gracefully, a stout footstool in front of it with a stitched heart on its upholstery. He pictured a young mother holding her baby, rocking and singing softly, and quick, hot tears filled his eyes.

The rest of the room had other such feminine touches. A table with chairs was covered with an oilskin cloth, and placed in its center was a bouquet of autumn leaves, pine boughs, and miniature cones.

He moved around the room, touching the signs of a life he'd forgotten. On the mantel rested an oval frame containing a daguerreotype of loved ones. Beside it were two floral china candlesticks, just like some he remembered his mother had at the Dearbourne Rancho. And in the corner of the room was a child's toy cradle, probably made by the child's father. In it rested a rag doll. He crossed the room and stooped to pick up the doll to have a better look.

He thought of Aislin. She'd had a doll like that once, and he remembered how it was smudged with years of little-girl kisses. *Oh, Aislin...sweet Aislin!*

"Stay where you are!" a voice growled in the dark.

Every instinct from his months of imprisonment was in place. Jamie dropped the doll and whirled, catlike, ready to pounce.

But before he could take a step, a gun blasted. A brilliant flash. A sulfur stench worse than death itself.

Pain hit him like a bright, flaming light, searing clear through him.

Jamie fell, spinning into a harsh darkness in which there was no light at all.

He was dragged back to Elmira, screaming. He'd been there. Didn't they know? He'd paid for his crimes, though he'd committed none. He'd paid by watching death. By watching things that were worse than death.

"Please," he pleaded. "Not again!"

Willie King, wielding a razor, came at him again, his rodent mouth open, yellow teeth moving. Jamie screamed. He'd already fought him. He no longer had the strength to fight him again.

He'd saved the bugle boy, Ben Haven, once before. A boy too young to be in prison, too young to see death. Jamie didn't know if he could save him again. He was so tired. So very weary. He sobbed loud and long, crying first to God, who he knew wasn't listening, then to his guards, who weren't either.

Little Ben cuddled beside him, reminding him of a young Spence, and he pulled the boy closer, trying to warm him.

He'd saved him once. He couldn't save him twice. Neither could God!

The boy closed his eyes, whimpering against Jamie. His chest rose, and his breathing was ragged and loud. But the men in the cell were louder. Jamie yelled, telling them to be quiet so Little Ben could rest, could sleep.

But no one listened. Not even God.

Now the Reb bugle boy cried out, sounding like a crippled kitten or pig about to be butchered.

The boy was starving. Willie King had taken every bit of his food, along with what belonged to the skinniest and weakest of them all.

When the mewing became so weak it could barely be heard, Jamie stuffed his own food into the boy's mouth. Before, he had chewed and gazed up with his dark-rimmed, too-bright eyes, thanking Jamie with his look. But now the chewing had ceased.

Jamie stuffed more bread into the little mouth. He moved the child's jaw up and down with his fingers, and rubbed his throat the way he'd seen Spence gentle a horse. But the child didn't chew. Didn't swallow.

"Eat!" he screamed at the little boy, no more than twelve years old. Too young to be in a war. Too young to be in a prison. "God, where are you? Why have you forsaken me?" Jamie screamed.

"Eat!" he said to the boy again. "Please, eat!"

Now the boy's face was still, completely still.

And there was no movement in his thin chest. No breathing. No heartbeat.

"I've killed him," he cried. "I've killed him with my own hands, stuffing food into him. Oh, God, can you forgive me for killing him?"

He was sobbing again now, and the other prisoners had gathered around him. They were trying to take the boy's body. Jamie fought them off, screaming at them that it was his fault the child died.

Again and again they reached for Little Ben. They wanted to drag him off with the other dead. Drag him by the feet across the maggoty swamps, through the slime.

No. Jamie whispered to Ben Haven that he would not allow it. He made a promise that he alone would carry him to his burial place. Later. After he'd properly mourned. Cried all the tears of his mama and papa and brothers and sisters.

He clutched the boy and rocked. To and fro he rocked, and he pretended that Ben was still alive. That he would open his eyes and say he'd just been funnin' with Jamie, funnin' the way Spence did when he was but twelve years old.

Then they came, the guards who gathered the dead. They pulled young Ben Haven from his arms. One of the scurvy-ridden, greasy-haired men pinned Jamie's arms while the others took the child. And they dragged him, just as Jamie had promised they wouldn't, through the mud and slime.

All that was left was the boiling marsh, crawling with vermin and maggots; and prisoners fainting flat from the heat; guards, little more than boys themselves, jeering as the Rebel dead were piled high, readied for mass graves.

He was left with the noise of thirty thousand prisoners, belly-kicked and beaten down. He was left with the smell of death. A stench that would never leave him.

Jamie sobbed again. How could they send him back to Elmira? How could he survive this?

He couldn't.

He knew he couldn't.

A sweet, warm, welcoming darkness enveloped him. And this time, he hoped there would never again be light.

Fifteen

There was silence in the room where Jamie lay, but outside, from somewhere in the distance, drifted the music of a light wind in the pines, the calls of birds, and in an outer room, the giggle of a tiny child. It was then he knew he hadn't been taken back to Elmira.

He tried to open his eyes, but the effort was too great, so he lay still, listening to the sounds of silence, listening to the rhythm of his own breathing. He was alive, though he couldn't quite comprehend why he was in this place instead of in Elmira.

So he lay quiet, trying to recollect how he arrived here. He remembered the trail, the long distance he walked. He remembered his hunger, his weariness, his bleeding feet.

Just then someone touched a hand to his forehead. He rested easier. The hand was familiar somehow, as if he knew it.

"Aislin?" he murmured. "Aislin…"

"Just rest now," replied the voice, and he knew it wasn't Aislin's. "Just rest."

He drifted back to sleep, and it was dark when he woke again. Before he opened his eyes, he knew it was night, but only because the pines, the birds, and the child were silent. The house was still, completely still. When he succeeded in opening his eyes, the dim light of a single candle greeted him.

He turned on his pillow, and his neck, his whole body ached with the effort.

A woman sat in a rocker near the bed, asleep, her head tilted slightly downward, an open book in her hands. He gazed at her, wondering who she was and how he had gotten here.

She was lovely, sleeping there in the candlelight, nestled against the high-back rungs of the wooden rocker. She was fair; her hair was pulled back from her face, light brown in hue, though it was hard to tell in the light from a single candle. A few stray tendrils had fallen loose, giving her an almost childlike look.

He attempted to sit up. A white-hot pain shot through his shoulder, pulsing down his torso, through the rest of his body. He caught his breath and waited for it to subside. It did, finally, but left him chilled, a cold moisture on his neck and face, and lying flat once more.

He closed his eyes. The woman's even breathing comforted him as no other sound had for months, maybe years. He fell asleep to the rise and fall of its softness.

The next morning, as sun poured through the window, Jamie opened his eyes, looking immediately to the rocking chair. But it was empty.

He attempted to raise his head from his pillow once more, thinking it was high time he removed himself from the bed. But again, pain shot through his chest. He fell back, weak, against his pillow.

There was a fall of footsteps on the slatted floor outside the bedroom, and he turned toward the door. The woman from the rocker the night before stepped into the room. She gave him a slight smile, more polite than friendly, as she approached him.

She put her hand on his forehead, just as he remembered her doing before, then nodded crisply. "Your fever's down today. That's a good sign." Her voice was low and soft. It brought him solace, just as her breathing had the night before.

"What happened?" he said, his voice hoarse from lack of use. He cleared his throat and tried again. "What am I doing here?"

"You don't remember?"

He tried to shake his head, then winced from the pain and let out a small moan.

She stepped closer. "You were shot," she said briefly. "In the chest. Here." She touched a place just below his left shoulder. It was bound with layers of bandages. But he winced again even at the featherlightness of her touch. "It was at close range," she said evenly, watching him with eyes the color of cornflowers.

"Is the ball…still there?"

"I dug it out myself." Her soft voice was matter-of-fact, not the least bit prideful.

"You?"

She nodded. "Who else?"

"There's no one else here?"

"Only Emma. My daughter." She paused, a bit uncertainly, he thought. "For now," she added.

"Your husband…is away at war?"

She studied him a moment before answering. "Yes," she finally said. "He is away."

"Fighting for the Union?"

"He is in a Union uniform," she confirmed.

Then he knew. She was the enemy.

"How did I arrive here?"

"You arrived of your own volition," she said, her expression revealing nothing.

"I don't remember anything."

She settled into the rocking chair. In the outer room, Jamie heard the child's happy voice as she played. Little snatches of songs drifted through the doorway.

"You broke into my house, sir."

Snatches of moonlight, a locked door, climbing through a window, came back to him. He swallowed hard. "I must have had good reason." It was the only thing he could think to say.

"I found you standing in my living room."

"Then it was you who shot me."

"Yes."

He let the information sink in. "Now you're waiting for the authorities to come get me."

"Authorities?"

He suddenly realized she didn't know about Elmira. Just then the child raced into the room, and he was saved from commenting.

"Who dat man, mama?" the little girl asked. "He awake?"

"Yes, he's awake, sweetheart," the woman said. "But we should find out his name so we don't have to call him 'that man.' Shall we ask him?" The woman's tone was decidedly softer with the child.

"What your name, man?" Emma demanded, sucking two fingers. Her face was round like her mother's, the same soft sweep to her cheek, the same light brown hair framing it.

"My name is Jamie Dearbourne," he said. "What's yours?"

"Emma Callahan," she said proudly. "An dis is my mama."

Her mother laughed, low and easy, as if she laughed a lot. "My name is Hallie Callahan, and I'm pleased to make your acquaintance, Mr. Dearbourne."

"And I, yours, ma'am." His words were more polite than his tone.

"An me, too," said Emma.

"Now, let's see to some soup for you," said Hallie. "It's been on simmer since dawn." She started to leave the room, but Jamie cleared his throat and she stopped.

"I don't know why I broke in here," he said. "I think maybe because I needed food. Maybe clothes. Whatever the reason, I had no call to do it. And I am sorry for the trouble it brought you."

The memory of his journey, its pain, its terrors, flashed before him.

"There's a war going on, Mr. Dearbourne," she said simply. "And war does strange things to folks. We don't any of us know ourselves well at times like these."

Emma had gone on ahead of her into the outer room, but Hallie hesitated at the doorway. "You had some days of delirium. You spoke often of someone named Ben Haven…"

For several moments he stared at her in silence. But instead of Hallie's face, he saw the faces of Union soldiers as they jeered, the faces of the prison guards as they dragged Ben Haven's body through the mud, the faces of the Kentucky thugs who sold him to the Rebel cause for a price.

Hallie was studying him as if reading something in his eyes, something that made him suddenly ashamed. He turned away from her, unwilling to have his bitter thoughts read by anybody. They were too vile.

She was the enemy. She and all her kind. Later, when she brought him soup, he ate in total silence, refusing to meet her gaze. She soon left him alone, and he heard her voice, soft and low, as she spoke to the child.

He fell into a troubled sleep once more, a blessed respite from his bitterness, and he remained in a dark and dreamless state until dawn.

Hallie Callahan was an honest and forthright young woman; she didn't practice beating around the bush about facts, nor did she expect anyone else to. She had no doubt that she'd find out where this Jamie Dearbourne hailed from and exactly why he'd headed onto her property, planning to rob her blind.

She stood in the bedroom, looking down at him while he slept, trying to figure him out. Beneath his bitterness was a raw vulnerability. And despair. A desperate sorrow, especially visible when he was deep in slumber. Of course, she thought with a wry smile, it helped to actually see his face. Before he had regained consciousness, she had cut his hair and shaved him with Charles's straightedge.

She had figured him to be a much older man, but once she'd washed off the trail dirt, she was surprised to see that he wasn't much older than she. But his face told her he'd seen enough tragedy for three lifetimes. She knew the look well.

He had entered her house with the obvious intent of stealing, and she now figured he was on the run, probably a deserter, though she couldn't tell by his manner or speech whether he was Union or Confederate. In Kentucky he could be either.

Right now he posed no threat. Goodness' sakes, he was at her mercy, bedpan and all. He slept in her husband's worn nightshirt, and he swallowed her food as if he hadn't eaten in weeks and wouldn't eat again for weeks to come. His scrawny body worried her some. He'd been close to starvation; she knew the signs.

No doubt he would have died if she hadn't taken him in, though the thought brought another ironic smile. She'd never shot a man before, and hoped never to again. But it was shooting him that had saved his life.

But still, he was a puzzle. There was something gentle about him, but it was buried so far under his pain that she figured even he didn't know it was still there.

She touched his hair, brushing it lightly from his brow. Now that it was washed, it was the color of sunlight and cornsilk, straight and shiny. He was not at all like Charles, who had been dark and ruddy-skinned, yet there was something about this man that touched her soul, just as her husband had. His thoughtful and earnest manner of speaking perhaps. Or maybe his gentleness of spirit, easily hurt by cruelty.

His night terrors told her he'd been hurt by such cruelty, and she remembered how Charles had suffered as well. Her own memories threatened her with terrors of their own, and she quickly pushed them from her mind.

Jamie announced a few days later that it was time to move on.

"I don't believe you can walk as far as the picket fence out front," Hallie told him plainly after he'd spoken his piece. "You haven't even made it to the privy alone yet."

He let out an impatient sigh.

Ignoring his bad temper, she went to his side and began to unwind the fabric strips from around his chest and arm. A bowl of clean water waited on a stand nearby, and some soft cloths were stacked beside her on the bed.

He didn't utter a sound as she pulled the last bandage off his wound. The ball had entered his chest at an angle, and when she had dug it from his flesh, she had worried that he might bleed to death. But she'd stanched the flow with tightly packed strips. Today they needed to be removed.

"You'll need to think about something other than what I'm doing," she said, knowing the pain would be excruciating. Then she explained what she was about to do.

Jamie looked out the window at something distant, perhaps just the sky, as she probed the packing. "You ever do this before?" he inquired as calmly as if asking if she'd ever baked a pie before.

She chuckled lightly, her fingers still probing. "You're my first," she said.

"That's comforting."

"You don't have much choice," she countered.

"Why'd you do it? Save me, I mean?" he demanded, still staring out the window.

"I didn't want a dying man bleeding on my rug," she said. He winced as she pulled out the first of the packing. The bleeding started again as the flesh was exposed. She pressed against the wound with a cloth, and he bit his lip. "Besides," she went on to keep his mind off the pain, "I figured maybe you'd earn your keep by doing some chores around here. That is, if I patched you up properly." She chuckled again. "You may have noticed there're some things needing doing."

His eyes were closed, and a sheen of moisture covered his face. "What all needs doing?" he muttered between clenched teeth.

"Oh, I've got quite a list."

"What's on the list?" he grunted.

"Hmmm. Fixing the shutters on the window you came in might be a start. I'd like to have them lock properly."

She thought she saw a hint of a smile.

"What else?"

"There's the gate out front."

"I'll fix it."

She laughed again, her tone light. "I think I could probably get you to agree to most anything right now, Mr. Dearbourne. You're beholden."

Another hint of a smile. "Name it. Just get this over with."

She worked in silence for a few minutes, aware of his ragged breathing and his rapid pulse. She needed to hurry. The pain was nearly too much for him; she could see it in his eyes. "And there are the winter apples," she said.

"Apples?"

"Yes. A dozen bushels."

"Why would a person have so many apples?"

"For putting up for winter."

"I suppose you need them peeled."

She quickly yanked out the final bit of packing, and at the same time said, "Every apple."

He drew in his breath and closed his eyes while she applied the new bandage and pressed firmly against his chest to stanch the new flow. "There, now," she said finally. "Nearly as good as new." She helped him to sitting, while she wrapped the new cloths around his torso and shoulder.

When she finished, he fell against his pillow wearily. "Now, what were you saying about being ready to leave?" She lifted the bowl and cloths into her hands to carry from the room.

"Maybe just a few more days," he said, his eyes closed.

She was tiptoeing from the room when he called out to her. "Bring in those apples, and I'll get started," he murmured sleepily. "But I'd prefer an apple pie instead of preserves."

She laughed. "The first apples will go to your pie."

She thought she heard him chuckle as he fell asleep.

By the time he'd awakened in the late afternoon, she'd peeled the first few apples herself and rolled out some dough, and the pie in the oven had filled the house with the fragrance of baking apples and cinnamon.

"You wanna have some pie?" Emma inquired at his door after knocking. Hallie stood behind her daughter.

He nodded his assent. "Then we'll help you to the table." She supported him while he stood. Pain shot through his feet, sores still raw from his time on the run. He leaned against her as they took the few steps into the great room and moved to the table.

Emma pulled out a chair, and he sat down heavily.

Hallie cut the still-steaming pie and brought him a healthy slice. Then she placed smaller helpings at her place and Emma's. Next she served him a mug of hot coffee.

This time there was no mistaking his smile. He looked first at the pie, then across the table to meet her gaze. "You didn't wait for me to peel the apples."

"There's plenty left," she said. "About eleven-and-a-half bushels or so."

His grin widened, and she saw a glimpse of the boy he'd once been, of the man he'd been before leaving for the war. "I'm much obliged," he said, his eyes on the pie.

He picked up his fork, and it was poised midair when Emma spoke up. "We tank God first," she said, "for all our blessin's."

"Yes, of course," said Jamie, replacing the fork.

Hallie took hold of his hand with her left and Emma's with her right.

"Heavenly Father," she said. "We bow before you, and thank you for being here with us…for keeping us close to your heart…for providing food for our table and blessings abundant in our home. Amen."

"Amen!" shouted Emma. She grabbed her spoon.

Jamie's gaze met Hallie's, and she noticed a darkness in his eyes.

Emma jabbered about the pretty day, telling Jamie how she helped her mama pick apples and how she wanted to go apple picking again and how Lucy, her rag doll, wanted a sister. A sister named Trudy. Or maybe Maude. Lucy couldn't decide which. Then after finishing her last bite of pie and wiping her mouth with a swipe of a napkin, Emma hopped from her chair and raced to her toy cradle in the far corner of the room. Soon she was humming to herself and rocking Lucy in her arms, paying no attention to the grownups.

"Oh, to have the heart of a child again," Jamie said quietly. "A heart with no more worries than what to name your doll." He didn't smile. Then he looked back to Hallie. "Or a heart with no more worries than lifting a sweet prayer to God."

"Do you think I have no worries?"

He looked sorry for speaking so plainly. "I'm sure it must be difficult waiting for your husband to come home."

She let out a heavy sigh, heavier than she intended. "Maybe it's those sweet prayers that see me through."

He shrugged.

"Do you believe in God?" she asked.

"Once I did," he said. "A long time ago." He laughed cynically. "I did my share of lifting sweet prayers heavenward."

"And now you're wondering what good it did you?"

He laughed bitterly. "Something like that."

"You must have suffered terribly in the war." Her voice was soft. "I'm sorry."

He put down his fork and stared into his empty plate. "It wasn't easy." Several moments passed, then he looked up at her again. "I was in prison, Mrs. Callahan, in a Union prison where prisoners were treated worse than vile swine."

She bit her lip, considering him. "I'm sorry," she repeated.

He let out a short, harsh laugh. "The ironic thing is, I wasn't even in the war."

"You weren't in the Confederate army?"

"No. I was captured in St. Louis, on my way from California to join up. Sold to a Rebel captain who paid so much per head for any able-bodied soldier he could get."

She reached for his hand, but he recoiled from her touch, and she withdrew it.

"Didn't take me long to see the captain was a traitor to the Rebel cause. I tried to escape, tried to get to an honest officer to report what I knew. Seems the captain didn't want it known that he was a traitor." He let out another laugh. "He had me watched."

"The captain was a Union sympathizer?"

He nodded. "Apparently there was more to it than just an exchange of men for money." He drew in a deep breath, and for a moment closed his eyes. The look on his face was bitter. "The captain was bringing in others who were Union sympathizers. I got mixed up in the bunch of new recruits."

"So these traitors would report back?"

"Yes. Also do what damage they could by working for the Union army while supposedly fighting for the Rebels."

"That's how you ended up in a Union prison."

"I knew too much. I was shot in the back, trying to get away." He paused, remembering. "Some old woman dug me out of my grave, ranting that I'd risen from the dead. I might have escaped, except for the attention she brought to the empty grave. By then the hills were swarming with friends of the traitorous captain. It didn't take them and their dogs long to find where I was hiding."

"Oh, Mr. Dearbourne, I'm sorry," she said.

The only sound in the room now was that of Emma singing a lullaby to Lucy.

"I was taken north to Elmira. I thought the trek would kill me. It took weeks. I was roped with other prisoners and forced to drag those who fell. Sometimes even those who died. It didn't kill me, but after I reached Elmira, I wished it had."

"You had nightmares about the place," she said gently.

"Oh yes. You asked me about Ben Haven—said I'd been calling his name."

"Yes."

He lifted his eyes to her, and she saw raw pain in them. "He was just a boy. Little more than twelve years old. Had been a bugle player somewhere out of Georgia. How he survived the march to Elmira…" he shook his head, but didn't finish the thought.

"He was the kind of boy who might be picked on in school. Teased for crying. But this wasn't a schoolyard. And the thugs who teased him called themselves soldiers. Soldiers on the same side. But they tormented the child mercilessly."

"You became his protector." Somehow she knew, perhaps because of the few glimpses she'd had into his heart.

"Yes. One of the men got a hold of a razor. He used it to take what he wanted from anyone, found it easy to take food from a child. And he did."

"So you gave Ben Haven yours."

"Yes, I did. Until the razor wielder caught on and started after me."

"I saw your scars," she said quietly, and he looked up at her. There was something deep and smoldering in his soul. Hatred, maybe? Sorrow? Shame?

"By then I knew the boy was dying. He was already starving, and now some of his wounds putrefied. There were maggots…" He fell silent, and moved his gaze to little Emma who was still chattering to her doll.

"I held the boy so he wouldn't feel alone when he took his last breath. I tried to feed him, but he refused. Almost as if he was willing himself to die. And I promised him I wouldn't let the guards take him from me." He looked up at her. "I promised I'd see to his burial myself."

"So you held him in your arms…"

"Yes." His voice was barely more than a ragged whisper. "And I prayed. I prayed that God would deliver this innocent child. Get him out of that place." He was crying now, and when Hallie reached for his hand he didn't pull away. "That boy should've been running in the fields with his friends, fishing or swimming in a creek, not dying in a maggoty, filthy marsh of a prison for a war he didn't understand."

Jamie bowed his head, and his shoulders shook with quiet sobs. Hallie stood and put her arms around him, holding him tight while he cried. Behind them, Emma was still talking to Lucy, explaining in detail to the doll how mamas made apple pies.

When Jamie lifted his head, Hallie scooted her chair so she was facing him and held both his hands.

"Did you ever think that God *was* with that child?"

He didn't answer.

"You were there. Your arms were wrapped around Ben Haven while he suffered. You never let him go. You fought to defend him. You gave up your food so that he could eat."

Jamie nodded.

"Don't you see? Your arms were those of God. Your defense was his defense. Your presence was his presence. Your love for the boy was his love. Don't you see?" Hallie was crying softly now as she spoke. "God was there. He sent you to that prison to be with that child."

Tears were running down Jamie's face unchecked.

"And he did get the boy out of prison. Ben Haven left the comfort of your arms to go straight into those of his heavenly Father." She was quiet a moment, her eyes still brimming with tears. For Ben Haven. For Jamie Dearbourne. "Maybe God brought you from California to be with that child in his hour of need," she said quietly.

"God knows where each of us is, even when we think we're lost. Ben Haven was his child. He was never out of God's arms. Neither were you."

Jamie stood suddenly, knocking his chair over. Emma looked up, startled. He wobbled uncertainly, and Hallie reached to steady him. But he brushed her away and limped into the bedroom without a word.

That night, he said, "I'll make myself a crutch if you've got some wood, then I'll start getting some chores done around here so I can leave."

"There're some planks of wood out back," she said. "I'll see if one might be suitable."

He turned his head away from her, and she could tell he didn't want to look in her face. She left him alone.

The next morning she brought the wood around to the front of the house, then found an old scarred table to move there so he could work. Next she brought a rusted saw, a hammer, and some nails. When she headed back into the bedroom, Jamie lay staring at the ceiling.

"I've brought you some wood for crutches," she said.

He didn't turn toward her. "Thank you. Just make a list and I'll not bother you as I work."

"I've already done that," she said, attempting to make him smile. But still he wouldn't meet her eyes.

"Now if you'll help me get to the wood you've brought, I'll get started." Wincing, he pushed himself up and swung his legs slowly to the floor, so that he was sitting on the edge of the bed. Then he leaned against her, wrapping a long arm around her shoulders, and she placed her arm around his spindly, thin torso.

"Mr. Dearbourne," she said as they moved to the front of the house, "I'm not your enemy."

He halted his hobbling gait and looked down at her, finally. "I know that in my heart, ma'am," he said. "But it's my head that keeps me from believing it."

"What I said yesterday, about God being with the child after all… I spoke from my heart." She halted on the porch and looked up at him. "I didn't mean to preach. I didn't mean to sound like I knew all the answers."

"I didn't think you were preaching," he said quietly. "But I did wonder how you knew all the answers when you haven't known suffering."

Quick tears stung her eyes. She shrugged his arm from her shoulder and nodded to the old table on the porch. "There's your wood. Make your crutch."

With that, she swept back into the house.

Sixteen

Jamie leaned against the fence post for support as he lifted himself to standing in front of Hallie's picket gate. It had taken only a single nail and two finger scoops of grease to ease the gate's swing and allow the latch to snap firmly. He was surprised that the small accomplishment brought him such pleasure. He picked up the handmade toolbox with his good arm and, steadying himself with the crutch, hobbled to the front porch, moving slowly, step by step, up the stairs. He pulled out one of the double shutters to repair the sliding bolt that hung sadly downward, rusted and useless.

Hallie had moved to the front door while he studied the latch. Now she stood, leaning against the doorjamb, watching him work. Late afternoon sunlight slanted across the porch, touching her face. She blinked in its brightness and held her hand across her forehead to shade her eyes.

In the two weeks he'd been with Hallie and Emma, he'd settled into the rhythm of their days. After a morning that seemed ready to burst at the seams with activity—Emma with her chatter and singing and laughter, Hallie with her milking and cooking and baking and sewing—the afternoon seemed to take on a slower pace, peaceful and quiet. He noticed that Hallie always took time to rock Emma before her nap, for cuddling, storytelling, and singing.

Though it was too personal to admit to Hallie, he waited with anticipation each day just to see the two of them together. For him, it was a time to watch the love in both their faces, a time to listen to love's music in Hallie's voice. A time to heal.

For those few minutes he pushed away the memories of Elmira. After the darkness, hatred, and terror to which he still felt captive, simply watching love from a distance filled his soul with light, even if only for a few minutes each day.

"It's good to see you looking stronger," Hallie said. She was still shading her eyes, and their cornflower hue had darkened in the shadow of her hand.

He nodded and turned back to the broken bolt.

"Have you given any thought to where you're going from here?"

He didn't look up. "I'll continue on west. That's all I know…or care about."

"To California?"

He shrugged. "Eventually."

"It's a long walk, Mr. Dearbourne."

His short laugh sounded harsh, even to him.

"I want you to take Broomtail."

He turned to her, finally. "I can't do that, Mrs. Callahan. I can't pay you, for one thing. And I can't leave you here in the wilderness without a horse."

"Broomtail is a gift, so you don't need to worry about paying. And Emma and I have no need for a horse. Besides, the old thing doesn't earn his keep." She smiled. "You'd be doing me a favor, taking him off my hands."

Jamie knew her last words didn't ring exactly true. She would miss the horse. It cost her a great deal to offer him. The gesture touched him, and he swallowed hard, to keep the lump in his throat from forming. He nodded curtly. "As you wish then," he said.

Then it struck him that he was so unused to kindness that he didn't know how to accept it. So he cleared his throat and tried again. "Thank you. I'm much obliged." He quickly looked away so she wouldn't see how her gift touched him.

She stepped closer and leaned against the porch railing, arms folded. "There's something else I've been thinking about," she said. "Something that may be of help to you."

He turned to her again.

"My brother lives in St. Louis. A few years ago he was part owner of a trading company that was making runs between Independence and Santa Fe. The company doesn't run the Conestoga trains with the same frequency it used to. But because of the war, there's still some trading. Last I knew, he was sending wagons to Santa Fe from time to time. I'm thinking he might hire you on as a muleskinner."

She had his full attention now. "Why are you going out of your way for me?" he asked, frowning. "Don't you know I'm your husband's enemy? I'm an escapee from a Union prison…one of *his* army's prisons. If he came home and found me here, he'd probably shoot me on the spot."

For a minute she didn't answer, just kept studying him with those cornflower eyes. "You are not the enemy," she finally said. "Neither am I yours."

He turned back to prying the rusted bolt from the shutter.

"Why are you so all-fired bent on *being* the enemy, Mr. Dearbourne?" She didn't give him a chance to respond. "Not all people are filled with the need to fight. There's goodness left in the world, despite what you've witnessed. There's goodness in people, no matter what's been done to you by some."

By now her raised voice had captured his attention, and he stared at her.

"You think you're the only one who's suffered. Let me tell you, you aren't!" She swiped at the tears that brimmed in her eyes as if she were angry that they'd chosen now to show. "There's a little girl inside my house who will never know the feel of her father's arms around her. Will never hear her father's laughter as he tosses her in the air in play. She will never know the security of a father who comes home at night and eats supper with his family or sits by the fire and reads to her. Or watches her grow and tells her how proud he is. She will never hear his voice say, 'I love you, Emma. Your daddy loves you.' Emma will never know any of those things, Mr. Dearbourne."

The young woman's hands were on her hips, and there was fire in her eyes. "And furthermore, I'll never hear him say those words to me either, Mr. Dearbourne. My husband won't ever be coming home again! Not today. Not a year from now."

She squinted at him. "You don't need to worry about him showing up and shooting you." She started to leave, then turned to look at him again. "Charles was strung up, hanged not far from here for helping a Rebel deserter to safety."

Jamie was so stunned he couldn't speak.

"You asked if my husband was a Union soldier, and I answered yes. But he never saw action, Mr. Dearbourne. He hadn't even been issued his uniform when he was killed.

"And as for suffering. You think you are the only one in all of God's creation who's suffered. Well, let me tell you, Mr. Dearbourne, you are wrong. I watched my husband hang. I watched his body twitch until his soul departed.

"We were together when he was captured. His captors taunted him by forcing me to watch. He begged them to let me go, but they would not." Her voice was low, and Jamie was ashamed that he hadn't realized her suffering. He started to speak, but she held up her hand.

"Let me finish, please," she said. "I loved him, Mr. Dearbourne. I had loved him since childhood. Now all I have left is Emma. I was pregnant when Charles died. But it was too early to know. Charles didn't even know that we were expecting our first child.

"And has it ever occurred to you to wonder why none of my neighbors stop by?"

He shook his head. He'd figured her place was too distant.

"Well, let me tell you. I am an outcast, and Emma, too, by association."

He finally spoke. "For what Charles did?"

"For what we both did."

"You helped the runaway too."

She lifted her chin defiantly. "Yes, I did. Forcing me to watch my husband hang was my punishment. It was also a warning."

He was overwhelmed by what it would cost her if he was discovered.

Her blue eyes locked on his as if reading his mind. "You're actually safer here," she said softly, "than most anywhere. As I said, my neighbors aren't very neighborly."

"That's why you don't go into town, why you offered me Broomtail." Suddenly he understood everything.

"I don't want Emma to know what it feels like to be shunned."

Jamie put down his tools and turned to face her. He hobbled slowly to where she stood by the doorjamb. "Can you ever forgive me, Hallie?" It was the first time he'd called her by her given name, and he hoped she wouldn't be offended. Somehow he didn't think she would be.

She stared up at him, unblinking, her eyes glistening with unshed tears.

"Please, forgive me," he said again. "I've been—"

Hallie shook her head. "Don't say another word. I know your bitterness without you telling me. And your pain. My words won't take that away. You'll need to forgive to get rid of all that's inside you, to heal. But I can't stand here and tell you when and how you can do that. No one can."

"You've forgiven those who killed Charles?"

She looked away from him, out toward the river. He wondered if it was the direction of the place her husband drew his last breath. "Yes," she finally said. "It took time. It took a lot of leaning on God. But I did it. I had to. For Emma as well as for me."

Hallie looked again into his face. "I didn't want my daughter growing up knowing bitterness and anger instead of love and compassion for others. In the end, that's what helped me forgive them all."

"Did you know the men…those who captured Charles?"

"Yes." Her voice dropped. "I did. We both did."

"That made it harder to forgive." It wasn't a question. He knew it was so.

"One was my husband's brother."

"Oh, Hallie…"

Again, her eyes glistened with moisture. "Forgiveness isn't ever easy, but sometimes—" Her voice broke.

Jamie wanted to pull her into his arms, but instead he just stood there, looking at her and thinking he had never seen so much compassion on a face in his life. It was as if her suffering had deepened, had widened, her capacity for love.

And he was drawn to that love in a way he couldn't comprehend. He only knew that it was a force stronger than that of a starving man for food, or a thirsting man for water, a blind man for light. It was all of those and more.

She seemed to understand his thoughts, for she said simply, "Healing will come, Mr. Dearbourne"—then she smiled, a wide and glorious smile—"Jamie. But you must let your Lord be your physician. No one else."

Without another word, she turned and left him standing alone.

Jamie placed the crutch under his arm and hobbled back down the porch stairs, down the pebbled walkway, and through the gate. He eased himself down on a fallen log and propped the crutch up against it next to him.

He was facing Hallie's house, taking it in—the yard, the garden, the orchard in back, all of it—with fresh vision. For nearly three years, she had lived here alone. She'd lived off the land with just an old milk cow. A bull. A few chickens. What she could grow in her garden or pick from her orchard.

It seemed to him that every part of it reflected something of Hallie Callahan. Her grit. Her will to go on. Her spirit. Her love.

It moved him with an emotion too deep for words. Maybe because everything Hallie touched also reflected life—her own, her child's, her God's, even her land's—and that was something he hadn't considered for a very long time. Life that could—would—go on.

Despite suffering and tragedy, man against man, brother against brother. Life would go on.

God created it so. Just as he created love. Just as he offered forgiveness. And grace. And mercy.

Mercy. Oh, how he needed God's mercy right now!

He turned from Hallie's house and pushed himself to standing with the aid of his crutch. Slowly, he made his way to the riverbank. The shadows were longer now, and the dark waters shimmered as a breeze gusted, kicking up ripples across its surface.

His last prayer had been when Ben Haven died. After that, he figured it didn't do any good to pray if God didn't hear…or worse, simply didn't answer. But could he pray now?

He lifted his gaze above the river and into the heavens. He tried to speak the words that were in his heart, about his anger toward God, his disappointment in other people, his fear of not making it home, his willingness to heal finally, and his need for mercy.

Above all, his need for mercy.

But his soul was utterly bereft of a single word that could be lifted in prayer. Too long had he held his emotions in check. Too long had he barricaded his soul's door…not just to humankind, but to his Lord. He wondered suddenly if he'd seen too much horror, experienced too much pain, to ever trust again.

Hallie had learned to trust, and it gave him hope that he might again. But perhaps her soul had been more open than his. Then the image of what she witnessed came to his mind, and he knew it wasn't true.

He stared bleakly at the river, its swirling eddies and glistening surface.

Still, the words wouldn't come.

Then a breeze kicked up in the pines to the east of the house, and there was a murmuring. He was reminded of the first morning he woke in Hallie's care. He'd heard the pines murmuring, the birds singing, and little Emma giggling. The musical blend of those sounds had warmed his heart before he opened his eyes.

The pines murmured again, and he sensed a Voice in the sound of them. A Voice he knew, but hadn't listened to in a very long time.

MY BELOVED, YOU ARE MINE. I KNOW YOUR GOING OUT, YOUR LYING DOWN. I KNOW YOUR EVERY THOUGHT, EVERY FEAR, EVERY HEARTACHE, EVERY SORROW. I HAVE HELD YOU IN MY ARMS, MY SON, JUST AS YOU HELD ANOTHER CHILD OF MINE. I HOLD YOU NOW.

I WILL NEVER LET YOU GO.

For a long time, Jamie stood looking out at the river, thinking that the darkness in his heart was so dense that it could swallow even the light from the sun itself. The familiar bitterness and terror were too entrenched, too comfortable, to let go. Perhaps too repulsive to admit even to God.

I KNOW YOUR EVERY THOUGHT, EVERY FEAR, EVERY HEARTACHE, EVERY SORROW.

Every vile and bitter thought, Lord? Every shred of hatred? Every black and hopeless nightmare?

I KNOW YOUR EVERY THOUGHT, EVERY FEAR, EVERY HEARTACHE, EVERY SORROW.

What if I hate myself for my fears? For my vile thoughts? For my inability to trust you? What if I hate you, Lord?

I HAVE LOVED YOU WITH AN EVERLASTING LOVE, MY CHILD. WITHOUT MEASURE. WITHOUT LIMIT. FOREVER.

Jamie buried his head in his hands and wept.

Exactly one week later, Jamie rose at dawn. Just the afternoon before, he had finished the chores on Hallie's list. Now it was time to leave. Winter was coming on. A light snow had fallen during the night.

Hallie had washed and ironed two shirts and a pair of homespun pants of her husband's and packed them in a worn saddlebag. She had also wound up an old quilt to tie at the back of his saddle for sleeping. He wore Charles's boots, and didn't ask if they were the same that he had worn when he died. They were sturdy and warm, and he appreciated Hallie's gift.

Hallie. He needed to leave quickly; if he didn't, he might not leave at all. Hallie's lively blue eyes made him never want to be anywhere except where he could gaze into their depths. The music of her voice made him never want to be anywhere except where he could hear it.

He had begun healing here in this place filled with love and laughter and joy. Maybe that was all there was to his feeling for her—gratitude for a fresh start. Besides, he told himself, she was the first woman he'd seen after nearly three years in prison. Of course he would be drawn to her.

And little Emma. So like her mother. He didn't want to consider that he likely would see neither of them again.

As he swung the saddlebag over Broomtail, who stood patiently near the front gate, and tied it securely, Hallie came out of the house. She moved toward him with Emma perched on one hip, a small bound package in her free hand. The child yawned and stretched, then smiled when she saw Jamie.

"How's my girl?" he said, and she reached for him.

He held her close while she circled one arm around his neck and held onto the kiss-smudged Lucy with the other. "You go?" she asked, peering up into his face.

"Yes, I go," he said, and knew his smile was sad.

"When you comin' back?"

His gaze locked on Hallie's, and he could see by her expression that this parting was as difficult for her as it was for him. "I don't know."

She poked a finger in Lucy's face. "Lucy don't want you to go."

He held the little girl tighter, thinking about Charles, about all that Hallie had said about Emma not having a father. "I don't want to go," he admitted, as much to himself as to the little girl.

"Den why you go?" Emma insisted.

"California is my home," he said simply. "The people I love are there."

"Lucy loves you. She's here," Emma said, still poking her little finger at the doll's face.

He swallowed hard. "I know," he finally said. He kissed the top of Emma's head, feeling the softness of her baby-fine brown hair. "I know." Then he handed her back to Hallie. Emma watched him solemnly and stuck two fingers into her mouth.

"Well, I guess it's time," he said, his gaze not leaving Hallie's face. He tried to memorize the hue of her eyes, the curve of her cheek, the tenderness in her expression as she studied him.

Broomtail, an old brown-and-white calico, was standing patiently. Hallie moved closer, and for a heartbeat, he thought she might touch his face. But she didn't. She just looked into his eyes without blinking. "God be with you, Jamie Dearbourne," she said at last.

He nodded. "And with you, Mrs. Callahan," he said, smiling. Then he caught her hand and lifted it to his cheek. For a moment he held it there with his eyes closed, feeling its warmth, its solid and feminine strength. He pictured her hands, rolling out dough for pies, ironing her husband's shirts for Jamie to pack, dressing his wound, caressing Emma's arm while she rocked and sang.

He let go of her hand, reluctantly, and raised his eyes again to hers. "May our Lord bless you and keep you always."

"And me, too," said Emma. She reached her little arms across the space that divided them, grabbed his ears, and pulled his head closer to hers. "I love you," she said. And she gave him a loud, wet kiss on the cheek.

He thought of Lucy's kiss-smudged face and wished he, too, could go without ever washing off Emma's kiss.

Then without another word, he swung a leg over Broomtail and winced slightly as he hefted his weight into the saddle. Hallie handed him the bundle she'd been holding.

"To sustain you, at least through today," she said, smiling. She had already packed as much salt pork and hardtack as he could carry. At his quizzical look, she added, "An apple pie, Mr. Dearbourne."

He nodded his thanks, and reining Broomtail toward the open gate, headed through. Soon he moved the horse into an easy trot on an Indian trail, some distance from the river. He had ridden for less than half an hour when he reached a bluff affording him a view of Hallie's house.

It showed bright yellow in a patch of winter gray land next to the water. A thin gray haze rose from the chimney, and he pictured the fire inside, crackling while Hallie fixed toast for Emma as she did every morning. He stared at the house for some time, unwilling to move on, unwilling to let go of even this last glimpse. There had been too much left unsaid.

Finally, he urged Broomtail back onto the trail, pressing his heels into the horse's flanks. He headed down the same trail he'd just left.

Only this time he headed for Hallie Callahan's.

SEVENTEEN

Less than an hour after leaving the Callahan land, Jamie rode back through the gate, and Broomtail halted, knowing he was home again.

Hallie must have been watching out the front window, because when he dismounted, she was already running down the porch steps, wiping her hands on her apron as she ran.

He opened his arms, and in a single beat of his heart, she ran to him. He grasped her around her waist with his good arm. And she circled her arms around his neck. She felt solid, standing there, holding him, loving him.

"I can't leave you," he whispered into her hair.

"I can't bear it either," she murmured, her face buried against his shirt. "But I know you can't stay."

"Come with me." He pulled back slightly to look in her upturned face. "Come with me to California! You and Emma."

She laughed, sounding like a schoolgirl. Then she reached up and touched his face with her fingertips. "Are you asking me to marry you, Jamie?"

He laughed, enjoying her directness. "Oh, Hallie! What joy you bring me!" He paused, about to propose properly, then he stopped.

Aislin. *Aislin!* He was already promised to another. But the ranchos, their families, Aislin herself seemed so far away. Of course he hadn't forgotten her; he just hadn't allowed himself to think of her as flesh and blood, as alive, as someone to go home to.

Hallie's face fell as if she'd seen inside his heart. Then she said quickly, "Before you say another word, the answer is no, I can't marry you. I can't go to California with you. This is my home. Emma's home that her father built, land he cleared. It's only right and proper I bring her up here."

"Hallie…" he began, but she shook her head decisively.

"I love you, Jamie Dearbourne," she said, her eyes steady on his. "But you have a lot of healing still to do inside. The time isn't yet right for you to choose wisely or with wholeness."

He reached for her, and she came into his arms again. "There's a room in your heart I don't think you've discovered yet," she murmured against him. "A sanctuary where you'll find strength and safety. And someday, complete healing.

"My prayer for you as you travel will be that you'll find that heart space, Jamie. Meet God there. Let him show you what else is in there. I think you'll be surprised."

She trailed her fingers gently across his wound. It still ached, especially to the touch, but he wouldn't have moved her hand even if it meant he would never hurt again.

She was looking deep into his eyes now. "You'll find love in that sanctuary, eventually," she said quietly. "But the healing must come first. You still have more than one wound in need of wholeness."

Jamie wanted to ask her to wait for him, but thoughts of Aislin wouldn't allow it.

Again, Hallie seemed to sense his thoughts. "When your healing is complete, your heart may change. Once you are home, around those people who love you…those you love… Well, things may be different."

He grasped her to himself, her warmth flooding through him like a life-giving charge. "How can I let you go?"

She pulled away from him then, and laughing lightly she said, "Why, Mr. Dearbourne, I don't believe either of us will ever let the other go. Even if I never see you again in this life, you will remain in my heart. You will be there always."

For several minutes he clung to Hallie in silence, then without another word, he mounted Broomtail and rode away from her.

Eighteen

Aislin awoke in a cold sweat from a terrifying nightmare: Jamie had been buried alive. She recalled the dream, staring into the whorls of ashen predawn fog, and realized it wasn't Jamie, but she, who had been buried. She could almost taste the soil in her mouth, feel the suffocating pressure of the dirt on her chest. She shivered and tried to pray. The fog, relentless now for weeks, made her unable to catch her breath. Her fear, so familiar, made her unable to lift her heart to God.

There was a dread she couldn't shake from her mind; it was with her more often than not. She needed to come to grips with Jamie's death, but couldn't. Not since the thugs told her there was a chance he might be alive. It was obvious they had been lying. But still the nagging doubts remained.

Trying to breathe slowly, she tossed on her pallet for several minutes, then finally decided to rise early and see to their morning routine.

She kindled the fire and arranged some dried branches over it. It caught, though it smoldered some in the damp fog. As she fanned it into flames, she thought of Jamie, wondering what it would be like to see him again after all this time. Would those feelings, long buried, surface again? Those feelings of love and adoration, contentment to be with him? Was he dead…or alive?

She considered whether it might be she who was buried alive. Daily, Spence captured her attention in a different way: the quiet strength of his character; the joy he took in simple things, whether it was spotting a new species of bird or teaching her to shoot his rifle. Yet she held him at a distance, buried her delight in him someplace deep inside, so deep that she hoped it would never be uncovered.

She poured coffee and water into the blue speckled pot and set it on the flat cooking rock. A dense, milky-white fog had settled close to the ground, just as it had every morning in the weeks since they arrived in the Valley of the Horses, and she could not see beyond the perimeter of their campsite.

They'd made camp at the south end of a shallow lake on slightly higher ground, in the shelter of a copse of willows. On the few afternoons that the fog lifted, they tracked the herds around the marshy lake and into the low-slung foothills. But when the fog clung resolutely to the ground, as it did on this day, they remained in camp, huddled around the fire. It was at those times that Aislin worried Scotty and the hands would be unable to find their meeting place.

The water in the coffeepot had just begun to boil when Spence rolled from his pallet and stepped to the fire. His hair was tangled from sleep, and he stretched and yawned. That was another of those delights she buried in her heart—the mussed and boyish look of him first thing in the morning.

He looked over at her. "You all right?"

She laughed, trying to cover her anxious thoughts. But Spence was watching her carefully. "The hard ground is giving me a bit of a glum disposition. That's all." She paused, aware his concerned gaze was still on her. "Though I must tell you," she continued, to give him something else to think about, "I'm worried Scotty might not find us in this fog. Don't you think he should have been here by now?"

Spence nodded and reached for the two blue speckled mugs. Using a heavy pad on the pot handle, he poured steaming coffee in each and handed one to Aislin. She wrapped both hands around it, staring into the contents to avoid looking into his face.

When she finally glanced up, he was scanning the skies as if looking for a break. "I've already done enough worrying about that for us both," he said, then took a long swig of coffee. "He and the ranch hands may be riding in circles, looking for us."

"How long should we wait?"

"As soon as the fog lifts, I think we need to track any herds we can, those we've already spotted." He'd recorded in a journal the whereabouts of some, mapping their trails and habits. "We'll wait only a few more days…" His voice fell off as he frowned in thought.

"And?"

He turned to her, rubbed his tangle of honey-hued hair, yawned again, then smiled sleepily. "Then the two us will herd as many of the horses as we can and head out for the Old Spanish Trail."

She met his gaze over the top of her mug. "Just the two of us…with say, a hundred horses or so?"

He chuckled. "I was thinking more like a thousand."

She almost dropped her mug. "That's impossible."

"I like doing the impossible," he said, not moving his gaze from hers.

"We'd better hope for help soon," she managed. "Two people on horseback, herding a thousand horses to New Mexico?"

"You forget my way with horses, m'dear," he said, still grinning. "I don't see it as impossible at all!"

Two days later, the fog lifted again enough to see across the valley to the nearby mountain range. They saddled up and rode out to look for Scotty and the hands, first riding southwest to the Tejon Pass, then back to the east and the foothills of the Sierra Nevadas.

They were turning back when Spence spotted a herd at the base of the mountains, and, urging Ruffian into an easy lope, headed toward them. Aislin followed on Silverheel, but slowed when Spence held up his hand as a signal. They walked the horses to a gentle slope, and observed the herd in the distance.

It was led by a powerful obsidian stallion. They watched as the beast kept an eye on the small herd. He arched his neck and lifted his feet high as he slowly circled the herd. He was magnificent.

Aislin and Spence urged their horses nearer, but the stallion caught their scent, and within minutes the herd had disappeared into a small rocky canyon.

The following morning the sun finally broke through, and Spence met Aislin's gaze over breakfast.

"You want to go after the stallion." She didn't need to ask; she knew what was causing the light in his eyes.

He nodded. "No time like the present."

As the sun turned the fog to mists that laced among the willows and cattails, Aislin mounted Silverheel, then followed Spence on Ruffian at an easy canter through the marsh grasses. He headed toward the place they'd spotted the herd: a desolate rocky canyon at the base of the Sierras.

Spence took the lead as they entered the narrow canyon. They skirted the lip of a sheer wall, winding along the trail made by the wild horses. Below them snaked a narrow river, its waters spraying over a boulder-strewn bed. Its rush and roil echoed off the granite like a low thunder.

Spence halted the sorrel and craned around in his saddle. "Up ahead," he said, as if barely able to contain his excitement. "I spotted the stallion. He's watching us. Ears back. Ready to protect the herd."

"Let's just hope they don't blast down this trail," she shot back at Spence. "I dare say, there's not room for us all."

He gave her a quick nod and a grin, and turned to urge Ruffian on again.

"It's not funny," she called after him, looking down the sheer drop to the ribbon of water below the trail.

Within minutes they had reached the apex of the canyon. Its slant was gentler now, and the trail wound down to the river where it widened into a pool fed by a waterfall.

Aislin moved Silverheel closer to Spence and Ruffian.

"Look at that." There was awe in Spence's voice, and she thought he meant the beauty of the water, the place itself. "Behind the falls," he said, pointing. "Do you see it?"

She narrowed her eyes in concentration. "See what?"

He turned to her. "There's an opening behind the falls."

She looked again, but still didn't see what he was talking about.

"There," he said again. "There's something back there. I know it."

Her gaze again sought the place behind the falls, but she saw nothing. "You're telling me the horses are behind the falls?"

"Remember when I told you I saw the stallion?"

She nodded. "It wasn't more than just a few minutes ago. Where is he now?"

"I'm not sure, but he must have given the herd some warning. They've disappeared. This is a box canyon—there's no other way out. At least I don't think there is, except for this trail."

Aislin glanced at the cliffs, the sheer slices of mineral-sparkling granite. The sun was higher than the canyon walls now, and hit the granite, as bright as millions of dancing diamonds. There wasn't a tree or flower in sight, but it was still one of the most majestic sights she'd ever seen.

Spence studied the waterfall, frowning in concentration. "I want to ride over," he said. "See if I can climb up to that."

"It looks dangerous, Spence. The trail is wet from the spray. Besides, we don't know if there's anything at the top. If the horses are back there, who's to say they won't come charging out and down the trail we're on?"

"Are you saying you don't want to go with me?" He lifted a brow in challenge, just as he had when they were children.

She grinned. "I just wanted to make sure you wanted to go with me! Follow me, great hunter!" She quickly urged Silverheel to take the lead, laughing as she headed the big mare down the trail to the pond.

Spence followed. They both dismounted at the pond, letting the horses loose to drink. The water fell from a height of more than fifty feet, and its spray created a mist above the pond. Every stone, every bit of sand, was slick from it. The trail leading upward looked even more treacherous from here.

She shaded her eyes, studying the waterfall. Spence was right. There was an opening, a cave of some sort.

Spence adjusted his hat against the sun, then motioned to the trail. The closer they got to the falls, the greater the roar; it made talking impossible. The slippery trail wound upward very close to the waterfall. Sometimes it shot straight up; other times, it took a horizontal course, sidewinding snakelike toward the cave. Aislin refused to look down as they climbed.

At the trail's apex, Spence stopped and looked back. Beneath his hat, tiny droplets had gathered on his eyebrows and lashes. He smiled, and it struck her that his face, with its expression of absolute joy, had never looked so beautiful.

"We're nearly there." He mouthed the words, since they still couldn't be heard above the roar of the waterfall.

She nodded and mouthed back, "Let's go!"

He climbed the remaining distance, now horizontal, to the opening, and she scrambled behind him.

Finally, they stood on a granite ledge, barely wide enough for the two of them, and inched their way sideways the remaining few feet to the waterfall itself.

Aislin held her breath, still not daring to look down. The spray was heavier here, more of a misty fog. She reached for Spence's hand, glad for the warmth of his fingers clasped around hers.

She tried to force from her mind the image of the stallion rearing in fear as they entered the cave. Or the herd thundering out of the opening. Trampling. Pushing. She shuddered.

Spence halted to look back reassuringly. At least that's what she supposed his reason was, until he pointed to a fissure just before the cave's entrance. She drew in a deep breath. They would have to jump across to enter the cave. Jump. And land solidly behind the water in the safety of the cave.

Safety? She pictured the wild herd. The stallion with his flaring nostrils. *Safety?*

Spence stopped again, and turning to her, mouthed instructions. She shook her head, unable to decipher a single word. Then she signaled with one hand for him to jump first. She would follow.

He squeezed her fingers once, then let go. Without hesitation he leapt across the fissure and landed solidly on the other side.

Aislin stepped to the abyss and made the mistake of looking down. It seemed to slice into the center of the earth itself. If a person slipped into it, there could be no rescue. A person would be wedged in abject darkness.

Her heart pounded wildly.

She sensed, rather than heard, Spence call her name. She looked at him instead of into the fissure. His gaze was locked on hers, and he reached out his arms. He would catch her. She took a deep breath, stepped back a few feet to get a running start, then flew across the distance between them.

Her first realization upon landing was that she was crushed against a laughing Spence who held her tight in his arms. Her second realization was that it was a wonderful place to be.

Laughing herself, she stepped back quickly and brushed herself off. They were now behind the deafening cascade. She turned in a circle, leaving the glorious sight of the wall of water, and looked into the cave itself.

To Aislin's surprise, it wasn't enclosed. And it certainly sheltered no horses. She glanced at Spence who was staring straight ahead into the back of the cavelike room, which opened to daylight on the other side.

As one, they walked to the opening, some fifty yards back from the waterfall. It became quieter the farther away from the falls they moved, and finally, by the time they stepped to the opening, which was little more than the height of a man and just as wide, Aislin could hear the sound of their footsteps echoing in the cave.

Spence reached the opening first and motioned her to hurry forward. She joined him moments later and caught her breath in surprise. "Oh, Spence…" she murmured.

There before them was a small, enclosed meadow, filled with winter grasses, buckeye, and redbud. To the north was a stand of slender pines, plush and green, and to the west, a pond, probably fed from the waterfall runoff.

And in the center of the meadow stood the wild horses, the stallion having placed himself between the herd and the intruders.

Spence glanced at Aislin and nodded. "We found them," he whispered.

"Now the trick is capturing them," she whispered back.

"There's an old Indian trick I've heard about," he said. "If I follow them at a distance for quite some time, then turn around, they'll follow me."

"Sounds like hocus-pocus."

"I've heard the Sobobas say that it works every time. I've just never tried it."

"You mean you're going to get them to follow us out of the cave…down that trail…back to our campsite?"

"You don't think I can do it?" He quirked a brow.

They were moving closer now to the brush at the edge of the meadow. Aislin imitated Spence's movements—sure, steady, quiet, and slow. "I'll believe it when I see it," she challenged.

Spence halted and stooped behind a thick tangle of manzanita. She crouched next to him, pulling back some of the spindly red branches. The stallion, his dark hide gleaming in the morning sun, circled the herd. He stepped high and proud, lifting his tail, seemingly conscious of being observed by Spence and Aislin.

Whispering, Spence explained the procedure. "Indians use this method for hunting any wild animal within bow-and-arrow shooting distance. If a man follows the herd, pressing them to move away for a distance, the prey become so curious about the hunter that when he turns to walk away from them, they also turn to follow."

She was astonished at the idea. "You mean they don't have to rope, or trap, or hurt the animals in any way?"

"If the Indians are hunting for food, I would say their prey will feel some pain."

She laughed lightly. "Well, of course." She turned back to the herd. "But in this kind of a hunt, the only pain will be fear."

His gaze was on the herd. "And maybe we can remove even that."

"It seems a shame to lead them from this beautiful valley to a life on the battlefields."

Spence winced as if receiving a physical blow. "I have considered that too." He looked back to her. "And only half of the horses we round up will actually survive the drive to New Mexico."

For a moment, neither spoke as they watched the grace, beauty, and power of the herd before them.

"I must try it," Spence whispered, not moving his gaze. Then he turned to her and grinned. "Be prepared to run, though, if anything goes wrong."

"You mean, if they charge you?" She tried not to wonder how they might escape from a couple hundred thundering tons of muscle and hooves headed their direction. She swallowed hard. "Just make friends with that stallion, Spence. And quick."

"I intend to, ma'am," he said, tipping his hat. Then he removed it and handed it to her. "Keep it safe."

"Keep yourself safe."

But Spence didn't answer. He was already slipping soundlessly toward the stallion. Aislin settled behind the wall of manzanita to watch.

Spence stood tall, walking slowly but fearlessly toward the big horse. She noticed Spence didn't make eye contact, and knew that if he had, the horse would feel challenged and might charge. Spence walked with a sure and graceful gait, unchallenging, curious. The horse responded in kind.

When Spence was within forty feet of the stallion, the horse's ears flattened, and his nostrils flared, but instead of charging, he danced backward away from Spence, who kept his eyes averted.

Spence's movements continued slow and dancelike in a silent language of movement. The sun was higher now, and its light filled the meadow. Aislin moved forward from her hiding place, her gaze never moving from the beauty of movement—Spence's, the stallion's, the herd's behind them. Hides gleamed in the sun, and there was a tangible, almost electric, sense of anticipation in the air.

The stallion now turned and walked purposefully away from Spence. The herd, almost as one being, sensed the change, and moved ahead of the stallion toward the furthest boundary of the meadow. For several minutes they loped, ears pinned back, nervous as they moved away from him. Spence was moving faster now himself, loping along at the same speed as the herd.

The stallion moved to take the lead, then circled back to the flank, to once again position himself nearer Spence. Aislin noticed the horse's ears were no longer pinned tight to his head; one now flicked forward, the other to the rear, as if to listen to both the herd and Spence at once.

Then Spence halted. He waited, watching, as the herd slowed to a nervous walk, then finally to a standstill, curious, alert. Slowly, he turned, then trotted back across the meadow the opposite direction.

Aislin leaned forward against some manzanita branches, almost afraid to blink lest she miss even a heartbeat of action. The herd's nervousness was palpable. Ears flicking. Heads held low. Still, Spence loped away from them. He didn't glance back or pay any obvious attention to the stallion. He just kept moving, agile, surefooted, across the meadow.

Then the stallion moved a few steps toward him. The herd turned and followed.

Aislin bit her lip, waiting, watching Spence's movement in the light of the mountain meadow, trying to fathom the behavior of the wild horses behind him.

The stallion loped behind Spence, though at a healthy distance, the herd bringing up the rear, some walking, some trotting. Spence sensed the horses' movements behind him, and flashed a wide smile in Aislin's direction. He ran on for several minutes longer, then slowed, and finally halted.

The horses matched his movement. When he halted, they also halted, though again at a distance. He turned around. They did the same. As he began running again, the herd moved as one before him.

Spence lifted his arms, hands spread. He turned slowly, his face heavenward as he followed the horses. There was a powerful grace in his movement. He danced as if thanking God for the beauty of this moment, for the gladness of creation.

He beckoned Aislin to join him, and she left her hiding place in the manzanitas, moving slowly, steadily, toward him. The horses were still moving away from Spence, the stallion in the lead.

Aislin stepped closer to Spence, and he reached out to grasp her hand. They ran together behind the herd, pressing them ever forward.

This time when they halted, the herd stopped and turned, almost as if anticipating the movement backward again. Spence caught her gaze and held it a moment before taking Aislin in his arms, turning her to some inner music. At first they moved slowly, almost as if in an ancient dance. Then, still moving to the silent music, they smiled into each other's eyes. They moved faster…and still faster…whirling and laughing like children, dancing for the joy of movement, for the joy of being together.

Behind them the herd stood like statues, and the stallion circled once more to stand guard.

Spence nodded to Aislin and, still holding her hand, moved toward the horse. At first the stallion skittered backward, then Spence began to speak softly, and the beast stood perfectly still again, waiting. Aislin kept her face turned away slightly to avoid eye contact and fell back to let Spence close the gap between himself and the stallion. He spoke soothing words. The stallion didn't move.

After a few minutes, Spence stood very close to the horse and slowly extended his arm to touch its neck. The horse reared back in fright, and Spence immediately stepped away. After a moment he tried again, and this time the horse didn't move. Spence touched the stallion's neck, stroking lightly, continuing his gentling with words and touch.

Quick tears filled Aislin's eyes as she watched man and horse. Spence spoke to the horse about everything from God his Creator to the lovely meadow home of the herd. Spence circled a few times, then rubbed the stallion between the eyes, the place that spoke the silent language of trust by the horse.

The stallion didn't shy away, merely flicked his ears. After a moment, Spence mounted the horse, bareback. The horse flattened his ears a moment, danced sideways a bit, then stood quietly.

Spence found Aislin's gaze and clung to it, just as he clung to the stallion's obsidian mane. She smiled and melted again into the brush at the side of the meadow to watch Spence direct the wild stallion with mere pressure from his knees and heels. The big horse responded, lively and wild, but never once did he buck or rear to unseat Spence.

For an hour, Spence thundered around the meadow atop the obsidian. Finally, he stopped near Aislin and slid from the stallion's back.

"If we spend this long with each horse," she said, "it's going to take us a long time to break even a thousand horses."

He nodded. "This won't happen again."

"Why not? I mean, other than the fact that we don't have the time?"

"We can't take this herd."

She understood before he started to explain. "They belong here."

He gazed back at the herd, at the stallion. "This valley must remain a secret when the others join us. I don't want one of these horses taken from here."

"A thousand wild horses couldn't drag the information from me," she said with a grin.

"Speaking of a thousand wild horses," he said, squinting up at the sun, "we'd better get on our way. Since we've ruled out this herd, we'll have to look for some others."

She glanced back to the meadow. "I could stay here forever." She felt his gaze and purposely didn't look up at him. "I don't think I've ever seen anything quite so moving. You really do have a mysterious way with them."

"Aislin," he said softly, and, placing his fingertips under her chin, lifted her face toward his. "How long are we going to avoid talking about what's between us?"

"It's Jamie who's between us," she said. "And we've done all the talking we can on that subject."

"We can't go on living with his ghost. Do you know what it's like for me?"

"We settled this, Spence," she said. "We agreed…"

But she didn't finish—Spence lowered his head and covered her mouth with his. Aislin melted into his embrace, feeling the warmth of his lips on hers. Images of Spence dancing with the horses filled her mind just as his nearness filled her senses.

She tried to push him away, but he held her firm. "But we can't…we mustn't," she whispered when she could breathe again.

"Jamie's dead," Spence said. "He's dead, Aislin. Dead!"

She pushed against him again, this time freeing herself.

"He's dead!" Spence, who was almost shouting now, reached for her again. "Listen to me, Aislin. I saw his grave. My brother's dead!"

He moved closer, grasping her hands in his. "We are the ones who live. We can't chase after a ghost. And we can't live with a ghost for the rest of our lives."

She lifted her eyes to his.

"I love you, Aislin. But I can't continue to live with my brother's ghost between us."

For several moments she couldn't speak. She just gulped in ragged breaths of air as if she had been running a very long time. "Jamie is not dead," she said, finally. "I have felt it in my heart since we first heard he might be alive. I—I dream about him. About being buried alive."

Spence stared at her without speaking. The cold expression in his eyes made her heart freeze.

At the same moment, loud shouts issued from the cave. They both spun around, dumbfounded. The uniformed Scotty MacPherson was the first to spot Aislin and Spence standing at the edge of the meadow.

He hollered into the cave behind him, then back to the couple.

Aislin looked up at Spence in disbelief. "How'd he find us?"

He shrugged and looked back. What they saw next was even more astounding.

"Sybil…?" Aislin breathed.

Her sister gave her a big wave and started running toward her with open arms. It took only a heartbeat for Aislin to respond. But before she took one step forward, Spence groaned.

There in the mouth of the cave stood the stately, gray-haired vaquero, Fraco Ciro, his eyes glittering even from this distance as he studied the herd and the prancing obsidian stallion.

NINETEEN

Scotty MacPherson strode toward Spence, hand outstretched. "Good to see you again," he said.

Spence shook the younger man's hand. "How did you find us?"

Scotty laughed. "It wasn't easy. First we were delayed at Fort Tejon, figuring we'd wait out the fog. Once we hit the valley floor, we circled the lake a few times. Saw your campsite. That's where we left the others."

Spence grinned. Scotty's words tumbled out as if he wasn't sure Spence would hold still long enough to hear them all. "But this canyon…" Spence reminded him. "Not easy to find."

He looked proud. "I had the idea of heading for higher ground to get a better view of the valley. Fraco, here, and I had just headed into the foothills when we spotted you off in the distance. Saw you disappear." He shook his head. "By the time we got to the canyon, you'd left. It took some doing to find the entrance. But once we followed the trail inside, we saw your horses below the cave."

Spence glanced back at the nervous herd before turning to walk toward the cave where Aislin and Sybil waited. "How many hands did you bring?"

Scotty frowned. "Not as many as you'd hoped for."

He nodded toward Sybil. "Plus one unexpected?"

Scotty held up his palms toward Spence and shrugged. "I didn't ask for that particular wrangler to join us."

Spence laughed. "You don't have to ask. She charts her own course. Always has."

"So I'm learning."

Fraco stepped forward and greeted Spence, stone-faced as ever.

"This herd one we are taking?" He nodded to the stallion and the herd behind him.

"No. Terrain's too difficult. There are others in the valley that'll be easier to herd."

Fraco assessed the meadow and the herd, his eyes darting from one to the other, then back again. "You are wrong," he said. "This is a box canyon. It is a perfect place to trap them. Once they head out of here, there is only one place to go. Downstream. We will place some of the hands behind them here to chase them out. Another group will wait at the mouth of the canyon."

"I said no." Spence stared at the man. He remembered the first day of the fandango, the man's treatment of the mustang filly in the pen. "We won't take this herd with the others. I want them left alone."

"As you wish," Fraco said, his granite face impassive. Spence started to walked away, but Fraco called out after him, "You need to keep in mind, *amigo,* that I am in no one's hire. Not yours. Not Sergeant MacPherson's. None of the ranch hands are any longer in Dearbourne employ or in that of MacQuaid Byrne."

Spence wheeled to look first at Scotty, who acknowledged the truth of the man's words with a slight nod, then at Fraco himself. "What are you talking about?"

Fraco stepped closer. "You don't know, do you?"

"Know what?"

Scotty filled in the painful details. "MacQuaid Byrne can no longer afford to pay his men. Fraco's right. None of the men are in MacQuaid's employ."

"And Rancho Dearbourne?"

"I didn't speak to your father, but according to MacQuaid, he was still planning to hang on as long as he could." Scotty stepped forward and placed his hand on Spence's shoulder. "When I arrived at La Paloma, MacQuaid Byrne had just received word about his loans being called in. There was talk of his being forced off the rancho. That was two weeks ago. I don't know what's happened since."

Spence looked to Aislin, only to see by her serious expression that

Sybil had already given her the bad news. Aislin turned, searching for him, and he nodded slightly, indicating that he knew. She turned back to Sybil, and the sisters walked slowly into the cave, arms around each other.

"We're too late, then, with our scheme," he said, turning back to the two men. But only Scotty remained nearby. Fraco had wandered into the meadow and was studying the stallion. As he approached, the big stallion exhibited more nervous behavior than in all the few hours since Spence and Aislin had found the herd in the meadow.

Spence tried not to be too concerned about Fraco's admiration of the horse and turned back to Scotty.

Scotty frowned. "Do you still want to go through with it?"

He nodded slowly. "I don't know what good we'd do by returning empty-handed right now." He pictured the families, loading their wagons and moving from their beloved homes. If there was any way possible to save the lands, he would do it. Odd that he was almost desperate to save the ranchos. Now.

Now that it was nearly too late.

"We can move forward with the plan, then." The younger man sounded almost too eager. "I know the road well. Perhaps we can save time and distance."

"We?"

Scotty colored slightly and shifted his gaze away from Spence. "I'll be traveling with you as far as Santa Fe, where I'm to report for reassignment in the east."

"The war."

"Yes, sir. The war."

Spence studied Scotty for a moment. "I'm glad you'll be coming along with us. We can use another good hand. And you know the area, right? The trails east?"

"Yes, sir," said Scotty, still looking uncomfortable. "Been on them once, but I reckon that's enough to find my way back."

Spence draped his arm over Scotty's shoulders as they turned to follow Aislin and Sybil into the cave. "Well, whether you can scout for us or not, I'm glad to have you along."

By the time they had climbed back down the trail beside the waterfall, it was obvious that Fraco Ciro wasn't following. Spence waited impatiently near the pond at the bottom of the falls. He met Aislin's gaze and saw she understood. A few minutes later, Fraco moved out from behind the falls and onto the trail. Carefully, he made his way down to the others.

Spence had just swung a leg over Ruffian's saddle, when Fraco, already mounted, moved his horse nearer to Spence. A lead-stocked quirt was hooked around his saddle horn, its braided-leather thongs looped in several coils, a menacing reminder of its use for striking a rearing horse.

"It is a fine herd in this valley," he said.

"It is," Spence agreed, "but this fine herd will stay in this valley."

Fraco flicked his eyes over Spence in a cold appraisal. "We will see," he said. Before the others could mount and join him, the vaquero reined his horse forward and onto the trail leading from the canyon.

That night, following a supper of venison stew fixed by Cook, Spence gathered the wranglers together and stepped onto a tree stump and called for their attention. Darkness had fallen, and the only light was from the glow of the nearby cookfire. Aislin and Sybil sat near the fire, and Scotty MacPherson stood nearby. One foot propped on a rock, he leaned an elbow on the same knee, facing Spence. Scotty seemed to be studying him with an unusual intensity as the men dropped their mess kits with Cook's Chinese helper and sauntered over in small groups toward the place where Spence stood.

"I understand you've come of your own accord, assuming that because of the ranchos' misfortunes and your subsequent dismissal, you're in no one's hire." There were some murmurs and nodding of heads, and Spence went on. "Each of you is expecting a portion of the proceeds from the sale of the horses once we reach Santa Fe, is that correct?"

Again, the men agreed.

"You need to understand that you are indeed in someone's hire, and that someone is me. Though you are working without immediate pay, you will be paid in full at the end of our run. You need to know that this is not an operation of every man for himself. We must pull together to be successful."

A few of the men exchanged glances, shrugged, and looked back to Spence.

"I take a man at his word. Your solemn oath is all I need from each of you—that you will support my captaincy until we reach New Mexico, sell the herd, and each receive your pay. Your word is your agreement to be in my hire."

There were nods of assent. Spence took a deep breath, looking over the crowd of faces before him. Some of the men had worked on one or the other of the ranchos since his childhood; others were migrants such as Fraco Ciro and his small band of vaqueros, who worked seasonally on ranchos up and down the coast.

From the rear of the group, Fraco Ciro and his small band watched with impassive faces. A couple of the vaqueros nodded and shrugged with Spence's last words.

"I give you my word that each of you will receive fair pay for the work done when we reach Santa Fe. The more horses we arrive with alive and well, the better your pay." He paused. "We'll be saddle-breaking the horses as we move. Since we hope to have some four to five thousand in our herd by the time we leave, and there are only forty-some of us, you can see that it will require several hours daily."

Erasmo, one of the men from La Paloma, spoke up. "Just how do you propose to do that? We know your reputation for talkin' to horses, and if you think you're going to get the rest of us to do that—" His voice was cut off by Bobbie Oakes and Parker Burnside, who hooted with laughter. Others joined in. Jake Polley scratched his head and snickered.

Spence held up a hand and grinned amiably. "I won't expect you to talk to horses. Truth is, I don't know any horse who'd want to talk to any of you!"

There was more laughter, this time with Spence, not directed toward him.

"I've got some ideas, however," he said when the laughter had faded.

"An effective way to calm a horse to rider is to break him in water. He can't struggle with the same strength. No cruelty done to rider or horse. Some of you have probably seen Indians breaking horses this way."

There were nods. Polley and Oakes exchanged nods.

"On those days we're near water, we'll break as many to saddle and rider as possible."

Fraco Ciro spoke up. "Rivers are empty now because of the drought," he said slowly, pointedly.

"The drought's in California," Spence said. "We'll be herding the horses out by week's end, heading them across the Tehachapi Mountains into the Antelope Valley to the Mojave River. Water will be scarce the few hundred miles of our trek. No doubt about it. But we'll be moving as fast as we can from water hole to water hole."

There was a lull, then Jake Polley spoke up. "What about bandits? Anything we can do to avoid 'em?"

"You've all heard the tales about Peg Leg Smith, the Ute chief Walkara, Bill Williams?"

Nervous laughter spattered across the group. Aislin and Sybil were sitting near each other and seemed to turn white-faced at the mention. Spence held up his hand to stop the speculation.

"The tales of these men have been grossly exaggerated," he said. "It's been a couple decades since they last raided any herds. Every time their stories were recounted, they got better. The thieves were meaner, the numbers of horses stolen got bigger. This is not to say we won't face our own dangers—or those that fancy themselves newfangled versions of Peg Leg Smith or old Bill Williams—but if we're on the lookout, keep together, body and spirit, we'll come out of this wealthier than we are going in."

There was a cheer, and Erasmo threw his hat in the air. Jake Polley and Bobbie Oakes did the same. Others whooped and tossed theirs. Except, Spence noted, the vaqueros in the back of the group.

"Tomorrow—" Spence said, holding up a hand to quiet the group. "Tomorrow, we begin in earnest. We'll spread out to round up the herds I've spotted so far, bring them back to camp for the night. Then the following morning, we head out. Once we hit the Antelope Valley, we hit mustang country. I figure we'll take as many mustangs to mix in with the herd as we can.

"Our maximum number is five thousand wild horses, gentlemen. Our minimum, four thousand." He looked over the group. "We want as many as possible to make it all the way to Santa Fe. Are there any questions?"

Parker Burnside, who'd been sitting near the fire, stood. "I got one. We sellin' to the North or to the South?"

Spence grinned. "I don't know about you all and where your sympathies lie, but as for me—I figure the horses will go to the highest bidder. We're in this for financial gain, not necessarily to help either side."

This time the cheers rose louder. Hats again flew into the air as Spence stepped off the tree stump. Some of the wranglers sauntered off toward where they'd left their gear, discussing what they planned to do with their profits; others huddled in small groups, talking about the roundup the following day.

Spence turned to Scotty, now walking toward him, his expression intent. "I thought it was understood you'd be selling to the U.S. Government," Scotty said.

"I don't believe I ever said."

"When you asked for the government to help by seeking my services as courier," Scotty continued, "it was indeed understood. Why do you think they're allowing me to accompany you? To sell to the Confederacy?"

"My agreement with your superior was to send you to Tejon from here with some broken wild horses to pay for your services. I didn't expect you to accompany us any farther than this, Sergeant. Whatever your superiors decided in my absence is nothing I agreed to, nor do I intend to."

Scotty looked uncomfortable, and Spence dropped his voice. "If you have a problem with my plans, Sergeant, I suggest you hightail it back to Tejon tonight."

"You owe it to your country," Scotty pressed. "Your country is at war, and we all must do our part. If you must take less profit than planned, then so be it. We all have to make sacrifices."

"You don't sound convinced, yourself," Spence said. The younger man didn't comment, and he went on. "You said you're heading east after Santa Fe?"

"I did."

"You'll be in the thick of the fighting then."

"Yes, sir."

"And are you convinced that's what you want to do?"

"What are you trying to get at?"

"Nothing, Scotty. I just notice you aren't the same young man we met up with at Tejon a few weeks ago." He paused. "I admire what you must do for your country. But I am just as adamant about being left alone with the decisions to be made about every detail of this drive—including the final arrangements in Santa Fe."

Scotty turned without a word and strode back to the remuda, to check his horse, Spence supposed, but also perhaps to think through his options. He decided he wouldn't be surprised if Scotty had ridden back to Tejon by morning. He didn't have long to speculate, because he was approached by Erasmo, Polley, and Burnside, who plunged immediately into more questions about tomorrow's roundup.

Aislin watched Spence with growing respect. Earlier when he spoke to the men, it was obvious that he was in absolute control. His father and others had crowned Jamie the natural leader of the two brothers, assuming that Spence's attributes counted for nothing.

Yet as she watched him, she was aware of his quiet strength. Maybe he didn't possess the flash and daring that Jamie had, but there was something compelling about the way he took control with good humor and grace. Not unlike his dealings with animals. Gentle. Solid. Persuasive.

Persuasive.

It was that attribute that bothered her, at least as far as she personally was concerned. She needed to distance herself from him as much as possible. It would be difficult, but not impossible. Spence did not intend to persuade her with his extraordinary gifts, and perhaps that's what made them, made *him,* so appealing. Everything about Spence was unintentional, unassuming, and utterly charming.

Spence sensed her gaze and turned toward her while he spoke with Erasmo, then after the older man left him, Spence strolled across the clearing to where she stood. She dreaded what she needed to say to him, and almost wished he wouldn't come near her.

"I've been waiting to catch you alone," he said. The warm timbre of his voice threatened to melt her resolve. "Especially after hearing about La Paloma."

It surprised her that she had shoved the news about La Paloma far from her consciousness because of the whirl of conflicting emotions she'd felt since Spence's kiss. Or perhaps because losing her family home was simply too painful to think about.

"Yes," she agreed. "We do need to talk."

He took her arm to escort her farther away from the night fire. "You heard about the loans?"

She almost winced. "I can only imagine what my father and mother are going through. This crazy scheme seems impossible…" Her voice trailed off. "Do you think there's really a chance we can get back in time to help?"

They stopped in a small clearing by the creek behind the cook wagon, now deserted. Someone had pulled out a Spanish guitar and was strumming lightly, the soft tones rising in the night air. The tule fog hadn't settled into the valley, and the sky was spangled with a million pinpoints of light.

Aislin leaned against the rear of the wagon, half sitting on the tailgate. Spence propped himself against the outside corner, half turned toward her, and hooked one boot over the opposite ankle. He gave her a slow smile, and the look of him in the moonlight broke her heart.

"First of all," he said, "I'm highly optimistic."

"Is there anything you *aren't* optimistic about, Spence?"

His grin widened. "Not much," he said, and she knew he was referring to something completely different than what her question addressed.

"I'm serious, Spence. What are our chances?"

"Once the roundup is completed, it will take us fifty trail days to reach Santa Fe. As soon as the transaction is made, we'll have some thirty days to make it back to California."

"We won't know what's happened by then. Everything…" her voice choked as she thought of her beloved land. "Everything could be gone."

"We'll not consider what might happen while we're gone. Only the task ahead for us," he said simply. His reply reminded her again of the solid and graceful way he headed into most things in life. Never once had she known Spence to wring his hands. This was no exception, and just knowing it brought her comfort.

She sighed heavily and, crossing her arms, looked up into the night sky. "We need to talk about what happened earlier…"

"I was out of line," he said quietly, and she spun around to look at him. "I wasn't listening to what you said. Mostly because I didn't want to listen."

"About Jamie."

"Yes."

"So you wouldn't have done what you did…I mean, you wouldn't have kissed me, if you'd known…I mean, if you'd known how I felt about Jamie being alive?" She felt a blush heat her face and was thankful for the dark to hide it. It was enough that she was irritated with her stammering; if Spence could see her bright cheeks, he would know how he affected her. Though she suspected he did know.

He stepped closer, and her heart hammered beneath her ribs. He wanted to kiss her again, but she knew he wouldn't. He considered her in silence.

She swallowed hard and started over again. "What I need to say to you, Spence, is that there can be no more episodes such as what happened this afternoon."

"I already said as much, Aislin."

"I plan to stay as far away from you as possible during this trek. And I hope you will honor my wishes and do your part."

For a moment, Spence didn't speak. She held her breath, not

knowing what to expect. Finally, she glanced his direction from the corner of her eye.

"Is that all?"

"What do you mean, is that all?" She turned to face him once more.

He was still chuckling. "I thought you were going to send me packing and head up this drive by yourself."

"You did?"

He was grinning and watching her with that unfathomable look of merriment in his eyes. "I did."

She thought over what he'd just said. "You sound like you think I could do it."

After a minute he sobered, then watched her with quiet consideration. He raised one brow. "Don't just think it, Aislin. Know it."

"Thank you for the compliment," she said, feeling strangely solid and grace-filled herself. "Thank you."

"But now back to your dilemma."

"My dilemma?"

He was smiling straight into her eyes again. The music from the guitar still played in the background. A breeze flicked the tendrils of her hair that had fallen loose from her braid. One long strand blew across her eyes. Spence leaned closer, reached for it, then hooked it behind her ear. He brushed her cheek with the backs of his fingers as he pulled his hand away from her face. She blinked, staring wordlessly at him. How could she possibly stay away from him when she wanted nothing more than to be in his presence?

"Yes, your dilemma," Spence said, crossing his arms over his chest, and recrossing his boots at the ankles. "If that's truly what you want— staying as far away from me as possible, I mean—I will certainly do my part." Now he was gazing up into the star-filled sky.

With the music of the night, the soft guitar now joined by a banjo, the breeze fluttering the slender willow branches, she thought how altogether lovely it would be for Spence to pull her into his arms, to dance, to… She pushed the unbidden image of his kiss from her mind, just as she had a dozen times at least since he'd swept her into his arms.

She cleared her throat. "You will? Honor my request, I mean?"

"Of course, Aislin. Your wish is my command."

"It is?"

He was chuckling again. "It's the least I can do for you allowing me to stay on, ma'am." He raked his fingers through his hair, the color of pale honey, even in the starlight.

She sighed heavily. "It's as it must be, Spence."

He stared at her, a slight smile playing at the corner of his mouth. Then he reached for her hands, tugged her to standing, and laced his fingers firmly through hers. They were so close, they almost touched, her face upturned toward his.

"It's as it must be, Aislin," he whispered. "As long as Jamie is alive in your heart, it's as it must be."

He looked into her eyes for several long moments. Then, finally, he bent his head and touched her lips with his; it was a touch as light as the wings of a butterfly. Aislin melted into his embrace and reached up to circle her arms around his neck, to draw him even closer. But Spence abruptly caught her wrists, pulled them away, and stepped back.

"That, my love," he said, "was simply my farewell." He arched a brow and gave her a quick half smile. Then he spun away from her and strode back through the wall of willows to the night fire.

"Spence!" she called after him.

But he didn't turn.

Spence was true to his word. During the following days of roundup he made sure he was never near Aislin, especially alone. And if he spoke to her at all, it was only in businesslike terms.

It was truly as she wished, and by the time the herds were ready to head out of the Valley of the Horses into the Tehachapis, Aislin and Spence had settled into a routine of speaking only when necessary and putting as much distance as possible between them every hour of their long days.

Aislin spent more time with her sister than she ever had in their lives, annoying as it was to listen to Sybil's complaints about every detail of life on the trail. Even so, she was conscious of every move Spence made. Her gaze followed him across the plains as he rode through the marsh grasses to scout new herds. She watched him as he wrangled, his hat pulled low against the sun, his posture relaxed in the saddle. And across the night circle when the banjo plucked, and he tapped his boot to the beat. And when he played the harmonica, watching her solemnly over the top of his cupped hands.

But their silence was truly as she wished. Whenever she thought otherwise, she uttered just one word to herself.

Jamie.

TWENTY

Spence kept a close watch on Fraco Ciro and his small band of vaqueros. From the first night, more often than not they removed themselves from the company of the other wranglers. Fraco was increasingly secretive about his whereabouts. And during the first few days of the roundup, his men rode out separately from the others, always returning with sizable herds, but they were close-mouthed about where they had found them.

The days were filled with the hard sun of an Indian summer and the dust from the hundreds of wild horses. Now that the fog had dissipated, at least temporarily, the rugged peaks to the east seemed etched against the sky, posing a formidable challenge to crossing with the massive herd.

They now had moved their base camp from the southern end of the lake to the foothills of the Tehachapis, near the pass across the mountains.

Early the morning before they planned to cross, with Scotty at his side, Spence rode out to scout the trail they would take through the pass. They spent the day mapping out the route and, on their way back to camp, dismounted to rest the horses just below the summit.

Scotty remained near the horses, scrutinizing the granite walls of the narrow pass while Spence walked to a lookout point and gazed at the valley, wide and golden-hazed, as it spread uninterrupted to the horizon. Closer in, below where he stood, camp was being set up. The cook fire burned, its smoke spiraling upward, and the company moved about, preparing for an early supper. The herd was off to the southwest, looking from this distance like one massive, rolling beast. The wranglers on first watch had already moved into place, keeping the horses corralled for the night.

As always, he searched for Aislin and spotted her heading to the remuda.

"It'll be hard to get them through here tomorrow," Scotty said, diverting Spence's attention. The younger man had turned and, frowning in concentration, was gauging the precarious gap. "We'll be lucky to make it through with seventy-five percent."

"We've got to do better than that," Spence said, now looking back to the valley below. He narrowed his eyes. It appeared that Aislin was leading Silverheel from the remuda. He waited a moment, watching as she saddled the horse and mounted.

"Something wrong?" Scotty stepped closer, following his gaze.

"It's Aislin," Spence said. "She's leaving camp, though I can't tell where she's headed."

"She knows not to leave alone past nightfall."

Spence watched her move her horse into a canter.

"Anyone else missing?" Scotty peered down into the valley.

Spence quickly assessed the group below. "I don't see Fraco and his band. Do you?"

Scotty pulled out a brass telescope, unfolded it, and swept it across the company. "They aren't there."

"How about Sybil? Maybe Aislin rode out to look for her sister."

Scotty grinned as he zeroed the scope onto the young woman. "I would have been surprised if that were the case. Nope, she's right there. Sitting off to herself, reading."

"*Godey's Ladies Book,*" mused Spence with a grin. "Bet you possums to yellow jackets that's the book she's studying."

Scotty studied her for a moment, then looked away from the telescope with an appreciative grin of his own. "How'd you know?"

"She and Aislin might as well be family. I can probably tell you the page she's poring over." He paused. "Try page 127— men's fashions."

Scotty went back to the telescope. "I can't see the page numbers from here."

Spence laughed. "I didn't think you could. Besides, I don't know exactly the page. But I know Syb; she's poring over the men's section."

"Men's?"

"Since she was knee-high to a chipmunk, she's fancied herself fit to marry a prince. Or at least the most highfalutin gentleman she can charm onto his knees."

"She wants a highfalutin gentleman?" Scotty swallowed hard and looked uncomfortable.

Spence laughed again. "It's a wonder that she wanted to come along on this drive. I'm still surprised she hasn't insisted on being taken home before we get out of reasonable distance."

"I got the feeling she didn't want to live with her parents and their, er, reduced circumstances," Scotty said, almost as if defending Sybil.

Spence smiled. "She's the most beautiful of the Byrne daughters, no doubt. But she's also spoilt as rotten as they come."

"What about the youngest daughter? What's she like?"

"Brighid." His voice softened. "Everyone loves little Brig. She lives in a different world than Aislin and Sybil. She's a dreamer, though her dreams are completely unselfish."

"Such as..." Scotty lifted the glass, and Spence noticed he was watching Sybil again.

"Such as, teaching the Soboba Indian children to read...that's just one of her dreams. Some of the others are even more of a wonder."

Spence nodded to the telescope. "May I have a look?"

"Sure, go ahead." Scotty handed it to Spence.

Spence squinted through the glass, scanning the landscape once more. He'd been watching Aislin on Silverheel while he and Scotty talked, and now he followed her more closely. She was heading north, skirting the foothills. He wondered briefly if she might be heading to the hidden valley they'd discovered several days ago.

He brought the telescope back to camp and searched again for Fraco Ciro. No sign of him. He moved the scope back to Aislin.

"Do you remember the valley where you found us the other day?" he asked Scotty. He still held the glass to his eye, watching Aislin, who seemed to be riding slower now.

"Of course," Scotty said, frowning.

"I think that's where she's heading." He handed the telescope back to Scotty, hoping he was wrong.

"I see her. Hard to tell from this perspective, but it sure seems like she's turning into a canyon. Might be the same one. Landmarks are different from up here."

"Fraco's missing too. So's his band."

"You thinking what I'm thinking?"

Spence nodded. "You ready for a hard ride?"

Scotty looked at the western horizon and squinted into the sunset. "We don't have much time before dark. That canyon…" He paused. "I would hope that Aislin's got better sense than to head in there at this time of night."

"If she's gone in there, I think it's for only one reason."

"Fraco Ciro."

"That's it."

"To go after that herd." Scotty glanced at Spence as they headed back to the horses. "You've just told me that Sybil's spoilt rotten; Brighid's a saint."

Spence swung a leg over Ruffian's saddle.

"And just what," Scotty continued as he mounted the brown, "would you say about Miss Aislin Byrne?"

Spence urged Ruffian forward and called back over his shoulder, "I'd call her either the bravest woman on God's green earth or…"

Scotty nudged the brown forward. "Or the most obstinate?" he finished.

"You don't know the half of it," Spence muttered.

A half-hour later, they'd skirted the foothills and galloped straight for where they had last seen Aislin. Dusk was falling, and the horses danced nervously when they halted near the river at the mouth of the canyon.

"You need to ride on to camp for help," Spence told Scotty. "Also some lanterns."

The younger man agreed. "You going on in?"

He nodded. "I can't imagine what prompted Aislin to head in alone this time of night, but it better be a good reason. I don't know what she's facing in there, but I'd rather she didn't face it alone."

Scotty gave him a half salute, and as he headed into the ashen darkness toward camp, Spence urged Ruffian into the canyon. The horse was skittish, so Spence took it easy, allowing the gelding to walk.

As they headed deeper into the canyon, the tall granite walls shut out all remaining light from the fading sunset.

"Oh, Lord," Spence said out loud. "We need your help. I don't know if Aislin is in danger, or even exactly where she's headed. Be with her this moment. Surround her with your Presence…your love."

He paused, patting Ruffian's neck to calm him.

"Oh, Lord! How I love her! She may never know how much. She may never know how I pray for her daily, sometimes hourly, that she will come to peace within herself…with you, Father."

The horse's hooves clopped along on the granite trail, and Spence slumped forward in the saddle, settling into the rhythm of Ruffian's slow and graceful gait.

"Strikes me, Father, that Aislin and I both face a darkness of another kind. A darkness we can't seem to find our way through. It all has to do with Jamie…our guilt, our fears, our lack of trusting you. Help us both through that darkness, Lord, just as you're helping ol' Ruf and me through this one."

Darkness was falling faster now, and he worried that Ruffian might sense his own unease with keeping to the trail. He thought about singing to the animal, then dismissed the idea just as quickly. Most folks already thought him daft for talking to horses. If he started singing to them too, he'd be laughed out of the company.

Chuckling to himself, he pulled his harmonica out of his pocket, played a few scales to warm up, then began a lively rendition of "Oh, Susannah!" to lift his spirits. The horse sauntered along, his hooves echoing on the granite trail. Spence tried not to think about the sheer drop to his left and instead considered the beauty of the moonless, starry night, the music of the rushing river accompanying his harmonica.

His eyes grew accustomed to the dark, and he hoped Ruffian's vision was adjusting as well. He patted the horse's neck, and began the lively chorus.

Oh! Susannah, Oh, don't you cry for me!
I come from Alabamy with a banjo on my knee.

Even Ruffian seemed more comfortable now, and continued his slow clip-clop to the beat of the music.

After a while he tired of "Oh! Susannah" and started into "I Dream of Jeannie with the Light Brown Hair."

So intent was he on the trail, enjoying the music, and praying for Aislin, that he almost didn't hear the voice up ahead. He took the harmonica from his lips and halted Ruffian, thinking it was his imagination. Then he brought the harmonica to his lips, hesitated, and frowned.

He heard it again.

Finally, there was no mistaking the sound, and he pressed his heels into Ruffian's flanks and the horse shot forward.

Aislin had ridden only a short distance into the canyon when she realized her enthusiasm had outweighed her common sense. Earlier, she had watched Fraco Ciro and his men prepare for a roundup. Each had tied a quirt to his saddle, the lead handles meant for beating a rearing and bucking horse; the long leather thongs, three on each weapon, meant for whipping.

She remembered Ciro's glittering eyes when he saw the obsidian stallion, the wild herd in the hidden valley. This was their last day in the Valley of the Horses; by tomorrow morning the outfit and their herds would head over the pass and into high desert country. If Ciro wanted the stallion, or the entire herd, today was his final chance to round them up.

She waited for Spence and Scotty to return from their scouting trek, long after Fraco Ciro and his men left camp on horseback. Finally, at sunset, she could wait no longer. She borrowed a rifle from

Erasmo, ignoring his cocked brow. "Thought I'd shoot a rabbit for supper," was the only explanation she offered. Her old friend Erasmo merely shrugged and wished her luck, though he did look worried as she rode off.

The sun was just setting when she reached the canyon, but halfway in the trail disappeared in the darkness, so she dismounted and led Silverheel by the reins as she felt her way along the granite wall.

There was no turning back, even if she had wanted to. The trail wasn't wide enough. Now she wondered if she had misread Ciro's intentions. Why would he head into this valley so late in the afternoon? And if she did find him, what could she do to stop him?

One woman with a rifle? She almost laughed at the thought. She hoped that Ciro's years of dedication to her father and to the rancho, even though it was seasonal, would count for something. Perhaps he could be persuaded without pointing a rifle at him. She couldn't imagine shooting a rabbit, let alone a man.

Then she remembered Spence and his wild, graceful dance with the horses. The stallion, obsidian eyes and hide, proud and powerful, had pranced behind Spence as if communicating in a language only they understood.

To imagine that same magnificent stallion with Ciro on his back, beating him into submission with a lead-handled stock, filled her with an anger that moved her farther into the dark canyon.

Spence was right. That horse, his herd, belonged unmolested in the hidden valley. She would do her best, short of shooting Ciro himself, to see that they remained there. So on she walked, slow step by slow step, in the dark, pulling Silverheel by the reins. She tried not to think about anything except the wild horses in the meadow as she moved deeper into the canyon.

The roar of the rushing water in the canyon below dropped away from her as they climbed. She had just rounded a switchback when she heard the harmonica in the distance. At first, the murmur of the water below made her believe it was just fanciful thoughts in this dark and lonely place.

Then she heard it again, and this time there was no mistaking.

Oh! Susannah! Oh, don't you cry for me!

She knew only one person who could play that tune with quite so lively a lilt. She halted Silverheel at a place where the trail was broad and safe, dismounted, then leaned against the granite wall to wait.

Soon "Oh! Susannah" drifted into "I Dream of Jeannie with the Light Brown Hair." She hummed along with him, though he was still at quite a distance. Then she decided she might scare the socks right off him if he came upon her suddenly, just standing there on the trail.

That's when she decided to sing along.

"I dream of Jeannie with the light brown hair…"

She was so enjoying the song and especially the notion that she was no longer alone on the trail, that she didn't notice Spence had stopped playing. And that she was singing quite loudly, quite completely…alone.

She stopped singing, and the sound of hooves echoed toward her.

"Aislin?" came the call from the darkness of the winding trail.

"I'm here, Spence. A ways up the trail."

"I can't see you."

"I know; I can't see you either."

"Keep singing," he said, and she heard the smile in his voice.

"You heard me?"

"It was like a siren's song."

"If that's the case, you might smash into some rocks along the way."

He laughed.

With his encouragement, Aislin again took up singing "Oh! Susannah." Silverheel nickered and shook her head slightly.

Finally, she saw the shape of him in the starlight. He pulled Ruffian to a stop and slid to the ground.

"I thought we made an agreement," she said, looking up into his face when he drew closer.

"You mean about not being alone?"

She smiled into his eyes. "Precisely."

But Spence didn't smile. Instead, he glared at her. "I was worried about you, Aislin. I saw you from the Tehachapi trail. I could see you'd come in alone."

She explained about Ciro's preparations and how she thought she'd seen him head into the canyon. It was too dark for her to tell, but she knew Spence was probably working his jaw in anger…first about her actions, now about Ciro's. She cleared her throat. "I brought Erasmo's rifle," she said. As if that would make a difference.

He turned to her with a blank look—or maybe it was the dim starlight—almost as if he didn't understand. "You did what?"

"I borrowed a rifle from Erasmo."

"What did you plan to do with this rifle?"

"Stop Ciro from taking the herd. What do you think?"

A smile played at the corner of his mouth. Even in the dim light she could see it. Or maybe she just knew him well enough to know it was there.

"If you're right, there are fourteen armed men in that valley, Aislin."

"I know."

She thought she saw Spence shaking his head. Then he said, "A minute ago, you said you thought Ciro went into the canyon."

"He headed this way."

"But you didn't actually see him enter?"

"I couldn't bear it, Spence. To consider what Fraco Ciro planned…" She didn't finish.

"But do you know for certain," he pressed, "that he or his men entered the canyon?"

"No," she admitted quietly. "I just remembered his eyes that day he spotted the stallion."

Spence seemed to consider her a moment. She waited for him to tell her how foolishly she'd acted, knowing his chastisement would be nothing more than what she'd already told herself. She'd blindly followed her instincts and put herself, and Spence, in great danger. A distance away, a coyote yelped, followed by another. Silverheel danced sideways nervously, and Ruffian nickered as if to calm the mare. Aislin braced herself and waited to hear Spence's disapproval.

"I believe you're right," Spence said. "You've done the right thing by following. I've thought all week that Ciro might head back here. Tonight's the logical time. He probably figured no one would expect him to herd the animals at night." He was quiet a moment, and the sounds of yelping coyotes and rushing river rose in the background. "I should have figured it out myself."

"You should have?" Her voice was little more than a squeak. She blinked. He believed in her judgment, even without proof of her reasoning. He trusted her.

"We've got men on the way," he was saying while she still stared at him in surprise. "I sent Scotty back for help and lanterns. We'll head in tonight. If we wait until morning, it may be too late."

"They can't get out without coming down this trail."

"I was thinking more of the damage they could do to the horses before we reach them."

For a moment they stared at each other. "I'm glad you're here, Spence," she said.

"Did you think I wouldn't follow?"

"I didn't consider that you'd know where I'd gone."

"I would search heaven and earth to find you, Aislin. Don't you know that?"

She stood there stiffly, looking into his eyes, trying not to consider the warmth that flooded her heart at his words.

Spence smiled gently and stepped backward a few steps. He settled onto the ground, leaned back against the rock wall, and patted the spot next to him. She sat down.

He draped one arm around her shoulders. "No need to dwell on the danger we face," he said. "It will arrive soon enough." With his other hand he pulled out the harmonica.

Aislin leaned against him and sighed contentedly, listening to the plaintive tones of the English ballad "Children in the Wood."

She closed her eyes as he played and felt the rhythmic thud of his heart. When the song ended, Spence rested his cheek on the top of her head. They sat without speaking, each lost in thought, and waited for Scotty and the men to join them.

⟭

Within the hour, pinpricks of light from at least a dozen lanterns bobbed along the trail as the riders moved slowly toward Aislin and Spence.

Spence looked down at Aislin tenderly. "You sure you want to come along? You could wait below the falls."

She stood and brushed herself off. "I wouldn't miss this for the world."

"I thought not." He grunted as he pushed himself to standing. "It will be dangerous. No doubt about it. We're slipping into the valley at night, and Ciro will attack before we have a chance to holler hello."

She grinned. "You plan to holler hello?"

"Might as well be friendly before we point our rifles at them."

"Spence, what if they're already breaking the horses?"

He looked grim. "Then it's war, Aislin. And it's Fraco Ciro who declared it. He's no better than a horse thief."

"And we'd better get ready for that war," she said, looking down the canyon. "The troops are here."

Scotty MacPherson's face appeared in the glow of the lantern he was holding. His men followed at a distance down the trail. Each held a lantern, and Scotty lifted his in greeting as he moved closer. Soon they had all gathered, single file, near Aislin and Spence.

"Any sign of Ciro?" Scotty asked without dismounting.

"No," Spence replied. "But we'll soon find out. I figure the band probably left their horses near the pond at the base of the falls." He went on to tell the others what to expect when they reached the falls, how they would make the ascent to the cave and hidden valley behind.

Within minutes the group was on the move once more, this time leading their horses, Aislin on point, Spence following immediately after.

"Spence, take a look," Aislin said after they had rounded the last switchback before the falls. She held her lantern over the side of the cliff. The rest of the men did the same.

Spence nodded solemnly to her. "You were right."

Below them, near the pond, was a small remuda of horses.

The trail was wider now, and without hesitation, the group mounted and rode swiftly down the trail to the pond and dismounted. Each man seemed to instinctively know his role. Scotty led the climb, Erasmo followed with a lantern, another ten wranglers behind him, each carrying a weapon and a few others also carrying lanterns.

Aislin began the ascent with Spence immediately behind her. This time she didn't consider the danger of falling as she had the first day she and Spence had climbed the trail. Instead, she climbed steadily upward.

Spence touched her arm and nodded to the cave. Scotty had already made it across, and the men followed one by one, each jumping across the granite fissure with ease.

Finally, it was her turn. Spence squeezed her fingertips just before she jumped. She landed with the grace of a deer. As Spence landed beside her, she looked up.

Scotty was gesturing wildly, holding his lantern high. The cave was empty. Not a bedroll. Not a cooking utensil.

Not a quirt.

Without speaking, they moved through the cave and out into the meadow, dark, except for the wranglers' lanterns. It was empty.

The wranglers lifted their lights and began searching the small valley.

There was not a single wild horse, not a vaquero, to be found.

TWENTY-ONE

Camila stood to rub her back, then wiped her hands on her apron. Brighid was kneeling beside her on the rock-hard ground, a short spade in her hand.

She looked up and shaded her eyes. "Mama, are you all right?"

Camila's gaze swept over the wide expanse of dusty land in front of the small adobe. "*Sí*, sweet child. I am tired, but just a little. It is nothing to worry about."

Brighid stood and moved near her mother. She circled an arm around her waist. "You've been tired a lot lately."

Camila laughed to soothe her daughter's fears. "It is the result of all those years of laziness," she said lightly. "Too many years with servants waiting on me hand and foot."

"Mama, you've never spent a lazy day in your life."

Camila reached up to pat her daughter's round cheek. "Your help, Brighid, is all that's seeing me through. I do not know what I would do without you."

Brighid looked embarrassed to receive such a compliment. She shrugged. "I do only as I wish, Mama." She knelt again and pushed her spade into the soil.

With a sigh, Camila settled onto her knees beside her daughter. "We will bring mint from the mountains to plant, also sage from the foothills. Soon this patch of hillside will contain herbs and spices among the finest to be found in all of California."

Brighid chuckled. "If anyone can make such a thing happen, it's you, Mama." She pulled out a stubborn clump of weeds. "I saw a patch of wild onions on my way to school yesterday. As soon as the soil is prepared, I'll bring a pailful back with me."

Camila stopped her tilling. "I worry about that school of yours, Brighid. Now that we are living in the adobe, the distance is great for you to ride. And you have to pass by the squatters." It hurt her to say the word. The day the Byrnes moved from La Paloma, squatters by the dozens had planted themselves on prime land, that nearest the river. Squatters who were coarse and profane, lazy and meanspirited.

Brighid smiled. "I have five students now, Mama. You must come visit sometime." She set her spade down, and her eyes shone as she related their antics. "You should see my latest, little Berto. He's the youngest of them all now, and very possibly the brightest."

Camila smiled at her daughter's enthusiasm. "How about the tribal council? You've been worried that with one word from them, their children will no longer be allowed to learn to read and write."

"I have more to fear from some of our neighbors. They're as adamant about keeping Indians from education as Southerners are about keeping their slaves from learning to read and write."

"That is another reason, child, not to ride alone to the Soboba village. Your father has already had unpleasant dealings with the squatters."

"I will be careful, Mama. I promise." Smiling, she went back to her spading.

Still, Camila worried, no matter her daughter's assurances. She prayed silently for her as they worked side by side.

When the sun was high, the sound of an approaching horse carried toward them. Shading her eyes, Camila gazed across the fields. It was MacQuaid on one of the three horses they were allowed to keep. A few minutes later, he dismounted near the house, then moved slowly across the dusty yard. The slump of his shoulders told her that he did not carry pleasant news.

He looked at her with the distant expression that too often settled on his face lately. It made her ache for him so, for the joys they had once shared.

"My husband," she said, standing to greet him. He kissed both her cheeks, European-style, as always, then nodded formally to Brighid. Mother and daughter exchanged worried looks.

He toed Brighid's spade with his boot. "No wife or daughter of mine should be on her knees in the soil."

"Papa, I enjoy working the soil," Brighid protested. She stood now to look him square in the face. "Since when are we too good for hard work? For as long as I can remember, you told my sisters and me that we needed to learn to work because life might not always be so easy on us."

MacQuaid's expression softened. "Aye, I did at that, lassie." His eyes swept across the bone-dry lands, the empty bed of Mystic Lake in the distance. "But I preferred that it be a choice, not a necessity."

"You looked to be bearing news," said Camila, "as you came across the fields."

He nodded. "I have indeed." Camila started to kneel down next to Brighid, but MacQuaid let out a loud burst of protest. "Can you not wait on that, both of you?"

Camila glanced up and smiled, then grabbed her daughter's hand and pulled her to standing. "I could use a rest. Let's sit on the porch in the shade."

"You could use a rest, lass?" MacQuaid was studying her, and she gave him a reassuring nod.

"Only in a manner of speaking, my husband. I enjoy sitting on our porch. I never had the time, nor the inclination, at La Paloma. This porch, now that you have made the repairs, is pleasant and restful. That is all I meant."

He moved closer and placed his arm around her as they walked. Brighid followed slightly behind.

"Now," Camila said, after they were seated, she and MacQuaid on the small settee that once rested beneath the century oak in La Paloma's courtyard, Brighid on the top step of the porch, leaning back against the railing. "What is your news?"

"I've just come from the Dearbourne's. Their property foreclosed yesterday."

"We knew it was coming," Camila said, her heart aching for their friends. "But I am so very sorry. What will they do?"

"This is the strange part, and, I think, one of Hugh's gravest mistakes."

"Having to do with where they'll live?" asked Brighid, always the one to bring news, good or bad, to simple reality.

"In a way, yes. Sara will live in Pueblo de los Angeles with a cousin who recently moved there."

"And Hugh?" Camila asked. "He will not be staying with Sara?"

"He's decided to ride out to join Spence and Scotty and the girls. He and Sara are leaving this afternoon for the pueblo, then he'll head on from there to the high desert and try to intercept the company on the Old Spanish Trail."

"To help herd?" Brighid sounded as astonished as Camila felt.

"Not just help, lass. He plans to take over the drive. He feels Spence will only make a muck of it. Thinks he'll fail and lose the only chance we all have of getting back our lands. I don't know what's come over him. I've never heard him be so hard on the young man."

Camila frowned. "How can he do that to his own son?"

"He can, and he will." MacQuaid was working his jaw. "I tried to talk him out of it. Told him that I am sure that Spence will be successful. I know that boy. He's got more intelligence and courage than any other dozen men you'd want to pick all rolled together. It may be quiet grit, but it's grit nonetheless."

"Why can't Hugh see it?" Brighid asked. "Everyone else can."

MacQuaid stared out over the dry fields. "Hugh has always favored Jamie, but there's something about Spence…" He didn't finish. He just shook his head sadly.

"Hugh changed after Jamie died. There's a new bitterness about him. Something I've never before seen in the man, for all our years as friends. Sometimes I don't think I know him at all."

Camila met her husband's gaze. "Are you thinking of going too, my husband? With Hugh, I mean."

"No," he said.

"I thought you might feel a responsibility for Spence—you love him like a son."

"Aye, that is for certain. Lovin' him like a son, I mean. But I canna leave you. Besides, I have my work at the rancho. It's all we have to put food on our table."

Camila breathed easier. "We need you here—*I* need you here and not just to put food on our table," she said softly. "But in many ways, I would rest easier about our daughters if you were with them."

MacQuaid nodded. "Yet I believe the lessons they are learning need to be learned without their papa lookin' over their shoulders."

"And that's the difference," said Brighid thoughtfully.

MacQuaid and Camila both turned to their daughter. "What difference?" they asked, almost in chorus.

"Your willingness to let us discover life's lessons, God's lessons, on our own. How different than Hugh riding out to take over Spence's venture. Even if Spence fails, isn't it better to fail on his own?" She rested her chin against her knees.

"There is the savin' of the rancho to consider," MacQuaid said, defending his friend. "I believe Hugh has that in mind, not any lesson his son might learn from failin' at the effort."

"But isn't that just the point? God's the one giving the lesson, which means he's the one who will be with Spence every step of the way, whether Hugh is there or not…whether the effort fails or not." She leaned back, looking at her mother and father earnestly. "And if the effort fails, does that mean that he failed God or failed to learn his lesson?"

Camila glanced at her husband. His face reflected the same awe she was feeling about their daughter's deep thoughts about God.

MacQuaid cleared his throat. "You are saying that in God's eyes, failing to keep the ranchos may not be failing at all?"

Brighid nodded slowly. "I wonder if we think that everything must turn out right—at least right in our eyes—for us to believe that God's directing us."

"If I'm understandin' your thoughts, you're sayin' success doesn't necessarily equal God's directing of our paths. And at the same time, failure doesn't necessarily mean he wasn't with us in that either."

Brighid was watching him carefully. "Even more than that, Papa.

Maybe the greatest blessings of all come not from success, but from learning to lean on our heavenly Father in times of our greatest troubles."

"Ah, my little Brig," said MacQuaid. "Just looking at your face, listening to your sweet voice, speakin' of God's direction and love—" his voice broke, and he moved his watery gaze out over the dry lands in front of the adobe. After a moment he continued, his gaze still distant. "Child, you've just made an old man who's lost everything feel he's the richest man in the world." He paused, looking again to Brighid with a gentle smile. "And maybe I am," he said softly. "Just maybe I am."

Camila reached for his hand, lacing her fingers through his. "We all are, my husband," she murmured, looking into his lined and weary face. "Richly blessed."

Brighid saddled the old roan, kissed her mother and father good-bye, and rode down the trail that led to the Soboba village, nestled in the San Jacinto foothills. She moved the mare into an easy trot as she headed for the river.

Clouds had gathered over the jagged mountain peaks to the north, and she wondered if they could be the harbinger of coming storms. She decided to ask the Sobobas if the drought might be coming to an end. People still spoke of their mysterious predictions of the drought a few years earlier. Yet it never struck her as unusual that the Indians read such signs as yellow jackets or blooming seasons to determine weather patterns.

She was already learning as much from her Soboba students as they were from her. The children chattered endlessly about everything from catching fish in the nearby weir, to building wickiups with thatches made of branches from the high mountains.

She was so busy watching the clouds and thinking about the Soboba children that she almost didn't see the men who'd stepped onto the trail several yards in front of her.

At first there were only two, then three more joined them. They stood, rifles in front of their chests, hats pulled low over their eyes, and neck scarves wrapped around their lower faces. They had appeared out of nowhere.

She pulled the reins back harder than she intended, and the roan reared in pain from the bit. Her own heart pounding, she calmed the horse and brought her to a halt directly in front of the menacing group. The horse danced sideways nervously.

"You might as well get down now, Missy," said the man standing in the center of the group. "Either that, or we'll shoot the horse out from under you."

She needed to do as they said or make a run for it. Brighid decided on the latter. She kicked the horse in the flanks. The animal reared again, and Brighid reined her hard to the left, away from the trail.

One of the men laughed, a low, gravelly sound, and a shot rang out.

The old mare stumbled, then crumpled to the ground.

Brighid tried to stand. To run. But her right foot was pinned beneath the horse. Struggling, and now whimpering from the pain, she looked up in fright as the men sauntered toward her.

"Well, now. Lookie here," said the man with the gravelly voice. "Ain't she pretty."

Still moving toward her, the others laughed.

"Help me!" she cried, clawing the ground while trying frantically to free herself. "Help me. Please!"

Silently, they circled her, staring. Their intent was written in their cold eyes.

She screamed. It was useless, but she screamed again. And again.

A rough hand covered her mouth. She bit down. Hard. The taste of blood filled her senses.

Then her world became a swirl of darkness and terror, until at last her mind sank into a velvet black sanctuary of nothingness from which she hoped never to return.

TWENTY-TWO

Spence headed across the low rugged mountains north of the Mojave River along the trail to Bitter Spring. He was scouting the route alone today, having directed Scotty to stay with the company because of the growing danger of raids by the Paiutes.

In the two weeks since crossing the Tehachapi Pass, the company had crossed high desert country to the river to follow its meandering path deeper into the desert. And now, after leaving the Mojave, they were headed east to the last oasis before crossing a forty-mile barren stretch. The danger increased daily—for the herds, the wranglers, for all of them. Lack of water was just one trial they faced.

Fraco Ciro, the vaqueros, and the herd of wild horses with their obsidian stallion had not been seen again, though Spence suspected they were following the company at a distance. When he and Scotty scouted the trail while still in the mountains, from a lookout point they saw the dust raised by another small herd following. Though no one spoke openly about it, there was a quiet recognition of the dangers they faced from horse rustlers and thieves. Their ranks had dwindled to fewer than thirty wranglers, now that they'd lost Ciro and his band. Spence didn't like to think about what that did to their defenses.

Of course, Spence considered wryly, that same band of vaqueros might be up to no good themselves. He figured Ciro's plans mirrored their own, perhaps with the exception of taking for themselves Spence's herd. Why would Fraco go to the trouble of herding mustangs for himself, when he could have Spence's for the taking?

He spotted the spring now in the distance; Ruffian, as if sensing the water, headed into a canter toward it without urging. Bitter Spring truly rose like an oasis out of the barren desert, surrounded by tamarisk and cattails. The closer they came to it, the more enchanting it seemed, the only verdant spot in the miles of flat desert landscape.

Minutes later, Spence dismounted and let Ruffian drink from the cool waters of the cattail-edged pond. Then he ambled around to the opposite side of the spring, knelt, scooped water into his hat, and poured it over his head to wash off the trail dust. After he'd had his fill of the surprisingly sweet water, briefly wondering who'd named it Bitter Spring, he pushed himself to standing. Ruffian was now munching on the tall grasses at the edge of the pond, so Spence sat down on a rock and pulled out a map Scotty had brought to him from Fort Tejon.

It had been drawn by John C. Fremont, who had taken this exact route two decades earlier. Spence studied the trail directly ahead, looking for water that would see them through to the next stopping place. There was none, just as he had figured. The herd had to cover forty miles before reaching water. Cook could carry enough barrels of water in the wagon for the wranglers and others. But the horses could not drink for forty miles—dry, dusty miles.

He considered the problem. If they rode the herd hard to reach water faster, the horses might die from the exhaustion of the ride itself, especially with the great thirst they were bound to have. Twenty miles was a hard day; thirty, even more difficult; forty, impossible.

He studied the map again to see if he'd missed a small rock spring, even a dry stream bed where they might dig for water. It was clear; the forty-mile drive was their only option, even though it was a certainty that they would lose many of the horses. He tried not to think of how they'd brought them from their valley home, only to let them die on the trail.

He stood and brushed himself off, then headed to Ruffian, who was grazing contentedly. He'd just swung a leg over the saddle and was preparing to turn the horse back to the trail when he heard a rider approaching, hard and fast, from the southwest.

His hand on his rifle, he remained mounted as he urged Ruffian into the cover of some low-slung sandstone rocks.

Within seconds, Scotty MacPherson rode into sight, craning around frantically until he spotted Spence stepping out from cover.

The younger man looked vastly relieved as they both dismounted and exchanged greetings. "I'm glad I found you," he said, leading his horse to the spring.

"Has there been trouble?"

Scotty held up a hand in a gesture that asked Spence to give him a minute. Then he stuck his head in the spring and drank as if the water might not be there tomorrow.

Scotty had never once disobeyed a directive, even though technically he was not subordinate to Spence. Their relationship was more a partnership. No, thought Spence, it had grown beyond that into an easy camaraderie. He trusted Scotty's sound judgment. The young sergeant wasn't afraid to oppose Spence's ideas, though he never said so around anyone else. He would approach Spence later to voice his opinions, perhaps try to convince Spence of his own tactics. Spence always listened, though he didn't always agree or act on Scotty's suggestions.

Scotty poured water over his head to wash off the dust, then gulped once more from the spring. Spence wondered, as the young man stood and brushed off the excess water, if he had simply taken it upon himself to go against Spence's direct order to stay with the herd or if something else had happened.

"What's going on?" Spence frowned.

"You'll have to excuse me, if I've done the wrong thing, stepped in where I shouldn't have, by coming to you."

"You'll have to tell me first what you've stepped into," Spence said.

Scotty raked his fingers through his bright orange hair, then replaced his soaking wet hat. "Well, you see, we've had some folks meet up with us."

"Fraco Ciro?"

"No, no. Nothing like that."

"Then what, man?" Spence was getting impatient.

Scotty looked at him solemnly. "I'm not sure what to make of it, whether I should have ridden out…or waited…or…"

"I promise to help you make sense of it, MacPherson, but you've got to tell me what it is first. What folks are you talking about?"

"They're from your rancho. Enough wranglers to make up for those we lost with Ciro. Also more supplies for the trail, brought on burros."

A slow grin spread across Spence's face. "I don't see why that's any cause for consternation on your part. That sounds like the best news I've heard lately." It was especially gratifying that his father believed in the trek enough to send additional support for him. "I'd say this is cause for celebration. But the way you're standing there, looking like your dog just died, I'd say…" His voice fell off, and he narrowed his eyes. "I'd say you've got more to tell me."

Scotty nodded. Water dripped from his hat, and he removed it, wrung it out, then replaced it at an angle. "Yes, sir. I've got more to tell."

Spence stepped closer. "What is it?"

"It's about your father."

"Did he come along?" The expression on Scotty's face made him think a calamity might have befallen him. "Is he all right?"

"Oh yes. He's all right. He's more than all right." Scotty paused as if gathering courage. "He says he's come to take over the operation. Wants to be sure it's done right."

Spence felt as if he'd just been hit in the stomach. It made him want to double over in pain. "He's what…?"

Scotty said again, "I hope I'm not poking my nose in where it doesn't belong, but I thought you should know before riding back into camp."

Spence looked back to the spring…the sunlight on the water, the breeze moving the cattails, the smoky color of the tamarisk.

And he thought of Jamie. Again. Always.

"What do you plan to do?"

"First of all, get on Ruffian's back and hightail it back to the herd."

"To confront him?"

"It's past time," he said simply, striding to Ruffian. "And something I should have done a long time ago."

Scotty mounted the brown. "He was pretty adamant about being in charge; this may get ugly."

Spence swung onto the sorrel. "It's been ugly for as long as I can remember. So that's nothing new."

"I'm with you, Spence," Scotty said as they urged the horses forward. "Don't forget that. I'll support you, whatever you decide."

Spence gave him a nod and mock salute as the horses moved into a three-beat gallop across the desert.

Spence and Scotty came over a slight rise. They were riding directly into the setting sun and shaded their eyes against its glare. The dust from the herd rose in the distance. Confrontation was minutes away.

As they continued across the desert, Spence tried to formulate a plan, but none would come to him. When challenged by his father, he'd always chosen a different path, a path that would lead away from confrontation.

This was different. He would not leave. He would not give up the plan he'd worked so hard to conceive, to accomplish.

The stakes were too high. The stakes had nothing to do with selling the horses and heading back to California in time to save the ranchos. No, not those stakes.

These had to do with Spence himself. He felt called to his task. Born to the task. If he gave it up because of his father, he would be giving up part of himself. Perhaps all of himself.

He didn't know if he had the support of his men. Instinctively, he knew his father would use every tool he could against him.

He gazed out at the horizon, the cloud of dust closer now, superimposed on a red-orange sunset. They were within minutes of intercepting the company.

First he spotted Aislin on Silverheel, and Sybil riding next to her. The herd and the wranglers were a ways behind them.

Then he spotted Hugh Dearbourne, on a tall silver-spotted Appaloosa, riding point as if he belonged there.

Spence urged the sorrel to move faster. He adjusted his hat against the slant of the now waning sun. He took a deep breath and headed straight for his father, who halted his horse. He saw that the entire company was slowing to a halt, the cook wagon, the wranglers and herd. Scotty continued riding until he met up with Aislin and Sybil, then he, too, stopped to give Spence time alone with his father.

Spence touched his hat brim in greeting. "Father," he said simply.

"Spencer," came the formal reply.

"I see you've brought us some needed hands. We lost Ciro a ways back, his men. Fourteen altogether. We can use those you've brought."

His father nodded, watching him carefully.

"I can use your help," Spence said.

"I didn't come to help. I'm here to take over."

"I am captain of this outfit. You've no cause to come in and try to run that which is already running well."

His father looked surprised. But there was also a meanness in his eyes, an expression Spence remembered from childhood. It made him more determined to stand his ground.

"I brought fifteen men with me."

"Is that a threat?"

"Maybe."

"A threat that you'll take them and leave us short-handed? Or that you'll turn them loose on my men to fight for your...captaincy?"

His father laughed. "Your men, son? Where are your men?" When Spence didn't answer, he went on. "The men who've been with you work for me. When I got here during your absence, it was as natural for them as bees searching for nectar to look to me for leadership."

Spence drew in a deep breath. The belittling was too familiar. He fought the urge to turn Ruffian and ride away from it all...from his father, the herd, the men...Aislin.

"Ready to back down, are you, son?" Hugh laughed, confident that his son would do his bidding.

"As I said, I run this outfit. I have from its inception. If you and your wranglers want to stay, you're welcome to. Your pay will be your part of the cut." He smiled amiably. "You can be foreman, if you'd like. But I am captain, and I'll thank you not to forget it."

"My pay?" His father threw back his head and laughed, as though he wanted the whole company to see how humorous he thought his son's challenge was. "You are going to offer me pay?"

"I will save the rancho. I don't know how. Or when. But I will, father. With this herd, my business transactions, I'll have the means to do so. And when I do, it will be in my name, not yours."

"Surely, you wouldn't…" His father was visibly flustered and stammered when he finally found the words, "…wouldn't do that to…your mother…to me." Spence noticed his father didn't seem to doubt his ability to do such a thing; he only doubted that he might have the effrontery to do it.

"The job offer is yours. Take it or leave it."

"Foreman?"

"Yes."

His father drew himself up tall. "I will not work in a subservient position to you—"

"Father," Spence said softly, leaning toward him in the saddle, "I would be careful if I were you. I will no longer take your criticism. You've been filled with nothing but venom toward me because it was me who lived, not Jamie. I felt sorry for you, for Mother, because of your loss."

"You don't know what you're talking about."

"Don't I?" His voice was low and earnest, but uncompromising in its intent. "I will not ever apologize to you or to anyone else for being who I am. If Jamie came riding across that hillside this moment, it wouldn't make any difference. It would not change who I am. And right now, Father, I am captain. Take it or leave it."

For several moments Spence gave his father a hard look, then wheeled Ruffian around, and rode back to the herd. He called out the signal, and the company started moving forward.

"We'll make camp tonight at Bitter Spring," he yelled back to Scotty. "Spread the word. We'll have to move 'em fast to make it by nightfall."

Spence took his place at point, and, riding with his usual easiness, his hat pulled low over his forehead, he passed his father. He wondered if the confrontation was over or, judging from his father's expression, if it was just beginning.

Hugh Dearbourne watched Spence ride off. He didn't know whether to be proud or dismayed at Spence's new sense of leadership. Proud that the boy was determined to see this impossible scheme through. Or dismayed that he might undermine Hugh's own commitment to see that the scheme fail.

He signaled for the fifteen men he'd brought from Rancho Dearbourne to fall in behind him. Oh yes, they'd ride with Spence and the herd. But his own plan was of far more importance than Spence's.

A momentary twinge of guilt caused his heartbeat to increase. He hadn't known until now that Spence cared for the land. But he quickly pushed the thought from his mind and breathed easier, telling himself that Spence would find his own way in life without the land.

He moved his horse into a canter. He'd been numb so long, nothing mattered—Sara, Spence, the rancho…even Jamie's death. As soon as this land transaction was complete with Boothe and Fitzwalter, his own dream would begin. Right now, that was all he cared about.

He would proceed with tonight's meeting with Fraco Ciro to see that Spence's efforts to save the ranchos failed.

⊰───⊱

The silver-haired vaquero was waiting for him in the rocky hills above Bitter Spring just past midnight. The moon was bright enough to light his path without a lantern.

"Amigo," Ciro said, shaking his hand. "We meet again."

Hugh nodded, and plunged ahead, unwilling to exchange pleasantries with the man who was formerly in his employ. "You know that

Spencer is aware you are following behind." He kept his voice low—sounds traveled easily and clearly across the barren desert.

"Of course." The vaquero smiled, teeth gleaming even in the dark. "I am counting on you, amigo, to offer protection for us from within. Just as we had planned."

"You will have to await my signal."

"To overtake your son and his company…with your help, of course."

"Since we're planning to take the herd to New Mexico anyway," Hugh said, "we might as well let the company do the work for us. I figure Spencer is planning to break the horses along the way. They'll bring a higher price in Santa Fe."

Ciro smiled again. "*Sí*. Your son must have his father's brains."

Hugh let out an irritated snort.

Ciro went on, "We will overtake them then, sometime before they reach Abiqui."

"Yes."

"And our agreement stands. We take the horses, sell them to the highest bidder, and split the money."

"Including the horses you've got."

The vaquero narrowed his eyes. "That was not part of our agreement, *amigo*."

"It is now. I'm giving you a small fortune in trail-broken horses. Call it my cut."

"The original split is your cut, *señor*." Ciro stepped closer, a menacing look on his face. He drew himself taller, his face appearing a deathlike gray in the moonlight. "You understand, *amigo?*" He drew out the last word slowly.

Hugh stepped closer. "We will have plenty of time to come to an agreement, my friend." His tone was cold, haughty.

But Ciro didn't back down. "It is as we agreed. Nothing less. I keep the majestic horses from the secret valley. The silver they bring is mine. Mine alone."

Finally, Hugh nodded, just to placate the vaquero. He would find a way to convince him otherwise at a later meeting. "All right then. You keep your horses. We'll split the others as planned in New Mexico."

The two men shook hands once more.

"I will let you know when it is time to attack the company."

"*Sí, amigo.*" Again the glittering teeth showed in the pale light. "My men and I will be following a few days behind. We will be waiting."

TWENTY-THREE

Jamie Dearbourne crossed the Mississippi on a raft of straight-trunked young pines he'd felled in the dark of night, Broomtail swimming alongside. He then followed the Big Muddy downstream toward St. Louis, skirting towns and settlements, traveling by night, sleeping in the shelter of deserted barns or foliage by day. The journey took him fewer weeks than he or Hallie Callahan had expected. Of course, Hallie's neatly penned map guided him through shortcuts and along little-traveled trails, helping him move faster. And now that he was nearly there, he hoped her brother might have a place for him on a wagon leading to Santa Fe, as Hallie herself had suggested.

Hallie Callahan. Just saying her musical name lightened Jamie's heart. During all his days of travel since leaving her, not an hour had passed that her name wasn't on his lips, her face in his mind.

But each step westward also made him wonder if Aislin still waited for him. If so, how could he reject her for Hallie Callahan? If Aislin had remained true to him all this time, he was too honorable a man to leave her standing at the altar. No, he realized, Hallie's wisdom had kept him from making a mistake that would have hurt Aislin to the core.

As Broomtail cantered on, Jamie considered that Aislin might have found another. He tried to picture her standing beside another bridegroom. But the image, even her image, would not come to him. After his capture, he had thought of Aislin and mourned for her. Once he was herded north to Elmira with the other prisoners, her image had faded. It was as if she had never existed. It frightened him, because others had faded too. Others he loved. His mother and father. Spence. The Byrnes.

When he saw Aislin, he now wondered, would all those feelings he once had—the tenderness, caring, sense of responsibility, sense of honor—return?

And he wondered if Hallie Callahan's image would fade. It shone brighter than the midday sun, and he couldn't imagine the soft curve of Hallie's face, the vivid blue of her eyes, ever fading from his memory.

He gave Broomtail a gentle kick and headed up a gently sloping hillside to gain a better view of the Mississippi and St. Louis, spread out lazily beside it. The river stretched and curved like a mud-green snake into the southern horizon.

The sight of St. Louis, the scent of the river, caused the memory of his capture—the saloon where he met the thugs, the helpless and sick feeling of being bound and tossed into the barge's hold—to again surge into his consciousness. He thought he might be sick, and quickly dismounted, gulping in huge breaths of fresh air.

He gazed at the town lying buried in a haze off the river and, after a few moments, urged Broomtail back onto the road. He'd concentrate on finding Hallie's brother. That was all that mattered now. All he could bear to think about.

St. Louis had grown since he'd last seen it. Lining its boardwalk were saloons, inns, smithies, mercantiles, chandlers, and liveries. Gun shops were tucked here and there between the other shops, though Jamie noticed their window displays were sparse because of the war. Most prominent was the Hawken Brothers Gun Emporium in the center of town. There was a sign in the window, promising top dollar for guns turned in.

Hundreds of dock workers, shopkeepers, and travelers, mostly families, milled about. A few stray Indians in buckskins sat on benches in the shade of the boardwalk cover. Music and laughter drifted from the doorways of the saloons into the street. And from hotels near the docks, the smell of frying catfish hung in the air. Carriages and wagons rumbled along the planked streets, and a few Union soldiers on horseback rode by, prompting Jamie to head Broomtail into an alley and wait until they passed.

Dressed in Hallie's husband's old clothes, he easily blended with the crowd. Still, he didn't want to take any chances. He headed straight to the last address Hallie had for Ransom Brown, her brother: a small white house two doors down from the Church of the Good Shepherd.

He found the church within minutes, the house not long after. It was the only white house within walking distance of the church. After hitching Broomtail to a nearby post, he stepped briskly up the stairs and rapped his knuckles on the door.

There was no response. So he knocked again. Still no answer.

The yard was overgrown. Weeds had overtaken the flower bed by the front door. The whitewash on the house itself was more gray than white. Paint peeled from the front door where he stood.

He knocked again.

This time the sound of slow footsteps carried toward him.

An old woman pulled open the door. She squinted up at him. "Yes?" she said, her voice quavering.

Hallie had said her brother lived alone, and he was disappointed, knowing immediately he had the wrong house. "I'm looking for a man named Ransom Brown," he said gently to the woman. He paused. "You don't happen to know where he lives, do you?"

Her brow was wrinkled as she peered up at him. "Well, now. I believe I do," she said. "But get down here where I can see you better." She reached up and pulled his face down where she could peer into his eyes. "You look kindly enough," she said after studying him a moment. She nodded slowly. "Kindly enough, indeed."

Jamie couldn't help smiling. "Kind enough to be told his whereabouts?" he asked as he straightened again.

"No, kind enough to come into my house and have some vittles," she said.

"You said you knew how I could find Ransom Brown," he reminded her.

She brushed away the comment with her small, narrow hand. "I said I know where he lives," she corrected. "Not how you can find him."

Before he could answer, she went on. "We can't discuss Ransom

Brown until we see about getting you something rib-stickin', child." Then she halted. "And we can't do that until I know your name."

Child? He grinned. It had been a long time since anyone had called him that. "My name is Jamie Dearbourne."

"Pleased to meet you, Mister Dearbourne," she said, sticking out her hand and giving his a vigorous shake. "Pleased indeed. And I'm Gertie Hill. Folks around here just call me Aunt Gertie." Her pronunciation made it sound like *Ain't Gertie*.

"The pleasure's mine, Aunt Gertie," he said.

She was squinting at him again. After a moment she gently pinched his upper arm, right through his shirt sleeve. "Not much between my pinch and your bones, son. You've been a long time without food."

"Yes."

"Then let's remedy that straightaway. You follow me now." She held open the door and he entered the house. With tiny steps, she led him into one large room, a great room, dominated by the fireplace at one end. The fire crackled merrily, and a heavy iron pot on a swing-arm rested above the flames. The aroma of whatever she was boiling in that pot made his mouth water.

Her wrinkled face pinched into a smile as she watched him. "Chicken and dumplings," she pronounced. "You can sit yourself down over there." She nodded to a table covered with a blue gingham cloth and a few blue willow dishes stacked at one end.

He started toward the table, but her small arm shot out and grabbed him with an iron-fisted grasp. "I wasn't finished," she said. "I was about to say, you can sit yourself down over there—after you wash up. And I'll show you where you can do that. You follow me now, son."

She hobbled with short, careful steps through another door and down a long hallway. He slowly followed her into a bedroom, grinning as he walked. A quilt-covered iron bed was at one end, a chest of drawers at the other, with a red, yellow, and blue braided rug between. The washstand was next to the room's single window, and its lace curtains billowed in the breeze. The rose-covered wallpaper was faded to a pale ivory, but it was as elegant a room as Jamie ever remembered setting eyes on. She gave him a crisp nod, then left him alone to wash.

A few minutes later, Jamie joined her in the great room, trail dust scrubbed from his face, dirt from beneath his fingernails. He wondered if she might inspect behind his ears. He couldn't stop smiling.

"Now you can sit yourself down," she said, nodding to his setting of flatware and blue willow dishes at the table. "I've already eaten, but I'll sit myself, and keep you company."

"Thank you," he said, taking his place. Steam rose from the chicken and dumplings in his bowl.

"Now, I believe you plumb forgot your manners," she said, standing at the end of the table and looking at him with small, bright eyes.

He tried to think what she might be talking about, then realized. Up he sprang and pulled out her chair. She settled into it like a queen, patting the little gray bun at the nape of her neck. "That's better," she said. "Now, Mr. Jamie Dearbourne, you may be seated."

He settled into the chair beside her and noticed that her hands were folded on the table in front of her. She seemed to be watching to see what he would do.

He grinned. "Would you like for me to pray?"

Her smile was as wide as the prairie heavens. "Well, yes now," she said. "I think that would be right nice."

He bowed his head, but before he began to pray, she took his big rough hand between her small ones. "There, now," she murmured, patting his hand as if he were a child again. "You may begin."

"Father God," he prayed, "thank you for leading me to this house. Thank you for the generous and loving spirit of this woman, your servant."

Hallie came to his mind, and he could almost hear her words. *When you held that boy, Ben Haven, your arms were God's arms, you were his voice. He wasn't in that prison alone. You were there. Did you ever consider that God wanted you to be there at that particular time, for that particular child? You may have thought you were alone in that prison, Mr.*

Dearbourne. But God was there with you. He was holding you, just as you were holding that child.

He considered this woman next to him, her hand warm in his. She'd brought him, a stranger, into her home, to feed and care for him as he'd done for Ben. *God was with you, even when you didn't know, Mr. Dearbourne!*

"Oh, Lord, I am so grateful for your loving care…" His voice choked, and he couldn't continue.

Aunt Gertie patted his hand and finished for him. "You direct our paths in ways we don't always figure on, Lord," she said. "You lead us to others of your children in need, you bring those in need to us." Her voice rose with gladness. "I'm so glad to be part of your great big family, God!"

She let out a satisfied sigh. "So very glad! Fact is, my Friend, I could sing praises all day long just about your goodness…" She paused again, then laughed. "Oh, and I almost forgot, Lord. We thank you kindly for this food you have so bountifully provided. Amen."

She looked up at Jamie. "Now, you can eat, child. You fill up while I tell you about Ransom Brown."

As he sliced his spoon into a dumpling, Aunt Gertie fixed herself a cup of hot water and honey.

"Ransom Brown was my boarder for a time," she said as she slid back into her chair. "Lived here nigh onto two years. Loved him like a son. God didn't see fit to bless me with children, though he's brought many across my path that I could call my own." She lifted her cup and took a sip.

"Well, sir. He'd come from Westport, just spitting distance from Independence where his freighting business was located. Brought his young wife, Susannah. Oh, my, she was a pretty little thing. And spunky. She'd traveled the Santa Fe Trail with him, lived in New Mexico for a time. She didn't know how to slow down, that one." She shook her head sadly. "And oh my, how they loved each other."

Sadness was sure to follow, he knew, because of Aunt Gertie's tone as she went on. "They were expecting their first child when they arrived. The freighting business had nearly died out because of the war. Besides, they wanted to raise their child in civilization, they told me."

Aunt Gertie noticed his nearly empty bowl, and stood to refill it, continuing her story as she did so. "But they'd only been here a short time—"

"They were to stay here, you mean, with you?"

"Oh yes. I met them at church, invited them right home with me that day," she said with a smile. "They said it was temporary. They wanted a house of their own…for the baby.

"They'd been here only a few days when…" Her eyes filled, and she pulled out a lace-edged handkerchief. "…when Susannah's time came."

"Time?"

She patted his hand. "Time to deliver, son. But something was wrong. She had a healthy little boy, as big and beautiful a child as I'd ever laid eyes on." She shook her head sadly. "Then Susannah fell to rantings. Her thin body shook with fever. She died in just a few days."

"And the baby?"

"The sweet angel died only one day after his mama. Whatever it was took her, took him, too."

Jamie laid down his spoon. "I'm sorry."

"Well, sir, it was a hard thing for that young man." She took a sip of honey water. "He loved Susannah. Said more than once, after her passing, how he'd planned to surprise his sister over in Kentucky with his new wife and baby. Family was important to Ransom. Told me how he hadn't the spirit in him to write and tell his sister what happened. Said she'd had enough grief of her own without adding his to it."

"Hallie Callahan."

She gave him a sharp look and cocked her head.

"His sister. Hallie Callahan."

"You know her, son?"

"She sent me here to find her brother."

"Did she now?"

He nodded. "I'm making my way west. She told me about Ransom's business. Thought he might have some ideas on how I could work my way along the Santa Fe Trail."

Aunt Gertie studied him a moment. "I think he'd like that."

"You haven't told me where I can find him. Is he here in St. Louis?"

"Oh no. He stayed almost two years. Lived right here with me while he grieved and healed."

Grieved and healed. From what Jamie had seen of Gertie Hill and her home, he couldn't imagine a better place to do both.

"Then not more than three weeks ago, he left to return to West-port. Had a grand new idea for a business. Gave him a spark of life that I hadn't seen in him since Susannah's passing."

"What business was that?"

"Horse trade."

"Horse trade?" He squinted his eyes in thought.

"Yes, sir. On the Santa Fe Trail." Her eyes brightened as if she'd dreamed up the plan herself. "Seems there are herds of wild horses in the West that wranglers are trying to move east for the war effort. Ran-som took it upon himself to start up his freight business again, only this time it's not goods he's packing along the trail. It'll be horses. Wild horses." There were little spots of color in her cheeks, and she sat for-ward in excitement as if it were her own adventure.

"You'd like to be there with him, wouldn't you, Aunt Gertie?"

She lifted her cup to her lips and smiled at him over the rim. "I'd give up my headstandin' to go."

"Headstanding?"

"Stand on my head every morning to get the blood to my head. Gives me a clearer mind throughout the day. But I'd gladly give it up for a ride on that kind of trail."

"Did you ever tell Ransom you wanted to go?"

She laughed. "Didn't think of it myself until after he'd ridden off." She paused, her smile fading. "Besides, what good would an old lady be on such a trek? Only trouble, I'd say. Only trouble."

This time he patted her hand. "I think you'd be a welcome addition to any trek west. As long as it wasn't too hard on you."

"Well, it's not worth the trouble to consider," she said with a flutter of her hand as if brushing away the thought. "Now, back to catching you up to him. He'll be muleskinnin' his way to Santa Fe in Conestogas packed to the hilt with goods to sell. Whatever profit he makes will buy the horses. Thousands of horses." She laughed, her good humor restored. "What I'm trying to tell you, child, is that you've got a good chance of catching Ransom. He'll be driving a team of mules. You'll be on horseback."

She glanced at his empty bowl. "You look like you could use another."

He grinned. "Yes ma'am, I believe I could."

Aunt Gertie stood to take his bowl. "You'll spend the night here, then I'll pack you a meal so's you can leave at sunup."

"I don't want to put you out." He pictured the room with the quilt-covered bed. "You weren't expecting company…"

Standing near the pot of chicken, she threw up a hand. "Laws. You're just another of God's children. One more he's sent my way. Put out?" She laughed. "Never!"

He smiled. "All right then. But I've got a question for you."

She ladled more large chunks of chicken and tender dumplings into his bowl and made her way back to the table with tiny, hobbling steps. "I don't think you'll ever fill," she said with a wink as she set it down in front of him. She fixed herself another cup of hot water and honey, then settled again into her chair. "Now, what's your question, child?"

"You speak of Ransom Brown like he's your son."

"That's true. Love him the same."

"You'd like to see him again?"

"I'm hoping I do sometime this side of the veil."

"Why don't you come with me?"

A wide smile spread across her wrinkled face. "I'd only slow you down."

"Do you have a buckboard?"

She looked at him thoughtfully, as if truly considering the notion.

Then, with a twinkle in her eyes, she smiled. "I have a better idea." She patted her hair. "One that I think will suit us just fine."

"What is that?"

"I've had a hankering for quite some time to take a steamboat up the Missouri."

"To Independence?" He thought of the cost involved. "I'm sorry. I don't think I can—"

She cut him off. "God sent one of his own to me. You're in his care, child. And part of that care might be for you to accept a gift or two along the way. Do you think you can set aside your pride to do that?"

He swallowed hard. "Yes ma'am. Since you put it that way."

"I've prayed for a little adventure in my life." She narrowed her eyes in thought. "And if I'm understanding you correctly, from the nearly starved look of you, you've been running. A long time. Maybe from prison. Maybe the law." When he started to speak, she shushed him. "It doesn't matter to me where you've been or what you've done. But if it's the Federals…or even the Rebs…you're hiding from…"

She paused, her eyes sparkling. "I'm thinking that you, dear boy, traveling with your feeble old Aunt Gertie, will not be confronted. You'll be my sweet and doting nephew, my traveling companion." She smiled triumphantly, as if glad to consider pulling the wool over the eyes of any authorities they might run into. "I've got the money for our tickets. We'll purchase them first thing tomorrow."

Feeble? Old? He almost laughed. She started to rise from the table, and he reached for her hand to stop her. "Will you come all the way to California with me? My family has room—"

"One thing I've learned," she said, interrupting him again, "is that I shouldn't plan too far ahead. Takes the adventure out of life. Just think, if I'd planned to take the trek west with Ransom, I'd have missed out meeting another of God's lambs. So, dear boy, I might go on to California with you. But most likely, I'll head back from Santa Fe with Ransom, maybe help with the cook wagon. I've had a hankering to ride trail with a herd of wild horses." She shrugged. "But then, you never know. I'd like to stick my bare feet in that big Pacific Ocean someday too."

She stood. "I'll see to packing my trunk."

He stood with her. "You won't need to give up your headstandin', you know."

She gazed up at him and laughed. "Well, now. I like that way of thinking, son. But you may be wrong. Standing on my head in a steamer's one thing. But standing on my head in a Conestoga's quite another."

As he cleared the blue willow dishes from the table, he heard her footsteps down the hall. She was humming as she went, a rattling, off-tune hymn. It was the most beautiful sound this side of heaven.

TWENTY-FOUR

In the pearl gray of dawn the following morning, Jamie hitched Broomtail to Aunt Gertie's wagon and loaded her trunk in the bed. She closed up her window shutters and locked her front door, then turned to walk toward the wagon.

Jamie smiled as he saw her. She was dressed completely in gray and white, from her worn straw hat with its froth of silk flowers to her slightly frayed velvet traveling dress and matching gloves. A tiny gold watch was pinned to her lapel.

She bobbed her head at him, the petals on her hat shaking. "I'm ready," she said, "though I barely had time for headstandin', so I'm not quite myself."

He chuckled. "One would never know it. You cut quite a striking figure, ma'am." He swept his hat off and gave her a small bow.

She took his arm and stepped slowly to the buckboard. He helped her climb to the front bench and seat herself. She held her face straight forward, her chin tilted upward, hat brim level with the horizon.

Jamie climbed onto the bench beside her and flicked the reins. Broomtail started forward and the wagon creaked and rattled as they pulled away from the small white house. Aunt Gertie didn't look back once.

They reached the dock by sunup and, shortly after, had purchased passage for the two of them and Broomtail to Independence.

"Now, son," Aunt Gertie said once the trunk was unloaded, "you take the buckboard to the livery on the corner. Get what you can for the old wagon. We'll buy a sturdier vehicle once we're in Westport."

"You've thought this through."

She looked up at him, the sunlight striking her face. "You have no idea how long."

A few minutes later, he returned with a fistful of money and Broomtail in tow just as the steamboat, the *Southern Belle,* began boarding passengers and freight.

Aunt Gertie waited, seated with hands folded, near her trunk. She waved her small gloved fingers when she saw him. Jamie signaled for a porter to see to the trunk, then he took Aunt Gertie's elbow to help her aboard.

A few Union soldiers lolled about, but Jamie kept his chin high as he escorted the wiry woman past them. At just the right moment, she halted in front of a group of officers and reached up to pat Jamie's cheek. Then she bobbed her head to the officers. They gave her a friendly look without so much as a glance at Jamie, then moved on.

"Haven't had this much fun in years," she said when they were out of earshot.

"Would you like to go to your cabin?" He thought she might want to rest from the excitement of the morning, and he worried that she might go beyond duty's call trying to help him avoid Union soldiers.

She glanced up at him as if he'd just asked her to ride the paddle-wheel. "Why, I don't want to miss a bit of this voyage. In fact, I do believe I'll have a cup of tea and sit and watch the water slide by."

"Yes, ma'am," Jamie said, chuckling. Somehow her request didn't surprise him. Nothing about Gertie Hill surprised him. In fact, everything about her delighted him. "One cup of tea coming up."

He found a small, round table with two chairs and pulled one out for Aunt Gertie. When she had settled into her chair and adjusted her hat, he left in search of tea.

Just then, the big paddlewheeler pulled away from the dock with a lurch. He turned to see Gertie rock precariously in her chair. The two officers she'd smiled at earlier were standing nearby and rushed to her side.

"Oh my!" she said, holding on to her straw hat as they caught her. "Oh my!"

Jamie was poised, ready to run to her aid, but halted when he saw the men pull up two more chairs, obviously at Gertie's invitation. If he bolted now, they might suspect him, so he blew Gertie a kiss and headed inside to look for her cup of tea.

When he returned, one of the men was leaning back in his chair, laughing at something Gertie had just said. The other looked about as if watching for someone.

He took a deep breath and headed to the table.

"Why, Jamie, thank you, child," Gertie said, her voice sweet as sugar as he set down the set down the steaming cup. She beamed at the officers. "This is the boy I've been telling you about. My favorite nephew."

Jamie nodded curtly, then pulled up a chair to sit at Gertie's elbow. "Glad to meet you," he said, when they'd exchanged names.

"Your aunt was just telling us you're taking her back to California," said Lieutenant Kenwood, the older of the two men.

Jamie glanced at Gertie, now sipping her tea. She raised her eyebrow and nodded slightly, silk flowers bobbing.

"Yes, that's right," he said, hoping his uncertainty didn't show. "Planning to head west on the Santa Fe."

"So she said." The younger man, who'd introduced himself as Captain Hugo, looked sharply at Jamie. "You look familiar," he said. "Have we met before?"

Jamie gazed at Hugo. He was right. There was something in the man he recognized as well. Elmira? Or the trek from Tennessee to New York? A number of Union officers had taken turns herding the prisoners north. Hugo might have been one of those. A shiver spidered down his spine as he stared at the man. "I think not," he said finally.

"I don't know…" He squinted at Jamie. "Where was it you said you were from?"

"I didn't say."

Aunt Gertie laughed, breaking into the conversation. "Well, now, where are you men headed?"

"New Mexico," said Kenwood. "We're joining up with our regiment in Independence."

"You'll be heading the same direction we are then?" Aunt Gertie asked, beaming. "That beats all, doesn't it, Jamie?"

He nodded. "Quite a coincidence." He could feel Hugo's eyes studying him.

"We'll be traveling with a Conestoga train. All we'll see of you is your dust," Aunt Gertie put in.

"That's true. We're a cavalry unit," Lieutenant Kenwood said almost in passing. His attention was on Jamie. "Where're you from, son?"

"California."

"I knew a prisoner once from California. Skinny kid," said Hugo. "Dead ringer for you." He studied Jamie with narrowed eyes.

"That right?" Jamie said, his voice calm, his heart pounding. He studied the man, searching his memory, the myriad faces, those who'd befriended him, those who'd beaten him. Nothing.

Aunt Gertie broke in, "Gentlemen, you'll need to excuse me. I'm feeling a bit lightheaded." She stood, swaying dramatically, touching her forehead with the back of her dainty, gloved hand. "Jamie, dear, will you escort me to my cabin? I do declare, there was too much sugar in my tea. I feel ready to swoon."

Jamie, standing beside her, took her arm. She leaned against him and sighed. The officers stood, alarmed, their attention now on Aunt Gertie. She touched Lieutenant Kenwood's arm. "Such a handsome man," she said, smiling weakly. "I bet your mother's proud."

He colored, looking pleased. "Well, ma'am, I couldn't say," he said.

"And you." She gazed up at Captain Hugo, towering above her. "You, son, look like such a brave soul. I'm sure you've made your mother proud in this war."

He met her gaze, shoulders back and chin jutting forward. "Ma'am, you make me proud to be a soldier," he said reverently. Then he lifted her hand and kissed it.

"Jamie," she said, faintly. "You'd better see me to my cabin, son."

"If you'll excuse us," he said with a nod to the two men, who parted like the Red Sea. His arm around Gertie's shoulders, Jamie moved slowly between them.

Once they reached her cabin, Aunt Gertie was back to her wiry, spry self. "Now it's time for you to tell me your story," she said. "And I want to hear it all. If I'm going to help you, I'll need to know where you've been and why."

"Do you need to rest first? It's a long story."

She laughed. "Of course not. Never felt better in my life." She removed her hatpin, then her hat, and patted her hair. "Now," she sighed, leaning back into a horsehair chair in the corner. "You tell me your story, son."

He sat in the opposite corner and began to talk. Her eyes were closed, and once when he hesitated, thinking she was asleep, she said, "Go on. I'm listening."

So he did. He told her everything. About leaving California. His capture. Being shot in the back. The long trek north to Elmira. The child, Ben Haven, dying in his arms. He told her about Hallie Callahan. And love. Also about Aislin. His promise to her.

When he'd finished, she was staring into his eyes. "It's quite a journey you've been on, child."

He nodded. "Yes."

"Hallie Callahan is right though."

"About healing?" He'd told Aunt Gertie everything Hallie had said about it.

"Yes."

"I know that now. I didn't think so at the time Hallie said it. But I know it now." He paused. "It's a good thing she didn't take me up on my offer to come with me to California. I don't know what to expect when I get there."

"Do you ask every lady you meet to accompany you to California?" She laughed merrily.

He couldn't help grinning. "Only those I fall in love with."

"Ah, go on now, child!" She looked pleased. Then she peered narrowly at him.

"What about forgiveness?" she said, leaning forward slightly. "You've endured pain and great suffering at the hands of others."

He swallowed hard. "Healing is one thing, forgiveness quite another."

"Maybe they're the same."

"It wouldn't matter. I can't forgive what was done to me. Or what was done to others." The image of Ben Haven's face wouldn't leave him as he said the words. The boy's starvation-swollen stomach. His skinny arms and legs. "I can't forgive."

"I thought not," she said, her eyes closed again. "I thought that about you."

"I know by your tone, you think I must," he said, almost angrily.

Her eyes were open now, looking right into his soul. "Your Lord did. And what was done to him was worse."

For a moment, he had no answer. Then he said, "But he was without sin. I'm a sinner."

"Have you ever heard of the gift of grace?" Aunt Gertie asked with a faint smile. "God's grace?"

"No."

"Are you a perfect man, Jamie?"

He let out a short laugh. "Of course not."

"I thought that about you too." She chuckled.

"What are you getting at?"

"Only this. If God can forgive you, why can't you forgive others?" She leaned forward, staring at him intently. "If he can give you the gift of grace—mercy, forgiveness, even love—why can't you give the same to others who are less than perfect?"

He started to sputter that she didn't know what she was talking about, that she hadn't walked in his shoes, suffered what he'd suffered, when he remembered Hallie. He had accused her of much the same thing, only to find her suffering had been worse than his. He didn't know Gertie's story; it would be wrong to judge.

"Maybe someday I'll come to that kind of forgiveness," he said gently. "But right now, Gertie, it's something I can't do."

Her expression was loving. "I know that too, son. But it's something you need to start thinking about."

"For healing?" He smiled at her wisdom.

"Yes. Now," she continued with a sigh, "with all the excitement of the morning, I do need to rest. Leave me, please, son."

"Shall I wake you for the noon meal?"

"Yes, child," she said sleepily.

He planted a kiss on her forehead before leaving her cabin.

"God bless you, child," she murmured just before he closed the door behind him.

The next few days were uneventful as the paddlewheeler made its way to Independence. Now that Aunt Gertie knew the subjects to steer clear of, any conversations with the Union officers were easily guided away from the war between the States to life in New Mexico, the Conestoga journey on the Santa Fe Trail, and the difficulties of the trail beyond.

On the morning of the day they would dock in Independence, Jamie was heading to Aunt Gertie's cabin when he ran into Captain Hugo. The man blocked his path.

"Excuse me," Jamie said, his tone pleasant.

"I remembered where I've seen you," Captain Hugo said, standing directly in front of Aunt Gertie's door.

Jamie halted, afraid to breathe. "That right?"

"It was on the march to Elmira. You were a prisoner. One we picked up at Fort Donelson."

"I don't know what you're talking about."

"You'd been shot in the back. A deserter, as I recall. Lower than pond scum."

Jamie stared at him, a whirl of emotion filling his senses. Fear. Rage. An overpowering desire to pound the man's face into pulp. His hands fisted. But he didn't answer.

Hugo stepped closer. "There a price on your head? You escape

Elmira? Now you're heading back to California?" He spat on the carpeted floor outside Gertie's stateroom. "Hiding behind the skirt of an old lady."

"Who you calling an old lady?" The voice seemed to come from nowhere.

Hugo wheeled toward Aunt Gertie's door. The little woman stood in the doorway, a pistol pointed at the man's chest.

Captain Hugo blinked in surprise. "Now, ma'am, I meant no offense."

"None taken," she said calmly. "Now, I want you to walk with us to the deck. You holler, and I fire. Got that?"

He swallowed hard and nodded.

"Good," she said. "Jamie, take his firearm. Then walk beside him just in case he tries anything."

Jamie, stifling a smile, did as he was instructed.

"All right then," Aunt Gertie said. "Let's go upstairs." She hung her straw hat over the hand with the pistol, keeping the barrel pointed at Hugo's back.

The captain was sweating freely. She nudged him with the gun, and he started forward.

When they reached the deck, Aunt Gertie smiled pleasantly at the few officers they met and nodded to a soldier or two. Jamie followed her lead and did the same.

"Over there," Gertie instructed, nodding to the disembarking gate. Jamie, walking close to the captain, turned him toward it.

"What do you plan?" Captain Hugo muttered.

"A lesson, that's all. Remember, I'm just a little old lady. No one to fear, sir. Not at all."

The captain snickered, and she jabbed him in the ribs with the barrel of the pistol. He sobered.

When they reached the gate, she said, "You may step over, Captain, if you'd be so kind."

He looked at her with a raised brow, and she waggled the hat-covered gun just enough so he was aware she still meant business. He glanced around, but none of the other passengers were paying any attention to them. Finally, he stepped over the railing.

"Now jump, sir," she said pleasantly. "I hope you can swim." She rammed the pistol closer.

He made a grab for it, but lost his balance and fell backward. He seemed too stunned, or embarrassed, to let out even the shortest yelp.

"Oh dear," Aunt Gertie said. "Man overboard. Oh dear. We'll need to inform the pilot."

Jamie simply stared at her in awe.

"Well, not too soon though." She glanced down at the small gold watch pinned to her lapel. "In an hour or so, we'll tell the captain we saw Captain Hugo jump overboard."

Still holding the concealed gun in one hand, she took Jamie's arm with the other. "I just hope the dear soul can swim."

TWENTY-FIVE

By midafternoon the *Southern Belle* had docked in Independence, the trail head of both the Oregon-California and Santa Fe Trails. Jamie hired a carriage and tied Broomtail behind, and they headed to Westport, arriving well after dark at one of the town's three hotels.

It wasn't until morning that Jamie set out to find Ransom Brown in the small, wind-kicked town and discovered it was mostly made up of vagabonds—muleskinners, guides, scouts, trail pilots—who paid little attention to the comings and goings of others and thus had never heard of Ransom Brown. He finally found a shopkeeper who told him that Ransom had rolled out three days earlier with his Conestoga freight company.

Because of marauding Indian bands and harsh weather, Santa Fe was still a dangerous route for travelers, but no matter, he and Gertie would need to follow immediately if they planned to catch the train. Jamie wondered how fast he could travel with the older woman in tow, and how safe he could keep her.

For the first time, he doubted the wisdom of his suggestion that she accompany him. Though as soon as he considered it, he had to smile. She'd saved his hide the previous morning. Who was protecting whom?

He headed back to the hotel, mulling over whether they should buy a heavy farm wagon or attempt the trek by horseback, then double up in one of the Conestogas when they reached the train.

When he brought it up with Aunt Gertie later that afternoon, she smiled. "Oh, that," she said. "I plan to go in a carriage."

"Carriage?"

"The finest we can buy." She settled onto the corner of her bed, primly folded hands on her lap. "A brougham. Doesn't have to be new. But I would like it to be presentable."

"One horse?" He thought of the old swayback Broomtail pulling such a thing.

"No. Let's buy three to go with Broom," she said sweetly. "Give the poor thing some company."

"I'm not sure that a carriage will work on the trail. It's rutted. Rough. You have no idea."

She dismissed his words with a flutter of one hand. "Oh my, son. I've read all about it. Susan Magoffin traveled the same trail in a carriage years ago. I read her memoirs. Tipped over only once. I'm certain that if that little thing could do it, we can."

She pulled out her purse, released the drawstring, and handed him a roll of bills. "Now, you go down to the livery and see what you can find for us. Hurry now, and when you return, we'll have supper."

Jamie swallowed hard as it struck him that he was taking orders from a woman half his size and older by decades. He was Jamie Dearbourne. Heir to Rancho Dearbourne. He'd ordered people around for years. His brother. Aislin. Her sisters.

He'd taken pride in his leadership, his ideas, his power, his answers.

Now this little lady was making decisions about how they were going to travel the perilous Santa Fe Trail. Gertie Hill. Standing here, bright eyes sparkling, lined face pinched into her familiar smile.

He threw back his head and laughed out loud. "Gert, you're priceless," he said. "Absolutely priceless."

She laughed, a low, rattling sound. "Glad you noticed," she said. She seemed pleased he'd called her Gert. Perhaps it was more fitting now that she'd be traveling the rough trail.

"I think you're right. We will travel in style. I'll go see what I can find." He paused. "Any particular color you have in mind?"

She smiled again. "Well, sir. I've always fancied gray."

"Then gray it will be." He headed out the door, still laughing. He hadn't felt so much peace since being with Hallie Callahan.

"I'll wait for you in the downstairs parlor," she called after him.

He was back within the hour, only to find that Gert had disappeared. He tried not to worry, but he couldn't help it. He paced the empty parlor, waiting. Finally she rushed in, cheeks pink with excitement.

"I got the rest," she said.

"The rest of what?"

"Our supplies."

"You did what? How did you...? I mean, you couldn't possibly carry..."

She raised her hand. "Everything will be delivered here by sunup tomorrow. I'm assuming that's when we want to leave."

"I thought we'd get the rest of our supplies tomorrow."

"No need. It's done." She brushed off her gloved hands. "It's all done."

Jamie sat down weakly on one of the flowered sofas. "What did you buy?"

Gert perched on the sofa beside him, reciting a litany of food supplies, cooking utensils, tents and blankets for sleeping, even a pot of bear grease for the wheels.

When she finished, he only asked, "Will there be room in the carriage for all that?"

She smiled. "No need. I bought a pack mule, too. Name's Lafayette. Beautiful shade of gray."

He sighed. "Is there anything you haven't thought of?"

She sighed, a long and satisfied sigh. "No," she said. "I do believe I've thought of everything."

Early the next morning, they met in the parlor. Gert was dressed in another gray traveling dress, covered with a long woolen cape. The straw hat was perched, straight as the prairie horizon, atop her gray hair. Ever the lady, even starting the difficult trek west.

True to her word, the supplies soon arrived at the front door of the hotel, and as soon as Jamie brought around the carriage from the livery, drawn by three sturdy grays and Broomtail, he helped Gert into the vehicle. Lafayette was tied behind as soon as his packs were loaded with their supplies, and Gert's trunk was strapped to the back bench of the carriage.

The sun was lifting over the horizon behind them when Jamie flicked the whip above the backs of the horses and the carriage rolled down the rutted dirt road leading out of town. Gert sat, eyes straight forward, gloved hands folded on her lap, silk flowers bobbing with each bump and sway of the carriage.

They arrived at Shawnee Wells by midday, stopped for their noon meal, then headed back onto the trail, hoping to make first water by nightfall. The horses moved slowly and surely along, the silence of the prairie broken only by their hoofbeats and the jangle of reins, once in a while the pop of the whip.

The sun gleamed on the winter-brown prairie grasses, and the winds whipped them into golden waves. Something about the expanse of the sky made Jamie think about the rancho lands at home.

For the first time since leaving Elmira, he was flooded with memories of the land he once loved more than life…riding his stallion across the fields and into the hills…looking up at the rugged snow-capped peaks that jutted into the purple heavens. He remembered how in spring the foothills were covered with carpets of wildflowers. Natural springs bubbled from the earth, attracting game; and farther down the mountainside, grass, greener than anything the East could boast, shot up tall and lush, a haven for great herds of California's mule deer.

And the ranchos—they almost seemed as one in his memory—the windswept lands, jagged and rocky cliffs, the rolling herds of cattle, the warmth of both rancho houses—his own, and the Byrnes's La Paloma, his second home. He pictured now, for the first time, riding onto his land. He pictured the welcome. His mother's arms. His father's proud face. And Spence, the brother he loved.

The carriage rocked along the rutted trail, and he glanced across the bench seat to Gert. Her eyes were closed against the slant of the sun, and she appeared to be resting.

He popped the whip lightly above the team as a prairie dog skittered from beneath the grass and across the trail. The horses calmed, and he went back to his reverie.

He was heading home, and now the reality struck him afresh. During his first few weeks of escape, his thoughts were on survival alone. Now, they were on life. He drew in a deep breath, taking in the scent of the sunbaked soil and fragrant grass. Yes, life!

Aislin. They were promised to each other. She'd told him she would wait for him forever. They would certainly marry as soon as he arrived home. He pushed all thoughts of Hallie Callahan from his mind and tried to focus on Aislin and the love he once had for her.

But try as he might, he felt no love; he pictured only emptiness where once her being occupied his heart. Her memory had faded so long ago that every sense of her was gone. The color of her eyes. The sweep of her hair. The outline of her profile.

Yet why did Hallie's come so readily to mind? He remembered her cornflower-hued eyes, the roundness of her cheek, the tint of her brown hair. And sweet Emma. He remembered holding her in his arms. There was still an ache where the child's head had laid against his shoulder.

"You're letting out troubled sighs," Aunt Gertie said, interrupting his thoughts.

He glanced toward her and smiled. "Don't tell me I woke you with them."

"Laws, no. I'm far too full of excitement to sleep." She frowned, her gaze fixed on him. "What's troubling you so, child?"

"The closer I get to home, the more I wonder how much has changed there."

"Life has probably gone on without you. Does that bother you?"

He grinned, squinting against the sun hanging like a red ball above the western horizon. "How is it you have me figured out so well?"

She laughed. "Comes from years of experience dealing with all the children God's sent my way."

"I am to inherit my father's land, marry the daughter of our neighbor and friend. Someday our ranchos will be one."

"Sounds like a big piece of land."

"It is…will be. The combined acreage will make the rancho the largest in the southern half of the state."

She reached up to tilt the brim of her hat to shade her eyes. "Is that what you want?"

"The land is part of me. I grew up exploring it from end to end, loving every rock and bush and sprout of grass on it." He laughed at the childlike admission. "Sometimes when I was in prison, in the middle of filth and vermin and the smells of the dying, I couldn't picture my family's faces, but I could picture the land. I could smell the dust after a summer storm, I could see the hills covered with wild lilacs and poppies."

He turned to her. "The land became almost a living, breathing person, calling me home."

"I always figured the greatest beauty on earth is patterned after heaven," Gert said. "After all, the Creator shows us himself with his creation. I wouldn't be ashamed of such a love for your land, child."

They rode for a few minutes without speaking. Finally, she said, "You told me there's a woman waiting for you there."

"Yes. Aislin Byrne."

"And do you love her?"

The carriage rattled along, pulled by the now-plodding, slowing horses. It would be time to feed and water them soon. He scanned the horizon for signs of foliage marking their next stopping place. But nothing broke the flat expanse of grasslands.

"I don't know. I'm hoping that when I see her, those feelings I once had will be there once again."

"What kind of love did you feel for Aislin?" Gert asked, studying him.

"We were expected to marry. We knew it from childhood, so we accepted each other on those terms. I think our love grew out of friendship."

"There's nothing wrong with that," Gert said, her face again turned westward. The sun hung closer to the ground, and she shaded her eyes beneath the hat brim.

"It doesn't really matter now though," he said. "I plan to marry Aislin as soon as I get back. We are betrothed. That fact hasn't changed. I'm a man of my word."

"Sounds honorable," Gert said, though her tone said otherwise.

He turned to her. "You don't think I should keep my commitment?"

"I think you should pray about such a step."

He chuckled. "In Gert Hill's eyes, I've got more needing fixing than not."

She didn't laugh, but turned to him with a steady gaze, her eyes still shaded by her hand. "We all do, son."

Honor and commitment. No matter what else had vaporized during his suffering, these remained, providing the very foundation of his life. They would not change. Neither would his pledge to Aislin Byrne.

In the distance, a clump of trees marked first water. He flicked the reins, and the team lurched forward as if smelling water. Their hoofbeats pounded the hard-packed dirt trail, and the carriage rocked precariously as the horses hurried to where they would strike camp for the night.

≈

For two days and nights, Jamie pushed the team as fast as he dared. He kept a close watch on Gertie, for fatigue or dehydration, but she amazed him by her endurance. At night, they spread their bedrolls in tents by a dried dung cookfire, and Jamie got up several times to add new fuel for Gertie's comfort. Every morning she rose at 4:30 to boil the coffee and begin packing up cookware and bedding for the coming trek.

On the morning of the fourth day, Jamie spotted a cloud of dust in the distance on the trail ahead. Gert glanced over at him with a grin. "You suppose that's my boy and his train?"

"Could be, though we'll not know for sure until we get closer." The cloud was too distant to identify whether it was made by wagons or troops or a marauding band of Indians.

They followed the cloud of dust all day, unable to close the gap between them. That night they camped in the shelter of a copse of willows near a spring. It was on a slight rise, and after dusk fell, the orange twinkle of cook fires glowed in the distance.

Aunt Gertie talked nonstop about meeting up with the train and her boy Ransom. But Jamie worried silently about the Union cavalry unit he knew was somewhere on this same trail.

They awoke to a band of clouds in the northern skies, and the nip of a gray, wintry morning. Aunt Gert had taken a chill during the night and, when she settled into the carriage, insisted on using two lap blankets.

The skies grew darker, and Jamie scanned them for the first signs of rain, hoping they'd find shelter when needed. By midmorning, the first large drops began falling, and soon the dry, dusty earthen trail turned to mud. Still, there was no shelter in sight. He finally halted the team because the strain of pulling the carriage through the mud was tiring them quickly, and he and Gert sat inside, listening to the rain beating on the roof and on the mud surrounding them.

Gert reached over and patted his hand. "Now, you must remember, child. Whatever stops us, stops them. Ransom is no farther ahead than he was this morning."

He grinned at her. "You've got a point there." *If it's Ransom ahead of us.*

The sun broke through within the hour. Jamie got out to check the vehicle. The mud was deep, but not deep enough to keep the wheels from turning. To be safe, he decided to let Gert drive the team while he levered the back wheels.

"Didn't think you'd ever ask," she said, chin tilted upward, hands taking the reins. He readied the lever, then gave the signal. Gertie flicked the whip as if she'd been doing it every day for years. The horses strained into their harnesses. She popped the whip again and yelled out, "Haw!"

Jamie worked the pole, and finally the carriage moved. "You sure you haven't done this before?"

She chuckled. "Just takes common sense." She popped the whip again, obviously enjoying herself immensely.

Jamie trotted alongside, then lifted himself up and into the carriage as it rolled onward. He looked over at Gert, ready now to take over driving. But, with a smile fixed on her face, she did not appear ready to hand him the reins.

"This beats all," she said after a minute. "I could be home sipping hot water and honey. Imagine."

Jamie leaned back in the seat, half closing his eyes. "Just wake me when we get there," he said.

A peal of laughter was his answer. And another pop of the whip.

By their nooning, they'd covered only a few miles because of the mud, and by sundown, only a pitifully few more. Jamie was disheartened. The longer they were out on the prairie alone, the greater the danger. He had hoped to join Ransom Brown by now.

He scanned the horizon for a resting place for their night camp. They headed up a slight incline toward a sparse stand of foliage, dark silhouettes against an orange-streaked sunset.

"Up ahead!" Gertie announced as they crested the hill. "Look!"

In the distance, just beyond the spring, was a circle of Conestogas. And off to the north, just a few hundred yards away, was a bivouac of the Union cavalry, their horses corralled beyond.

TWENTY-SIX

By the time the wild horses reached the Green River, one quarter of the herd had been lost, a few to Indian raids, some to hunger and thirst. Hundreds went lame, even though the mustang hooves were as strong as iron. Still others died from exposure in the frigid cold of the mountains.

Sybil complained so often that there wouldn't be enough to sell for a profit once they reached Abiqui, that everyone from Spence to Cook threatened to leave her someplace along the trail if she didn't keep her opinions to herself. She thought it silly that Spence kept defending the numbers, saying that he had planned to lose at least half by the end of the trail. For someone who loved horses so much, she thought he was being downright careless. Of course, it wasn't the loss of life that bothered her half as much as the loss of profits. Profits that would make the difference between success or failure in restoring Rancho de la Paloma to her family.

She nudged Rachelle to a gallop and sighed as she pictured the rancho. Odd, it wasn't her bedroom—its stylish Parisian furnishings, her lovely wardrobe filled with gowns—that she thought about. It was the century oak in the courtyard! Wonders would never cease, she thought with a laugh. Of course, she would never admit to anyone that it was the oak she missed the most, the stone benches beneath it, the sound of the fountain and the birds that gathered around it.

She slowed Rachelle as they reached the Colorado River, its banks winter bare and covered with a sifting of fresh snow. Sybil had ridden out ahead of the others, impatient with the slow-moving herd. Aislin, who had been riding behind her, now closed the distance between them. Scotty had left earlier with a couple of the wranglers—Bobbie

Oakes and Parker Burnside—to scout a place to ford the river. Sybil was hoping she might cross paths with the scouts, especially with Scotty MacPherson, and she was mildly annoyed that her sister had seen fit to follow.

She slid off her horse near a sand spit that allowed the river to pool and let Rachelle drink. Behind her, Aislin dismounted.

"Spence warned you about riding off by yourself," Aislin chided as she led Silverheel to the water.

Sybil lifted one shoulder dramatically. "I'm within shouting distance."

"This is Ute country. The rule is travel in groups of two or more at all times."

"I'm looking for a place to bathe."

Aislin rolled her eyes. "You're saying bathing is more important than safety."

Sybil grinned. "Better dead than dirty." Then she gazed at the frigid water and shivered. "Though I'm not too sure about this. We may have to break ice by morning." Her breath fogged in front of her face.

Her sister just shook her head.

"I'm so tired of cold water." She patted her hair, though she didn't know what good it did. It was in its usual braided tails. And no fashionable hat, or even ribbon, adorned it. "I've got an idea. If we start now, we can heat enough water for a bath. Kettle by kettle over the cookfire."

"What are you planning to use for a bathtub?"

"Cook has an old barrel. I saw it in the back of the wagon. I'll ask if we can use it."

"You'll end up smelling like salt pork."

"But warm salt pork." Sybil sighed. "It would be worth it. Besides, I brought a bottle of Parisian Mist for just such an occasion."

Aislin shook her head and laughed. "All right. You get someone to bring the barrel. I'll start a fire to heat the water."

"Don't tell me you're going to join me."

Aislin grinned. "A warm bath would do wonders."

"What about being away from the company?"

"We're the only two women. I wouldn't want to bathe any nearer the others, would you?"

Sybil shrugged. "You're beginning to see things my way."

Aislin laughed. "Heaven help us, Syb. If that's the case, we'll all be in trouble."

Sybil swished through the brush, heading back toward the noise of folks setting up camp. The smell of woodsmoke and pine filled her nostrils. She shuddered, wondering if her clothes and hair would ever be rid of the smell. Day and night, the smell of woodsmoke. And on the trail, horse hides sweating in the sun. Yes, one whiff of Parisian Mist would make her feel like a real woman once more.

She'd stepped deeper into the brush when she heard the crack of a breaking twig behind her. She halted, the hair on the back of her neck standing on end.

A moment later, a large doe soared from the brush. Sybil laughed at her fear and moved on. She walked only a few more yards when she heard the distinct sound of footsteps again. Light footfall on damp, snowy ground. She frowned. Why would anyone be following her?

Growing impatient, she spun around, hands on hips, to face her follower.

A split second later, the brush parted, and a tall, mangy Ute brave moved out, his black eyes challenging her gaze.

She swallowed hard, but kept her hands on her hips. "Are you following me?" she demanded, fully aware he probably didn't understand a single word.

He walked closer. She wondered if she should scream or faint or act indignant. She chose the latter. "What are you doing here, following me?" she growled, hoping to sound menacing.

He kept coming, but she narrowed her eyes and held her ground. "You go away now," she said, her heart pounding. "Go away." She fluttered her fingers at him as if at a pesky mosquito.

He grunted unpleasantly, still approaching.

Sybil didn't want to slide her gaze from him even for an instant, but she wondered how many companions he might have hiding in the brush.

"Go away." He was close enough for her to smell him, and his odor nauseated her. She cleared her throat. "Go away now."

He halted barely an arm-length away. "Come." His smell was over-powering.

She spun around, only to have him catch her left braid and yank her backward. She let out a yelp as he pulled her toward him.

Then there was silence. Utter silence. Her heart pounded wildly. He still held her hair fast, and she couldn't turn.

"I'd let go if I were you," said a voice behind her. And she heard the click of a pistol cocking. "Now!" said the voice she knew was Scotty's.

The Ute hand released her braid, and she stood upright, brushing herself off indignantly.

Scotty held his gun to the warrior's temple. "Now, back away. Slowly. That's right." He waved the barrel at the brave.

The Ute, with defiance in his black eyes, turned and, without another sound, disappeared into the brush.

Scotty watched him go for a moment before turning back to Sybil. "You shouldn't be here alone."

She nodded mutely, her heart still pounding.

Scotty stepped closer, concern now showing in his eyes. "Are you all right?"

Sybil stared at him, realizing her time for fainting into Scotty's arms had passed. And it had been such a wonderful opportunity. She swallowed hard and nodded.

He was standing very near her, and her heart pounded, though now not from fright. "You shouldn't be out here alone. You've heard Spence's orders."

"Ye-es," she croaked, then cleared her throat and tried again. "Yes, you are absolutely right." Then she frowned. "But what are you doing here?"

"I saw Aislin by the river. She told me you'd headed this direction." He spoke with cool authority. "It's easy to let down our guard when we're so close to our destination. Even your sister should've known better than to follow you alone." He holstered his gun, removed his hat, then raked his fingers through his hair. "You put her in great danger as well." He replaced the hat. She loved the rakish angle of it on his carrot-hued locks.

"I'm sorry." The words weren't a normal part of her vocabulary, but for Scotty, she might be willing to utter them seventy-times-seven.

"You're trembling," he said, his voice husky.

He was right. Her teeth chattered as well. But not from cold. Or from fear. He was staring, and the look in his eyes was as soft as a caress.

"You're cold."

She nodded, not trusting her voice.

"Would you like me to hold you? Maybe you'll stop your shaking."

She didn't think so, but when he opened his arms, she stepped into them with a deep sigh. She rested her cheek on his coat, enjoying the scratch of the heavy woolen fabric against her skin. She sighed again, listening to the pounding of his heart.

He wrapped his arms around her, and after a moment he rested his head on hers. This was one time she was glad she hadn't worn a hat.

Slowly, he pulled back and gave her another of his tender, caressing looks. Her heart turned over.

Scotty swallowed hard, and when he did, his ears wiggled slightly. She loved how they did that. "Sybil," he said, "I've been meaning to tell you something for weeks now…"

"You have?" Her teeth were still chattering.

"I've…well, I've been wanting to talk with you. I mean privately."

"You have?" Through the years when she dreamed of the man who would someday declare his love, she'd practiced her poetic, flowery answers. Words to pass down to her great-grandchildren. Here it was, about to come, and she could only stand here, teeth chattering, uttering inane repetitions. She cleared her throat again. "You have?"

"Yes." There was high color in his cheeks beneath the freckles.

"Um. What was it you wanted to talk to me about?"

"You are lovely," he blurted out. "Just about the loveliest woman I've ever seen."

"I am?"

"If I could, I would declare my love for you this minute."

"You would?" Then she frowned and stepped back. "Well, why can't you?"

"I'm heading to war."

"I thought you were heading to Abiqui."

"My orders are to proceed east immediately after. I'll report to a cavalry unit in Santa Fe. I'm not sure where the unit is heading, only that it's straight to wherever we're needed most."

She brought her hand to her mouth. "But I thought you were coming back to California with us. Maybe not with us. But at least back to Fort Tejon."

"I received my orders just before we left. I'm sorry."

"Must you go?"

"Of course."

There was something in his eyes that looked uncertain. "How did you get to California in the first place? You're from New York." *New York.* How she loved the sound of the words.

He laughed lightly. "Well, no one knows how it happened. I thought I'd be in the thick of battle by now. When I joined up, that was my intent."

"I'm glad it happened." She felt unexpectedly, uncharacteristically shy. Her cheeks felt hot. "I mean, the mistake. I mean…"

He stepped closer and reached out to lift her chin. They gazed at each other without speaking.

Finally Sybil drew in a deep breath. "So many have died in the war. I don't want to think about what might hap—"

"Don't say it, Sybil. Or even think it. My duty lies with my regiment, no matter where I'm sent."

"You said that if you could, you would declare your love." Her voice was barely more than a whisper.

"And I meant it."

"But you're leaving. What does that have to do with love? I mean, declaring it or not declaring it?"

"I don't speak lightly of such a thing. If I speak to you of my love, then I will also ask for your hand in marriage. Since I can't do the latter, I can't do the former."

"But what if I want you to anyway?"

He laughed softly and touched her cheek with his fingertips.

"Can't we speak of it, then you could carry my handkerchief…or something…with you into battle? I'll wait for you, then someday you'll come riding back for me…" It sounded so romantic.

"Love is more than that, Sybil. Until I know my future, I can't tell you my feelings."

She stared at him for a moment. "Well, there's nothing stopping me from telling you mine."

He grinned.

"I think I love you, Scotty MacPherson." She tilted her chin upward, still unblinking, and looked into his eyes. "You can't stop me from loving you just because you're about to ride into a war that you've no business riding into." She brushed the tears from her eyes.

"That's the nicest thing anybody's ever said to me."

"*Nice?* Is that all you can say?" she sputtered. "*Nice?*"

He laughed and stepped closer. "If you must know, Sybil, there's not an hour, not a minute that goes by that I don't dream of holding you in my arms. Dream of covering your face with kisses. Dream of whispering 'I love you' in your ear."

"Kisses?" She felt her cheeks flame again.

"Yes, kisses."

"Oh my."

"But I can't say any more. At least, not yet."

"Couldn't you just kiss me once? I mean, it would be a nice memory to hold while I wait for you to make this declaration."

He chuckled, shaking his head. "But I will hold you in my arms once more if you'd like—to keep you warm."

"I would like that very much," she said.

He opened his arms, and she stepped into his embrace. For a moment they stood very still, and he tightened his arms around her as if he never wanted to let her go.

Then he pulled back slightly and placed his hands on either side of her face. He bent very close and touched his lips to hers. She let out a small sigh and circled her arms around his neck.

"I thought we couldn't kiss," she breathed after a moment, "until you declared your intentions."

He sighed deeply and kissed her again. "My intentions are to love you for the rest of my life," he said, finally. And when she looked up into his eyes, she saw they were filled with anguish. "I just hope, my love, that our lives are long and full."

She understood his meaning, and quick tears rose to her eyes. She stood on tiptoe and touched her lips to his again.

Scotty saw Sybil back to night camp, then rode out with Spence to check the herd.

"We've got only a few weeks to go," Spence said as they rode. "I'd like to break the rest as we cross the Colorado."

"It can be done," Scotty said. "Each man can take several turns crossing."

They rode in silence for a few minutes.

"Something bothering you?" Spence studied him carefully.

Scotty shrugged. A lot was bothering him, but he didn't know how much to tell his friend. It was hard enough to have let his heart be captured by Sybil Byrne, now that he was on his way into the thick of battle. But he also had his orders to turn over the herd to the army as soon as they reached Abiqui. He glanced at Spence. The man needed top dollar, yet the army was about to double-cross him by taking the herd, paying him nothing but an IOU, due sometime in the future.

The plan was for Scotty to head into Santa Fe as soon as the herd reached Abiqui. He'd contact the major in charge, and troops would be sent to take over the trail drive from that point on.

How could he do it? How could he *not* do it? He was an honorable soldier, an honorable man. If he disobeyed orders, he would be court-martialed. So much for heading into the glories of war. He'd be heading straight to prison. If he obeyed orders, he would betray his friend. The ranchos would be lost after all. He would lose Sybil.

But maybe there was another way. An honorable way to get his orders changed back to California. He grinned at the thought. His love for that fiery young woman might just make him smarter than the entire Union army. He grinned. Yes, it just might.

Spence was staring hard at him. "You sure there's not something you need to tell me?"

"Nope. Just thinking this horse can take yours any day." He kicked the brown to a gallop, and with a whoop and a holler, rode like the wind across the mesa.

Behind him, his friend was laughing out loud, hard on his heels atop Ruffian, the big bronze sorrel.

TWENTY-SEVEN

Darkness had fallen by the time Spence and Scotty returned. Aislin sat outside her tent near the cook wagon. Bedrolls and tents were scattered around the fire, and Cook was ladling venison stew into metal cups as the men lined up for their portions.

Aislin lifted a spoonful of stew to her lips, savoring the scent of sage and wild onions. Spence headed for the cook wagon, metal cup in hand, and she watched as his gaze sought hers; then he headed her direction.

He greeted her with a nod, took a seat on a nearby stump, and dug his spoon into the stew. Their time together on the trail had grown into one of comfortable companionship. Without speaking of it, they both had made a concerted effort never to be alone together. Spence honored her commitment to Jamie, and for that, she was grateful.

They'd spoken often of their plans, once they reached New Mexico. Spence would return to California with the funds from the drive, racing as quickly as possible to save the ranchos. They agreed there would be no time to spare.

Aislin was equally adamant about continuing east to search for Jamie. Spence had protested, wanting to accompany her as originally planned. But the funds from the drive were safest in his hands, she had explained. And besides, her search for Jamie was a personal quest. It was better that Spence not be along.

Her only concession was to promise that she would allow Spence to help her find an appropriate and safe escort for her journey.

"How much longer till we arrive in New Mexico?" She took another bite of venison.

"We'll spend a few more days here, crossing with the herd. Then,

I'd say, perhaps another three weeks to reach Abiqui. Depends on the weather."

"You've been successful, Spence. I'm proud." She smiled at him as she scooped another spoonful of gravy.

"Don't speak too soon. We've got another hundred and fifty miles or so to go."

"I overheard some of the men talking about how you've taught them to break horses."

He laughed. "It's not original, but it works. We've got one more chance to break the rest crossing the Colorado." He took another bite of stew, obviously savoring it as he chewed. "It'll take some doing. We've got several hundred head trail broken but not ready for saddles. Taking them across the river will be enough to settle them, providing each has a rider."

"I'd like to try it."

He smiled into her eyes. She knew she should look away, but couldn't. "I'm serious."

"Pick your mustang, m'dear, and the river's yours."

"I may surprise you and do just that."

He sobered. "It'll be dangerous."

"I know. I'd like to do it anyway."

Spence dug into his stew again. The glow from the night fire made his hair glisten, turned the stubble on his jaw gold.

"I see your father watching you sometimes," she said. "I think even he's impressed with what you're doing."

Spence's expression turned to a scowl. "Sometimes I think he cares, but most of the time I feel he's up to something." He shook his head. "Can't explain it. Just feel he's biding his time, waiting for the right opportunity…"

She set her cup on the ground beside her. "To attempt to take over the drive again?"

"Most likely. It's not like him to give up on something he wants to do."

Aislin saw Hugh sitting on the other side of the night fire, alone as usual. "I feel sorry for him."

Spence turned to follow her gaze, taking another bite of venison as he did so. He nodded slowly. "If he'd give me half a chance…"

Aislin touched his arm, then retracted her hand. "You've given him many, Spence."

He looked at her over the top of the metal cup as he scooped the gravy with his spoon. "Have you noticed how he doesn't join in with the rest of us when we speak of home…the ranchos?"

She laughed lightly. "You, Syb, and I are always talking about the land. Our memories of it. Our love of its beauty. Even its harsh climate."

"But my father never joins in. It's as if it's already in the past and will forever stay there."

"Maybe he doesn't speak of it because he's not the one trying to save it."

"We could be partners in this, if he'd just meet me partway."

"Have you tried talking with him, Spence? Maybe sometime when the two of you are alone."

"He seems to make a point of staying as far away as possible." Then he hesitated, as he placed his empty cup on the stump beside him. "Strange, though, he approached me a few days ago about learning to break horses, my way, in the water. Wants all his hands to have a try at it. Said they'd meet me at the river with the rest of the herd tomorrow."

"Maybe he's finally seeing the value in what you do. In who you are."

Spence turned to her, seeming to consider her words. He shook his head slowly. "I know my father, Aislin. He's got something else in mind. I also know I need to be on guard."

He reached for her empty cup, then stood to take them both to the cook wagon. Erasmo, on the other side of the circle, picked up his fiddle and began playing a lively "Arkansas Traveler." She tapped her foot to the beat. Soon Jake Polley joined in with his fiddle, followed by Bobbie Oakes strumming his guitar. Spence came back, settled onto the stump, and pulled out his harmonica. He gave her a quick grin before he started to play.

She folded her arms around her knees and listened to the voices and laughter carrying across the fire circle. The music of the harmonica rose above it all, and for just a heartbeat, Spence watched her above the instrument cupped in his hands.

Spence turned away, unable to bear the look of firelight in Aislin's eyes. He had hoped for the first weeks of the trek that she would release Jamie's memory, accept his death, and allow her heart its own direction. But, stubborn as always, she still clung to the idea that his brother might be alive. Not even the rigors of the trail, the terrifying hopes and fears about the ranchos, could change her mind.

Meantime, he fought a war within himself, a war between honoring her commitment to his brother and taking her into his arms and showing her what real love was all about. Not love based on childhood memories. Promises to the dead. But flesh-and-blood love.

So far honor had always won the battle. He didn't know how much longer it would. He slid the harmonica over his lips, aware of her nearness. He closed his eyes to block her image, only to find it was still there, emblazoned on the backs of his eyelids. In his mind. In his every thought. In his heart.

Finally, unwilling…unable…to gaze on her even once more in the glow of the fire, he stood, placed the harmonica back in his pocket, and, without another word or so much as a glance her direction, walked to the far side of the fire circle.

Scotty saw him coming and gave him a mock salute as Spence threaded his way through the bedrolls, saddles, and tents. "I was just about to come looking for you, friend," the younger man said, standing up.

"Something wrong?"

"Just got through talking to some of the hands, those who rode flank earlier today. Seems they've spotted another herd behind us."

"I can tell by your worried look, you don't mean just another wild herd of mustangs."

He shook his head. "No, this herd is accompanied by wranglers."

"How many head?"

"Several hundred. A thousand, maybe. Good-sized herd."

"How far back?"

"They were close enough to identify a couple of the wranglers."

Spence knew then why the worry. "Fraco Ciro?"

Scotty nodded. "Not him, personally, though he may be part of the group. But some of his vaqueros were spotted."

"Did they appear to be gaining on us?"

"Too early to tell."

Spence felt the prickly sense of someone watching him and turned to see his father's unblinking gaze. It occurred to him that he might have something to do with Ciro's band following. He wondered if his father was waiting for him to fail.

"Strikes me as odd that Ciro would choose the same route," Spence said, turning back to Scotty.

"Maybe he did it for the same reason you did—more water along the way."

"The Mojave Trail is faster."

"Not many would consciously attempt this route through the mountains, especially this time of year."

Scotty stepped closer and dropped his voice. "Do you think someone in our group told him our route?"

"Or has been in communication with him along the way?"

"Who would do it?" Scotty glanced around. "What would be the point?"

"Money. Pure and simple. Any of our hands might think a greater profit could be made by turning over the herd to another bidder. A bidder that isn't a part of either army, Confederate or Union."

He noticed a look of discomfort cross Scotty's face, and he wondered if his friend might be the turncoat, then dismissed the thought just as quickly. A turncoat wouldn't have warned him of Ciro's approach.

"Tomorrow we cross the river. It'll slow us down to the point of Ciro's herd catching us."

"I thought of that."

"We'll need to post some men to guard the herd."

"Are you sure you want to take time to break the horses while we cross?"

Spence considered herding them across all at once, riderless, taking them on to Abiqui to be broken in the traditional way. They wouldn't fetch as high a price. He pictured the horses thrashing and bucking in the water, learning to accept their riders without pain and terror. "We'll proceed as planned," he said. "With guards."

"That'll be fewer to break the horses as we cross."

"We'll just take longer."

The younger man looked worried, but didn't argue. "I'll call for more guards in the morning."

"We'll start across at sunup."

Scotty nodded and gave him a salute. "You're the captain."

Spence started to head for his tent, then changed his mind and turned back to his father.

Hugh watched his son approach and stood to greet him.

"Father…" Spence stuck out his hand to shake his father's. "As foreman, you're to report anything unusual to me."

"I've been doing my job," his father said, his tone defensive.

"I've just heard we're being followed." He met his father's critical gaze without blinking.

"Just heard about it myself."

"You should've told me immediately."

"I said, I just now heard about it."

"Did you also hear who it is?"

"No."

"Fraco Ciro. Is there anything you haven't told me about Ciro and his band?"

"What are you suggesting, son?"

"You tell me."

His father lifted his chin, with an expression of both pride and defiance.

"Why did you come on the drive?"

"Perhaps to witness your success."

"I don't think so."

"Why do you say that?"

"You've kept your distance. That, I give you credit for. But you make no effort to make the drive easier for any of us."

"And should I?"

"Are you hoping I'll fail? For some obtuse reason that only you know, I wonder if you want me to fall flat on my face."

"I don't know what you're talking about."

Spence studied the man for a moment. All he wanted was love. Acceptance. To be looked at with pride.

Finally, he shook his head slowly, swallowing hard. "I wish things could have been different between us. There's so much…" but he couldn't finish. So much he wanted from his father. So much he wanted to give. Instead of speaking, he just looked into his father's eyes, still hoping for a glimpse of warmth.

His father looked away.

⬥

That night Hugh Dearbourne sent one of his men to tell Fraco Ciro to meet him the next morning before daybreak at an outcropping of red rock just west of camp.

When Hugh awoke, a light snow was falling. He hoped his footprints wouldn't be seen leading away from camp to the corral where he saddled the Appaloosa. Once mounted, he headed west into the forested and rocky hills.

Just as instructed, Ciro waited. He was atop a powerful black stallion, a stark contrast to the slant of the falling snow and the red of the rock walls behind him.

The vaquero nodded as Hugh reached him. "So it is time for the attack, *amigo?*" Both men dismounted.

Hugh faced Ciro, hesitating to speak. With just one word, he would destroy Spencer's dream, his hard-earned efforts, and both ranchos. For weeks now, Hugh had been fighting his misgivings about the confrontation. He'd been fighting the images of Spencer struggling to save what was rightfully his in the battle between Ciro's men and those of the company. And Hugh's men would be the deciding force, led by Hugh himself.

Before watching Spencer head up this drive, he wouldn't have believed the young man had such grit. Now he wondered how he could have thought the boy would walk away from such a challenge.

No. Spencer would fight. Hugh knew it as well as he knew his own name. And for the first time in the boy's life, he feared for him. And surprisingly, admired him. Was proud of him.

"Amigo?" Ciro prodded. "You have not changed your mind?"

Still he didn't answer, just stared at the man. He had asked for the meeting with the full intention of seeing his plan through. Why couldn't he utter the words?

"What is the matter with you, *amigo?"* Ciro hissed.

"I need to know if your men are ready," Hugh said, feeling sweat bead on his forehead.

"Of course they are. They have been all along. We will attack now, if that's what you have come to tell me." He nodded beyond the red-rock hills. "They wait, already mounted…over there."

"We'll let the herd cross, then decide when and where…exactly."

"Decide?" Ciro spat the word. "That sounds like no plan has been made."

Hugh let his gaze dart to the hills. As if seeing his nervousness, Ciro stepped closer. *"Amigo,* you do not plan to double-cross me."

Hugh finally let out a long pent-up sigh. His breath fogged in front of him. "There will be no attack."

"What?"

"I said, there will be no attack. That's what I've come to tell you." He stepped to the Appaloosa and started to mount. "Actually, consider it an order. You will not attack." He glared at the vaquero with the same expression he had used many times when the man was in his employ.

Ciro grabbed his arm, and swung him backward. "You come here to cheat me out of what's mine?"

Hugh pushed the man away and moved back toward the horse. He swung his leg over the saddle and looked down at the stunned vaquero. "It was never yours, *amigo…*" He drew out the Spanish word as a taunt.

As he turned the Appaloosa toward the trail, he wasn't surprised when he heard the cock of a rifle behind him.

Perhaps he had expected it all along.

Spence rose in the pale light of dawn and woke Cook to clang the triangle. The company dispensed with a morning cook fire and coffee, and instead packed their belongings quickly and headed the herd toward the river.

It was obvious that a storm was settling on them. A flurry of light flakes was falling, and by the time the herd reached the sand spit where they planned to ford, it was coming down at a stinging slant.

Spence urged Ruffian to the water's edge. Scotty appeared beside him, barely visible through the snow.

"Still think we ought to try breaking 'em as we go?" He was peering into thickening flurries. "Barely see the other side."

Spence stared across. "We can do it."

"You think the men are up to it?"

He nodded. "I'll promise extra wages for each horse they break in the river."

Scotty laughed. "Well, then, maybe I'll try my hand at it as well. Several times across."

Spence glanced back at the herd, the few dozen in the lead heading for the river. "Guards posted?"

Scotty nodded to a piñon-covered incline. "Up there. But I doubt they can see anything beyond twenty-five feet."

"At least our tracks will be covered before Ciro gets here."

"That's about all this white stuff is good for," Scotty said.

A moment later Spence turned Ruffian back to the herd, searching for his father to give him, as foreman, some last-minute instructions for crossing. Hugh wasn't with the herd or any of the wranglers, so Spence, though puzzled, headed back to the river.

When the herd reached the sand spit, Spence shouted out directions for riding them across. To all who wanted to take a turn at water breaking he promised extra pay. A whoop went up, and the men headed to the riverbank to take their turn.

Half the herd was driven to the east side, then men on both sides plunged back into the water, astride the bucking mustangs. The process was repeated until hundreds of the horses pulled out of the river, the fight in them nearly gone. Hundreds more waited; it would take all day to finish the breaking.

Sybil and Aislin rode up beside Spence, one on either side.

"We're ready," Sybil announced with a grin.

He craned in his saddle to look at her. "Don't tell me—you're going to try it?"

She nodded. "Betcha possums to bumblebees, I get across without mishap."

He glanced at Aislin, who shrugged. "I know better than to argue with Sybil," she said. Then she smiled. "Besides, I plan to go over with her."

The sisters exchanged scared but triumphant glances.

"I'll go with you."

Sybil narrowed her eyes. "As long as it's for the ride, not for keeping watch over us."

He laughed. "You ready?"

"Didn't I just say we were?" Sybil grinned at him.

"Let's go then. We'll take our horses to the east side, then ride back on the mustangs."

Sybil let out a screech and headed Rachelle into the water. Aislin and Spence followed, plunging their horses into the frigid river. Minutes later they emerged on the opposite side, Aislin and Sybil laughing and shivering with cold.

"We're only halfway," he reminded them.

"M'ladies, choose your mounts," he said with a bow toward the nervous horses.

"No tack at all?" Sybil said, her eyes big.

"No bit, no harness, no reins," he answered. "You hang on to the mane." He paused. "You don't have to go through with it, Syb." He hoped she wouldn't. But he knew if he said so, she'd do it for spite.

She bit her lip. "I'll take that one," she said after a moment, pointing into the herd.

But before Spence could give the order for three horses to be taken into the water, there was a commotion from the west side of the river. He squinted through the snow flurries, barely recognizing the shadowy figure of Scotty as he yelled and gestured.

"Stay here," he ordered, then, mounting Ruffian again, he plunged back into the water.

He emerged again on the west bank, water sheeting off Ruffian, and headed for Scotty, mounted on the brown. "What's going on?"

"You've got to come quickly."

"What—"

"It's your father, Spence." Scotty called back over his shoulder, as he threaded his way through the herd still awaiting their crossing.

"What's happened?" He nudged Ruffian in the flanks, urging him to move faster. "What's happened to my father?" His heart was pounding.

"He's been shot. Hurry! I'll fill you in as we ride. But there may not be much time, Spence."

They were clear of the herd now, and he followed Scotty up the trail at a gallop. "What do you mean, there may not be time?" he shouted at his friend, once Ruffian had caught up with the brown on the trail.

Scotty glanced over at him, his face stricken. "He's dying, Spence."

TWENTY-EIGHT

Spence halted the sorrel and slid from the saddle near a copse of snow-covered piñons. Erasmo, Jake Polley, Bobbie Oakes, and a few others stood near the shelter of a blanket strung across some trees. They stepped back as he approached. Scotty followed.

He saw the blood-stained snow and knew the wound was serious.

"Father," he whispered as he knelt beside his father. There was no answer. He reached for Hugh's hand and held it between his.

"How bad is it?" he asked Erasmo, who stood nearest.

Erasmo's lined face told him more than words could. Spence turned back to his father.

"Father, can you hear me?" Still, there was no answer. "Would you leave us alone?" he said to the others without looking up.

There was the sound of shuffling as they moved away.

Spence lifted the blanket that covered his father. Dark blood slowly seeped from a hole in his chest. Judging from the ragged look of the flesh, Hugh had been shot from behind. The hole was from the bullet's exit. Spence pulled off his bandanna and tried to staunch the bleeding with it.

Hugh's breathing was ragged and shallow, his face the color of old snow. "Let me go, son." Hugh's voice was barely more than a whisper.

Spence bent over his father.

Hugh's eyes were open now, and Spence was struck by their abnormal clarity. "I'm not worth saving."

"Don't—"

His father lifted his arm, and placed his hand on Spence's. "You don't know what I've done."

"I don't care what you've done. I just want you to live."

Hugh closed his eyes, and for several moments didn't speak. Spence thought he'd slipped into unconsciousness again. "I'm dying," he said after a time.

"No," Spence said. "I'm not going to let you."

"Let me go."

"You think I'll fail at this, too?" Spence growled. "At saving your life?"

His father's eyes flew open. "What—"

"You're ready to let me fail at just about everything I attempt. You assume that I don't have what it takes."

There was a spark of fire in Hugh's eyes. Just what Spence wanted to see.

"I already told you. That's not an option. You may think I'll fail, but I'll prove you wrong, Father. Once again." His tone was arrogant, but he didn't care.

His father's lips curved on one side. He coughed, groaned, coughed again. Curiously, he seemed ready to laugh. "So like me after all," he wheezed. "Just like me. Stubborn as the day is long."

Spence removed his coat and laid it over his father. "Tell me who did this to you," he said to distract him from the pain.

"Ciro," came the clenched-teeth mutter. "We were in cahoots. But I figured you guessed it."

"I did," he agreed calmly. "What kind of a deal did you make with him?"

"We were going to take the herd," Hugh grunted. He was shivering now, the tremors worsening. Spence wiped the perspiration off his forehead. "I wanted you to fail."

"Why, Father?"

"The ranchos…a deal I cut with some bankers…" His voice drifted off. "But I couldn't go through with it." He drew a raspy breath and was silent for a moment as if trying to find the strength to continue. "But there's still time. With me dead, the deal is null and void. You get that money and hurry back. There's to be an auction, but now it'll be fair game. You can buy back both ranchos."

"You knew Ciro would kill you if you backed out of it."

His father stared at him without answering, then closed his eyes. "Sara," he cried out. "Sara! I'm sorry. I'm so sorry." He lay very still for a moment, then whispered, "Spence?"

"I'm here, Father."

"I can't see you."

"I'm right here beside you."

"Where's Sara?"

"She's back home."

His father was crying now. "But her home is gone."

"We'll get it back. You'll be well again. We'll ride back to California, Father. Together. We'll get the rancho back."

"Sara?" Hugh called again. "Is that you? Hold me, Sara. I'm afraid."

"I'm here, Papa."

"Jamie?"

"No, it's Spence."

"Jamie's dead."

"Yes, Father."

"I've lost everything. Everything…everyone…I ever loved."

"I'm here, Papa. You haven't lost me."

His father's eyes were still closed, his breathing labored. Spence noticed the wound near his heart was bleeding again. "It wasn't the money, son. Just power."

"Power?"

"I thought it would stop the ache I felt inside…" His voice broke.

Show him mercy, child.

Hugh seemed calmer now, clearer of mind. "I was to meet Ciro at the river today. We'd work together to see that the herd couldn't cross. We planned a stampede. Planned to take the herd.

"Can you forgive me, son?"

Show him mercy, child.

"Why?" was the only word he could utter. "Why?"

"I needed you to fail. It was part of the plan."

"You always thought I would fail on my own. Why was it different this time?"

"I never knew you before. Never saw that strength in you."

"Then what happened? What went wrong?"

"I couldn't do it, son. I've been watching you. You made me proud. I said that you were like me. I misspoke. You're ten times the man I am. Hundred times." Then he seemed to chuckle and cough at the same time. "And you're not even my son."

Spence didn't think he had heard him correctly. "What?"

Hugh moved his pain-filled gaze to Spence's. "Haven't you guessed by now?"

"Guessed what, Father?"

"Sara...your mother. She was..." He coughed again and began to cry.

"She was what...?"

"Something happened to her, son. Something awful...years ago..."

"What do you mean, Father? I don't understand."

"It wasn't her fault. But I blamed her because she went out alone. Unprotected. Some men..." There was a wrenching sob that wracked his body, and he shuddered. "She begged me to love you. What happened wasn't her fault or yours. But I couldn't forget...I could never forget..."

Spence felt he had been pierced to the heart. A wound deeper than his father's. Images of Hugh's bitterness swept over him—his father's deep caring for Jamie, his indifference and anger toward him. His mother's deep sorrow. Now he understood. His pain was greater for it.

But now Hugh was calling for Sara again, crying for her, crying about how sorry he was. "Oh, my sweet Sara. Forgive me, my darling. Forgive me."

Spence bowed his head and wept. For his mother, his father...for them all.

Then Hugh spoke again. "I'm cold, Spence. Colder than before." He stared into his son's eyes. "Will you hold me, son?" He drew in a ragged breath. "Will you forgive me, son?"

The man who'd never once taken him into his arms or loved him lay before him, filled with pain and heart anguish. The man who'd asked Spence for a forgiveness Spence didn't think he could give.

SHOW HIM MERCY, CHILD.

Spence bent low over his father and gathered his broken body into his arms.

"That's better," Hugh said weakly. "I'm so cold."

"You're going to make it, Papa. Remember what I said. I'm not going to let you die." Tears were rolling down his cheeks.

"Son?"

"I'm here, Papa."

"Spend your energy getting back the rancho. Undoing my wrongs...not saving my life." He fell quiet for several moments. "One more thing."

"Yes, Papa."

"Marry that little gal."

"Aislin?"

"Who else?" His soft laugh came out in a wheeze. "She's loved you all along, you know."

"It was Jamie," Spence reminded him.

"I used to watch the three of you. It might've been Jamie she thought she loved. But there was something between the two of you..."

"You watched me?"

There was a hint of a smile on Hugh's pale lips.

Outside the shelter, the snow was falling thicker, heavier. Spence held his father close to stop his shivering. But it didn't stop.

"You didn't answer me, son. About..."

Spence knew what he was asking. *Forgiveness.* He stared into the bleak, white sheath beyond the shelter, rocking his father as he would a child.

SHOW HIM MERCY, CHILD.

"I...need to know..." Hugh whispered.

But the words could not leave Spence's lips. He thought of all the years he wanted, needed his father's love. Jamie and his father, together, laughing. Hugh's pride showing in his eyes. The camaraderie, the love they shared. *Mercy?* Spence was the one who needed mercy!

SHOW HIM MERCY, CHILD. JUST AS I SHOW YOU MERCY.

FORGIVE, AS I FORGIVE YOU.

"Son?"

"I'm here." His face was wet with tears, but still he could not speak the words.

"Forgive me…" He breathed the words so quietly that Spence had to bend close to his father's lips to hear them.

Finally, he answered, "I forgive you." And he pulled him closer. "I forgive you, Papa." Hugh took his last breath, and still Spence held him.

He heard the approach of riders outside. Aislin was the first to reach the shelter. She entered and knelt by Spence's side, wrapping her arms around him as he cried.

TWENTY-NINE

Camila moved quietly to her daughter's bedside in the small adobe. Brighid looked up and smiled as she approached.

"How are you feeling this morning, *mi cariña?*"

"You worry too much, Mama. I'm better every day."

"Sara's coming to visit this afternoon. Would you like to sit with us for a short while?"

"Of course. Shall we have tea outdoors?" She pulled the covers protectively under her chin, seeming to shrink further into her feather bed.

Every day Camila suggested that Brighid rise, but the answer was the same. Her daughter agreed, smiling as though nothing was wrong, but when it came time to leave her bed, she made up excuses. Still smiling. Still agreeable. But refusing to rise.

That's when the fear in her eyes was most pronounced. Fear, along with a fixed smile on her sweet, round face.

Camila settled onto the edge of the bed beside her daughter. She reached for her hand. "It's been weeks, now, but you are still healing, *mi cariña.* You will continue to heal."

Brighid gave her another bright smile.

"You don't have to smile, child. I know there's deep pain inside your soul. The most difficult kind of pain to heal. It is all right to cry."

Brighid turned her face away from Camila. Her lips were set in a straight line. If only they would tremble. If only the tears would come. But she hadn't shed one tear since the night Camila and MacQuaid had found her near the trail, body and spirit so pitifully broken. She'd stared at them, unseeing, as if numbed by a pain too deep for comprehension. Her beloved horse was lying dead beside her.

"You are loved, my child." She repeated the words dozens of times a day. She showed her in actions many times more. "You are loved."

Still Brighid stared unblinking at the adobe wall. Camila squeezed her hand. "*Niña,* if only I could take your pain…"

Brighid finally turned back to her mother. "I think tea on the porch would be lovely today with Sara. Perhaps I shall borrow one of Sybil's frocks. I wonder if I have matching gloves. Do you know, Mother?"

Camila felt the sting of tears behind her eyes. If only Brighid could cry. Wail. Shout at God. Shake her fist. Then perhaps she could get past the awful numbness. She brought her daughter's hand to her lips, held it fast, and kissed it tenderly.

"Did you know, sweet child, that there's nothing that happens to you that doesn't pierce God's heart first? You are his beloved child." These were other words she spoke often and lovingly to her daughter, hoping that some portion of their truth would penetrate the barrier Brighid had erected around her heart.

But as usual, Brighid stared at her with a vacant look, then after a moment gave her another of her dazzling smiles. "Well, of course I am," Brighid said. "But now, would you see about Sybil's frock?"

<hr />

That night just before sunset, Camila sat with MacQuaid on the front steps of the adobe.

She reached for his hand, and he turned, meeting her eyes. There was a new and unfathomable depth in his gaze these days. A look filled with pain. Sorrow. And strangely, also strength.

"When we arrived in this land, we saw only pleasant times ahead," she mused.

He nodded. "Aye. It's good we cannot see too far into the future." His gaze swept across the valley in front of them. "We came here so filled with hope. We planned to raise our family on this land, to build the finest rancho this side of the Rockies…"

She laughed softly. "We did both."

He turned back to her. "So much is uncertain. I have no doubt that the land cannot be saved. It's too late for that. I have visited the offices of Boothe and Fitzwalter too many times to count, only to be turned away at the door. I've heard rumors that both properties have been placed under government control." He stood and moved to lean against the porch railing. "This land seemed somehow tied into God's promise for us through the years, visible evidence of his blessings."

"Maybe that's why it was taken away," she said quietly, rising to stand near him.

He turned to her, frowning. "I serve God openly. Love him. Raised our daughters to love and serve him…"

"And now you are wondering why he took away all that we worked so hard to keep?" He nodded slowly as she went on. "You see, I do not agree that it is or was a reward for our loving God. For our serving him." She paused. "Neither are our tragedies cause to think we are being punished."

A shadow darkened his face, and she knew he was thinking of Brighid.

"Then why…" His voice fell off. "Why, my Camila, has our Lord seen fit to put us through this?"

"You do not carry the thought far enough. When you say 'put us through,' you are saying our troubles are temporary."

He nodded slowly. "You think they are not?"

"Our Brighid will take a very long time to heal."

His hands fisted as she spoke of their youngest daughter.

"We may never call La Paloma home again. We may never live anywhere but in this small adobe." She paused, looking out across their beloved land. Oh, how she loved it! Even in its barren winter state. Even in its years of drought. Golden grasses waving in the breeze. An orange sunset glow settling across it. Lavender mountains fading one into another like petals on a silver rose.

"If we did not love our land, the sacrifice of praise would not have meaning."

"Sacrifice of praise?"

She smiled gently. "There is a passage from the Book of Habakkuk that says,

'Although the fig tree shall not blossom,
neither shall fruit be in the vines;
the labor of the olive shall fail,
and the fields shall yield no meat;
the flock shall be cut off from the fold,
and there shall be no herd in the stalls.'
"Oh, my husband, listen to this:
'Yet I will rejoice in the LORD,
I will joy in the God of my salvation.
The LORD God is my strength,
and he will make my feet like hinds' feet,
and he will make me to walk upon mine high places.'

"Do you see what our Lord is telling us?" She did not await his answer before rushing on. "He is asking for our sacrifice of praise in the midst of heartache and pain. Because if we give him that…" She paused, searching his beloved face. "If we give him praise now…it is not land or riches he rewards us with."

Behind MacQuaid the sky was turning a golden red. He leaned against the railing, his feet crossed at the ankles, his gaze locked on hers.

"Do you not see? God is rewarding us with feet that can tread upon serpents, tread upon the rocky places and not falter.

"He's giving us feet that will take us to the high places."

Her eyes filled, and MacQuaid's image shimmered, almost disappearing into the hue of the sunset.

"You said, from this adobe, that looking to God's hills would give us strength. But that is only part of God's promise. We need to have the strength to walk those hills. And that very strength comes from rejoicing in our God and King when the fig tree fails to bloom. When all around us seems little more than confusion. Pain. Sorrow."

MacQuaid had stepped closer to her now. He touched her face with his fingertips, so tenderly it caused fresh tears to spring to her eyes.

"Camila, my love," he said, his voice low and hoarse. "What did I do to deserve you?"

Then he gathered her into his arms.

THIRTY

Ransom Brown was remarkably like his sister, Hallie Callahan. The pale brown of his hair. The round slant of his cheek. On Hallie, Jamie thought, the effect was utterly feminine. On Ransom, it merely emphasized the strength in his broad face, stocky build, and open demeanor.

He was friendly from the first moment he set eyes on the two, grabbing up Gertie Hill like a rag doll and whirling her in his arms, then shaking Jamie's hand with equal exuberance.

By the time they'd ridden together on the trail for one week, Jamie felt he'd known the man for years. At the end of two weeks, they spoke openly of their pasts—Ransom's loss of Susannah and their baby son, Jamie's years in the Union prison. After they'd been on the trail for a month, Jamie was ready to tell Ransom how he felt about Hallie. He didn't know when he'd broach the subject or what exactly he'd say. He only knew that he wanted Ransom to carry a message back to his sister. Even if Jamie never saw her again, he wanted Hallie to know he had loved her and had thought of her every day since their parting.

Aunt Gertie's carriage had been dismantled and loaded into the rear of a Conestoga. She took turns riding with the muleskinners, sometimes driving the mules a ways herself along smoother sections of the trail. The men in the company each claimed Aunt Gertie as a blood relative.

Today, six weeks into their trek, she climbed onto the bench with one of the oldest muleskinners in the company, a man referred to as the Reverend because of his propensity to quote Scripture in place of talking. He was a handsome man, face tanned the color of elk skin, hair straight as a stick and white as cotton. Aunt Gertie beamed as the Reverend clucked to the mules and the wagon pulled out in the lead. She craned around and waved to Jamie and Ransom sitting on the bench in the next wagon back.

Ransom popped the whip over the team's backs, and the wagon lurched forward. They spoke for a while about the weather, the pile of clouds up ahead, then moved to the subject of the Union troops that had traveled with them for a while earlier, before riding on ahead. They could still be seen from time to time in the distance.

Ransom seemed to figure out early on that being in close proximity to the cavalry caused Jamie great discomfort. Without saying a word, Ransom slowed the company when the troops were spotted ahead. Jamie was grateful. He'd seen enough of Lieutenant Kenwood on the *Southern Belle* to last a lifetime, and hoped never to run into Captain Hugo again. If the man had gotten himself out of the river and somehow caught up with Kenwood and the cavalry, Jamie might find himself on his way to a Union prison instead of Santa Fe.

Jamie glanced at Ransom. "Got any idea when we'll get to Santa Fe?"

"If the weather holds, maybe four weeks."

"How long will it take for the turnaround?"

"Horses will be waiting for us. Mostly coming from the West. California. Nevada. Good sturdy stock. Hooves like iron. Some mustangs. Some a mix."

"You've got to sell the freight and the wagons first?"

"My partner in Abiqui will have this company sold before we get there." He laughed and flicked the whip. "Good man. He moves fast. He'll have bid on the best herds in the bunch. Have 'em ready to roll when we are."

"You care whether they go North or South?"

Ransom turned to Jamie. "Do you?"

"I suppose I'd rather see them go to the Rebs, if I had a choice." He paused. "Actually, if I thought it would make a difference in calling a halt to the war, I wouldn't sell to either side."

Ransom nodded. "You've got a point." Then he chuckled. "Though I suppose one might argue that selling them to the stronger side might bring an earlier end."

"Which side is that?"

"Folks say it won't be long now. The tide has turned in favor of the Union."

"They were saying the same thing before I left California in '61. Then, it was the Rebs who would thoroughly rout the Federals."

They rode along without speaking for a while. The jangle of wagon tongue and chains and the squeak of leather yokes could be heard above the dull thud of mule hooves on the hard-packed ground.

"I'm sure you know," Ransom said, "that New Mexico is occupied by Union troops. Santa Fe will be swarming with soldiers."

"I figured as much."

"There's probably a price on your head, even here."

"Only if it's discovered where I've come from."

"A number of my men know."

"I realize that. They seem a trustworthy bunch." He looked out across the flat, arid land. "Besides, I plan to leave your company before we get there. Make my way alone to the trail west."

"You've got a job with me if you want it. Be happy to have you along on our return trek."

"Herding horses?"

"The same." Ransom nodded in Jamie's direction. "Ever wrangle?"

"I grew up on a ranch. More at home in a saddle than in a chair." He laughed. "Thanks for the offer, but I've got obligations in California. Need to continue on west."

"Obligations?" Ransom cast a quick glance at Jamie. "As in romantic obligations?"

Jamie didn't smile.

"You don't look too happy about it." One of the wagon wheels hit a rut and the rig swayed. "Whoa!" He popped the whip above the mules, and they plodded on.

"There's a woman I'm betrothed to…back in California."

"I don't detect any joy in your voice." Ransom stared straight ahead. "It should be an occasion of great joy—returning to her after all this time."

"It's been years since I've seen her. I've changed. I don't know anymore…"

"If you love her?"

Jamie nodded. "She's beautiful inside and out. I'd be crazy not to love her."

The mules plodded along. "Does she know you're coming?"

"She probably thinks I'll be in prison until the end of the war."

"Is there anyone else?"

The question surprised him. He glanced across the bench at Ransom, who was studying him with an intent gaze. He knew his friend had guessed about Hallie.

He nodded. "Yes."

They rode along without speaking. Finally, Ransom said, "Well, are you going to tell me about my sister?" He chuckled.

Jamie grinned at him. "She's a good woman. Beautiful, too."

"I can't disagree with you there."

"I asked her to come with me back to California. Thought for a minute she might."

"Then you remembered the other woman you're to marry."

"Actually, Hallie sensed it and turned me down. She said that I won't know who I love until I'm through healing."

"And are you? Through healing, I mean?"

Jamie kept his eyes on the horizon, and he pondered how far he'd come since leaving Elmira. Not in distance. But to finding that solid place in his heart—what had Hallie called it?—that sanctuary where he'd meet God, meet himself. He nodded slowly. "I've still got a ways to go, but I've come a distance too."

Ransom nodded. "Haven't we all been on that same journey?"

"When you return, are you planning to go visit Hallie and Emma?"

"I'd like nothing more."

"When you see her…will you tell her how highly I regard her? That there is not a day goes by that I don't think of her, her words of wisdom, her love of God?"

"I'll tell her. She'll be glad to hear we met."

"Someday, maybe you could bring her to California...with Emma..."

Ransom turned to look him in the eyes. "From what you've said, my sister has feelings for you. Maybe deep feelings. If she figured that you're heading into a marriage where there isn't love...then she'd never set one foot inside California, especially near you and your bride." He was looking straight forward again. "I know Hallie," he went on. "That's something she wouldn't do."

Jamie knew her well enough to know that her brother's words were true. He was sorry he'd mentioned it.

<hr/>

The days passed, one fading into another, as the wagon train snaked its way across the prairie; fording the Arkansas, the Cimarron, the Corrizo Rivers without mishap, wagons floating and bobbing, bullwhackers shouting and cracking their whips; fixing broken axles, metal wheel rims, and tipped-over wagons; seeking shelter from the sudden rains, then making their way through knee-deep mud; stopping for a buffalo hunt as they passed the great, rolling, thundering herds and feasting for days on the roasted meat.

From time to time, they were followed by small bands of Kansa, Osage, or Shawnee for days at a time, the sounds of their drums at night blending with the fiddles of the muleskinners.

By the time they were well along the Cimarron Cutoff, the teamsters took to walking by their teams to give the weary beasts some rest. They passed Rabbit Ear Mountain, then forded the Canadian, the last river before reaching Santa Fe.

Jamie knew he wouldn't be with the company much longer. As soon as they reached the Sangre de Cristo range, he would set out alone, head along a wilderness trail to Taos, Abiqui, and the Old Spanish Trail.

The nights grew longer and the weather grew colder, snow often covering the trail. The teamsters wore buffalo robes by day, slept beneath them at night.

Jamie didn't have long to worry about Aunt Gertie taking a chill; the teamsters fought over who would present her with a buffalo robe of her own. She was so proud of the garment that Jamie and Ransom laughed that she might never take it off, no matter how high the temperature soared.

A few days before they were to pull into Santa Fe, Jamie saw the Sangre de Cristos to the west. He was driving the lead Conestoga that morning, Gertie sitting beside him, straw hat level, as usual, with the horizon, its silk flowers faded and tattered but bobbing jauntily. She was wrapped to her chin in the luxurious buffalo robe.

She spotted the distant mountain range at the same time he did and fell quiet as they approached.

The wagon wheels creaked, the rig swayed, and the mules plodded along the bright sunlit trail.

"I once told you God didn't bless me with children of my own," she said after a few minutes. "But he's seen fit to bless me mightily with others of his children."

He nodded slowly. "Can't bear the thought of our parting, Gert," he said.

She grinned at him from her side of the bench. "I have to say, I've done a fine job raisin' you," she said.

He laughed. "You've done a fine job raising all your children, I'd wager."

"God only gives me a short time with each of those he sends my way, but I take pleasure in every minute they're with me."

"You've done a fine job helping me along my journey," he said.

"Wasn't me, child."

"You still standing on your head?" He wanted to carry that image with him forever. Along with her spunk. Her joy. Her love.

She laughed, the creaking, raspy laugh he loved. "In the privacy of my own wagon," she said. "Some of the muleskinners tell me that if it'll help them be as feisty as I am when they're my age, they plan to start."

"I may join them."

"Have you come to a conclusion about what you'll do once you're home?"

"You mean about Aislin?"

"Yes, son. Seems the most important decision you'll be facing."

"I've thought of nothing else. Every day I imagine how it will be to see her again. I wonder if, as Hallie told me, when I'm through healing, maybe the images of those I loved at home will flood back into my heart. That maybe the love I had for Aislin will return as well."

"What about Hallie?"

"She'll be with me forever."

"Will you tell Aislin about her?"

He studied the trail ahead, the startling blue of the New Mexico sky, the etched Sangre de Cristos. "A portion, perhaps, of who she is, what she did for me." He turned to Gertie. "But I will never tell her everything that was in my heart."

Aunt Gertie nodded. "And part of your commitment to Aislin must be putting Hallie from your heart forever."

"That may be the hardest part of all."

It took three more days to reach the foothills of the Sangre de Cristos. On the morning Jamie was to leave Ransom's company, the two walked out to the remuda where Broomtail was saddled and waiting. A pack mule stood nearby, laden with food and supplies for the trail.

"I can't thank you enough for all you've done," Jamie said, shaking Ransom's hand.

"Sure I can't entice you to wrangle your way back with us?"

"The land's calling me home," he said easily.

"You may find it changed. Those you left behind changed."

"Not as much as I have." He laughed.

They spoke of the trail through the Cristos. "It will take you at least a week to get to Abiqui."

"Any chance I'll run into you there?"

"Probably not. My partner is handling the trade in Abiqui. He'll take delivery, then swing the herd north of Santa Fe to meet me."

"This is it then, my friend." Jamie shook his hand again.

Aunt Gertie appeared from around the end of the Conestoga and moved toward them with her tiny, hobbling steps. Jamie gathered her, buffalo robe and all, into his arms. "You recognize the mule?" She smiled up at him.

He turned to study the beast a second time. "It's Lafayette."

"One and the same. My gift to you," Gertie said, immensely pleased.

"I'm going to miss you," he said.

"You asked me a ways back to come see you in California."

He laughed. "Would you come?"

"You just try to stop me." Her eyes were bright. "I've been talking to the Reverend about that very thing. He wants to see that big Pacific as much as I do."

Jamie couldn't stop grinning. "You mean it?"

"You're not going back to St. Louis with me?" Ransom asked.

"Oh, laws," she said with a laugh. "What's a woman to do? So many choices." She paused. "Of course, I've got plenty of life left in these old bones. No reason why I can't do both. Return to St. Louis now, head west again someday."

Jamie looked into her beloved face. "When you do, you've got a home with me for as long as you like. Just don't wait too long."

"I believe I'll take you up on that," she said. "I don't know when or how, but I'll get there."

"Meantime, you'll write?"

"I never learned," she said. "But you're written in my heart, child. Always will be. Don't ever forget it."

"And you're in mine, Gert," Jamie said. He gave her a fierce bear hug, feeling a sting behind his eyes. He quickly turned to shake Ransom's hand once more, then mounted Broomtail.

With a wave, he nudged the horse to a walk, Lafayette trailing along behind. At the trail head, he turned and waved. Ransom gave him a salute, and Aunt Gertie tilted her straw hat.

Within an hour he'd headed into a thick forest of piñon pines, and the Conestoga freight company was no longer visible.

Thirty-one

During the weeks following Hugh Dearbourne's death, Fraco Ciro, his vaqueros, and the small herd captured in the hidden valley followed blatantly close to Spence's outfit. Through the forested hillsides, along meadows and across rivers, they stayed almost within shouting distance.

Aislin watched Spence move through his days on the trail as if without any feeling except anger over his father's death. He barely spoke to her or anyone else, had not acknowledged her presence in any way since the day she held him in her arms at his father's deathbed.

She noticed his growing agitation with Ciro's taunting presence, and she feared a confrontation. By the time the company was within a few days of reaching Abiqui, she was certain of a showdown. Spence was raging inside, and the thought that his father's killer seemed to be mocking him as he followed was obviously too much for him to bear.

Ciro rode the powerful obsidian stallion now, sometimes riding close enough to Spence to make sure the younger man knew the horse's identity. She knew it broke his heart to remember the magnificent beast in the valley behind the waterfall.

Aislin tried to speak to Spence about Ciro's behavior, in hopes that talking about it might diffuse the seething just beneath the surface. But whenever she drew near to him, whether they were alone or surrounded by others in the company, Spence turned away.

Finally, one night after everyone had headed to their tents and bedrolls, she sought him out. He was just going into his tent, and turned, stone-faced, as she approached.

"I need to talk with you, Spence. It can't wait."

He stared at her. "What's it about?"

"It's about…well, you…" she faltered. "I mean, us…" She started again. "It about what's happening." She knew she'd muddled it and let out a deep sigh. "I'm not saying this well, am I?"

He continued to stare, expressionless. "I'm sure it can wait. We've got a long way to go on the trail tomorrow. Need to get an early start."

"Spence, please…" She touched his arm, imploring him, but he removed her hand.

"Go to bed, Aislin. Whatever it is can wait." He turned to leave her.

Aislin stood, watching him disappear into his tent, then finally turned back to her own.

Sybil joined her a few minutes later inside their tent, sliding under her covers, teeth chattering loudly, muttering about the frigid weather and her cold feet.

"Syb?" Aislin said as she extinguished their lantern. "Have you noticed how close Ciro's following now?"

"Scotty mentioned it too," she said, teeth still chattering. "You think he's up to something?"

"If he's not, Spence is."

"What do you mean?"

"Ciro killed Hugh," Aislin said. "Spence may be planning retribution."

"Why doesn't Spence just head out after him?" Sybil asked. "Confront him?"

"I think he's biding his time."

"Maybe he's waiting till we get to Abiqui. Get the law out here to help him."

"That's the Spence of old. Not the Spence of now."

Sybil didn't disagree.

"He seems to be waiting for the right moment." Aislin turned to her sister, propping herself on one elbow. "I worry that he'll do something he'll be sorry for later."

"Why don't you talk to him?"

"I've tried. He's completely alone in this. Wants to keep it that way."

"He loves you, Aislin. He may not talk to anyone else. But he'll talk to you."

"He loves me?"

In the dim light, she saw Sybil turn toward her, head propped in her hand. "You don't know that?"

"It's not what I want, so it really doesn't matter. Spence knows that."

"No wonder he won't talk to you."

"His silence has nothing to do with love."

Sybil was still staring at her. "Why don't you ask him?"

"He won't talk to me. I told you…"

"Go to him. Right now. Go to him, and tell him you have to talk."

"I just came back from his tent. He turned his back on me."

"Ask him if his silence has to do with love, Aislin. Bet you possums to yellow jackets, he'll talk."

"Right now?"

"Now. Go!"

Aislin reached for her heavy woolen cloak and wrapped it around her. Shivering, she pulled on her boots, then grabbed the lantern on her way through the tent flap.

"And don't wake me when you come in…" Sybil whispered sleepily as Aislin let down the flap from the outside.

She made her way through the sleeping camp to Spence's tent. The only light, besides her own dim lantern, was from the wranglers watching over the herd a distance away. She shivered, thinking of Ciro and his band. How they might sneak into camp…steal the horses…

She pushed the thought from her mind, dwelling only on talking some sense into Spencer Dearbourne.

"Spence!" she whispered loudly at his tent flap.

Only silence greeted her.

"Spence!"

Still, there was no sound from inside the tent.

"Sp—"

A hand touched her shoulder from behind.

Lantern poised, she spun. Ready to knock whoever it was across the head.

It was Spence. "Looking for me?" For the first time in days, he was smiling.

She let out an exasperated wheeze. "You scared the life out of me."

His smile widened. He didn't apologize.

"We need to talk," she attempted. Again.

"You're not going to give up, are you?"

"No."

"Do you want to come in?" He nodded toward the tent.

"It's not very private."

"What you have to say is private?" He raised a brow.

"Yes." She was staring into his eyes, noticing how they reflected the starlight.

"Shall we walk a ways from camp then?"

She nodded. "Yes."

He reached inside the tent for his pistol, strapped the belt and holster around his hips. It was the first time she'd noticed he wore a firearm. With one arm, she held the lantern up to light their path. He took her other hand and guided her through the maze of bedrolls and saddles serving as pillows.

Soon they were out of earshot of those sleeping in the night circle, but he continued leading her along a forested path to the box canyon where the horses were corralled. The wranglers watching the herd sat near a fire at one end of the canyon; Spence guided her along the canyon at the other side.

After a few minutes, he nodded to a tree stump, and she sat down, setting the lantern beside her. Spence put one foot on a nearby flat rock and leaned slightly forward, his forearm resting on his knee. There was a new boldness in his assessment of her.

She swallowed hard.

"You had something to say to me," he said. "Something private."

"Yes," her voice came out in a squeak. "Yes," she tried again. "I did. I mean, I do."

He kept watching her, but nothing about his demeanor seemed familiar.

"It's about Ciro."

"What about him?"

Her words rushed out. "I see the pain in your eyes. I know how you feel about him…what he did to your father…and now with the wild stallion…"

Spence held up a hand to stop her. "None of this is your affair, Aislin. You may think you know me." He narrowed his eyes. "But in reality, you don't. You never have."

He'd never spoken to her with this tone. This cold tone.

"Spence, I…I just want to help."

"Help, Aislin? Help me do what?"

She was confused. "I fear that Ciro may try to take the horses…" Her words fell off lamely.

He laughed, but there was no mirth in the sound. "Ah, of course. I should have known, Aislin, the true reason for your moonlit visit to my tent."

Her cheeks flamed. "Moonlit visit?" He made it sound tawdry.

But he went on as if he didn't hear her. "If the herd is stolen, all is lost. Our grand scheme to save the ranchos is over. Your beloved land is lost to you forever, as is Rancho Dearbourne to me."

She stared at him, unbelieving. "How dare you speak to me like this!"

"It's about time someone did, Aislin." His tone was so cold that she shivered.

"Spence…" she whispered, wondering why hot tears filled her eyes. "What's happened to you?"

"To me, Aislin?" He stared at her, his face like polished marble, cold, beautiful in the moonlight. "Maybe I finally grew up. It took my father's death, it took losing you, to realize that I was living in a make-believe world. A world where I wanted to be the beloved son. I wanted to be the prince to win the hand of the princess…" He looked away from her, back toward the herd. "This is reality. Getting the herd sold in Abiqui. And if possible, my princess, winning your precious land back for you. Nothing more. Nothing less."

"Are you going after Ciro?"

"Not in the way you might think, my dear. I plan to be perfectly law-abiding. But he will pay."

"When?"

He ignored the question. "Earlier tonight," he said, "you told me you had something to say…about us." His smile seemed somehow twisted.

By the look on his face she could see that the subject was closed. Perhaps forever. So be it. She shrugged. "I merely wanted to talk to you about our venture. And, of course, my worry about you going after Ciro before our transaction is complete."

Again, the twisted smile. "You don't need to worry on that account. My plan is to see the herd into Abiqui within the next two days. As soon as that 'transaction' is complete, I'll head out."

"That's only a few days from now."

He nodded. "Yes."

There was so much she wanted to say. Ached to say. She wanted to beg him not to leave. Or to take her with him. But instead, she sat in silence, looking into his face.

"Why aren't you going back with the others?" she finally asked.

There was a hard glint in his eyes. "Just call it unfinished business."

Ciro. The gun in Spence's holster. The agony he was going through because of his father. Her thoughts ran together, and her heart feared for what he might do.

"And you'll be heading east?" he asked, interrupting her thoughts.

"Yes. I plan to find transportation to St. Louis. Look for Jamie from there." She let out a pent-up sigh. "Erasmo said he'd escort me. See I come to no harm."

"And Sybil?"

"She wants to return home." She smiled. "It seems that Scotty may be returning to California. He and some of the wranglers will see her safely through."

"Scotty's orders are to head east to the war."

She smiled. "It seems love may have changed his mind."

"Love?"

"You haven't noticed?"

"Scotty and Sybil?"

She laughed softly, relieving some of the tension between them. "Who would have thought the two of them…?"

Spence turned away and didn't comment.

She stood and stepped closer to him. "So it seems our grand venture is about to come to an end."

He turned toward her, now standing upright. "I'll be gone when you return, Aislin."

"What do you mean?"

"Providing I get to California in time, I'll place the ranchos back in our families' names. My mother will take over running Dearbourne, I hope with your father's help and advice. Then I'll be heading out." He gave her a genuine smile at last. "I'm putting aside some of the money to buy a spread someplace else. Breed horses."

"I may not see you again." She was stunned by the thought. Spence had always been part of her life. She'd thought he always would be. Even if she found Jamie alive, Spence would always be there.

"It's likely."

Her eyes were wide.

He took her hand, lifted it, and kissed it where Jamie's ring still graced her finger. The half-smile returned as he studied her. "I wish you every success, my dear, as you search for my brother." He paused, still staring into her eyes. "And when you find him, I will pray for God's blessings on you and your family."

Quick tears sprang to her eyes. She pulled her hand away.

"You're no longer required to marry a Dearbourne to keep your land. When you come to Jamie, it will be for love. But as an added blessing, the lands will be joined. Think of it. Your children, yours and Jamie's, will inherit one of the largest ranchos in the state. And their children after them."

He chuckled softly. "There is some irony in it all. Your children will carry the Dearbourne name. Even the name Rancho de la Paloma will eventually fade. Your land, Jamie's land, will be known as the Dearbournes'." He paused, still gazing into her eyes. "I'm just sorry it took me so long to see your passion for my brother had a basis in fact."

"What do you mean?"

"Since you began believing that he lives…I've begun believing it myself." He narrowed his eyes. "How could a passionate belief such as yours be based on a dream only?"

She nodded. "Yes."

"I'll walk you back to your tent."

She didn't move. "So this is it? This is good-bye?"

"I won't be leaving for two more days."

"Spence…" His name came from her lips in a ragged cry. "I don't want you to go. Please. We never had a chance…"

Again, the cold stare. "It's too late, Aislin."

He reached down, picked up the lantern, then took her elbow to guide her along the trail back to camp.

Through the night, Aislin tossed on her pallet, unable to erase Spence's image from her mind.

Spence lay awake long into the night. He thought about how he'd spoken to Aislin, the bitterness with which he'd treated her. It broke his heart, but it was for the best. What he'd said had been half true. The real truth lay someplace within himself and the knowledge that he wasn't even a Dearbourne by blood. The families had always planned that Byrne and Dearbourne heirs would inherit the Big Valley.

He laughed to himself. What a sham it would be to marry Aislin under the false pretenses of producing such an heir. And if it was true that Jamie lived…well, their union would bring proper heirs to the land. He was the illegitimate son of the Dearbournes. Perhaps no one but his mother was left to know. And of course, he himself.

He stared into the black night with the words he'd uttered to Aislin playing in his mind. *I wanted to be the beloved son…the prince to win the hand of the princess…*

Well, Aislin had chosen her prince. The rightful heir to Rancho Dearbourne. Jamie. As always, Jamie, the beloved son.

⸻

The following morning just past dawn, Spence asked Scotty to walk with him as he headed to the box canyon. "I hear you may be accompanying a certain young woman back to California." One look at Scotty's face told him Aislin had been right. He was in love.

Scotty nodded. "I've been meaning to tell you."

"Is there more?"

"More to my story, you mean?"

Spence nodded. "I figured it might've had something to do with your orders."

"You knew?"

"I guessed."

"Why didn't you say something?"

"I could see you were having a battle of some kind inside yourself. Early on it wasn't any of my business. Of course, if you'd gone through with turning us over to the Union forces in Santa Fe, it would have become my business."

"Put me in quite a dilemma. I'm not one to run from danger—as far as heading into the war, I mean. But turning on my friends is another matter."

"Glad you thought so."

"I was to try to convince you to sell to the Union troops."

Spence laughed. "I remember you mentioning it once."

"I guess I didn't try too hard."

"Maybe because you knew we'd get an IOU instead of cash?"

"That didn't give me much incentive, knowing how much you needed the money."

"I'm glad you're coming back to California. The state needs more good men like you."

"I'll need to ride into Santa Fe. See if I can get my orders reversed. I've come up with a reason to be sent back to California."

"What's that?"

"I figure I'll tell them how badly I'm needed at Tejon."

Spence chuckled. "I bet they've heard that before. Strikes me that you may still get sent to the battlefields."

Scotty grinned and reached in his pocket. "Ever see one of these?"

He held out a gold nugget, as big and gleaming as Spence had ever seen. Spence let out an appreciative whistle.

"Found this in a stream in the hills behind Tejon. Had planned to save the place for myself. Return to mine it someday." He chuckled. "But I've decided the U.S. Army might be interested enough to let me lead them there."

"Seems you may be letting a fortune in gold go for the price of love."

Scotty threw back his head and let out a peal of laughter. "Can you think of any better reason?" Then he sobered. "There's no doubt in my mind that the love of Sybil Byrne is far more precious than gold."

Spence halted. "Something tells me trail dust won't have settled when you go to her father seeking her hand in marriage."

"It's true." The pale skin beneath Scotty's freckles had turned crimson.

Spence grinned. "Congratulations."

Scotty's smile widened. "And you? I've seen the way you look at Aislin. Any chance you'll follow my lead?"

"Not a chance, my friend. Not a chance."

Two days later, the wranglers herded the horses into a corral just outside Abiqui. As Aislin walked toward the enclosure, an open meadow surrounded by piñon forest, she considered the stark beauty of the west face of the Sangre de Cristo mountains looming above it all.

By midafternoon, a price would be offered for the herd, to be accepted or rejected by Spence. And now, as she walked closer, she watched him moving among the horses, unaware of her presence.

He stroked the neck of a nervous mare, speaking to her low and soft in that way he had. He rubbed the beast between the eyes, still whispering, rubbing slowly. The horse calmed.

Aislin remembered the foal on the bald mountain above the rancho. Spence had doctored its injured leg, then carried it like a baby to its dam in the wild herd. And the obsidian stallion behind the waterfall. Spence had walked with the herd, and they had responded, following him, walking in front, then behind, in some sort of ancient dance. She had never seen anything filled with such grace. Beauty. Strength. In Spence's face. In his every turn, every loping step.

But it wasn't the horses who filled her heart with memories. It was Spence. How many times had she considered him so?

How could she let him go?

Spence seemed to sense her gaze and looked up. She inclined her head slightly, and he went back to caring for the horses.

She stepped closer, leaned her elbows against the rough-hewn fence, and propped her chin in her hands, still watching his every move.

Spence met her gaze evenly. There wasn't a flicker of emotion in his eyes.

"Spence," she called out to him. He sauntered to the fence, lolled against it, regarding her. "What time are you leaving?"

"The agents have sent word they're on their way. The bidding should be finished within hours. As soon as it's done and the draft due us complete, I'll be heading out before sundown."

She reached for his hand and lifted it to her cheek. Her eyes flickered closed for a moment as she felt its rough warmth, its solid strength, and remembered its gentle touch.

When she looked up at him again, Spence was staring at her, his eyes smoldering with some deep emotion that held no hint of affection.

She wanted to take him in her arms and beg him to look at her again with love, or at least with friendship. Hadn't they once agreed to remain friends?

"We once spoke of friendship," she said, still holding his hand. Curiously, he hadn't pulled it away.

Spence laughed, a low harsh sound, and when he spoke his words shot out like gunfire. "Friendship, Aislin? Did you really think that would work between us?" Now he withdrew his hand, that strange half-smile, half-smirk on his face.

It struck her that he treated his horses better than he was treating her. "Why are you doing this? Why now?"

"I told you, Aislin. It's over. Whatever it was I've had for you through the years—love, attraction, fascination for the impossible…" He smiled. "Whatever it was, it's finally gone." He paused, staring at her. "Friendship, my dear, no matter what I said to you in that regard…friendship can never be part of the equation."

Tears came unbidden to her eyes. "But our families go back…"

Again, the harsh laugh. "My father betrayed yours. You didn't know that, did you?"

She caught her breath. "I don't believe it. My father loved yours."

He cut her off. "It seems my father held many secrets. And he loved the idea of power more than friendship, more than family, more than the land we all thought was so beloved."

"Oh, Spence."

"Before he died, he asked me to undo his wrongs." He paused. "With God's help, I'll undo as many as I can."

"Don't tell my father, Spence. Let him believe in Hugh."

"That's one thing we agree on. There's no need to destroy one man's love for another. As to his other secrets…no one will know those either."

Her eyes brimmed, and Spence's image wavered before her. Once he would have handed her his handkerchief or wiped them for her. Now, he made no move to do either.

"Our families will go on, just as I told you last night. When you find Jamie and marry, the generations to follow will know nothing of Hugh Dearbourne's traitorous heart." He touched her cheek with the backs of his fingers. "They'll know nothing of how you were once loved by a man who would have given his life for you."

She grabbed his hand, held it fast. "Spence, I…"

Again, he interrupted, pulling his hand away. "I said *once* loved, Aislin." He looked down at Jamie's ring on her finger and touched it lightly. "*Once.*"

Hot tears trailed down her cheeks, dripped from her chin. He met her gaze, and she brushed her wet face, almost angrily.

"This is good-bye, Aislin. Isn't that what you came out here to tell me?"

She didn't trust her voice to speak. She swallowed hard and nodded. *How could she let him go?*

She tried to pull Jamie's image into her mind, but it wouldn't come. She stared at his ring, turned it, then looked back to Spence.

He seemed to be waiting. For what, she didn't know. He'd made it perfectly clear how he felt.

She swallowed hard again. "Then it's good-bye," she whispered.

His expression seemed to soften as if she had made it easier for him to go.

"There's just one more thing I ask…"

He frowned.

"Would you hold me, Spence? Just one last time?"

He studied her for several long moments, then nodded. He swung a leg over the fence, and hopped down to stand beside her.

She fell into his embrace, and he held her tight while she sobbed. While she was pressed against him, she memorized the sound of his heartbeat, the scratch of the wool of his jacket against her skin, the press of his cheek resting on the top of her head.

Finally, he set her away from him, gave her one last, very long look, then turned abruptly and strode away.

By midafternoon, just as Spence predicted, the buyers' agents descended on the corral, inspecting the horses. Some wanted demonstrations that the horses were broken. Spence himself rode several to prove the point, to the obvious approval of the potential buyers.

Aislin watched from a distance as a deal was struck with an agent whose partner waited in Santa Fe, then listened as Spence called the wranglers together to congratulate them on their success. He handed out their pay, and the laughter and conversation grew more animated as the men counted their money and talked of their plans.

The agent who bought the herd then announced that his partner was heading into Santa Fe with some Conestogas to sell for running a freight business on the Santa Fe Trail. Several of the men, who'd been busy counting their money, were interested, Erasmo among them. After he grinned in her direction, Aislin wondered if that was how he planned to escort her east.

Finally, Spence walked over to where Scotty, Sybil, and Aislin waited. "We've met with success, my friends," he said proudly. "Sybil and Aislin, I can give you your portions now, or I can return to California, money in hand, to buy back La Paloma."

"You ride back fast as lightning with our share," Sybil said. "You didn't even need to ask."

He laughed. "Just wanted to make sure." He paused, counting through more of the bills and coins. "There's some extra to split," he said then. "Aislin, I assume you'll want your share for your journey east." He dropped a portion of the money into a canvas bag.

She nodded, and he placed it in her hands, then put the remaining cash in a separate bag for Sybil and Scotty. "Perhaps a nest egg for the future," he said to them with a grin.

Within a half-hour, the herd was gone, along with a number of the wranglers, who were heading to Santa Fe with the agent to inspect the Conestogas.

Some of the remaining men, Cook included, would return to California with Sybil and Scotty. Though it wouldn't be an easy trek, it wouldn't be at the lightning pace that Spence said his company would keep. Jake Polley, Bobbie Oakes, and Parker Burnside, all eagle-eyed sharpshooters, would accompany Spence to help guard the money.

She feared retribution was the real reason for splitting up the westward-heading companies. Spence hadn't mentioned Fraco Ciro.

But the look in his eyes told Aislin that he hadn't forgotten him, even though no one had spotted the vaquero or his band during recent days. She worried that Spence might take a detour—no matter the lost time on the trail—and go after his father's murderer.

At last, Spence swung a leg over Ruffian's saddle. The wranglers mounted and waited for the signal to leave, a train of pack mules behind them bearing disguised money bags and trail supplies.

The sun was just setting as Spence met Aislin's gaze one last time. He adjusted his hat, the brim low over his forehead, and inclined his head slightly in her direction.

A smile played at one side of his mouth as he beheld her for one long moment. Then he gave the signal to move out.

The bronze sorrel headed into the piñon forest. Never once did Spence turn in the saddle to look back.

THIRTY-TWO

Plesae come with us, Aislin," Sybil pleaded. "I promise, you'll love the little town of Abiqui. Scotty's already ridden through on his way back from Santa Fe. He says they've got a mercantile." She sighed. "It's been too long since we've bought real soap."

"Soap?" Aislin laughed. "I suppose you think you'll find French-milled soap in New Mexico."

Sybil gave her a pretty pout. "Dresses…maybe?"

Aislin shook her head. "Something tells me that even if they do, it'll be poke bonnet and calico fashion."

"Well, it doesn't hurt to look. Please. Say you'll come with us."

Aislin had no desire to stroll arm-in-arm with Scotty and Sybil. Their long gazes into each other's eyes, their heavy sighs and flirting glances would only serve to remind her of her own empty and loveless life.

But a trip into town would help get her mind off missing Spence. "All right," she finally said. "I'll go."

The sun was high in the stark blue heavens when they rode from camp. It took them barely half an hour to reach the town, which was little more than a few squat adobes housing a trading post, the mercantile Sybil had mentioned, a smithy, a hotel with its downstairs saloon, and a barbershop located in a central plaza. Two liveries and a single church constituted the rest of the town's offerings.

Sybil and Scotty were lost in each other, so Aislin sent them on their way to shop at the mercantile while she explored the town.

Sybil let out a squeal of delight, and Aislin glanced back to see her sister pointing to a hat in the mercantile window. Smiling to herself, she strolled slowly around the plaza, glancing in shop windows, stopping now and then to talk to shopkeepers.

The church, a small adobe the color of sand, was set apart from the rest of the plaza. The structure was perfectly square, except for an arched facade that held a plain white cross at its highest point. A thick adobe wall enclosed the church, a tall and solid wooden gate at its center.

The barren tops of a stand of aspen trees reached skyward behind the gate, and as she walked closer, the sounds of splashing water from fountains carried over the wall. She closed her eyes, taken immediately back to La Paloma and the courtyard she loved.

She tried the gate, but it was locked. In no hurry, she rounded the entire length of the enclosure, looking for a place to enter. There was none, so she strolled on past the plaza toward a nearby creek.

Though the winter day was crisp, the sun was bright, and soon even her cloak was too much. By the time she reached the creek, she'd removed it and was carrying it over one arm.

She walked upstream for a few minutes, enjoying the solitude and beauty. The creek was lined with more of the delicate, barren aspen trees, along with scattered willows and pines. She found a clearing, spread her cloak on the ground, and settled onto it. The sounds of the water falling across moss-covered rocks calmed her ragged spirits. She thought again of the church courtyard and decided that before she left with Scotty and Sybil to return to camp, she would try again to gain entry.

Meanwhile, she closed her eyes, seeking solace in the leaf-mold scent of the place, the music of the water, the warmth of a small patch of sunlight touching her shoulder.

Spence's image returned in the quiet of the place. Spence smiling. Spence moving with grace among the horses. Spence holding her for the last time.

She bowed her head and cried for him again, for what they'd lost. The sun rose higher, but still she remained in the clearing, listening to the water's song.

━◆━

Jamie had been on the wilderness trail through the Sangre de Cristos for nearly a week when he arrived in Abiqui. He figured he was distant enough from the Union troops to chance taking a room for a bath and a night in a real bed. He'd be on the trail to California for weeks to come. He might as well have one last indulgence of comfort.

He rode Broomtail down the middle of the main street, Lafayette trotting along behind.

The sun was straight up, and he smiled at the dazzling sight before him. The Abiqui adobes that made up the central plaza seemed bathed in light, and at its center, atop a church, rose a white cross on an arch. The look of it stunned him.

He halted Broomtail and stared for a moment. It was the first church he'd seen in months, and the thought of stepping inside appealed to his restless soul.

But first things first. He headed Broomtail to the hotel and dismounted. After arranging for a room, he took Broomtail and Lafayette to the nearest livery then headed back to the hotel and requested that a bathtub and some hot water be brought to his room.

An hour later, he dressed and combed back his wet hair, grinning to himself as he squinted into a small, cracked mirror above the washstand. Hallie Callahan had given him his last haircut and shave three months ago. Now his hair hung to his shoulders, his beard fully covered his face.

He still looked gaunt, probably had no more meat on his bones than when Aunt Gertie pinched his arm the first time they met and, with her horrified expression, declared him too scrawny for words. He squinted at his reflection, wondering if he ought to take the time to visit the barber before heading down the Mojave Trail. But just as quickly he decided there was no need. Who would he see other than Broomtail and Lafayette?

He headed from his room to the downstairs lobby. "Can you point me to a good eatery?" he asked the balding man at the front desk.

"Miss Thornton's boardinghouse on the corner has the best fare around these parts," the man said. "You might want to stop in and let her know you're coming for dinner. She likes advance notice."

"I'll do that," Jamie said. "Thank you kindly."

The man nodded and went back to his ledger. Jamie stepped out the front door and down the street. He found the boardinghouse without trouble, let Miss Thornton know to expect him, then strode the short distance across the plaza to the church.

The bell in the tower struck four o'clock just as he arrived at the gate. As he paused, listening to the mellow tones, a rattle of keys clanked against the metal latch from the inside of the courtyard.

A moment later, a robed priest pulled back the heavy gate. "Greetings," he said with a thick Spanish accent.

"May I visit?" Jamie asked in Spanish. He hadn't spoken the language since leaving California. Instantly, he thought of Camila.

The priest nodded. "I am Father Martinez," he answered in Spanish. "I'm glad you've come." He stepped back, inviting Spence to enter the courtyard.

"Thank you, Padre."

Jamie walked in, his gaze taking in the fountains, the slender aspens scattered about, the rock pathway leading to the front double doors of the church. A moment later, the priest led the way through the doors and into the dark, empty sanctuary. Candles graced the altar and shadows flickered on the whitewashed walls. "Stay as long as you like, son," the priest said before moving silently from the room. He closed the doors behind him, and Jamie was left alone.

Jamie walked to a long pew near the front of the church and settled into it. The hush was palpable, and he sensed God's presence in the simple structure. He slipped to his knees to pray.

Aislin heard the bell toll four o'clock, stood from her place of reverie near the creek, and strolled slowly back to the plaza, reluctant to leave.

She passed the church and glanced at the gate, now open, and she hesitated for just a moment before moving on. She was sorry she'd spent so long by the creek and had not allowed time for visiting the simple adobe structure. She shaded her eyes from the slant of the sun and gazed up at the white, rough-hewn cross, superimposed on an almost purple sky.

Soon she heard Sybil's contagious laugh, followed by Scotty's low chuckle. Her sister's beauty and Scotty's orange hair made them stand out, even at a distance. She waved as they hurried across the plaza toward her.

"I want to take a look inside the church before we go," Sybil announced breathlessly once she reached her sister. "It reminds me of the San Gabriel mission at home."

"It's getting late," Aislin said. "We need to get on the trail before dark."

If she'd expected to appeal to Scotty's good sense to back her up, it was quickly evident that if Sybil wanted to jump over the moon before heading back to camp, he would have agreed. Sybil dimpled a smile and reached for his hand, pulling him with her.

Aislin let out a defeated sigh and lagged along behind them. The young couple stopped at the gate and waited for her to catch up with them. They stepped into the courtyard.

"Reminds me of home," Sybil said in a hushed voice. "The solid look of adobe, maybe the fountain."

They walked to the entrance and opened the door. Aislin stepped in first; the others followed. It was dark inside the sanctuary, and for a moment, the three stood, letting their eyes adjust to the dim light. The scent of burning candles filled the air, and there was something about its simplicity that touched Aislin.

"There's someone up there praying," Sybil whispered in Aislin's ear. She pointed to one of the front pews.

Aislin saw the figure bent in the attitude of prayer. Shoulder-length hair and a thick beard on his face. She touched her finger to her lips and whispered, "Let's not disturb him."

Scotty placed his hand beneath Sybil's elbow and turned her toward the door. Aislin followed, closing the sanctuary door behind her.

When they were once again in the courtyard, Sybil turned slowly, arms outstretched, near the fountain. "If I close my eyes, I can almost believe I'm at home," she said. Then she looked at Aislin. "I wonder how long until Spence actually gets there…gets the property back in our name?"

"The question is, *if* he gets it back," Aislin reminded her. "We're hoping and praying, but we won't know for sure until we get there."

They moved to the gate, then out into the plaza. They'd walked a few steps when Scotty turned back. "Maybe I'd better close the gate," he said. "I didn't see anyone watching over the place."

Aislin and Sybil stood near a boardinghouse with a sign hanging in front, proclaiming a Miss Thornton as the proprietor in scrolled letters.

A few minutes later, Scotty joined then again. "The man who was praying in the church was just coming out. He told me he would see to the gate." They walked a few steps farther. "He's a man who's seen some ragged edges of life."

"How could you tell that by one look?" Sybil asked.

"Had a hollow look to him, like he's not too far this side of starvation."

Aislin halted. "We should go back. See if there's something we can do. Maybe offer food…"

Scotty shook his head. "I should've added that he's also got a tough look to him, like he's used to taking care of himself. I doubt he'd cotton to us even asking."

She shrugged and glanced back at the man, now heading across the plaza to the boardinghouse. She shook her head sadly. "I still wonder if we should offer…"

Sybil turned to look, studying the man for several moments, then added, "Makes you wonder what could cause a man to fall into such disregard for his physical appearance."

"You two obviously haven't been around folks traveling these trails alone. They tend to turn into mountain men, holding no regard for the niceties of life…such as French-milled soap." He chuckled, as if proud of Sybil's penchant for niceties.

"We just got through traveling these same trails," Sybil countered. "Not one of our wranglers ever looked like that."

Scotty stopped and smiled into her face. "That's because of you and your sister, my love. Didn't you realize every man was up at the crack of dawn, shaving and combing because of you two?"

Sybil giggled. "Well, I'll be," she said. "I never even noticed." Then she touched his face. "Well, make that, I never noticed anyone but you."

The two of them stood, staring into each other's eyes. Aislin cleared her throat. "I do think we need to get our horses and ride to camp."

Scotty and Sybil turned, almost as if surprised to see her. "Oh yes, that," Sybil said with a pretty flutter of her hand.

They headed to the mercantile where they'd left the horses tied. Aislin quickly mounted, and Silverheel danced sideways in the street as Sybil swung a leg over Rachelle's saddle and Scotty followed suit on the brown.

"Aislin, I bet you possums to yellow jackets you don't know what Scotty's horse is named."

Aislin rolled her eyes. "I really can't imagine." She didn't add that she really didn't care.

Scotty and Sybil exchanged glances as if what would follow was either the cleverest or the funniest name in the world.

"Well, I'm listening," she said, nudging Silverheel to a walk.

"Brown!" Sybil said with a peal of laughter. "Just plain ol' Brown."

"Whoa, Brown!" Scotty said as if to demonstrate the wonderful simplicity of the name.

But Aislin was no longer listening. Her gaze had locked on the rangy figure of a man, lolling against a post outside the boardinghouse. The same man they'd seen in the church.

She slowed Silverheel as they approached. He seemed to have heard the laughter, Sybil's distinctive giggling, Aislin's voice joining in, the repartee. He turned toward the three riders as they passed, perhaps longing to be a part of the group, she thought.

The horses pranced a bit as they headed along the plaza toward the edge of town.

Aislin turned in her saddle to catch another glimpse of the man's face. It was leather-dark from the sun and covered with hair the color of dusty wheat. But there was something about him. Something familiar.

He had moved from his relaxed stance to upright, now facing them. The horses continued their lively canter down the street, Sybil and Scotty still laughing, absorbed in each other.

"Stop!" Aislin finally called out, halting Silverheel as she did so. "Please, stop!"

Scotty and Sybil exchanged a look. "What's wrong?" Sybil asked.

"The man," Aislin said quietly. "The one we saw in the church…he's over there, watching us."

Scotty and Sybil turned in their saddles to follow her gaze.

"He looks…" Aislin didn't finish. She just stared. "Sybil, what do you think? Do you see a resemblance…?"

The man made his way toward them, moving slowly, but carrying himself in that proud manner that Aislin remembered so well.

Jamie.

THIRTY-THREE

Aislin slid from Silverheel's saddle and stood perfectly still as Jamie moved toward her, the distance between them lessening with each step.

He stopped in front of her. He didn't speak. Or move. Around them rose the sounds of voices and horses and jangling rigs, but still they stared without speaking.

Finally, Jamie reached for her hand and, taking it in his own, touched the ring on her third finger. He studied it for several long moments, then raised his eyes and smiled. It was the same smile she remembered from long ago. In that instant, her heart, her mind flooded with memories.

"Ceallach," he said softly, and her heart melted.

Sybil stepped forward with an expression of astonished delight. "Well, if you two can't get on with a proper welcome," she said, "I figure it's up to me!" She threw herself into Jamie's arms.

Sybil's exuberance broke the stunned silence. Laughing, he pulled her into a hearty embrace. Then she stepped back, looked in his eyes with a grin that covered her entire face, then gave him another bear hug.

"Jamie Dearbourne in the flesh!" she said. "We thought you were dead!"

"Dead?" He looked at Aislin over Sybil's shoulder. She confirmed it with a nod.

"This is Scotty MacPherson," she said proudly, reaching for her intended's hand and pulling him forward.

"What are you doing here?" Jamie asked, once the introductions were made.

Aislin still hadn't spoken and, for once, was glad for Sybil's excited chatter. Her sister eagerly told Jamie of the rancho troubles, the scheme to save the land, how Spence, the wranglers, and his father—she halted midsentence, and looked frantically to Aislin for help.

"Syb," Aislin interrupted gently, "I think Jamie and I need some privacy. Why don't you and Scotty return to camp. I'll—" she smiled at Jamie, then turned again to her sister. "*We'll* follow later. Do you mind?"

Sybil looked relieved. She gave Jamie a quick kiss on the cheek, then grabbed Scotty's hand and headed for the horses.

When they were gone, Jamie took her arm and they began to stroll slowly across the plaza toward the church, the silence between them awkward.

"Jamie," she began at the exact instant he said, "Aislin." They laughed, and said, "Go ahead," together.

Aislin stopped walking and turned to him. "This is difficult," she said. "I never…" She paused before going on. "I never really believed it, but we all assumed that, well, you were dead. Now here you are, standing in front of me. It's such a shock, I don't know how to act, what to say."

"It's been almost three years," Jamie said. "I feel the same way."

They started walking again. The sun was on its downward slant, its light clear and golden, and the air was turning colder. They walked past the church, following a footpath that wound to the creek.

"I need to tell you about your father."

Jamie stopped. "I knew from the look on Sybil's face that something had happened. Tell me."

"Do you remember Fraco Ciro?"

"Of course."

"He showed up with some of his men to help us herd the horses back in California. Had a falling out with Spence, then left, only to follow at a distance. Apparently, he planned to take our herd when we arrived at the Colorado River."

"My father was with you?"

"He and some of the Dearbourne wranglers joined us after we were on the trail."

"That doesn't sound like my father. I mean, to join Spence in a scheme like this."

"He wanted to take over for Spence. He thought he could do a better job."

"And did he?"

They were walking again, and she hooked her arm through his. It felt natural. "Spence wouldn't let him."

Jamie grinned. "He held his own?"

She looked into his face. "Better than that, Jamie. He ran every part of the operation for the two-thousand-mile drive."

This time Jamie laughed. "Good for Spence." Then his smile faded. "You still haven't told me what happened to my father. He is all right?"

She drew in a deep breath. There was no easy way to tell him. "He was shot, Jamie," she said softly, "defending the herd." She couldn't bear to tell him the whole truth.

Jamie halted and stood silent, staring, uncomprehending. "No…" he finally uttered. "It couldn't have been that long ago. If it was the Colorado, I mean."

"Only a few weeks."

He looked heavenward in his pain, closing his eyes. "After all this time. Three years…" He moved his gaze back to her face. "Within days of seeing each other after all this time."

"I'm so sorry," she said, touching his arm. His eyes held such pain that she almost looked away. "Oh, Jamie," she murmured.

In one swift movement, he pulled her into his arms and held her as if she might disappear again forever. A low, heart-wrenching sob erupted from him, and he pulled her tighter, burying his face in her hair.

Aislin had held Spence in the same way when Hugh died, and the irony struck her now. A strange calm filled her. All questions now were answered. Questions about her future. Jamie's. Spence's. How right she'd been to insist that Jamie lived, that she would remain true to his memory, his love, their betrothal.

Spence's words about her marriage to Jamie, his words of blessing on their children, their children's children, came to her now. It was as if he had somehow accepted that this moment was in her future. This moment, when his brother would again rest in the comfort of her arms.

"Aislin…" Jamie pulled back and looked her full in the eyes. His own still glistened with tears. "I'm glad you're here. I'm glad you were the one to tell me."

"I wish it didn't have to be so," she said. "I wish I had only good news to tell after all this time."

He frowned. "Is there something else?"

Spence's image filled her mind, an image so beautiful and strong, so utterly overpowering, that for a moment she couldn't speak. She closed her eyes to chase it away, to regain her composure.

"Aislin…?" he repeated.

"No," she finally whispered. "There's nothing else."

With his arm still draped around Aislin's shoulders, the two began moving once more toward the creek. He sighed deeply, thinking how Hallie had been correct in her caution. One look at Aislin's ring finger told him she had waited. What a fool he would have made of both himself and Aislin had he brought Hallie Callahan and little Emma with him from Kentucky.

The sun had slipped behind the mountains to the west, and dusk was falling.

"Tell me what happened after you left me," Aislin asked.

"I left California so full of glory, so full of myself." He was ashamed to consider his arrogance. "I was sure I'd win every battle single-handed."

"I remember." She laughed lightly, and he squeezed her shoulders.

"Before I had the chance to volunteer for duty, I was captured. Herded with others—trail guides, muleskinners—just as innocent as I was to the battlefield, sold like slaves to the highest bidder." He paused, looking at the dark mountains where the sun had just set. "I was shot in the back when they assumed I was trying to desert." He laughed, bitterly. "I was actually heading to report a crooked captain who was working for the enemy."

She slipped her arm around his waist as they walked along the creekside. It reminded him of when they were children, the easy way they had with each other then. Chasing. Laughing. Carrying on. Talking endlessly.

Jamie went on to tell her of the trek to Elmira, his time in prison, his escape, and how he made his way to St. Louis. He didn't mention Hallie Callahan. Somehow, he wanted to keep her memory private for just a while longer. Instead, he told her of Aunt Gertie, her head-standin' ways, her love of driving the big Conestogas, her parting gift of the mule, Lafayette. He also told her about his friendship with Ransom Brown.

When he'd finished, twilight had fallen, and the temperatures dropped. Aislin shivered, and he pulled her closer, taking pleasure from her warmth. For a while they stood, looking back at Abiqui. Candles and lamps were now lit and glowed through small windows in the adobes. The look of Hallie's house in the dark returned to him. The way its light had seemed a sanctuary from the dark, the physical darkness outside, the darkness within him. Her fireplace. The flicker of candle-light as she rocked Emma and sang to her.

But that was behind him. He would always look back on those days as God-ordained to help him heal. His commitment now was to Aislin, and as he glanced down at her upturned face, his heart flooded with affection for his longtime friend.

He smiled gently. "I'd made arrangements to have supper at Miss Thornton's. Shall we see if she can set an extra place?"

Her face softened. "I would like that."

"There's one more thing."

"What's that?"

"Do you mind waiting while I get a shave and a haircut?"

"Right now?"

He nodded. "I can't accompany a beautiful woman to supper looking like this."

She laughed lightly. "How about if I come along to see that it's done properly?"

He chuckled. "That sounds more like something Sybil would say."

"You remember us all well," she said, taking his arm as they headed along the plaza.

His felt his smile fade. "I do," he said simply.

An hour later, they strolled from the barber's, Aislin's hand tucked in the crook of his arm, along the boardwalk back to Miss Thornton's boardinghouse.

After he'd helped Aislin into her chair, he seated himself across from her. He had watched her in the mirror while the barber cut his hair, and he had wondered how many times after his capture he had tried to remember her face. How many times had he searched his heart and mind, only to find her image had completely vanished?

Now, staring across the table at her, he questioned how he could have ever forgotten what she looked like. She was as beautiful as ever with her luminous gray eyes filled with curiosity, her dark hair pulled into a braid, tendrils escaping, just as always. She hadn't changed.

But he had.

"You're different," she said, as Miss Thornton bustled toward them with two bowls of steaming soup. When the proprietress had left them, Aislin stirred her soup absently, watching him carefully.

"I was just thinking that you hadn't changed." He lifted his spoon. "But how do you think I have?"

"Perhaps it's just that you left a lighthearted boy. You've returned a man." She paused, thinking. "You always had the attitude that the world was yours, to enjoy, to direct if need be."

He laughed. "And now?"

"There's a settled sense about you."

"Settled?"

"That maybe, with all you've been through, you've come to a different understanding of the world and your place in it." She lifted a spoonful of soup to her lips. "An acceptance."

"Or resignation…" he added.

"That must be hard for you, Jamie, if resignation is what you're feeling."

"I've learned some hard lessons. Some I needed to learn…about myself, about others. But also lessons I'd have been better off not learning, especially about my fellowman."

Their conversation was easing now, and her expression told him she felt it too.

"Those things I saw, experienced, in prison…a man can't go through something like that and come out unchanged."

"It would be easy to be angry, bitter. But I don't see either of those in you, Jamie."

"My journey's been long," he said, without further explanation. She seemed to understand his reluctance to discuss it and didn't press him for details.

A comfortable silence fell between them as they continued eating.

"Aislin," he said after a few minutes, "about the years that I was away." He paused, meeting her gaze. "I'm glad you waited. I wasn't sure that you would—even without thinking me dead. Three years is quite a long time."

"We made a commitment, a lifetime commitment, Jamie. I wanted to marry you before you left, if you remember?"

"Yes, I remember."

"I never forgot my promise to you." She reached for his hand and stroked it as she spoke.

"And neither did I."

She seemed at a loss for words momentarily. Then she gave him a gentle smile and pressed his hand. "You saw the ring," she said. "I've never taken it off."

He traced the outline of her hand, lightly touching the small, gold band. How long ago that day seemed when he'd slipped it on her finger.

"I had planned to search for you…" She stopped, seeming to gather her thoughts before going on. "Rather than returning with Spence and the others to California, I planned to head east."

He wondered if it was his imagination or if there was a flicker of emotion in her eyes when she spoke his brother's name.

"I was planning to leave from Santa Fe with Erasmo—"

"I remember the man," he said.

"I didn't know exactly where to start, only that I knew I had to find you."

Her loyalty touched him. "I had no idea…" His voice broke. "Tell me about the ranchos," he said, wanting to change the direction of their conversation. "How were they going to save them if this horse drive hadn't come up? Was there a…an alternate plan?"

Her cheeks flushed just a bit, and her eyes seemed to brighten and then quickly fade. "Ah, Spence and I discussed marriage," she said with obvious discomfort, "though only because we thought it might help save the lands."

"Spence?" He'd never pictured the two of them together.

"It would have been a marriage of convenience."

"I see."

"I never removed your ring, even then," she added.

Miss Thornton interrupted, setting plates of roasted meat and potatoes in front of them.

They finished eating, and he smiled into Aislin's eyes. "It's a beautiful night for a moonlight ride."

She glanced out a nearby window. "It is. Strange how winter in New Mexico can be so beautiful. Even at night the air seems crisper, clearer."

"It's not long till spring."

"We'll be arriving home in time to see everything in bloom."

"A nice time of year for a wedding."

She didn't brighten at his words. Merely nodded and agreed with him.

"If Spence arrives in time to buy back the ranchos," he said, "it will be quite a celebration."

"And a homecoming," she added. "Though Spence himself won't be there to greet us."

"Why not?" Again, he noticed something undefinable in her expression.

"He's got a dream to start a horse ranch. He said he would head out as soon as the ranchos are secured in your family's and my family's names."

"I'll figure out where's he gone," Jamie said. "I don't want to get married without Spence standing up with me."

A pained expression crossed her face, then it quickly disappeared. "Absolutely," she said. "Though, knowing Spence, he may disappear never to be found again...that is, if he's of a mind to."

"You probably know him better than I do by now," he said, watching her carefully.

But she merely smiled. "Could be," she said with a light laugh.

A half-hour later, they mounted their horses and, with Jamie carrying a lantern, made their way slowly along the trail leading back to camp. As they approached, sounds of the wranglers' voices filled the air, punctuated from time to time by Sybil's peals of laughter. Firelight twinkled through the trees, and pine smoke lay close to the ground, scenting the air.

Aislin halted Silverheel a hundred yards before they reached the night circle. Jamie stopped right behind her, and they both dismounted. For a moment they stood very close together.

He reached for her, and she stepped closer. He placed a hand on either side of her face and gazed into her eyes, then he bent to kiss her. But she pulled away from him.

"Can you give me time?"

He needed it perhaps more than she did. "Of course," he said. "I shouldn't have pressed—"

She interrupted. "I need—maybe we both need—time to fall in love all over again, Jamie."

He nodded slowly and laced his fingers through hers. "We'll have time on the trail to work on it."

"Make that a lifetime," she corrected, her voice soft. "A lifetime to learn to love each other."

"Until tomorrow, then?"

"Yes," she said. "Tomorrow."

He watched her lead Silverheel through the trees. She turned just before reaching camp and blew him a kiss. Her face was beautiful in the pale glow of lantern light.

Aislin tossed on her pallet that night, unable to sleep. Her heart went out to Jamie. She knew he wasn't telling her everything he'd been through. How could he? The horrors of his life in prison must have been unspeakable. He'd glossed over them as if they were nothing. She wondered if he would ever open his heart to her completely.

She twisted the ring on her finger. Things weren't right between them, though she chided herself for her own impatience.

How could she expect their love to be as strong as it had been when he left?

He was different, even admitted he was different. Strangely, though, his differences should have made him more attractive to her. He'd lost his sense of arrogance, his self-importance. Those qualities she'd disliked but chose to overlook even as a child.

She fluffed her pillow, socked it, then fluffed it again, turning on her opposite side.

She would make it work—the marriage, the love. She'd been committed to Jamie for all these years. She wouldn't give up on him, on them, now or ever.

She pictured their wedding, perhaps in the courtyard of La Paloma, under the century oak, the fountain bubbling, bougainvillea cascading from the upper balustrade.

Sybil would stand with her, also sweet Brighid. Her wedding gown would be of Irish lace. She would wear her mother's white mantilla.

The wedding party would stand under the oak, waiting for the bride to step down the terrace and move toward her groom.

Yes, the thought was beautiful…until she pictured Jamie, watching her walk toward him. He said he wanted Spence at his side.

How could she walk down the aisle toward Jamie, if it was Spence's gaze she sought?

Thirty-four

The weeks on the trail were agonizing and slow for Aislin. There was no herd to drive, only a small remuda of spare horses to give their own a rest from time to time and a string of pack mules, led by Jamie's Lafayette. Yet they moved, it seemed to her, with greater deliberation and caution than before. The Mojave Trail was not as heavily traveled as the Old Spanish and, because of it, was more heavily populated with marauding bands of Indians, horse thieves, and robbers.

Every day, she and Jamie treated each other with great concern and respect. Every night, she cried herself to sleep. Every morning, she woke with a renewed determination to make their betrothal, their coming marriage, work.

She had spoken to no one about her doubts, but one night, just a few days from the California border, Sybil plopped down on Aislin's bed pallet.

"When are you and Jamie going to get over treating each other like distant kin?"

"Distant kin?"

"Don't tell me you haven't noticed."

"We're trying, Syb. Honestly. Trying to make it work."

"Oh, I can see you're trying. Too hard, in my estimation."

"It's just not the same. I think Jamie's feeling the same way, but we just can't talk about it."

"Have you tried? I mean, tried to get to the heart of your doubts?"

Aislin shook her head. "We talk about everything else but ourselves. Our feelings. It's as if it's a closed door."

"Maybe you should tell him about Spence."

She narrowed her eyes. "What about Spence?"

341

"That you love him." Sybil tilted her head and set her lips in a no-nonsense manner.

"I've never said I love Spence."

"It was obvious to everyone around you, Aislin. The entire trek to New Mexico."

Aislin drew in a sharp breath. "I never intended…"

"Oh, I know you never intended to fall in love with him, nor he with you, for that matter."

"Spence doesn't love me."

"Ha! He certainly gave every indication he would lay down his very life for you." Hadn't those been Spence's exact words to her? Sybil's arms were crossed over her chest, and she seemed very much the elder sister at this moment. "You were probably the only one who didn't see it."

"He wouldn't have left if that had been the case." She settled down beside her sister. "Syb, you should have seen how he behaved toward me. It was appalling."

"And why wouldn't he?" Sybil shook her head. "For someone so clever, Aislin, you're one of the most dull-witted women I've ever come across."

"What are you talking about?"

"Spence! Think a minute about how he felt. Here you are, pining away after his brother; dead or alive, you're pining after the man."

"We were betrothed."

"You were children. Jamie was gone, thought dead. You hung on to his memory just so you wouldn't have to consider that a real flesh-and-blood man, not a boy, loved you."

"You're saying I hung on to Jamie's memory to protect myself from Spence?"

"Yes. I'm saying exactly that. Jamie was safe. Known. The favored son. The heir to his father's lands. Spence was none of those things."

"You have no idea what you're talking about." But her heart caught in her throat with the truth of her sister's words.

For a moment, neither one spoke.

"I loved Jamie," she finally said.

"Did you hear what you just said?" Sybil frowned. "You said loved, not love. As in the past. Not the present."

"I was talking about the past, not the present," she said.

Sybil shook her head. "You're making a terrible mistake."

"It's between Jamie and me. We'll work it out."

"Maybe I should tell Jamie about Spence."

"There's nothing to tell."

"I think there is."

"Promise me, Syb," she said, taking her sister's hand. "Promise me that you will not ever breathe a word of anything you've just said to Jamie. His faith in humankind has been damaged. If he thought I'd been unfaithful, even in my heart, it would destroy him."

"I think you're wrong. I think you both need to be free of this charade you're carrying on. You need to try honesty."

"Promise me, Sybil Byrne, that you won't say anything."

Her sister stared at her. "All right," she finally said. "But I—"

"Hush, now," Aislin said. "I know what I'm doing. So does Jamie."

"Just one more thing."

"I'm listening."

"If you want this love between you and Jamie to work, maybe it's truth that you need to build on. Maybe you need to confess your doubts, let him do the same. Give yourselves the freedom to come together with honesty."

Aislin squeezed Sybil's hand. "When did you become so wise?"

Sybil laughed. "Well, now. That's a switch. Me, Miss Scatter-brained-and-Silly? Me, wise?" She laughed again, but looked pleased.

"I will do as you say, Syb. Maybe you're right."

"I *know* I'm right." Besides looking pleased, Sybil now looked arrogant. Aislin pushed her over backward on the sleeping pallet, and they both collapsed in a heap, laughing.

The following day as Aislin rode beside Jamie they spoke, as usual, about everything except the two of them.

"Jamie, I have a question for you," she finally said, when they had lagged a bit behind the rest of the group.

He glanced over at her and nodded. For a moment the only sounds were those of the hooves on the trail.

She took a deep breath and blurted it all out at once. "Do you have any doubts about our marriage—about me—your feelings for me?"

He looked surprised, drew his horse to a halt. She halted Silverheel, and while the horses danced a step or two on the trail, he looked into her face. "That's quite a question, Aislin, after all this time."

"That's why I'm asking it."

He fell silent a minute, then looked away as if praying or carefully choosing his words. Or both.

"Please be honest," she said. "I think it's honesty we need with each other right now."

He turned to her again. "I do have doubts," he said. "Not about you or your love. But about me. I've changed, and I don't know if I can ever love you the way I used to...the way you deserve to be loved."

"I understand," she said softly.

"Does it bother you that I can't...well, love you...at least not yet, in that way?" He searched her eyes.

She remembered Sybil's words. "Maybe we need to discover a different kind of love. Maybe the love we had was that of our childhood. Something we grew into without thoughts of it ever changing. We hadn't become ourselves yet."

She reached for his hand, and he nudged Broomtail closer so he could take her hand in his.

"We might have had to go through this even if you hadn't left."

"Rediscovering our love, you mean?"

She nodded. "We've talked about falling in love all over again, but we were thinking of the past, recapturing those giddy feelings of young love. We're no longer children. Maybe those same feelings can never be recaptured."

"Giddy love? Is that what you remember?"

"And it was grand," she said with a smile, remembering. "Our Gaelic fort on the hill."

"Ceallach," he said, meeting her eyes.

"It was romantic, but we were little more than children playing when you asked me to marry you."

"Even as I was riding off to war, I was almost playacting the childhood stories we made up. The glory and honor of it."

They nudged the horses to a walk again now, but kept them at a slow pace. The others rode farther ahead on the trail, the mule train following behind.

"It's a different kind of love we need to discover in each other, Jamie," she said, feeling wise in her assessment.

"It strikes me," he said, grinning at her, "that we shouldn't need to spend so much time trying to figure out what it is we're missing."

She looked at him gratefully. "I was thinking the same thing."

"It also strikes me that giddy isn't so bad when a man and woman think of each other." He chuckled, gazing steadily in her direction.

"I wonder," she said.

"Giddy, such as when your heart turns somersaults at the mention of your beloved's name. Or you see starlight in your beloved's eyes. Or hear your beloved's voice in the wind."

She clamped her lips together and they rode in silence for a while. From the corner of her eye, she could see Jamie watching her.

Finally she spoke, quoting a verse from First Corinthians, "When I was a child, I spake as a child, I understood as a child, I thought as a child…"

He gave her a sad half-smile, and finished the verse for her. "But when I became a man, I put away childish things."

"Exactly," she said.

He laughed lightly. "I don't think the apostle Paul was talking about courtship and marriage."

"He was talking about love," she countered.

The horses' hooves thudded on the hard soil as they moved on. "Have you prayed about this…our coming marriage, Aislin? Our life together?" he asked after a moment.

"No. Have you?"

He nodded. "Yes."

She halted Silverheel again. "I've tried, Jamie. But there's a heartache so deep in me that I find it difficult to express my feelings. I don't understand them myself."

He moved his horse closer and looked her straight in the eyes. It struck her that their honesty was bringing them closer together, but it was also painful. It was as if a knife was poised and ready to slice between them.

Tears welled in her eyes. "I'm sorry," she mumbled. "I don't know what's come over me."

"Don't apologize, Aislin. I've been wanting to have this same conversation for a long time."

"You have?"

He nodded. "Tell me about that heartache. What's causing it?"

"I can't…tell you." She let her gaze drift away from him.

"I thought this was to be our time of honesty."

She closed her eyes, and the tears spilled down her cheeks. She could no longer keep the truth from him. "Spence…" she whispered. "Because of Spence."

"Spence?"

She didn't dare look at him.

"Spence?" he repeated.

Finally, she opened her eyes. He was staring at her with anything but a look of hurt, disapproval, disappointment. He was grinning ear to ear, as if it was the best news he'd ever received.

"Spence?" he almost shouted. "Spence?"

She put her hands on her hips. "You've said his name at least five times. What's so hard to believe about that?"

"Four times," he said, his eyes bright with what seemed, impossibly, to be delight.

"Excuse me," she said. "But this is hardly the reaction I expected. Where's your injured dignity?"

"Oh, sweet Aislin," he said. "If you only knew…" He looked heavenward and released a deep sigh.

"Knew what?"

"First, tell me about Spence. What's happened between the two of you? Why did he leave?"

She gave him a tremulous smile. "You, Jamie. That's what happened. I remained true to you, and he did the honorable thing by removing himself from my life."

"He didn't even know I was alive."

"He knew that you were to me, and that I was determined to find you."

"Oh, honey, I'm sorry." He reached for her hand with more warmth than he'd shown her since arriving. It was as if the old Jamie was back. Flesh and blood. Heart and soul. "Tell me everything."

"Are you sure you want to hear it?"

He nodded, that impossible smile still lighting his face.

"I think I can sum it up in three little sentences."

He was still grinning. "Go ahead, but I think I know which three."

"My heart turns somersaults at the mention of his name," she whispered, as if to Spence himself. "I see starlight when I look in his eyes. I hear his voice in the wind."

Jamie nodded slowly. "I think we have a serious problem on our hands."

"I know."

"I don't think we can marry under these circumstances."

"I agree."

"It's the last thing we should do."

"I couldn't agree more."

He laughed. The horses were standing impatiently, stepping sideways a bit, tossing their heads. "Perhaps we should catch up with the others," he said.

"I'm confused, Jamie," she said as they rode. "Your reaction isn't what I expected. Is there something you need to tell me? Something about a love of your own?"

He studied her for a moment, as if trying to decide how much, or what, to say. "Someone once said I won't know who I love until I'm through healing," he finally said. "I'm just discovering how true that is."

The horses trotted along the trail. "Who was it who said it?"

"Hallie Callahan." He met Aislin's curious gaze with another wide smile. "A very wise woman from Kentucky."

Jamie felt as though a pressing weight had lifted from his shoulders. Aislin had ridden ahead of him, and he watched her in the fading sunlight. He loved her. Oh yes. And he probably always would. But it wasn't the kind of love—he laughed, remembering how they had both repeated the words—that had anything to do with somersaults, starlight, or wind.

He watched her ride, picket-straight, long braid swinging, to catch up with the others. He was letting her ride away from him, letting her go forever, and with his blessing. Then he looked at the small gold ring in his palm, the ring she had handed him before riding off.

Father, he prayed, *you've brought us this far. Take us where we need to go. All of us.*

He thought of Hallie Callahan, little Emma. *Hold them in your arms. Keep them safe…until we meet again.*

I've come a long way, Lord, but as I face the journey ahead, I know that you're not finished with me. Not finished with any of us.

Spence came to his mind, and he pieced together what he knew of his brother. He'd never been prouder. It took a big man to do what he'd done—save the ranchos with sheer grit and dogged determination; walk away from the woman he loved out of loyalty to her and to his brother; start a new life, leaving home, lands, and Aislin behind.

And, Father, he prayed, *cause your Presence to be known to him, wherever he is. May he know your abundant love, your mercy, your healing.*

Again, his gaze fell on Aislin riding jauntily on Silverheel ahead of him. *And this woman, Lord. Give her the desires of her heart.*

I love her! And I love Spence. Bless them both…now and forever.

THIRTY-FIVE

Aislin was in the lead as the small band headed across the pine-covered crest of Cajon Pass, then wound along the mountain toward Big Valley. She drew her horse to a halt directly above the valley, and the others moved their mounts to stand beside hers.

Sybil let out a low whistle. "Will you look at that?"

"Looks like the drought is over," Scotty said.

He was right. The valley was alive with growth—lush, green grasses and wildflowers of every hue.

"California…" Aislin said, her voice in a hush. "I've never seen it more beautiful." She turned to Jamie. "We're home, my friend."

He nodded. "No one's as glad as I am."

"Well, you never saw it in the drought—" Sybil said, hurrying to fill him in on every detail.

"Syb," Jamie interrupted with a laugh.

"Yes?"

"I really don't want to hear how bad things were here." He lifted a teasing brow.

"Oh. Well, I can see your point," she said. "I'm sure you think I'm whining. And of course, compared to what you went through—"

"Syb, enough!" Aislin said.

Sybil gave Jamie a playful poke in the arm. "Now, haven't you missed me?"

"Actually, yes. I missed having a little spoiled, bratty sister to push around!" Before the words were out of his mouth he nudged Broomtail to a gallop.

Sybil let out a good-natured yell and took off after him, whooping and hollering. The two raced through the grassy fields, Jamie holding his

349

hat above his head, his legs sticking straight out from the swaybacked horse.

Sybil caught up with him and grabbed the hat as she raced by, crowing like a rooster.

"You're sure you want to marry my sister?" Aislin asked Scotty with a grin.

"I've never seen such a bunch. Plus I never had brothers and sisters," he said. "All this liveliness will take some getting used to." But his expression told her he was loving every minute of it.

"Now you've got two new sisters…" She wanted to continue, "and a couple of brothers," but she didn't go on. It might be that the Dearbournes would never be part of the Byrne family.

The group settled down to an easy trot for the remaining short distance to the ranchos. Jamie fell back to ride beside Aislin as they approached Rancho de la Paloma.

When the familiar horseshoe gate came into sight, she slowed Silverheel to a walk and Jamie followed suit.

She turned to him. "The last word we had of any of the family was when your father joined us. He said your mother was living with friends at the Pueblo de los Angeles, and my parents and Brighid had moved to the adobe, which was no surprise. Sybil was already packing to move with them when she changed her mind and left with Scotty."

"I say we try the rancho first," Jamie said. "Let's hope that Spence made it back in time."

"I'm almost afraid to ride in."

"You're worried about someone else being there?"

"Living there," she corrected. "What if it's now someone else's home? I don't know if I can bear it."

He gave her a gentle smile. "You've said that more times than I can count, yet you bear most things quite well, I've noticed."

She laughed. "You would know better than anyone."

"I would, Ceallach." He raised a brow. "I chose the name 'warrior maiden' well, don't you think?"

The others had now drawn up their mounts, and a sense of anticipation fell over the group as they stared down the rutted road. Stands of trees and rolling hills blocked the hacienda from view, so they would have to wait until they were closer to know who was in residence.

"No time like the present," Sybil muttered and kicked Rachelle into an easy canter. With her back straight, her chin lifted high, she looked every bit the ranchero's daughter.

Aislin chuckled at her impertinence and followed suit, her own back straight. If another family was indeed in residence, at least she and her sister had this one last proud ride down the winding driveway leading to their former home.

She pressed her knees into Silverheel to pull up even with her sister. The two of them rode side by side. The hacienda now rose in the distance—glistening whitewashed walls, with the bougainvillea cascading across the roof and onto the front verandah, sycamores spreading a bright green canopy across the close-cropped grass in front. Flowers spilled from terra-cotta pots that flanked the walkway to the entrance—great frothy bunches of petunias and daisies and violets.

Oh yes. No matter who lived there, the evidence was everywhere that the drought had broken. God had poured his abundance of life-giving water on this thirsty land.

They reached the verandah and slid from their saddles. Aislin glanced back, relieved to see that the others had halted, giving her and Sybil time to discover for themselves what had happened to their home.

Sybil grabbed hold of Aislin's hand as they climbed the front stairs. "I'm scared," she whispered.

Aislin pressed her hand and reached for the heavy brass knocker.

She rapped it once, twice…a third time.

Finally, soft footsteps could be heard coming to the door. A few moments later, the door opened.

Josefa, their maid since childhood, looked stunned, and after a moment of silence, her words spilled out rapidly in Spanish.

"Wait," Sybil said with a laugh. "I haven't heard Spanish for so long, I can't understand you."

Josefa was crying now, and instead of repeating her words, pulled both Aislin and Sybil into her arms, rocking them as she had done when they were babies.

Aislin pulled back. "Mother and Papa…are they here?"

"*Sí, sí, sí,*" Josefa cried. "Yes. They are here. Follow me." She led the way through the entry, through the doors to the other side, and onto the terrace above the courtyard.

MacQuaid and Camila sat beneath the century oak. It was as if they'd never left the place.

For a moment, they stared dumbfounded at their daughters. No one uttered a word.

Aislin, with Sybil's hand still in hers, stepped down the terrace stairs toward them.

Silently, MacQuaid, Camila at his side, rose and pulled them into an embrace, and they stood, mother, father, and daughters, with arms wrapped around each other, crying.

Finally, MacQuaid pulled back. "Aye, my lassies, 'tis good to see you."

Camila smiled through her tears, her arms still circling the waists of both her daughters.

"Spence got here in time then," Aislin said, hoping for news of him.

"Aye, lass, that he did." MacQuaid met her gaze. "But he left soon after. He saw his mother safely from the pueblo back to Rancho Dearbourne, and after a few days, he was on his way again."

Her heart seemed to stop beating. "Did he say where?"

"No," Camila added. "He seemed not to want anyone to know."

Before Aislin could absorb the reality of his leaving, Sybil spoke up. "We have Jamie with us."

MacQuaid and Camila frowned, unbelieving. "Jamie?" MacQuaid said slowly.

Aislin nodded. "Yes. We'll explain later, but why don't we invite the others in?" She looked to Sybil, knowing she'd want to be the first to tell the news about Scotty. "Do you want to get them?"

Sybil ran across the courtyard to the terrace and let herself out the front entrance.

"Where's Brighid?" Aislin asked, turning to her mother and father.

They exchanged a solemn look. "She has fallen ill," said Camila. She frowned, seeming uncomfortable.

MacQuaid stepped up and wrapped his arm around his daughter's shoulders. "She had a tragic accident," he said quietly. "It involved some of the squatters who lived here awhile. She was on her way to the Soboba village. I told her to be careful, not to go alone. But the men…" His voice broke. "They shot her horse. They…" He couldn't finish.

Aislin searched her parents' faces and knew the unspeakable had happened to her little sister. Hot tears of sorrow and anger filled her eyes. Her voice choked, and she swallowed hard. "I want to see her."

"We will take you," MacQuaid said. "When she sees you and Sybil, perhaps it will help."

But Aislin knew from the bleak expressions on her parents' faces that they didn't believe it.

A few minutes later, Sybil returned in a flurry of chatter and laughter. She pulled Scotty by the arm, and Jamie followed behind. Again, there were greetings and hugs and exclamations of wonder over Jamie's return.

Then Sybil cleared her throat dramatically. "Papa, Scotty has something to ask you."

MacQuaid inclined his head, frowning. "About what, son?"

Scotty scowled, though not too seriously, at Sybil. "I really had planned to do this in private, Syb."

She dimpled prettily. "But I can't wait a minute longer. Please. Please, sweetheart. Ask him now."

"Sweetheart?" MacQuaid repeated. "What is this?"

"Ah, sir, I, ah…" Scotty began, the white skin beneath his freckles flaming as red as his hair.

Sybil couldn't wait. "He wants to marry me, Papa!"

MacQuaid chuckled. "Well now, does he?"

Scotty recovered, cleared his throat, and started again. "Sir, I would be most honored to have your daughter's hand in marriage. I, ah, we, that is, ah… We've prayed about this, and well, ah, we…"

Again, Sybil jumped in. "He's trying to say we love each other!" And she threw herself into Scotty's arms and kissed him soundly on the lips.

Scotty turned an even brighter shade of red, and Aislin thought she saw his ears wiggle.

While everyone was caught up in their excitement, laughing and talking, Jamie caught Aislin's gaze. He smiled into her eyes, then blew a kiss as he headed toward the terrace. She hurried to catch him before he left.

"You're on your way to see your mother?"

"Yes."

"Jamie…just now, were you thinking about us?"

His smile was tender. He touched her cheek. "Yes, Ceallach, I was."

"It could have been us making the same announcement."

"No." He shook his head. "God gave us wisdom to understand that we don't have that kind of love."

"Will you be staying on in the Big Valley?"

"For now, yes."

"But someday you'll go back to Kentucky?"

"How did you guess?"

"It was the way you said 'Hallie Callahan' that first time," she said.

"You'll like her, Ceallach."

"Then will you hurry and fetch her, please?"

"She's got a little daughter named Emma." His eyes seemed to mist as he thought of her.

"Go after them, Jamie. Don't let love slip away."

He drew her into his arms. "We both almost did." He held her close for several moments, then he pulled back. "And you?"

"I plan to go after Spence."

He grinned. "If anyone can find him, it'll be you."

He kissed her on the cheek, then turned, taking the terrace stairs two at a time. At the top, he looked back and winked. "Remember…somersaults, starlight, and voices in the wind, Ceallach," he said. Then he turned and was gone.

Before dark the same day, MacQuaid hitched a team of horses to the carriage and pulled up to the front of the house. The mood was somber as Camila, Sybil, and Aislin entered the vehicle.

"How long has Brighid been like this, Mama?" Sybil asked.

"Since the accident, child. She seems to have put it from her mind and now lives in a different world."

Aislin settled against the leather seat of the carriage, feeling each bump and sway as her father drove. "Why wouldn't she leave the adobe?"

Her mother sighed. "Somehow she thinks she will be safe there. Whenever we have tried to move her, she screams and cries, clinging to the doorway. It is the closest to grieving that she comes. We decided to let her stay there. Buena stays with her, cooking and taking care of her."

"Maybe we can help," Sybil said, her voice sounding young and scared.

Aislin reached for her sister's hand and held it fast the rest of the way to the adobe.

The carriage halted just beyond the small house. "Where was she heading when it happened?" Sybil asked.

"She was riding to the Soboba village," Camila said. "The children were waiting. She had been reading them stories and teaching them how to write their names." MacQuaid held the carriage door open, and Camila stepped down.

"Do any of her friends come out here to see her?" Aislin asked as they walked closer to the house.

"There are very few people she will see," Camila said, stopping at the front door. "Sara has been a blessing. She has been here almost daily…since she found out. She even drove here from the pueblo."

"And Brighid was happy to see Spence," MacQuaid added.

"Spence came?" Aislin looked up at her father.

He smiled. "Every day he was still in the Big Valley. Sometimes he came to read to her, or tell her stories about the trail. She loved hearing about gentling wild horses." How like him. Of course he would do that. Healing was what he did best.

MacQuaid knocked on the door, and while they waited for Buena to answer, he turned again to Aislin. "The last day he was here, he brought a wild foal for Brighid to see. Carried it into her room and laid it on her bed. Taught her how to gentle away its fear," MacQuaid said, then turned his attention to Buena, who smiled and invited them into the room.

Brighid looked up from where she sat, her back propped against pillows. She smiled at Sybil and Aislin as if she'd seen them every day for the last six months.

Aislin grabbed her little sister and gathered her into a hug. "Oh, my sweet Brig," she whispered tenderly. "How I have missed you."

Sybil sat on the opposite side of the bed, tears filling her eyes. She tried not to let them show and blinked them away.

Brighid looked from one sister to the other, her eyes luminous and clear, as if confused to be receiving such attention.

"I've been planning for a wonderful ball," she said conversationally. "Syb, I must ask your permission, however, to wear the dress you just ordered from New York. Please tell me I may."

Sybil glanced at Camila, who gave her a quick nod. "Well, yes, sweetie. Of course you may," Sybil said to Brighid.

Brighid looked relieved and fell back against her pillows again.

"I'm getting married, Brig," Sybil began, searching her sister's face for signs of understanding.

"And have you ordered your gown?"

"No, I haven't. But I'd like for you to be in the wedding. We'll order you a special gown to wear." Sybil bit her lip. "It can be your favorite color. What is your favorite color, Brig?"

"It must be white," she said. "I can only wear white. Everything must be white." She was twisting her bedclothes now.

Aislin took her hands and held them in her own. "I love you, Brig. We want you to get well and come home with us."

"I am home," Brighid said, her hands relaxing, her smile returning. "I entertain here every day. I serve tea on the porch. Ladies from all over Big Valley come to call."

Sybil bent low to look Brighid in the eyes. "Did you know your children miss you?"

"Children?" she said. "I have no children."

"The Soboba children," Sybil pressed.

Brighid looked stunned, as if a moment of complete clarity had returned. Then she began to tremble. "I think it's time for you to leave," she said, drawing herself up tall. "Tea will be served on the porch later if you would like to return."

She lifted her hand to smooth her hair, but it was shaking so violently that she instead hid it under the bedclothes.

Sybil and Aislin each embraced her again, then left the room. MacQuaid and Camila stayed a few minutes longer before joining them in the carriage. The ride back to La Paloma was subdued.

Sybil rose before dawn the following morning and, feeling sorry for the overworked Rachelle, saddled one of her father's horses. By dawn, she was on her way to the Soboba village near the river.

The Indians locked their dark-eyed gazes on her as she entered.

"I need to speak to your chief," she said in Spanish to a young woman about her age.

The woman stared, unsmiling, but motioned for Sybil to come. Sybil slid from the saddle and followed the woman. After a few steps, she turned and told Sybil in Spanish to halt.

Sybil did as she was bidden, and presently an older, dignified man with skin the color of leather stepped toward her. She swallowed hard, feeling vulnerable. But Brighid's sad image was seared in her mind, and she put all thoughts of herself, her own safety, aside.

"I have come for your help," she said in Spanish.

He nodded.

She took a deep breath and told him what had happened to Brighid on her way to teach his children.

When she finished, there was no emotion on his face, and she wondered if he'd understood her.

He turned to leave, and she stepped up to him. "Please," she said. "Bring the children to the adobe. Let my sister see them. Maybe they will make a difference. Tomorrow, please."

But he made no indication that he heard or understood.

So she returned to her horse, mounted, and rode back to La Paloma, telling no one where she'd been.

THIRTY-SIX

"I plan to ride out to the adobe. Introduce Brighid to Scotty," Sybil said at breakfast. "Aislin, would you like to come with us? I want to spend the whole day with Brig."

Aislin lifted her coffee cup and took a sip before answering. The sorrow of her sister's state pushed all other plans—riding to Rancho Dearbourne to visit Sara, to pay her respects after Hugh's death, to discover if Sara knew where Spence had gone—from her mind. Of course she would ride out with Sybil and Scotty to spend the day with Brighid. Finding Spence would have to wait.

She nodded. "When are you going?"

"I want to take her drawing paper and charcoals," Sybil said. "That was once her favorite pastime. I thought we'd leave as soon as I gather them together."

Aislin smiled. "While you're doing that, I'll fix a basket of Josefa's cinnamon rolls. Brig always loved them." She ached that it was so little to offer, when Brig needed so much.

An hour later, Scotty, Sybil, and Aislin rode across the Big Valley. The sun was now high in a bright sky, and the abundance of growth and wildlife seemed a harbinger of hope, with sparrows, scrub jays, and bright finches warbling their spring songs, red-tailed hawks soaring above it all.

Aislin let Scotty and Sybil ride ahead of her. A doe soared from a nearby thicket, followed by two spotted fawns. Startled cottontails and ground squirrels skittered beneath the brush.

She drew in a deep breath and lifted her eyes heavenward. She was home. In spite of the sorrows they'd found at the end of the hard journey, she was home. She whispered a prayer of thanksgiving.

Then she thought of Spence and wondered again where he might be. She wanted nothing more than to saddle up a fresh horse and ride off to find him.

Her heart urged her to go, to ride like the wind toward him. But where? For all her brave words to Jamie about finding him, she had no idea where to begin. She fought tears of frustration.

The sun warmed her face and dried her tears, and she tried to put her longing for Spence from her mind as she moved her horse into an easy trot.

They arrived at the adobe minutes later. They were surprised to see that the Dearbourne carriage, still hitched to a single gray horse, was parked by the side of the house.

When they entered, Sara stood to greet them. She'd obviously been sitting with Brighid. And though there was no visible change in the younger woman's vacant stare, Sara's face was filled with compassion—and with hope—as she looked upon Brighid. She gave her a quick kiss on the forehead and promised to return the following day.

Then she stopped to embrace Aislin before heading to the door. "It's good to see you home again," she said in the soft voice Aislin loved to hear. "Spence and Jamie have filled me in on all that's happened."

Aislin slipped her arm around Sara's waist. "I'll walk with you to the carriage."

Once outside, they spoke for a few minutes about Jamie and Spence, the ranchos, their journey home. Aislin noticed that as they talked, Sara seemed someplace distant, as if she was considering broaching a different subject. Aislin hoped it had to do with Spence's whereabouts. "Do you know where he's gone?" she asked as Sara stepped toward the carriage.

Sara turned, her dark eyes searching Aislin's. "Jamie didn't tell me why the two of you decided not to marry." She hesitated. "But it's because of Spence, isn't it?"

Aislin nodded. "Yes," she whispered. "I love him. But I don't know how to find him…to tell him."

Sara looked sorry. "He didn't say where he was headed. Only that he knew he must leave."

"Because of me...and Jamie. Only that's not—"

Sara interrupted. "There is something else, Aislin." She frowned, as if considering how much to say. "There was another reason he felt he had to leave." She smiled gently. "Someday you will know...but it's not yet time."

When Sara rode off in the carriage and Aislin again entered the adobe, Brighid was as pleasant as she had been the day before, but just as distant.

She had already set aside the drawing materials without so much as a glance, and she was chattering brightly with Scotty about dressing in white for the wedding. Then she exclaimed over the cinnamon rolls when Aislin removed the cloth from the basket. Scotty read to Brighid for a while, and Sybil showed her some old copies of *Godey's Ladies Book.*

Aislin, trying not to dwell on what Sara had just told her, sat next to Brighid, telling her of their journey to New Mexico, about how Spence had led them so valiantly and sold the wild horses for a profit.

"Wild horses..." mused Brighid dreamily. "Spence told me about the mustangs. Did you know he brought a foal, let me pet it?" Her hand moved in a circular motion.

"Yes, Brig. Papa told us." Aislin caught Brighid's hand and rubbed her forearm, much the same way Spence caressed horses. "Did Spence say anything else about the wild horses?"

Brighid smiled brightly. "He showed me how to gentle the foal."

"Did he say where he might be heading when he left?"

She shook her head slowly. "He wants to start a horse ranch."

"I know. But did he tell you where?"

"He's planning to breed mustangs with other horses. Make a sturdier breed." Brighid sounded so natural, so coherent as she spoke of the horses, her eyes less vacant.

As the day progressed, Sybil's spirits seemed to fall. She studied the landscape outside the window and several times stood on the porch, her eyes shaded, looking east.

It was almost sundown when Scotty went out to stand by both sisters on the porch. "I really thought they might come..." Sybil said.

"Who, Syb?" Scotty looked at her curiously.

"I wasn't going to tell you, either of you." She shrugged, looking from Aislin back to Scotty. "But now that it's obvious they're not coming, I'll tell you my wild scheme."

"Wild schemes seem to run in your family," Scotty said, draping his arm around Sybil's shoulders. "And whatever—whoever—was supposed to come, I wouldn't give up yet."

Aislin looked east where Sybil's attention had been fixed all day. Then she smiled, understanding in an instant what Sybil had set about to accomplish.

"Syb," she whispered, "are you waiting for some visitors? Soboba visitors?"

Her sister turned to follow her gaze, a look of amazement dawning on her face. "Well, my stars," she said in awe. "I reckon Scotty's right. Our schemes sometimes work out after all."

Moments later, the small band of Indians—made up of five somber little girls, two young braves, three young women, and the tall, dignified chief—stood stone-faced before the adobe.

Sybil went to the chief and gave him a look of deep gratitude. *"Gracias."*

He gave her a curt nod, then said something to the children. They stepped forward shyly.

"Come with me," Sybil said, taking two of them by their hands. The others followed, as did Aislin and Scotty.

Brighid looked up in surprise from her bed. At first she seemed uncomprehending, then she focused on the children's faces. Her hands began to tremble, and Aislin whispered a prayer that she would remain calm, that she would not be frightened or frighten the children.

She gazed into their faces, but this time the vacant smile didn't appear. She spoke their names, her voice soft. "Aiyana…Aponi…Ogin…Tala…"

As she said each, that child came to her and stood very close to the bed. "My children," she said, reaching out to touch their hands, one by one. "I have missed you."

The children stared, uncomprehending. Then she smiled and repeated what she'd said in Spanish.

For the first time, the children smiled back at her. One spoke, then another. The other three joined in, and all began to speak at once, chattering in a mix of Spanish, Soboban, and English.

Brighid laughed and held up her hand. "Have you forgotten your lessons?"

They shook their heads.

"Then let's speak in English."

The children nodded and started over again, this time speaking in broken English.

The little girl named Aiyana stepped closer, pronouncing each word very deliberately. "Tell us a story, Miss Byrne. We miss your stories."

Sybil spoke up, "Brighid, would you like to teach the children outside? The porch would made a grand school."

But the fear showed in her eyes. Deep. Pained. Stubborn. She shook her head. "No, I can't walk."

"We'll help you," Scotty said.

"No!" Brighid almost shouted. Her hands were trembling again. "Maybe the children should leave now." She smiled her vacant smile. "I must get ready for tea. Syb, please bring me the lace frock with the rosebuds. Do you know the one?"

The children seemed confused, except for Aiyana, who, with a determined look on her face, spoke again. "Miss Byrne, please tell us a story."

The child's voice seemed to pull Brighid back to reality. "All right," she said. "I have a new story for you."

There were ahs of delight. Brighid patted the bed. "Come," she said. "And listen."

The children settled quietly onto the floor, looking up at her. Brighid adjusted her pillows so that she was completely upright. "All right," she said. "Once there was a young Soboba brave who had a gift for healing horses."

The children nodded.

"One day this warrior—we'll call him Taima—found a beautiful herd of horses in a secret cave behind a waterfall."

Aislin's heart skipped a beat. Obviously, Spence had told Brighid about the herd they'd found.

"Well, one day a bad warrior from another tribe stole the horses. This man planned to take away their wildness and sell the horses to another tribe far, far away from the horses' home behind the waterfall."

The children sighed. "Oh no," cried little Aiyana, her hand over her mouth.

Brighid's face was animated, and she seemed perfectly natural. Scotty and Sybil glanced her direction, and she gave them a small affirming nod.

"But Taima loved the horses, and he decided that even if he had to give his life to save them, he would do so. He followed the bad warrior across the Big Valley, across the mountains, across the many rivers to the place of beautiful highlands.

"Then Taima waited until the time was just right. Until the bad warrior felt himself full of boast and bluff, unable to be defeated. He waited. And waited. And waited. The crow landed near him on a fence and said, 'It's time.' But still he waited. The hawk called down from his circle in the sky and said, 'It's time.' But still Taima waited. The snake slithered from beneath a rock and said, 'It's time.' But still he waited.

"Finally, a golden-eyed mountain lion leapt from some willows and said, 'It's time.' Now, Taima knew the voice of the lion, and he knew that it was indeed time to fight the bad warrior."

The children were sitting forward now, their eyes not leaving Brighid's face.

"Then what happened?" asked the little girl named Ogin.

"Taima asked the lion to go with him into battle," she said.

"And did he go?" asked Ogin.

"Yes, because the lion had been Taima's friend for all his life. He knew everything about Taima."

"So he knew how to help him get the horses?" asked Aiyana.

"Exactly how to help," Brighid said. "So Taima and the lion followed the trail of the wild horses into a deep, dark forest. They found the bad warrior and the herd in a small valley. The herd was guarded by other warriors, giant warriors."

"What did they do?" breathed Ogin, her eyes wide.

"What do you think a lion might do to frighten bad warriors?"

"I think he would roar," Ogin said in a hushed voice. "A huge, long roar."

"You are exactly right," Brighid said with a smile. A very natural smile. "That's what the lion did. It was a roar so loud that the mountains shook. Rocks rolled down and hit the bad warriors on their heads."

The children laughed. Aiyana clapped her hands.

"But the horses were not hurt."

"I bet they were scared though," said Ogin.

"Not a bit, because do you know what happened?"

"No, what?" the children breathed in unison.

"As soon as the lion finished his roar, the lion skin fell away. He wasn't a lion at all. He was a beautiful stallion the color of obsidian."

Aislin smiled, thinking of Spence telling Brighid the real story.

"And then what happened?" Ogin asked.

"This is the best part of the story," Brighid said. "Taima herded the horses together. With the help of the magnificent stallion, he brought them away from the dark forest, across the many rivers, across the mountains, across the Big Valley to their home…"

Smiles lit the children's faces and they cried in unison with her, "in the secret valley behind the waterfall."

Aislin's heart caught in her throat. Of course. Spence had left with the men who could best help him retake the herd from Fraco Ciro. Her father had said Spence had a wild foal with him on the last day he visited Brighid. On his way out of the Big Valley.

She knew where she would find him!

She gave Sybil and Scotty a quick hug and whispered where she was headed. "This is nothing short of a miracle, Syb," she said, looking at Brighid's face as she talked with the children. "And it's due to you."

"It's a step," Sybil whispered back. "She's got a long way to go."

"You did the right thing, sending for them," Aislin said, squeezing her hand. "It's going to take a while. If they could come every day…"

Scotty stepped forward. "We'll see that they do."

Aislin moved across the room and bent to kiss Brighid. A moment later she ran from the adobe to fetch her trail supplies from La Paloma and talk Erasmo into escorting her.

She had to reach Spence before he left the valley behind the waterfall. Because after that it might be too late.

THIRTY-SEVEN

Spence had taken his time herding the horses back to the meadow behind the waterfall. After their trek to New Mexico and back again, the horses needed time to rest and heal. He'd led them first to the high desert to graze, then into the Valley of the Horses for another few weeks of fattening on the tender spring grasses.

They roamed in wider circles as they became stronger, and finally, he noticed they seemed to sense their nearness to home. Two weeks ago, he had led them to the entrance of the canyon, then watched the obsidian stallion take his family from there.

Spence had followed on Ruffian, more from the sheer pleasure of watching the herd than from any sense that they still needed him. Then he camped in the cave at the entrance to the meadow for another two weeks.

Every day he thought of moving on. Every day the peace and beauty of the place kept him from leaving.

Today, however, he finally decided there could be no more delay. He had already saddled Ruffian and packed the saddlebags with his camping gear. He planned to head out within the hour.

But his heart wasn't in it. After he left Aislin that last time, something inside him died…the deep sense of joy that he'd always taken from her presence. Now it was gone, and it was time to move on, get his mind on new endeavors. He hoped that once he began his new life, she would fade from his memory, from his heart.

It was midmorning, and the horses grazed in the sunlit meadow. He stood to one side watching them, remembering how he and Aislin had found them together. How he had run with them, then beckoned

Aislin to join him. Together they had danced with joy across the meadow with the animals.

He walked out to be with the herd once more, first walking up to the stallion, patting him on the neck, rubbing his gleaming coat. Once he had taken him back from Ciro, he'd unbuckled the saddle, tossed it aside, and vowed that the horse would never be ridden again.

The big stallion stood silently as Spence whispered to him, telling him about freedom, about the beauty that was his, about the God who'd made him so magnificently. Some of the others gathered around, and he walked among them, whispering, patting, gentling.

The foal who'd been born on the trail from New Mexico and started life so frail came to him and nuzzled his hand. Spence bent to rub its back and neck. He thought of Brighid, the spark of life that had flickered in her eyes when she had touched this same foal.

He prayed for her healing, as he did each time she entered his thoughts. It was ironic—he loved each of the Byrne daughters in a different way, had always considered himself part of their family. Yet Brighid was now connected to him with an unbreakable fiber of compassion because her pain was so like what his own mother had experienced. He thought of how Sara had wept when he told her of Hugh's death and that he knew the secret about his conception.

Sara had gathered her son into her arms and cried until it seemed there were no more tears to cry. Spence had wept with her. When it was done, the pain he'd seen in her eyes through the years seemed to lessen.

He turned to walk among the horses once more, knowing it would be his last time in this place, his last time with them. Then it came to him that Ciro had found a different way out of the secret valley the night he disappeared with the horses. He stopped and scanned the canyon walls.

Was that a cavern in the canyon wall on the far side of the meadow? He squinted, studying the place. Even from this distance, it appeared to be an opening, more like a wide tunnel than a cave, perhaps a shortcut into the Valley. He returned for Ruffian, mounted, and rode through the herd toward the cavern.

⇒◆⇐

Aislin left Erasmo at their campsite in the Valley of the Horses. She found her way to the canyon entrance with no trouble, remembering that the last time she was on the trail it was as dark as midnight. As she rode, she hummed "Oh! Susannah," thinking how Spence had played it on his harmonica that night, and she had sung it back to him so he'd know she was nearby.

She hoped she wasn't too late. It had been a month since Spence left the Big Valley, according to her father and mother.

She nudged her horse to move faster along the trail. The sheer rock walls seemed less intimidating than they had the first time. The slices of granite, the sparkling minerals catching the sun, the stark majesty of the cliffs, all seemed familiar and surprisingly welcoming.

Soon the roar of the waterfall could be heard in the distance. She shuddered, thinking of climbing its steep rock face without Spence behind her. Leaping over the crevice at the cave's entrance without Spence to urge her to forget her fears.

She rounded the last switchback above the pool fed by the waterfall. It was just as she remembered. Beautiful. Terrifying. Magnificent.

She'd hoped to see Ruffian where they'd left their horses by the pool, but there was no sign of him, not even hoofprints in the sand. She urged Silverheel down the incline, dismounted, and left the horse to drink and graze while she headed up the cliff to the meadow.

She looked up at the narrow, rocky trail leading to the waterfall. The wet sheen of the rocks caught the sunlight. She swallowed hard, lifted a quick prayer heavenward, then headed toward the trail.

She knew better than to take a paralyzing look below her, so with Spence's image goading her on, she climbed upward, one handhold, one foothold at a time.

Reaching the top, she held onto a scraggly stick of a pine, and focused on the jump she needed to make to the cave behind the falls.

She swallowed hard again. Prayed again. Then, eyes closed, she leapt.

And landed with a thud in the cave.

The moment of euphoria quickly vanished. She had expected to see a bedroll and saddle, even Ruffian himself standing nearby. She rolled over, then pushed herself to her knees and stood. Brushing herself off, she looked around.

Nothing.

She walked through the cave into the meadow beyond, hoping that Spence might have pitched camp in a different place. There before her, in the dazzling sunlight, was the herd. The obsidian stallion, ears flicking forward and back, sensed her presence. He placed himself nervously between her and the other horses.

So she'd been right. Spence had rescued them from Ciro. He had returned them home. But she was too late.

She walked out to the herd. Spence had been there with them, maybe only days ago, and it was that thought of his presence that drew her. She walked to the stallion, and he stood very still, eyeing her as she approached.

She whispered to him, the way she'd seen Spence do. She touched his neck, felt its warmth, drew in the scent of sun-baked hide. She ran her fingers through his mane, still whispering, still gentling the beast with her touch.

And she thought of Spence, how foolish she had been to let him go. She buried her face in the stallion's mane, thinking of Spence as he had been in the valley that day.

"Aislin?" It was his voice. For a moment she didn't move. Then it came again, almost as if on the wind. "Aislin."

She lifted her head and turned.

He stood quite still, facing her. He looked as stunned as she felt. He made no move to come closer.

"I—I thought you were gone. I mean, I figured where you'd come.

That you would return the horses to their rightful home. But I couldn't get here any faster," she said. "I came as fast as I could."

"What's wrong? Has something happened?" Now he was walking toward her.

"Well, yes. Everything's wrong." She took a deep breath. "What I mean to say is—yes, something has happened."

He was standing very close now, and she looked up into his eyes. Her knees went weak with what she saw there.

He looked worried. "Is it my mother?"

"Oh no, Spence. I'm sorry for misleading you. It's nothing wrong, I mean, nothing like that…"

"What is it?"

"It's Jamie."

"Jamie?" Now his eyes glinted dangerously.

"He's alive."

"Alive?" The glint disappeared, replaced by wonder, then the dangerous spark returned.

She nodded. "Yes," she whispered. "Your brother is alive."

"You came all the way here to tell me that?"

"Well, not that only," she said, her eyes filling with tears.

"Aislin, I'm glad my brother lives, but forgive me if I don't congratulate you." He glanced behind her as if expecting Jamie to appear.

"Please listen to me, Spence." Her heart was thudding and skipping and somersaulting all at the same time. And her knees threatened to buckle.

He turned again to her.

"I'm trying to tell you. Jamie lives but, Spence, it's not him."

"Not him? What are you saying?"

"It's not him I love."

He stared at her, almost as if he hadn't heard her.

"I said it's not him, Spence."

He touched her face, trailed his fingers along her jawline until they reached her chin. Then he tilted it upward slightly. "You've come all this way to tell me it's not Jamie you love?"

She nodded.

"Then, Aislin," he whispered, his lips close to hers, "there must be something else you're here to tell me."

She nodded, looking at his lips instead of his eyes. "Yes," she breathed.

He inclined his head, waiting. She moved her gaze to his eyes again. "You told me once that I'm no longer required to marry a Dearbourne, and that when I marry it will be for love, not for increasing our lands in the Big Valley."

"I did," he said.

"You said, however, if I marry a Dearbourne, as an added blessing our children would inherit one of the largest ranchos in the state. And their children after them.

"What I came here to say was that if I marry a Dearbourne, as an added blessing our children will inherit the greatest love a family could give them. It really has nothing to do with the land, the Big Valley."

"When I spoke about the inheritance, I was speaking about Jamie. Not me."

She went on as if he hadn't spoken. "You also said that the Rancho de la Paloma name will eventually fade."

"I said that," he murmured, clearly not concentrating on her words. "But again, it was Jamie—"

She touched his lips again to shush him. "Spence?"

"Hmm?"

"I came here to tell you that I love you. That it will be our children God will pour his blessings on. And I don't care a fig about Rancho de la Paloma or Rancho Dearbourne. Whether their names remain for generations or for only a day. I just care about you, about being in your arms until the day I die."

For a moment he didn't say a word; he just drank in the look of her with his eyes.

"Spence?"

"Yes?"

"Will you hold me? I don't think I can stand up one minute longer."

He threw back his head and laughed and pulled her into his arms. Holding her close, he looked down at her upturned face. "I found the other entrance to the valley."

The sunlight slanted across his face, and she swallowed hard at the beauty, the love she saw there.

"It's just big enough to bring in a wagonload of timber. And a few loads of adobe bricks."

"Timber...and bricks?"

He nodded, his grin widening. "We wouldn't want the materials for our new ranch brought in through the waterfall."

"The workers might get hurt leaping across the crevasse," she said, thinking she might not ever stop smiling.

"We wouldn't want that," he murmured, his gaze locked on hers.

"It's the perfect place to call home," she whispered.

Then with a shout of joy, he twirled slowly, holding her in his arms. In the sunlit meadow, they moved among the horses. With grace, with beauty, in a dance of love.

Beloved Friends,

Thank you for traveling with me on the journey through *When the Far Hills Bloom*. California is the place of my birth and the setting for my own life story, and as you may have guessed, one of my favorite places to write about.

When I'm writing, I spend most of the time in our mountain getaway near Idyllwild, California. My office window faces east toward the snow-peaked San Jacinto mountains, the same view as mentioned in the book. And when I hike a mile or so out to a rocky "bald" mountain overlook—the same where Aislin and Spence found the injured filly—I can see the "Big Valley" where I've placed the ranchos. Each time I don hiking boots and windbreaker and head out to the place, I'm in awe of the wonder of God's creation. How blessed we are, my friends, to live in such a world!

Two books will follow *When the Far Hills Bloom*, continuing the family saga. Watch for *The Blossom and the Nettle,* the story of Aislin and Spence's son and a feisty woman from New York who has some very different plans for land she inherits near his cattle ranch. She has a dream of raising oranges, of all things, and brings a few hot-house varieties by stagecoach to this barren land. And he, a bookish cowboy, thinks she's out of her mind. Watch for the sparks to fly when these two meet.

I love hearing from you. You can write to me at either of the addresses that follow. Also drop by my new website. It's full of information about upcoming books, research trips, photos, and information for ordering any of my books—even those written as Amanda MacLean.

Love to all!

Diane

Write to Diane Noble:
P.O. Box 841
Sierra Madre, CA 91024-0841
E-mail: diane@dianenoble.com
Visit my website at www.dianenoble.com